HEART'S AWAKENING

PAIGE BRANTLEY

ZEBRA BOOKS
KENSINGTON PUBLISHING CORP.

ZEBRA BOOKS are published by

Kensington Publishing Corp.
850 Third Avenue
New York, NY 10022

First Printing: December, 1995

Printed in the United States of America

AT LONG LAST . . .

Sancha regarded Hugh wide-eyed. "What can you not endure?" she asked in a voice hushed and nervous with excitement, even though she knew exactly what he meant. The mere touch of his hands had sent an involuntary tremor of delight coursing through her body, urging her to twine her arms about his neck and press against him.

Hugh's heart beat wildly. His hands slid downward to caress the curve of her hips, and, bringing his face close to hers, he answered in a low tone, almost speaking into her mouth. "That you are the subject of my every thought. I think of you every moment of the day, only you and nothing else."

"What then is the remedy?"

"Either I must have you, or I must make a bed for myself in the abbey."

"Would you not prefer to lie in your own bed?" Sancha whispered.

"Only if I might have you."

Sancha stared into his eyes, blue-grey and smoky with desire. *He is asking me,* she thought, and recognized the restraint in which he had held himself for her sake. Now, it was only as nature intended that she should touch her parted lips to his, inviting him to take possession of her mouth.

Hugh needed no more inducement than the cool, shy brush of her lips. "Tonight," he mumbled, his voice no more than a deep, rustling whisper, as his hands drifted down her back.

"Yes."

HEART'S AWAKENING

She plucked a daisy white and vain,
The petals fell like summer rain,
"I love him not, I love him true,
Alas," she cried, "What am I to do?"
Sunshine today, tomorrow snow,
One moment laughter, another woe,
"I love him true, I love him not,
And I, betwixt the two, am caught."
PB

One

Anno Christi 1400

"Touffu! Touffu!" A trio of girlish voices coaxed the curly-coated little dog, but he would not relinquish the colorful felt ball. Around and around he ran, leading a merry chase, wagging his tail and artfully dodging the giggling girls. At last the pup leapt upon the velvet-draped bed and into the arms of his laughing mistress, the queen of England.

"What wickedness is this?" The reproachful voice of the Dame de Coucy cracked sharp as a whip. Striding swiftly across the bedchamber she lunged forward and snatched the curly-coated lapdog from the young queen's hands.

Deep in the scarlet-draped bed, little Isabelle, whose childish face was flushed with fever, started and stared in stunned silence. The Dame de Coucy had taken the girls by complete surprise. Their laughter choked off, and they looked for all the world like naughty children who had been caught out.

"Here!" the Dame de Coucy said, her voice brimming with spite. "Go! And take this filthy beast with you!" With a look of loathing, she thrust the wriggling white puppy into the arms of Dominique de Severies.

"Madame needs rest, not mindless chatter!" the Dame de Coucy sharply reprimanded the trio of wide-eyed ladies-in-waiting. "Go!" Her voice hissed between her teeth, and, with a gesture not unlike a peasant shooing hens, she herded the three young girls from the chamber.

Marie d'Ormonde, recently turned sixteen, stumbled a little on the train of her gown as she retreated across the chamber. Her fair freckled face was splotched with anger.

Beside her was Alene de Canneville, barely fifteen, her round face set in a pout. Short in stature and plump, she was not so blond as Marie. Her eyes and hair were of a soft, self-same shade of brown.

The third of the ladies was Dominique de Severies, known to her friends as "Sancha" and soon to celebrate her sixteenth birthday. The Dame de Coucy referred to her, and not in a kindly fashion, as "the little siren." There was a certain sauciness in her smile, and she took the eye. It was impossible not to notice her for, though she was not a classic golden beauty, she stood out vividly in any company with her brilliant eyes, thick black curls, and complexion of snow and roses.

Halfway across the chamber, the girls hedged and glanced back defiantly. But the de Coucy woman swooped forward, hustling them out through the chamber door, and slammed it after them.

"I hate her!" Marie whispered hotly, forgetting herself. She had not even looked about the antechamber to see if there was a servant to overhear her words.

Alene, slower to anger as all else, looked around before she spoke. "She gives herself airs! The de Coucy hag is naught but a jailer!" Even so, Alene pronounced her indictment in a hushed voice and glanced about again for unseen ears as they entered the solar.

Daylight poured through a brace of lancet windows, and ramps of dust-stricken sunlight illuminated the immense tapestries, where heroic huntsmen and their hounds pursued the hart through fanciful forests of glittering golden trees.

Sancha walked between Marie and Alene, keeping her thoughts to herself. She cooed to the little dog in her arms and stroked his silky fur. "Poor Touffu," she sighed. "And poor Madame the queen. Perhaps we will be permitted to see her tomorrow? The rash is fading," she asserted, and braving a smile, looked to the others with encouragement. "I think Madame the queen will soon recover. We must think of ways to cheer her. We could devise a guessing game. Madame loves games."

"How can you think of merriment," Marie remarked, "when all about us is treachery!"

Sancha did not reply at once. It was true. The queen and her ladies-in-waiting were no more than prisoners. Oh, they were grandly kept, but prisoners all the same, surrounded by Henry Bolingbroke's jailers and spies. It had been so since the day King Richard had fallen into Bolingbroke's hands. Richard was now imprisoned, no one knew where. And if there was news of him, it was kept from the queen. It was an easy enough chore. The little queen's once huge retinue was gone, sent away. Only three of her ladies-in-waiting, the youngest, had been permitted to remain because they were more easily handled, and only because the eleven-year-old queen had pleaded and cried so pitiably.

"What other choice is left to us?" Sancha finally said, cuddling the little dog. "If we might give Madame a moment's happiness, surely some good will come of it. She has known so little happiness."

"You are right," Marie conceded, putting aside for the moment her fears for their safety. She smiled halfheartedly, suggesting, "I could play the lute for her. Alene would sing, wouldn't you Alene?"

"Oh yes!" Alene's plump face broke into a smile. "Or Sancha could draw funny pictures, as she did in London. It is Madame's favorite game."

Sancha giggled at the thought of her invention, the silly animals dressed in courtier's clothing and each meant to represent a noble of Bolingbroke's court. Pigs and geese and cows, made funnier still for the outrageous stories about them she, Madame, Marie, and Alene had concocted.

Sequestered in their chamber, Sancha, Marie, and Alene passed the remainder of the day laying elaborate plans for the morrow. Their evening meal, as always, was brought to them.

Later, while the spring evening yet glowed with a rose-tinted light, the servingwomen came to undress them for bed. A lanky varlet, whose task it was to take the little lapdog for air, came and returned, and afterward, the lamps were doused.

Hours later, Sancha was roused from a sound sleep by a strange noise. She sat up suddenly in her bed and blinked. Again she heard the noise, a scritching, not unlike the sound of mice. Confused and yet half-asleep, she glanced at the other two beds which lined the wall of the rectangular chamber and saw the darkened, slumbering forms of Marie and Alene. All was silent. It was then Sancha noticed Touffu was not at the foot of her bed.

Once more she heard the scritching noise, and with it a whimpering sound. She turned swiftly and saw Touffu scratching at the door.

"Touffu!" she called in a whisper. The little dog halted its assault, and cocked its furry head at her. But an instant later it returned to its furious scratching, pausing only to whimper and snuffle the air beneath the chamber door.

"Touffu! Come here!" she commanded, her voice hushed. "Come here!" she coaxed. The little dog paid her no mind; indeed, he seemed to redouble his efforts. Annoyed, Sancha climbed from bed, groped for her slippers in the darkness, and, jamming her feet into them, padded to the door.

As she stooped to grab Touffu, a splash of light fell beneath the door and she heard the musical sound of bells, little tinkling bells. She fancied them to be hawking bells, though perhaps not; it was such a queer, silvery sound she could not say. Sancha stood up and strained to hear, but she could hear nothing more, only Touffu's determined scratching.

Overcome by curiosity, her hand moved to the latch. She opened the door but a crack, enough to feel a draft of air. The passageway was black as doom, but the waft of breeze still held the tarry odor of a torch. Her eyes quickly became ac-

customed to the utter black and she noticed that the servant
who normally stood watch was nowhere to be seen.

While she stood staring into the darkness, Touffu shot from
between her legs with the agility of a fleeing demon and
streaked off down the passageway. "No! Touffu!" she called
quietly, almost in pantomime, and sprinted after the curly little
beast. Sancha knew that she, indeed all of them, Madame the
queen included, were forbidden to roam about the palace unattended, but all Sancha could think of was Madame's little
dog. If Touffu was lost, how could she tell the queen? The
little dog was all that was left for her to love.

Sancha gathered up her night shift and gave pursuit. Touffu
bounded on, ignoring her muffled cries, dashing through the
unilluminated passages and past a superfluity of doors. Like
a willow-o'-the-wisp, the curly white pup darted down a winding stairs and into a shadowy gallery where the walls were
hung with weapons. Sancha nearly caught him there. She felt
her fingers brush his curly fur, but he darted away into another
passage and through the door arch of a low-beamed chamber.

Sancha hung back at the door. Caution sent a shiver up her
spine. Inside the chamber, torches burned in the wall brackets,
flooding the room with a ghostly light. Silver platters filled
with fruit and meat sat upon a lengthy table near the hearth,
and on a nearby chest, a wine ewer and a clutch of goblets
gleamed in the mellow light. Sancha hesitated and looked
about the room. She saw no one. The chamber, despite its
flaring torches, was uninhabited, save for the curly-coated pup
that roamed its length, sniffing at everything and wagging his
stumpy tail. Sancha rushed in just as Touffu raised a leg against
a smaller table draped with a gold-embroidered cloth.

"Naughty, no, Touffu!" she scolded softly, but too late. The
deed was done. Quickly, Sancha gathered the pup into her arms
and turned to flee. A distant tinkling of bells all but stopped
her heart, the same queer, silvery sound she had heard earlier
in the passageway. The musical jingling was followed swiftly
by a mutter of voices, vague and indistinct, but certainly male.

Footfalls echoed from the direction of the gallery and, with her every heartbeat, grew louder, nearer.

Sancha's breath caught in her throat. There was no time to go! And if she stayed? A sob of panic escaped her lips. Desperately, she scanned the chamber's shadows for a hiding place. In the unforgiving torchlight there was none, save for the small table before her. Quick as a rabbit in a hedge, Sancha ducked beneath the long embroidered cloth. She crawled far back against the wall, clutching the wriggling pup and pulling her night shift about her legs. The air beneath the table had a peculiar, musty smell and cobwebs veiled her face.

A spate of loud conversation, hearty laughter, and the trample of boots heralded the men's entry into the chamber. They milled about in boisterous knots and stood before the hearth. Their words shot past her frightened ears, bold, dangerous-sounding, and full of bravado. There was, however, no mistaking one voice that rose above the others. It was that of Henry Bolingbroke, he who had publicly forced his cousin, Richard, to hand the crown to him.

They were very close, and Sancha had only to crane her neck a bit to see past the edge of the gold-fringed cloth. It was an odd view, like that of a small child. But she had been correct, for there with his broad face and powerful physique was Henry Bolingbroke, surrounded by half a dozen of his cronies. Some Sancha recognized from Richard's court, others she did not know.

All at once they gathered round the table to view some novelty. Sancha strained to see what object had so completely captured the men's attention. One man shifted his position, another stepped forward. What Sancha saw through their midst caused her jaw to drop with horror. She clenched her eyes and sucked in her lower lip to keep from screaming.

Suddenly the sound of bells jingled in her ears. Sancha started, and the little dog squirming in her arms broke free.

* * *

On the morrow, Marie was the first to awaken. She saw at once that Sancha was not in her bed. A cursory search confirmed that she was nowhere in the chamber, nor was Madame's little dog, Touffu. Marie was of a nervous nature, always expecting the worst and seldom disappointed. She rushed to the other bed.

"Alene! Alene!" she cried, vigorously shaking the plump shoulder protruding from the coverlet. "Sancha is gone!" she cried. "Something terrible has happened, I am certain of it!"

Alene was not one to do anything quickly. She sputtered, still half-witted with sleep, and sat up yawning. Marie rattled on distractedly. When Marie's words at last penetrated Alene's sleep-numbed mind, she pushed her hair from her eyes and mumbled, "Where has she gone?"

Marie sighed helplessly. "I don't know! Touffu is gone as well."

"But how? When?"

Marie could only shake her head and wring her hands. Soon Alene was as distraught as Marie. The pair spoke in rapid, frightened whispers, imagining all manner of tragedies. Mercifully, they had not long to speculate.

Before the servingwomen came to help them dress, the Dame de Coucy appeared at their chamber door. The lanky varlet was two steps behind her, clutching the wayward pup in his arms. She came in quickly, directing the varlet to put down the pup and leave.

"Where is Sancha?" Marie questioned.

De Coucy gave her a cold look, as if she had not heard. "See that this foul little beast does not escape again. It has been the cause of enough grief."

The little dog cowered, pressing against Alene's legs. She bent over and scooped the curly pup into her arms.

The Dame de Coucy took several quick steps toward the door, when Marie, forgetting the respect due a lady of de Coucy's station, indeed, forgetting all civility, demanded,

"What have you done with Sancha? I shall tell Madame the queen that you . . . . !"

"I have already informed Madame of the lady de Severies's unfortunate accident," de Coucy said with a brusque, almost rude impatience.

"Accident? There has been no accident!" Marie accused.

The Dame gave her a poisonous smile. "Oh, yes, and there is the cause of it, that wretched dog."

"I do not believe you!" Marie cried.

"Nor do I," cried Alene, her eyes ablaze with anger.

"Believe as you chose, it will change nothing," de Coucy said with satisfaction, repeating, "The lady de Severies stumbled on the stairs last night and did herself a grave injury. She is in the care of Bolingbroke's physician." After which, the Dame went briskly to the door, ushered in the servingwomen, and hurried off as if she had urgent business elsewhere.

Marie and Alene put on a courageous face before the queen. She had quite enough to weigh down her young heart. But as children are apt to do, Isabelle saw through their charade. That day she spent long hours in the chapel praying, and more hours moping about her suite. The fate of her dear lady-in-waiting weighed heavily on little Isabelle. Even the company of Marie and Alene, with their games and songs, could not bring a smile to Isabelle's young face. Nor could the antics of her little dog coax her to laugh.

Two

Several days passed into the shadows of the great castle at Windsor. Below its hundred steps, the dirt course of an ancient road crossed a small tributary of the river Thames. There a wooden bridge stood on stone and timber piers, around which the sluggish brown water eddied and flowed. Near the shoreline, newly formed sandbars glistened in the dazzling spring sunlight, ridged where the current had formed them, and glittering gold where their sands disappeared beneath the slow-moving water. In the distance, little islands overgrown with osiers and clad in vivid green dotted the stream.

Below the bridge the banks of the waterway were thick with sedge and reeds, and sloped steeply for a short distance before broadening into a marshy clearing of sorts at the foot of a meadow. Here children frolicked at the water's edge and a number of women, with their skirts tucked up above their knees in peasant fashion, had waded into the chill water to wash clothing.

The youthful shouts of the children, the glancing sunlight, and the chatter of the women as they toiled added a pleasant tranquility to the April morning—a tranquility that was soon to be shattered.

Beneath the trees, Dominique de Severies ran blindly. Her lungs burned as if afire and the calves of her legs ached with exertion. Flashes of brilliant, blinding sunlight burst through the canopy of new green leaves. Brambles tore at her flesh and snagged her night shift. Gnarled tree roots lay across the narrow path like snares, slowing her frantic pace. She stumbled, losing a slipper.

The crash of brush and the pounding footfalls of her pursuers rang in her ears. She twisted, stabbed her foot into her slipper, and plunged on like a hunted animal. Her thoughts were tortured and dark. There was something she must do. But what? She could not recall. She knew only that her pursuers must not catch her.

Before her the path broadened, soft with bracken, moss, and wood sorrel, and turned steeply downward. Sancha shortened the course by clumsily slipping and sliding down the damp earth of the banks. Her pursuers were very close now. The muffled thud of their boots pounded against her ears like blows, and she could hear plainly their grunted exchanges and the heaviness of their breathing.

At last she stumbled from the wood and there before her, like a glimpse of salvation, was the level course of a road and a wooden bridge. She did not dare glance back. She ran toward the bridge, her trembling legs threatening to crumble beneath her. Only after she had reached the midpoint of the span did she see a man on horseback approaching. He, too, wore the scarlet-and-white livery of her pursuers. She halted and, glancing back, to her horror, saw three others come bounding from the wood and onto the bridge. She stood there, exhausted and gasping for breath. She could run no further. Her mind reeled with panic. "No!" she sobbed. "They must not catch me!"

The women and children below the span saw only the young girl poised at the bridge's rail an instant before she plummeted into the stream and vanished beneath the murky waters.

A chorus of shrieks rent the bright air. Women and raggedly dressed children dashed along the stream's edge, shouting for help. Seemingly from nowhere, as if conjured up by their piercing cries, two men dashed down the sloping bank, through the thick growth of sedge and reeds, and dived into the water. A moment later, another man slid down the bank and splashed into the stream after them. Now three men thrashed about in the brown water, shouting back and forth as they dived and surfaced, searching for the girl in the tattered night shift.

The horseman on the bridge dismounted and leaned from the rail to better view the unfolding drama. After what seemed an interminably long time, though in truth it was no more than a few brief moments, the stockiest of the three men bobbing about in the stream, shouted, " 'Ere! 'Ere! I've got her! Lend a hand!" Atop the bridge, the man leaning over the rail watched intently as the girl was dragged to the surface and slowly towed toward the shoreline. A cheer went up from the onlookers, and they crowded round as the men hauled the half-drowned girl through the reeds and onto the muddy bank.

Sancha awoke coughing and strangling. She was drenched to her skin, trembling with cold, and only vaguely aware of the great commotion raging around her. A circle of faces looked down on her, shouting and asking questions. Hands pulled and tugged at her. Sancha's lips moved frantically, but her voice would not obey. It seemed that only she was aware of the great cold darkness that threatened to close over her, and, before she could find her voice, she slipped again into unconsciousness.

"Poor lamb," one peasant woman murmured to another as they watched the men struggle up the bank with the limp and unresponsive girl.

"They said she was crazy!" a young boy announced as he darted back to join the onlookers. "She's crazy, the devil's in her head," he added, making a silly face and positioning his fingers like horns as he jigged about. A broad-bosomed woman boxed his ear and jerked him to one side. "Shut your mouth afore the devil hears you, ya little heathen!"

"Aye," the woman beside her said. "He be searching for loose tongues and empty heads!"

A short time later at Windsor.

A clatter of hooves in the small, walled court of the apartments drew Thomas Swynford to the window. Sunlight lay upon the embrasure and the cool air was scented with the heady musk of spring. Below, his villeins milled about. Bernard, seated astride a palfrey, held the girl before him. One of the men had wrapped a cloak about her.

Swynford's broad chest rose and fell. A profound sigh of relief escaped his lips. "By the saints!" he exclaimed. "They have found her!" The other man present in the room, Marcus Crowl, surgeon to the usurper king Henry Bolingbroke, came quickly to the window. He did not like what he saw.

The girl appeared unconscious. Her head lolled forward and she looked as though she was dripping wet.

Swynford had also noticed. His brow furrowed with concern, and in a hushed aside, muttered, "What's the matter with her?"

Crowl gave only a grunted response, turned on his heel, and dashed from the chamber. Swynford rushed after him, following him swiftly down the stairs.

In the foyer several servingwomen crowded the doorway, whispering among themselves. There was a shuffling of feet as the men entered. The hush of voices subsided upon seeing the girl's sad state. Water dripped from her muddied night shift and her skin was the color of ashes. Gone was her pink-and-white prettiness. Her long dark hair wound in coils and tangled about her face, and her lips were blue with cold. One among the women gasped, "Lord God! She be dead!"

"Hold your tongue!" Crowl snarled, shoving the woman aside and pressing his fingers to the girl's throat.

The other men hung back at the door. "There was nothing we could do," they mumbled, twisting their felt caps in their hands. "She ran like a cat afire."

Bernard, with the bundled girl in his arms, nodded in agreement. " 'Tis so," he swore, his voice raspy with effort. "She jumped from the bridge afore we reached her." Muddy water pooled on the floor beneath him. His shoulders were beginning to ache from effort. He shifted the girl's weight in his arms.

"We drug her out quick enough," he stammered, glancing fearfully to his master, like a dog who had misbehaved.

Swynford was deaf to his villein's words. He saw only the girl. She seemed to be breathing, but she was white as flour paste. He watched aghast as the surgeon's long bony finger lifted an eyelid. "She is not . . . ?"

"No, of course not," Crowl, the noted surgeon, replied in a testy voice. "Delphine!" he shouted to the broadest of the women. "Fetch a bowl of warm water and some toweling." To Bernard, straining with the girl in his arms, he instructed, "Here, bring her this way," and led off down the corridor.

When Sancha awoke, it was to a sense of still being lost in a dream, awake and yet unable to escape the imaginary world of sleep. She had no memory of being pulled from the water, lifted upon a horse, and conveyed to the chamber. She recalled the bridge and the cold weight of the dark water, but all the rest was blank to her. She did not recognize the people hovering over her, nor the man holding a cup to her lips.

She drank, hardly knowing what she did. The liquid was thick, cloyingly sweet, and tasted of violets. Time stood still. The faces of the people around her began to melt like wax and flow together, and the mingled sounds of their voices garbled so that they seemed to be jabbering in some strange tongue. Before her eyes the walls of the chamber warped and buckled. She raised herself suddenly on her arms, then tumbled backward into blackness.

Before taking leave of the chamber, Crowl sternly cautioned the servingwomen. "She must have the elixir without fail. Once of a morning and once of an evening. Without fail," he stressed. "Do you understand?" They stood about with downcast faces. "Do you understand?" he reiterated in a still sterner voice.

The tight-lipped women responded with murmurs and nods. They were terrified they would yet be punished for leaving the girl unattended. It had only been for a few moments, and no one had told them she might wander.

Crowl had no sooner stepped from the chamber when a hand dropped on his shoulder.

"We must talk," Swynford said in an undertone, guiding the surgeon toward the solar. Once they were beyond earshot of the servants, Swynford accused, "You told me she would be unable to find her way from her chamber!"

The surgeon's shoulders lifted in a shrug. "I underestimated her resistance to the drug. It will not happen again." His sly gaze followed Swynford as he crossed the room to a sideboard, where he filled a pewter cup with wine from an ewer.

"Wine?" Swynford offered. Crowl declined. "I have increased the dosage," he remarked.

Swynford turned swiftly to face him, wine sloshed from his cup. "She must not die!"

"There is no danger. She will not lose her life. Her mind perhaps, but that can only be to our advantage."

Swynford took a draught of wine and rolled it over his tongue before swallowing. "You are certain? And she will recall nothing, nothing at all?"

"Yes," he assured, "as certain as I am of tomorrow's sunrise. However, she must have the elixir twice each day, that is vital."

"I will see to it." Swynford took another mighty draught of wine. "I wish to God this were ended!" His nerves were in a terrible state.

"It is," the surgeon reminded him with a smile. "Even the girl's uncle believes she is mad. His only fear now is for his own daughter's marriage contract. He will not wish it known that 'brain fever' has reared its monstrous head in his branch of the Valois family tree. He will do all in his power to influence the queen in favor of the marriage."

"Bah! The queen is a child. How does one reason with an eleven-year-old brat?"

"Do not underestimate de Severies. He is a countryman of the queen, and more importantly, his daughter's future is at stake. He will know which persuasions to use. Besides, I am told the little queen is fond of him. Was it not he who brought her the lapdog from France? A present from her mother, Queen Ysabeau."

"Accursed mongrel," Swynford mumbled into his wine cup. "Damnable dog was the cause of all this."

"It will soon be made right," Crowl reminded him. "Has Canby's bastard agreed to wed our little patient?"

"A servant has been sent to fetch him from London," Swynford replied, toying with the wine cup. He looked up suddenly, distractedly, and gave a snort of laughter. "According to Canby, the boy would marry the bloody dog for a fief!" With that, Swynford drained the cup and returned to the sideboard. His nerves were in shreds. He ran a hand through his thinning hair. "It is not his willingness that troubles me. Christ's blood," Swynford swore, slamming his fist down on the oaken chest, "there are too many heads on this beast, too much that might go amiss. If word of this gets out, we shall all hang from the gibbet!"

"Calm yourself, Thomas. Perhaps I should leave some elixir for you, something to mix in your wine tonight."

"Save your poisons for your gullible patients."

"As you wish." Crowl chuckled. "I must go now to inform de Severies of the morning's events. Perhaps it will prompt him to renew his efforts with the queen. Good day, my friend." At the door arch, the surgeon paused. "Twice a day, she must have the elixir morning and night."

"Yes, yes. Do you take me for a fool!"

Three

The following morning, Martin Sims, a young soldier in the pay of Lord William Canby, entered the duke of York's encampment outside London. Daylight was just breaking as he cantered his horse into the meadow. All about him cookfires were being rekindled and men crawled from tents. The bitter, blue tang of woodsmoke added a pleasant sharpness to the cool spring morning.

Martin wasted an hour talking to this man and that before discovering Hugh Loxton was not in the camp. As he led his horse through the rows of tents, Martin met a boy leading several horses to graze. The boy was a talkative sort and told him that Loxton, along with a group of young friends, had gone into the city the day before.

"You'll likely find them swilling ale and harrying the tavern maids," the boy laughed, wanting to appear older and wiser than he was. "Look for the sign of the Gold Ram or the Crescent," he advised. After Martin had put his foot in the stirrup, mounted, and turned his horse about, the boy called after him, "Hoy! You might try the Blind Rook."

At seventeen, Martin Sims was a sturdy-built, sensible lad, not given to flights of fancy or idle gawking. But he had never been to London. The immensity of the city staggered him. His eyes were hardly big enough to take it in. Everything he saw was a wonder to him, the huge fine buildings, the milling crowds, the great bridge that spanned the Thames. He saw as well the gaunt, angry faces of the poor, the beggars, the cripples, and smelled the city's bowels in the stench of the refuse-littered streets.

From merchants and street vendors he found his way. In talking to them he learned that there was a sickness in the city, a scourge, brought on by the lack of rain or some said the retribution of an angry God.

On half a dozen street corners Martin saw men selling marigold petals from sacks, carolling it as a cure for the red pox and doing a brisk business.

When at length he found the Gold Ram, the tavern reeked of vinegar. A huge iron kettle filled to its brim bubbled on the hearth. Coming in from the air, the sharpness of it all but cut Martin's throat. "It cleans the air," the tavern keeper told him. " 'Tis an evil thing, the red pox. Many have died. The only good it's done is to run off the crazy French king's daughter. Sent her 'an her wastrel court scurrying off to Windsor, it did!"

Martin listened patiently while the tavern keeper condemned the state of affairs in England. "Bolingbroke is no better than Richard," the man sneered. Like many who had at first cheered King Richard's usurper, he, too, was now dissatisfied. For though Bolingbroke held the crown, taxes were no less; indeed, there was talk of more and higher taxes. It seemed a crown could not be seized without expense. There was also Richard's queen, the daughter of the mad French king, Charles.

It was a sore point with many, and the tavern keeper was no exception. "She's kept in splendor while people starve," the man went on, angrily. When the better part of his bile was spent, Martin asked, "Where might I find a tavern called the Blind Rook?"

"You'll get naught but watered ale," the tavern keeper warned him. "Though if you've a taste for slop, the stinking hovel be two streets east. 'Tis like a blink odor, you can't avoid it!"

Avoid it or not, Martin had a rare time finding the tavern. More than once he had cause to murmur the tavern keeper's words with annoyance as he wandered up and down a maze of mean-looking lanes and alleyways. It was some long time before he spied a tavern sign among the host of others. The wooden sign creaking in the breeze displayed a black bird perched upon a bony skull. Unlike most peasants, Martin could read a bit and he fancied the red painted letters spelled out, Blind Rook.

With a nudge of his heels and a jiggle of the reins, Martin headed his horse into the alleyway beside the tavern. The din of noise from the street subsided. The building on his right was a cobbler's shop and he could hear the rhythmic tapping of a hammer. It was dim and cool in the space between the buildings.

When he came again into the sunlight he could hear voices from the tavern's kitchen and saw a lot where patches of bare earth peeked through meager grass. Close by was a ramshackle stable, and beyond the attendant manure piles lay a stretch of weed-choked waste ground and a ravine. Where the ravine fell away, a pair of oaks, perhaps a century in growing, towered above a host of sapling trees. A sprinkling of wildflowers, yellow and purple, nodded amid the weeds, and in the distance, he could see the rear walls of another row of shops.

Martin dismounted. He did not at first notice the stable boy. His clothing was the same dull shade as the bare earth where he sat, cross-legged in the sunshine, intently peeling the bark from a twig. Before Martin could call to him, an explosion of voices swiveled his attention toward the rear of the tavern.

A door jolted open and a gang of young men burst into the lot, shouting and laughing. In their wake came a trio of fair-haired tavern girls, looking as if they had just been roused from bed. They trotted out through the patchy grass, clutching their skimpy shifts, all squeals and giggles and soft white flesh, a sight that was all the more startling for the harsh spring sunlight.

The young men looked to be soldiers, though not common yeomen. Martin thought it more likely they were knights, judging by their handsome longbows, fine leather boots, and silver spurs. That they had been a long while drinking was also clear, for they were loud and full of boasting. All had shed their leather jerkins, and some their shirts. Through the lot they went, jostling and parrying with the longbows, pummeling one another and hooting with laughter. Leading the unruly procession was a stout youth with short-cropped hair, yellow and fine as gosling down. His belly jounced as he jigged along, waving his bow before him. Something white, a scrap of linen, fluttered from the tip of his longbow. As the pack of young men drew nearer, Martin saw that the trophy, borne like a banner, was a woman's camisa, and he wondered which of the girls was without hers.

"To the stiffest shaft goes the glory!" the white-haired youth cawed, halting before the nearer of the two oaks and raising the trophy on the tip of his bow. Once, twice, thrice he leapt before he succeeded in snagging the flimsy garment on a high limb.

A flurry of laughter and broad crude remarks followed the men back up the lot. They gathered around several empty ale barrels, bragging and brandishing their longbows. Bets were made. The scantily dressed girls mingled among the men, their voices strident with excitement.

Martin's horse gave the reins a tug. The beast's determined attempt to browse on a clump of weeds brought Martin rudely from his thoughts. He looked about and saw that the stable boy, a skinny lad with tattered baggy hosen, was too busy watching to pay any mind to business. Martin led his horse into the stable and found an empty stall. He was not long inside and, when he again stepped into the sunlight, he saw the contest was about to begin.

The stable boy, still rooted to the spot where Martin had last seen him, stared with rapt attention as arrows were passed from hand to hand. Martin thought them to be Cheshire arrows, for they were sleek, flighted with grey goose feathers and looked to be a cloth yard long. Though, to Martin's eyes, even the finest arrows in the world could not compare with the sight of the nearly nude girls.

They hovered about the men like pale butterflies fluttering from flower to flower, touching and teasing. Their lips were full and red and they chattered and laughed, tossing their shoulders so that their rounded breasts threatened to escape from their shifts. Martin was tempted to stay and watch, but he had a message to deliver. Reluctantly, he struck out down the alleyway, toward the tavern's front entrance.

Inside the Blind Rook a crowd had gathered about a scruffily dressed soldier who stood atop a table, vilifying the usurper king. Ill dressed as the man was, his voice had the timbre of an orator. "Brothers!" he shouted. "Henry Bolingbroke rode to London on our backs and how does he repay us? With taxes and more empty promises! He has murdered Richard, our rightful king by the grace of God, and sent his body off to Langly in a farm cart!" The ruffian's long hair hung in greasy ropes and bounced defiantly over his shoulders as he continued his attack. "Bolingbroke claims the crown by gift. By gift, brothers! He swears barefaced that Richard gave the crown freely and without compulsion." Each time he paused, discontented rumblings, murmurs of agreement, rose from the listeners. "His words are lies, all lies! Our sweat and blood bought him his crown! And while our wives and children starve, he fawns at the feet of the French king's daughter. Tell me who has paid for her silken gowns and jewels? We have, brothers, you and I!"

Martin threaded his way through the crowd, wondering if Henry Bolingbroke would find the crown so pleasing, now that he possessed it. A year before the people had cheered him; now, they spoke against him in the taverns and even on the street corners.

Some even claimed Richard had escaped and that the body of a changeling had been shown to the people. There were rumors of him everywhere and the tale went that he was plotting to retake his crown.

At the far end of the room, where the wine and ale was sold from a high table, Martin found the tavern keeper leaning on his elbows, listening. Once Martin got his attention, he asked, "Have you seen any knights wearing York's badge?" His inquiry elicited only a momentary sidelong glance from the man, and slight gesture of his head, which seemed to indicate the tavern's kitchen.

Martin made his way slowly through the press of people. There was no one about in the kitchen, save for the ever-present swarms of flies. The air was humid, thick with grease, and the stench of rancid meat. Four or five workers, a man and several women, stood just outside the door, watching the contest in the back lot.

An arrow was loosed just as Martin wormed his way through the clutch of kitchen workers. He heard its telltale thrumming sound and raised his eyes to see the shaft lodge itself in a limb just to the left of the fluttering white camisa. A collective roar went up, and among the knights, laughter, and loud, good-natured attacks on each other's prowess.

The jeering died out somewhat as another among the knights strode up to take his place. He bowed elegantly and made a great show of sighting in his prey before he nocked his arrow.

Martin, not wishing to wait for another round of cheers and hoots, took the opportunity to gather his best baritone. "Be any of you called Hugh Loxton?" he asked, looking round.

The majority of the men had seated themselves on logs drug from a stack of firewood and stood on end to serve as stools. Heads turned.

"I am," said a voice to Martin's right. "Who asks?"

Martin jolted round to face an affable-looking young man, broad-shouldered with fair hair, and seated on an upturned log. More truthfully, Martin saw only the half-exposed breasts of the girl bent over him, her hands resting possessively on the muscular shoulders beneath the rumpled linen shirt.

With some difficulty, Martin tore his gaze from the girl's chest. "I am but a messenger, sire, sent by your father."

"My father!" Hugh Loxton gave a hearty laugh. "And who might he be?" A riffle of laughter swept through the group, for all knew Hugh to be the bastard of William Canby, lord of Redesdale.

A girl with ribbons braided in her tousled hair looked Martin up and down, and the man poised to loose the arrow, paused, and lowered his bow.

Martin, much disconcerted, swallowed hard and stammered, "William Canby, lord of Redesdale."

Hugh grinned, taking in the faces around him. "If this is a joke, I swear I shall have someone's hide in payment."

Martin drew the missive from his battered leather jerkin and went over to where the young man sat. "Upon my word, sire, it is no prank," he said, and offered the letter as proof.

Hugh unfolded the stiff linen paper. His eyes moved rapidly over the dark, sloping script.

"What does it say?" one of his friends asked. "Yes, tell us," the others clamored.

The tavern girl clinging to his shoulders slid her arms about his neck and, leaning forward, whispered into his ear.

Hugh brushed her aside, absently, as one might a pesky child. He stood up, holding the paper before him, and announced with a comical air, "It says, that my beloved father desires my presence." He paused, smiled roundly, and, in a voice thick with sarcasm, said, "He who has ever had my welfare at heart, now wishes to claim me before God and king. Ah, but here is the rub, only if I present myself at Windsor without delay."

"You must go at once!" The stout young man with the white hair shouted. He was known as Darcy and his mouth was every bit as large as the rest of him.

"Don't listen to the rogue!" a youth with a large moustache advised. There was a round of laughter.

"Darcy's an eye to winning the gold today," declared a tall, bare-chested youth. "He's more angles than a worm!"

Nearby, a swarthy young man with thick dark hair and a

tavern girl upon his lap, remarked, "If it's truly put, you should go. With a name you might snag yourself a rich widow, a fief perhaps."

Once the joking was set aside, advice came from every quarter.

Hugh turned his gaze on the messenger, demanding, "Who put you up to this?"

" 'Twas Lord Canby, himself," Martin insisted. "Before God, it was he and no other."

Hugh accepted his word, for the moment. He could not conceive of anyone carrying a prank to such limits, though neither could he fathom the reasoning behind William Canby's written words.

Within the hour Hugh had collected his leather jerkin, sword, and scabbard, and settled his account with the tavern keeper. Inside the inn, the noisy political discussion was still in progress. Outside in the lot, the hotly debated contest continued. Hugh bade his friends farewell and walked with Martin to the stable. It was midafternoon when they passed through the city's Aldgate and rode west into the sun.

At Windsor, the day dawned with low and threatening skies. The gloom was such that at noonday the lamps in the palace were still burning. Such was the case in the apartment of little queen Isabelle.

It was there that Sir Charles Grainger, chamberlain to newly crowned king, Henry Bolingbroke, once again expressed his profound regrets to the frowning child. "The sight of your unfortunate lady-in-waiting," he intoned, "would only cause Madame undue distress."

The answer was, no. The little queen's plea had been refused. Indeed the velvet gloves were off, and for all practical purposes Isabelle of France was Henry Bolingbroke's prisoner.

Grainger, a stout man with greying hair, lost no time in pressing his case. "Our noted surgeon, Messire Crowl, has assured me that the young lady's mind is damaged beyond mending. As Madame has been advised, the lady was found at the foot of a staircase. Messire Crowl is certain that an injury is responsible for the loss of her senses. Brain fever is his diagnosis. He has attended other such cases, and tragically, the mind may not be healed. There is no remedy, save by God's infinite mercy or the intervention of the saints."

Isabelle of France sat still as a statue, her small jewel-laden hands folded in her lap. She was fond of cosmetics, and her painted face and red rouged lips made her appear even more childish and forlorn. She did not completely understand the chamberlain's words. Despite the four years she had spent in England, her command of the language was poor.

Presently, she twisted her body in the chair, and whispered to the two young ladies-in-waiting who stood behind her.

She did not trust Henry Bolingbroke's chamberlain, even though much the same tale had been reported to her by her mother's courtier, de Severies. She had no reason to doubt his words or his motives. He was in fact the uncle of Dominique de Severies, her stricken lady-in-waiting. Even so, Isabelle was unwilling to relent. After the hushed conversation, she turned to Grainger and said querulously, "I do not understand your objections."

Grainger drew in a deep breath and began anew. The Dame de Coucy, whom Bolingbroke had placed in charge of the little queen, sat against the opposite wall, before a tapestry depicting the martyrdom of St. John the Baptist. She interrupted Grainger and, with a smile suggested, "Might the queen's ladies be permitted a visit? I would accompany them." The Dame de Coucy sought only to placate the little queen, to settle the matter as quickly as possible. After all, the remaining ladies-in-waiting were but impressionable girls, barely in their teens. They would see the sick girl's pitiable condition and report it to the little queen, much embellished no doubt. But most important of all, little Isabelle would believe them.

Grainger saw at once the merit of her thinking. Nonetheless,

he harbored a great dislike of the Lord de Coucy's second
wife. She was imperious and given to overstepping her bounds.
Grainger sent her a glassy look, but too late. Isabelle had
grasped her words. Now, the little girl was determined to have
her way.

Even Grainger's most skillful ploys could not dissuade her.
It occurred to him that he despised children. It was all he
could do to control his growing frustration. He promised nothing, and only reluctantly did he agree to take the request to
Henry Bolingbroke. When the interview ended, his face was
quite red. At the door arch he sent a last furious glance at the
Dame de Coucy, and stalked from the chamber, grumbling
beneath his breath.

Four

Hugh Loxton and Martin Sims were among the crowds of courtiers and tradesmen who entered Windsor's walls that dreary April day.

Fully ten years had passed since Hugh Loxton had last seen his 'father.' The occasion had been a tourney in the great city of York. Hugh had been a lad of barely twelve, a squire to one of the young Neville lords. The memories returned, of days filled with dust and horses, gaudy pennants, and glittering armor. Hugh's most vivid recollection, however, was of the envy, the suffocating anger that welled up in his chest when he saw William Canby riding onto the lists with his two sons. It was a hurtful memory, one that conjured up the long-dead past. Images returned, as indistinct and faded as the ink of an ancient parchment. Fragments of his childhood flashed to mind, the rough weave of his mother's clothing, his hand clutching her skirt, and the sight of his grandfather laid out to be buried.

Hugh left Martin with the horses. At the door of Canby's apartment, he announced himself to a manservant and was ushered inside. Hugh was at once aware of an unseen, but loud and heated discussion. The ruckus seemed to be coming from a chamber at the end of a short hallway that led from the foyer. The manservant directed him to follow and led off in that direction. He was an older man, white-haired and possibly deaf, for he seemed oblivious to the bawled obscenities that fairly rang off the walls.

The scathing pitch of the argument rose with every step

Hugh took. A shrill voice called out, "We are your sons! He is naught but the get of a filthy poacher's daughter!" Another voice, ragged with rage, accused, "You disgrace our dead mother!"

Hugh heard it all quite plainly, and the words affected him like fat thrown into a fire. A hot surge of anger rose with his pulse. He wondered why he'd come. By the time he reached the door, he was suffocating with hatred and his blood pounded in his temples.

The servant poked his head inside the chamber door and, in a voice louder than Hugh would have expected, announced, "Hugh Loxton, my lord."

The three men inside the chamber fell silent. Lord William Canby was the first to speak. "So you are Hugh Loxton. Come inside. Have you any recollection of my sons, Gilbert and Walter?"

The air of the room was charged with animosity. Hugh gave a curt nod of his head as he entered. He knew them well enough, and from what he'd overheard, their opinion of him had not been altered by time. It was with some small sense of satisfaction that Hugh noticed he was half a head taller than either of them.

Gilbert, the formidable elder brother, had grown heavy. He glared at Hugh from across the room, his face dark with anger. The younger brother, Walter, slow-witted, with ginger-colored hair and a pronounced Adam's apple, muttered beneath his breath with an air of righteous indignation.

"My sons are here from the north to attend Bolingbroke's parliament," Canby said with a wry smile and a sidelong glance filled with meaning. "Today they have come to dispute my sanity, as well as my decision to claim you, and having failed on both accounts, they are about to take their leave."

The remark goaded Gilbert to take a menacing step forward. "Do not do this, Father, I warn you!"

Willam Canby turned on him angrily. "You dare to threaten

me, you ungrateful wretch? All you have is what I have given you!"

"A lie!" Gilbert countered. "What you possess came to you through our lady mother's dowry!"

"And if I had not defended it for thirty years? Who would its master be today, answer me that?"

"I pray for you, Father!" Walter shrieked from beside his brother; his ratty ginger-colored moustache twitched with emotion. "That God may forgive you for the sin you have committed against our mother!"

Canby's heavy features shaded purple. "Get out! Out! Both of you, out of my sight!"

The pair retreated, but not without hurling a last volley of protests. Gilbert was the loudest. "It is our birthright you are squandering on this son of a whore!"

The shouting contest at the threshold ended when William Canby gave the door a mighty heave and slammed it shut. The pair's voices could still be heard as they ranted and raved down the hallway toward the outer door.

Inside the room, the silence was startling. Canby turned back, squaring his shoulders. He smiled and said, "They do not like the idea at the moment, but they will warm to it. They have little choice." He drew up before the young man and studied him a moment. "Do you know that I am your father?"

"So I have been told, my lord." The muscle in Hugh's jaw was strung so tight, he could barely form the words.

Canby circled him slowly, searching for some hint of himself, some replication. "Are you not curious as to why I have offered to claim you?" he asked.

"I expect you will tell me, if you wish me to know."

Canby smiled, more from surprise than amusement. "I am told you have been knighted?"

"Eight years past, my lord."

"Then you have done well by the Nevilles?"

"I have made my own way."

Canby detected a note of stubborn pride in the deep voice,

the determined line of the young man's jaw. Obstinacy, he wondered, or mayhap a grudge, for the humiliations of his childhood? "Without my intervention," he reminded the youth, "you would have been a peasant, and bound to nothing grander than a plow."

Hugh felt the blood rush to his face. "What you did was for the sake of your own soul, not for any love of me."

"Perhaps, though it does not lessen what I am offering you, legitimacy, the Canby name!"

There had been a time when Hugh would have gladly sold his soul to Satan for the privilege of claiming the Canby name. But that was long ago. "I have a name, my lord, that of Loxton."

Canby made a snorting sound. "You are an arrogant pup. You must take the name to gain the wife. If the bargain does not suit you, go! There is the door! Why do you hesitate?"

"You have not called me from London to send me away. We are wasting time. What is it you want of me?"

Canby turned to face the window, suppressing the smile that twitched at the corners of his lips and casting his gaze over the mild green hills and blue arch of sky. He was satisfied at last that he had found some hint of himself, of his own immortality in the brash youth. "A husband is needed for one of the queen's ladies," he said from over his shoulder. "The fief is borderland, but the dowry is £2000 in gold. There is also a church benefice as a reward, a prebendary. I am told the abbey's income is nearly £500 per annum." After a moment, he added, "The fief is known as Evistone and adjoins my holdings in Redesdale."

"You have two sons, why have you not offered it to one of them?"

"As fate would have it," Canby said, moving away from the window, "they have already taken wives, one a Percy heiress, the other a Mowbray."

Hugh felt sweaty beneath his clothes. He was still angry.

"How is it possible that I can be offered a church? I am not ordained, and if I accept your proposal, I too shall be wed."

"An abbey," the elder Canby corrected. "Such an arrangement is not unheard of," he said with deliberate slowness. "Surely you must know, that which pleases our lord Bolingbroke also pleases God."

Hugh understood. Now he was even more suspicious. "Who is this lady-in-waiting to the queen?"

Canby paused at the table, tapping his fingertips impatiently on the wooden surface. "The niece of Arnaud de Severies, the French king's representative."

"Her family approves of this arrangement?" Hugh asked, clearly skeptical.

"Yes!" Canby answered at once. "They are eager to find a suitable match." He then paused, regarding his bastard son with an air of reflection. Weighing his words, he decided how best to broach the subject of the lady's illness. "Of course, there are certain terms. They desire assurances that she will be well cared for, and you must swear faithfully to keep her in the north, away from court."

"What flaw has she?" All manner of unpleasant images flashed through Hugh's thoughts.

"None of which I am aware, only that she has become an embarrassment."

"She is with child," Hugh concluded.

"No. It is a more delicate matter even than that. She has been stricken with brain fever. She is not violent," Canby hastened to point out. "I am told she suffers from a sort of melancholy. Still, her dowry is more than generous, and if you do not accept it, another will. What say you?"

"Might I have a day to consider it, my lord?"

"No, it must be now, now or not at all. I must have your answer."

Hugh's gaze fell across the contracts lying on the table, land and wealth, far beyond his wildest dreams. He had lived in want too long. He was like a starving dog, offered a haunch of meat. He could not resist it.

Hugh inclined his head. "I will accept." He said the words before he fully realized that he had, and just as quickly doubted the wisdom of his choice.

"You could not do better. No land is finer, nor freer than the north country," Canby told him as he leaned forward to watch the youthful hand produce the sweeping letters upon the parchment.

Had he not been so intent on scratching out his name with the worn stylus, Hugh would have agreed, for it was the land where he was born. He knew it well, though it was a child's memory. He had not set foot in the border country for many years, ten perhaps. As for the manor house and abbey at Evistone, those he had never laid eyes upon. Evistone had been disputed land even then, passing endlessly in bloody battles from Scots to English and back again. Hugh laid the stylus aside, looked up, and asked, "Might I view the lady before the marriage?"

Canby glanced at the contracts, the flowing script. The boy had a deft hand. "I may be able to arrange it," he said, agreeing to do what he could, but cautioning, "the girl's uncle wishes the marriage to proceed with all speed. He awaits only the queen's permission."

"Richard's queen? She is a child, is she not?"

Canby shrugged. "She's wiser than her years. In any case, the de Severies's girl is in her service. She must agree to the match." Canby gathered the parchment, then addressed him directly, "Have you an escort, servants?"

Hugh nearly laughed. After his merry sojourn in London, he barely had money to stable his horse for the day. "No, my lord."

"You have no squire?"

"I cannot afford to feed one," Hugh answered honestly.

"That is all in the past," Canby murmured, making off across the room to a cabinet. From a small, cleverly fitted door he drew a leather pouch. It jingled with coins as he recrossed the room. "Here is a hundred pounds," he announced, dropping the pouch on the table. "Thirty of it are in pence and shillings. You must hire an escort, some servants, and purchase a char for your journey north. Do it this day."

Hugh reached out and claimed the pouch. It had a weighty feel to it. He stowed it inside his jacque and turned to go.

"Where will you be staying?" Canby asked, thinking ahead, realizing that he might need to locate his bastard son on short notice.

"The armory." Until that moment, Hugh had not the funds for anything finer.

"Fair enough, you will be easily found. Ah, yes, before you go. What did you think of the boy I sent to fetch you from London?"

"Martin Sims?" Hugh replied, for he had a good memory for names.

Canby glanced up from the parchment, where a hitherto overlooked phrase had caught his eye. "Is that his name? Yes, him," Canby muttered, for he had several hundred such young men in his service, cotters' lads the bulk of them and trained for little else than brawling. "Will you accept him as a squire?"

Hugh had not even considered it, although the boy had seemed levelheaded enough, a decent sort. "I don't know. I suppose he'd do."

"Take him then, as my gift to you." Canby's rugged features softened to a near-paternal air. "Keep in mind what I said about the escort. Make them stout men and well armed. There, that is all I have to say. Go to it, you have no time to waste; matters may move quickly."

At the armory stable, Martin offered to fetch their horses. "No," Hugh said to him, "we will walk." Hugh had no intention of shouting out his affairs for all to hear, and such would have been the case had they been on horseback.

Strolling leisurely they made their way past the stables and out the postern gate. As they walked, Hugh told Martin what he had need to know.

Martin was clearly delighted by the news that he was now a squire. In a matter of two days he had risen to a position which he had formerly seen as unattainable. He was still marveling over his unexpected good fortune as Hugh explained the chore that lay ahead.

Windsor was almost provincial when compared with the vastness of London and its seething sea of humanity. Though as if not to be outdone, tidy Windsor had its share of meanness in the narrow, twisting streets and clutter of houses that huddled about the castle's grey stone walls. The city was larger than Hugh had first thought, even to its sizable colony of beggars and cripples, who skulked in doorways and along the foulsmelling back lanes.

Turning from the main thoroughfare, Hugh and Martin mingled in the procession of tradesmen, carters, drovers, and pedestrians who made their way through the grimy streets toward the market. There amid the multitude of stalls, their progress was slowed by the press and mob of people. Baskets of fish, spring vegetables, cloth, herbs, spices, and all manner of goods were laid out on the ground on blankets or stacked in stalls.

Dead rabbits still in their skins and geese whose necks had been wrung hung from poles, while live ones sat trapped in wicker baskets. The squeals and grunts of beasts and clamor of human voices was loud and constant, as vendors and buyers haggled over pennies with a gusto that bordered on bloodlust. Noisy clutches of children dodged before their path, laughing and chasing. Drovers sold pigs, sheep and beef, and strings of horses neck-roped together were tied out for the inspection of prospective buyers. It seemed to Hugh that anything a man might want could be had there, for a price.

Hugh's first act was to choose a tavern. He found one near the market called the MERRY MAID. From there he hired several lads to run through the market and the village streets shouting, "All ye able-bodied men! Good wages and cotters' plots to be had in the north! Come to the MERRY MAID this noon!"

The plan succeeded far beyond Hugh's wildest expectations. By midday the tavern was jammed with a shoulder-to-shoulder crowd of freebooters and rabble, men and boys, old and young, all eager to seek a better life in the north.

"Sweet Jesu!" Martin whistled softly through his teeth. "How will you know who you chose, an' who you didn't? After you seen a dozen, they all begin to look alike."

It was a valid observation, one Hugh had not considered. Just then a tavern girl in a flimsy red woolen kirtle with a string of gaudy, painted wooden beads strung about her fat neck squeezed past. Hugh caught her by the meaty arm. "What will you take for the beads?" he asked.

She gave him a brazen smile and suggested, "We can bargain up the stairs, my good sire."

" 'Tis the beads I want, nothing more. I'll give you a shilling."

"They be my favorite," she protested, clutching at the beads which encircled her fat neck. "But maybe for two coins."

Martin eyed his master as if were daft. "Not her and a string of pearls," he muttered, soft as the voice of conscience.

"A shilling," Hugh stated flatly.

"Aye," a boy standing nearby piped, "it's more'n she'd steal off drunks in a week!"

The fat tavern maid sent the boy an evil look, and relented. "A shilling," she agreed with a sour twist of her lips, as she lifted the necklace over her head.

Hugh plucked the colorful strand from her hand, and slapped a coin into her upturned palm. "Have you a knife?" he said to Martin, who gave a bewildered nod of his head.

"As I choose a man," Hugh directed, "cut a bead from the strand. Caution him to keep the bead as proof that he was chosen."

For several hours, Hugh talked his way through the queue of men. In the end he chose twenty. A few had soldiered. One

was a burly fellow called Rumald, whose mother had named
him for a three-day-old saint. Among the others were an ap-
prentice ironmonger and a harness maker's helper. A third boy,
known as Donel, who had been let out to a wheelwright for
a pittance and a bed, knew where a char could be purchased
for a fair price.

The chosen were for the most part young and with no hopes
of bettering themselves. All told a like story. A garrulous tan-
nery lad remarked, "There's naught in Windsor for the likes
of me, an' London's worse." With anger he told how he had
gone off to London to seek his fortune only to return in a
fortnight with nothing to show for his effort but bruises and
a broken jaw. "I was robbed and left for dead." He was small
in stature, but shrewd and knew of a man in the market with
a string of sound horses who was desperate to sell the beasts
in order to pay a debt.

By day's end Hugh had struck bargains all over Windsor.
Some wise, some by his own admission not quite so astute.
Those he shrugged away. All in all he had accomplished what
he had set out to do, and for a cheaper price than he had
anticipated.

Taking leave of the horse dealer, Hugh and his squire sauntered through the market. It was all but deserted. Only a few
merchants remained, those who had come from the surrounding countryside with carts. They sat in groups, passing wineskins and leather ale jugs, tending their cookfires and talking
over the day's profits.

With evening upon the village, Hugh and Martin strolled
toward the palace, weary of mind and limb and decidedly hungry. Hugh debated taking a meal in one of the taverns, but in
the end determined the wine and the food from the palace's
kitchens would be more palatable.

Martin agreed, at least in principle, remarking, " 'Tis free
at the armory." So with grumbling stomachs they walked on.
The route Hugh chose led through an alleyway lined with taverns and like establishments.

Here the streets were as crowded as they had been at midday. The scent of roasting meat, the clamor of voices, and the bright red glare of torchlight filled the spring evening with a sort of sensual excitement. It was a stimulation made more acute by the women gathered beneath the torchlit entrances, calling to passersby in enticing tones.

There were women of all varieties, some large, some small, all displaying their curves in the torchlight, the soft flesh of their shoulders, a glimpse of breast.

Hugh and Martin continued on up the squalid alleyway, pressing their way through the crowd, their spurs jingling at their heels. Where another darkened alleyway lined with squalid hovels led toward the palace's postern gate, they turned, walking side by side.

In the foul-smelling darkness Hugh caught sight of a huge and shapeless humped form lying in the shadows. "Have a caution," Hugh warned, thinking it was a trap, for thievery was a fact of life. Martin nodded, his hand going to the hilt of his dagger.

Five

Suddenly the blackened mass jerked as if with alarm, and separated into two distinct forms—a man's prone figure upon the slippery, putrid ooze of the alleyway and a woman's. Surely a woman, for Hugh and Martin saw the outline of her hips, the fullness of her skirts. The pair lunged forward.

Martin overtook the fleeing form, grappled with her, and pinned her to the rough beam-and-mortar exterior of a hovel. He and the girl collided with a loud thump, rousing the householder, who cursed at them through the meager walls.

Hugh's voice rang out a warning. "Watch your gut, she may have a knife!" He halted and squatted on his heels beside the downed man. The victim was middle-aged and fat, a merchant, judging by his fine clothing. At first Hugh thought him dead. His face was colorless as a lump of dough.

The sound of Hugh's voice roused the merchant. He stirred and tried to raise himself on his arms. He began to blabber words, but they were so slurred by drink, Hugh could not make out what the man was trying to say.

"Yes, absolutely, my friend," Hugh agreed and sat him up against the wall of a house.

A short distance away, Martin wrestled with the girl. She was no match for him and presently he dragged her back along the alleyway, impervious to her struggling and the filthy insults she flung at him.

Hugh had been watching the scuffle. When he looked back

to the fat merchant, he saw that the man had passed out once more.

Martin swung the girl forward like a sack of grain. "Is he dead? She had his purse!" he stated, jangling the coins as proof.

"No," Hugh chuckled, "but drunk enough to fool a grave-digger."

"I never touched him!" the girl shrieked.

"A likely tale!" Martin shouted into her hard, harassed young face. Giving her a sound shaking, he demanded, "What did you hit him with?"

"I never! He fell over, he passed out, that be the God's truth!" she screeched, breaking into tears.

"They'll cut off your pretty white fingers for that!" Martin promised with a cruel exactness, as he passed the plump leather purse to his master.

Hugh jounced the purse in his palm as if to gauge its worth, then stuffed the purse inside the man's muddied velvet jacket.

"Someone else'll have it no sooner than you turn your back!" the dirty girl squalled, attempting to free herself with a violent shrug. Martin gave her arm a savage twist and she winced with pain. "Shall I turn her over to the provost?" he asked.

"No need for that," Hugh said, rising to his feet and looking the girl up and down as best he could in the darkness. She was young, a short, sturdy girl, with a round fleshy face. "What is your name?"

When no answer was forthcoming, Martin gave her a shake and snarled, "Speak up!"

"Alyse," she said through her clenched teeth, unwillingly, and with a stubborn, sideways glance. Another violent shake, prompted her to add, "Alyse Watsdoughter."

The surname brought a hint of a smile to Hugh's lips. Martin laughed, for in Saxon it meant "sweaty man," a peasant. In the darkness the girl glared at them, with anger, or perhaps with fright. For she knew having one's fingers chopped off was no idle threat, nor was it the first time she had been accused of thievery.

"There's no shame in honest sweat." Hugh told her, querying, "Are you as industrious as your name?"

"Aye," Martin answered for her, "what she don't squeeze out of them when they're between her legs, she steals from their purses later!"

Hugh silenced him with a glance, and continued, "Where are your kinsmen?"

"They be in Surrey. An' 'tis not true, what he says; I didn't always do this. I came here last summer, an' I had a proper place in the kitchens," she insisted, jerking her head toward the palace. "I was turned out for stealin', but 'twas a lie. I didn't steal nothing. 'Twas the butcher, 'tis him what's guilty as sin. He steals the lord's meat and sends it off to sell in the market. Oh he be the devil. He misuses all the girls. He hurt me, hurt me more'n once! An' when I threatened to tell about his thievin', to stop him from using me, he accused me a stealing some mutton, but 'twas a lie!"

Behind them the merchant began to babble drunkenly once more. Hugh ignored him. The girl watched the drunken merchant, fearfully. Her tongue flicked across her lips.

Hugh believed her tale, why, he could not say. Perhaps it was her solid stance, the ring of simple truthfulness in her country brogue. "I've need of a maidservant for my lady wife."

Her gaze jolted back. "Me, sire?"

" 'Tis you I've asked."

"Aye," she bobbed her head. "I would, 'an gladly," she said, her gaze darting nervously from the handsome young noble to the drunk who was now struggling to rise. "You'll not give me to the provost?"

"No, but you must come with us. Let her go, Martin." Hugh directed. He turned and began to walk away.

Martin dropped his hand, releasing the girl. He shook his head in wonderment and followed after his master, half-expecting the little slut to bolt and run.

She stood her ground, too confused to flee, fearful of the babbling drunk, of punishment. "Where are you going?" she called after them.

"To the armory," Hugh answered.

She hesitated, then tore after them. When she came even with the pair, taking two steps to their one to keep abreast, she asked, panting with exertion, almost pleadingly, " 'Tis not a trick?"

"No," Hugh replied. "I've had my fill of dishonesty today."

"Where be the lady, then?"

"She is sickly and in the care of a surgeon, but in a few days, perhaps less, we shall be traveling north to the border country. I need a woman to care for her, one I can trust to do my bidding."

She kept step as they approached the gate, her mouth open, gulping air, but silent.

Martin saw her furtive glance as they passed the entrance to yet another alleyway. "What he says is true, you stupid goose." Martin had no idea why he'd said it, for if she had darted away, he would have considered it well and good to be rid of her. He was even less pleased when a few moments later, inside the palace walls, his master left the filthy girl in his charge.

"See that she has a bath," Hugh instructed. In the leaping torchlight, he saw that her greasy fair hair hung in ropes. He had already noticed her ragged clothing and decidedly unpleasant odor. "Tomorrow," Hugh said, producing a coin from his jacque and passing it to Martin, "take her to the market, to one of the rag women and find her something decent to wear."

"Yes, sire," Martin answered.

Hugh last saw his squire walking resignedly toward the stables, the ragged girl trailing after him. Hugh went on to the armory. As he pushed through the door, the noise and the smell alone told him that the daily meal was being served. The hall was crammed, humid with the mingled scents of food and human bodies.

The tables where the common soldiers ate were filled to overflowing, and some men were even standing. The single oasis was the tables at the rear of the hall near the blazing hearth, where the knights sat laughing and taking their meal. A number of varlets scurried to and from the kitchens, serving food and wine. Here, there was space aplenty on the benches.

Hugh selected a seat away from the heat of the hearth, sat down, and was soon drawn into the conversations around him. Between talking and listening, he had eaten only a small portion of his meal when a youthful page approached the tables.

The boy was weedy in appearance, tall and thin with a skinny neck and protruding eyes. He looked about, squinting, as if he were searching for someone. At last he called out, "Hugh Canby?" in a shrill prepubescent voice.

Hugh washed down the cud of bread he was chewing with a slug of ale. "Here!" he responded with a slight motion of his hand. The boy edged between the tables and, drawing near, whispered, "Lord Canby wishes to speak to you at once."

Hugh grunted a response and continued to eat, out of obstinacy, as much as a need to fill his empty stomach. He had waited nearly twenty-four years for his father to recognize him. As far as he was concerned, the old boar could damn well wait till he finished his meal. When he looked up a short time later, the boy was still standing there, staring at him with his bulging eyes. "Why are you waiting? Go?"

"No, sire." The boy's Adam's apple bobbed up and down. "I am not to return without you!"

Hugh said nothing more and went back to his meal. The boy stood there, shifting from one foot to the other. Finally, in disgust, Hugh abandoned the remainder of the beef pastry on his platter. He stood up, drained his cup of ale, and followed the boy out into the dank spring evening.

At that hour there were few people moving about the palace grounds. Hugh and the messenger crossed the lower ward at a brisk pace, their footfalls ringing off the flagged stones. They had walked a fair distance into the middle ward, when the boy halted abruptly. Hugh walked on a few strides before realizing it.

"This way, sire," the boy said with a jerk of his head, explaining, "I was told to bring you to Lord Swynford's suite."

Hugh knew Swynford only by reputation, and at best it was an unsavory one. He was Henry Bolingbroke's half brother. It was said he had a penchant for brutality, and that he had been King Richard's jailer at Pontrefact Castle. Hugh and the boy entered the palace from the portico below the new tower and made their way through the palace's darkened galleries. Hugh's attempts to pry more information from the boy came to nothing. Either the boy was as dull as Hugh had at first suspected or he had been warned to keep silent.

A long, twisting staircase led from the galleries to a lengthy passage, dimly lit, and lined with court apartments. In all they met fewer than a dozen people in the passages, for the most part liveried servants and pages.

Swynford's suite was in a newer section of the palace, where every so often the pungent scent of new lumber reached their nostrils. Inside the apartment a number of servants milled about the foyer. Among them was a lanky varlet who held a small white dog in his arms. Hugh and the messenger's arrival sent the little dog into a fit of frenzied barking, which continued until the lanky handler clamped a hand over its muzzle.

Hugh was directed into the solar, where he found his father of less than a day and a man, whom he presumed to be Thomas Swynford, talking quietly. The conversation came to a sudden halt as Hugh entered. At the door arch, he inclined his head. "My lords. I trust I have not kept you waiting overlong."

William Canby stepped forward and, with a jovial laugh, pummeled Hugh on the back. "Of course you have, you young swine. Where the devil have you been?"

"Eating my supper."

"There, by God," Canby said with a chuckle, "at least he is honest about his poor manners."

"That alone is proof of your paternity," Swynford quipped,

as he signaled to a servant standing by the wall to fetch a goblet of wine for his guest. "I am Thomas Swynford," he said to Hugh. "It was I who alerted your father to the opportunity presented by the de Severies family."

Hugh gave a brief nod of his head. "I am indebted to you, my lord."

The smile remained, but when he spoke again, Swynford's voice had lost all hint of geniality. "Indeed, you will do well to keep that in mind," he said, pausing, his fingers playing nervously with the stem of his goblet as if he were choosing his next words with great care. "From your position of Evistone you will have a rare view of the border country. Our king, my kinsman Bolingbroke, is in need of clear-sighted young men."

The man drug out his words interminably. Hugh could bear it no longer and, in frustration, offered, "I shall do my utmost to hold the border against the Scots, my lord."

"Oh I am certain you will," Swynford retorted with a sigh. "Dear God!" he exclaimed, "Were it only the Scots who look with greedy eyes upon my kinsman's crown."

Swynford's glance flicked to the manservant as he handed a goblet of wine to Hugh, and his next words were spoken more rapidly. "Since we shall soon be interrupted, I will put the proposition to you bluntly. Before this day, your loyalties were with the Neville family?"

The statement, phrased as a question, left Hugh no choice but to respond. "That is true, my lord."

Swynford had a peculiar habit of twisting his lips into a grimace each time before he spoke, as if in warning, like a dog just before it bites. "If you accept Evistone, you must disavow all masters, save one, and that be our gracious king, Henry Bolingbroke." Swynford's fingers stroked the goblet's stem as he spoke. His gaze lengthened, and though Hugh could not see his 'father' from where he stood, he sensed the byplay between the two men.

"The northern barons hold themselves aloof," Swynford

stated. "They keep their own counsel, and it is known by all that some among them consider themselves as worthy to wear the crown as Bolingbroke. Therefore it is vital," Swynford continued, "that the king be kept well informed. All that you see and hear, any scrap of gossip which comes your way, you will pass on to my messenger. Accommodate me in this and you shall be rewarded handsomely." Once more the odd grimace cramped his features, and he promised, "Far beyond the paltry dowry of the lady de Severies. Do you understand what I am saying?"

For a long uneasy moment, Hugh said nothing. He understood perfectly. He found the idea somehow repulsive. He was being asked to gain men's trusts and then to betray them, to act as an informer. But at this stage he could hardly refuse, nor was he, to his profound shame, willing to abandon the dreams he had coveted for so long in order to spare his noble convictions. "My lord Bolingbroke may depend on my candor," he replied, forcing a smile.

Swynford's features relaxed, as if a great weight had been lifted from him. "Excellent. Have you any questions?"

"There is one problem, my lord," Hugh was quick to point out. "How shall I contact you? The distance is great, and if it is known that I . . ."

Swynford's words cut across his. "Have no fear. My courier is a man of many talents. He will find you, and you alone shall know his identity. Now, I believe you were promised a look at your future wife."

Six

William Canby set aside his wine goblet. "I'll show him the way," he offered, laying a hand on Hugh's shoulder and guiding him into the hallway. Once they were outside the chamber, Canby murmured, "You've done well. My God, 'tis unnerving. You are so like me twenty years ago." Hugh made no reply.

A half dozen strides brought them to the door of the sick chamber. The room was crowded with women, save for the court physician, Crowl, who stood beside the sickbed like a guard. He looked swiftly to the door as they entered, acknowledging Canby with a nod of his head. Just as quickly he returned his attention to the conversation at the bedside where two young ladies-in-waiting hovered over his patient.

One of the young ladies, a fair-haired girl, held the patient's hand and pleaded, "Sancha, dear Sancha it is I, Marie. See, here is Alene. Do you not recognize us?" Marie had tirelessly repeated the words over and over for nearly an hour. Her eyes glistened with tears. At last, she sighed and looked up to Alene with a tortured expression.

"We have come to visit you," Alene told the pale face amid the bed linen. There was no response. Still, Alene hoped and, with a smile, attempted to make her voice cheerful. "Madame the queen sends her prayers. She is sick with worry for you, Sancha. She prays morning and night for your recovery. Please speak to us, Sancha," Alene pleaded, her voice breaking tearfully.

Nearby, the Dame de Coucy, flanked by serving women, looked on, regarding the emotional scene with an expression of cold detachment.

From between the huddle of heads and shoulders, Hugh caught only a glimpse of a pale face deep in the shadows of the bed's draperies. His least hope of securing a closer view was dashed by yet another impassioned plea from the young, fair-headed lady-in-waiting. Whatever it was she had said, for she spoke in French, sent the bedridden girl into a gale of weeping and whimpering, and the physician quickly ushered everyone from the room.

As the crowd exited the chamber, Hugh dropped back and fell into step with his father and the scowling physician. "Does the lady recognize no one?" Hugh asked, determined to learn the extent of the girl's debility. From what little he'd witnessed it appeared hopeless, and the thought of being saddled with a raving maniac for untold future years suddenly disturbed him.

The hallway was jammed with people. Hugh was forced to repeat his words to make himself heard above the noisy departure of the de Coucy woman, her servants, and the two sobbing ladies-in-waiting. In the foyer, the little dog began to yip and howl.

The physician, Crowl, inclined his head. "Yes, I am very much afraid that is the case, messire. Even in our enlightened age the human mind remains as much a mystery as it was in the times of Galen and Hippocrates."

"Look to the bright side," William Canby remarked. "At least she will not meddle in your affairs."

A shadow of a smile brushed Crowl's lips. "He is right, you know."

Hugh ignored their remarks. It was answers he wanted. "What is the cause of her illness?"

His query elicited only a shrug from the physician. "Who can say? At first I believed the affliction was the result of her falling and striking her head. But now, well, I simply do not know. Surely the seeds of madness were always present, for the lady is of Valois blood. Perhaps the fall kindled the illness, as in the case of the mad King Charles."

"You say she fell and struck her head?" Hugh asked.

"Oh yes, though it was hardly more than a bump, superficial at the very worst, scarcely enough to cause a bruise."

Hugh was about to pose another question, but Swynford was waiting for them in the foyer. The crowd had exited, though it was still possible to hear the faint yipping of the little dog.

"Now that you have seen her," Swynford said, "have you any second thoughts? If you have, now is the time to speak."

"No," Hugh lied. He could not very well say what he was thinking, that all of it disgusted him.

"The wedding may take place as early as tomorrow, that is agreeable to you?"

"Yes, of course."

"Then I will bid you good evening messires."

Hugh walked a short distance with the stranger who was now his father. It was not from design, rather that they happened to be going in the same direction.

"A wife is but a dowry," William Canby said with a philosophical air. "No one will censor you for taking mistresses."

"Just as you did," Hugh suggested, unable to suppress the sting of resentment he felt.

William Canby laughed. "Do not be so quick to condemn me, you young hypocrite. Once you are a lord, there will be many a woman eager to come to your chamber by night and cosset and kiss you. I daresay you will not refuse them, no more than the next man." Canby drew to a halt. "Here our paths part. Go with God. We will speak on the morrow."

"Good night, my lord," Hugh intoned, though he would have much preferred to tell him to go to hell.

A steady drenching rain fell on the morrow. In Windsor's chapel, Mass was being said, and in the court apartments, Arnaud de Severies arrived, breathless, at Thomas Swynford's door, insisting he must speak to him at once.

Swynford, roused from his bed, came bleary-eyed into his solar. "What in God's name has happened now? No, do not say it, not yet." Swynford collapsed into a chair. A servant hastened to put a goblet of wine in his hand. He took a deep draught. "Well?"

With a flourish, de Severies produced a document. "I have it!" he crowed victoriously. "Isabelle's approval, the marriage can be finalized today. I say today, because it would be best to consummate the union before Isabelle has a change of heart. She will be en route to Havering within hours. Her entourage is gathering in the inner ward at this moment."

"Bolingbroke is sending her to Havering?" Swynford rubbed a hand across his eyes. He was yet groggy, somewhat annoyed that he had not been informed. He did, however see the wisdom of removing Isabelle from sight, what with parliament soon to convene at Westminster and rumors flying of Richard's escape, idiotic tales of his cheating death, and of Bolingbroke's attempt to pass off a changeling's body in place of Richard's.

"I, too, am bound for Westminster this afternoon," the Frenchman confided, anxiously mentioning the matter of his own daughter's betrothal. "There are papers to be signed. You can not imagine the complications, she in France and I, here in England. I must handle everything through couriers. It is maddening." Above all, de Severies feared scandal. "I shall not breathe easily until my niece is safely wed and away," he said, as he rose from the chair in preparation to leave. "Any hint of 'illness' in the de Severies branch of the family would be a disaster," he reiterated, and again at the door, he asked, "You are certain the wedding will take place today?"

Swynford assured de Severies in his most placating tones. "All is arranged, there is only the matter of the priest pronouncing the words. Do not worry, my friend, by this time tomorrow, the young lady will be on her way north, never to be heard from again."

Swynford was still congratulating himself on his coup, when his servant returned with Crowl, the court physician.

"So it is arranged?" Crowl accepted a goblet of wine from a servant. Normally, he did not take wine so early in the day, but this was a cause for celebration.

"Yes, it all went just as I planned. Now our only problem is getting her to the chapel. If we cannot do that, there will not be a marriage. She must be able to stand before the priest, and say the words. That is the law."

"Calm yourself, Thomas, I am not without alternative methods. My knowledge of such substances is complete. If one does not produce the desired effect, another will."

Two rooms away, Sancha awakened to find herself in a strange bed, she knew not where. She made a valiant, but futile attempt to rise. She drew in a deep draught of air and, frowning, willed herself to concentrate.

Objects in the room came slowly into focus. With great effort she raised herself on one elbow and grasped at the bed's green velvet draperies. Crushing the cloth in her hand, she pulled herself upright and gazed about the chamber.

She saw only a stout servingwoman seated on a bench before the hearth. The woman appeared to be dozing contentedly, her double chin resting on her bosom. With more stealth than she believed herself capable of, Sancha slid to the edge of the bed and touched her bare toes to the chill of the chamber floor.

The effort left her trembling, suddenly dizzy. *Where am I?* she wondered, helplessly. She had never known such a feeling of unreality. It was as if she was trapped in some terrible nightmare, one from which she could not awaken. None of it made sense to her, not where or why or how she had come to be there.

Dazed and unbelieving, she gazed at her surroundings. She

had but a dim recollection of the room. That room, or another very like it, though not as it appeared to her now, but filled with people. Strangers, who stared at her and asked her questions. There had been voices, too many voices, as if they had all been talking at once.

I am in London, Sancha thought. *But where are Marie and Alene? And Madame, where is Madame the queen?* She closed her eyes, battling the dizziness that threatened to overwhelm her senses. Swirling lights flashed before her eyes, and with them a sudden vivid memory of sunlight and trees.

A wave of nausea swept over her. She steadied herself by clinging to the bed's draperies. She clung there, moment to moment, willing herself not to be ill. When the worst of it had passed, she took her first faltering steps toward the door. Her only thought was to find Marie and Alene. There was something she must tell them, though she could not remember what it was. Cautiously, she released her grip on the draperies. Without support, her legs trembled, threatening to buckle beneath her.

She took another teetering step before the room began to tilt crazily. All her senses seemed to desert her, she shut tight her eyes once more, praying for the vertigo to pass. But when she lifted her head, all before her eyes rippled like water. Her hand shot out, clawing the air, groping for the bedpost, but finding only empty space.

The sound of Sancha's body striking the chamber floor brought the slumbering woman from her nap. Wide-eyed with surprise, the stout maidservant lunged from the bench with a violent start and began shouting for help.

The frantic voices of several women swirled above Sancha as she was lifted back into the curtained bed.

"There, there, demoiselle, you must not test your strength too soon," a masculine voice said.

Sancha stared at the long, angular face hovering over her. "Who are you?" she whimpered. "Tell them to let me go. I must go to Madame the queen."

"You must first recover your strength, demoiselle. You have given us many anxious hours." He smiled at her and, taking her hand, seated himself on the bed. "Do you not know who I am?" he asked.

"No," she cried. "Please help me, I must go to Madame."

"Of course you shall, all in good time. I am, Crowl, the court physician, and though you may not be aware of it, I have helped you for some days. There was a time that even I despaired for your life. You see, you have been unconscious for a very long time, since you fell on the stairs. You do recall the accident?"

Sancha could only shake her head in bewilderment.

He smiled, reassuringly. "No? Well, it is of no importance. You must not trouble your thoughts over it. You must devote all your strength to recovering your health in time for your marriage on the morrow."

Sancha gave a cry of protest. She knew of no betrothal, no marriage contract. Madame Isabelle had promised.

Crowl exhaled, making a tsk, tsking sound and patting her small hand. "You do not recall that either? Surely you recall the young man? In your distress, you called his name many times. Did she not, Delphine?"

"Oh, yes, messire, many times."

"He has visited you without fail."

"No! You are lying to me! Madame would not do such a thing. She promised. She would not send me away!"

"Madame the queen chose the young man herself. She was very pleased with her choice, as you should be, demoiselle."

Sancha shook her dark head in furious denial. "No! I do not believe you! I must speak to Madame the queen."

"That, I fear is impossible. Madame Isabelle has been removed to the safety of Havering. Here, you must drink this."

"No!" Sancha refused. "I demand to see Madame."

"I have already explained to you, Madame is no longer at Windsor."

Windsor? Sancha did not understand. How could she be at

Windsor? She was so terribly confused. "My uncle de Severies, I must see my uncle. Send someone to fetch him!"

"Of course, demoiselle. But first you must drink this."

Perhaps it was the manner in which he forced the cup to her lips, or the cloyingly sweet smell of the liquid that roused her resistance. "No!" she shouted, flailing her arms and knocking the cup from his hand.

Crowel's face went white with anger. "Foolish little cow!" he muttered, grappling with her and seizing her wrists. At his call, several servants burst into the room and converged on Sancha. Her screeching cries and frantic struggles were soon put down by the servants. Half a dozen sweaty hands gripped Sancha's body as the physician twisted her long hair about his hand, jolted her head back, and poured a measure of the sickening sweet liquid down her throat.

Sancha choked and gagged, struggling to free herself, but to no avail. In a matter of moments, the grey mist filled her mind once more, and she was lost to dreams, awake, yet unaware.

Later in the solar, Swynford berated the physician, "Suppose something of this sort happens at the chapel?"

"Faith, Thomas. In another hour, she will be led as easily as a lamb."

"I pray you are correct," Swynford muttered, "for both our sakes."

Seven

Hugh awoke long before daybreak. A groggy hand drawn thoughtlessly over his jaw was enough to tell him that he was in need of shave. With his leather satchel slung over his shoulder he set off for the chamber adjacent to the latrines.

There, rainwater from the armory roof was caught by means of troughs and funneled into stone vats. One had only to twist a spigot to draw a pail of water. It was quite a luxury. The only drawback to the arrangement was the close proximity of the latrines. Without a breeze, preferably a stiff north one, the stench was almost overpowering.

Bumbling in the semidarkness, Hugh located an oil lamp. But it required a dozen or so determined attempts and a spate of oaths before he managed to ignite the wick with his flint striker. There was precious little oil; for the most part it was the wick he was burning.

By the wavering light, he took a polished metal disc and a small, straight-bladed knife from the satchel. Twice he readjusted the angle of the polished metal disc, seeking a more accurate view of his jaw. The actual act of scraping away several day's growth of beard was a mindless chore, one which afforded him the opportunity to reflect on the events of the past few days.

In one fell swoop he had gained a fief, an abbey, and a rich wife. It was a heady feeling to suddenly possess your heart's desire. The most remarkable part of his incredible success was that it had been passed to him as casually as if it was a sugared cake. *Why?* he wondered The thought bedeviled him, buzzed at the back of his consciousness like an annoying gnat. Perhaps distrust was bred in his blood. He was, after all, the grandson of a poacher, born among peasants and possessed of the same simple cunning, the knowledge that nothing in life comes cheaply.

Why, then, had he been chosen? The question haunted his thoughts. Normally such lucrative plums were saved for political favorites, those who had performed some great or—as the case more often proved—dubious service for the king. Admittedly his agreement with Swynford fell somewhere to the left of honor, though it hardly seemed worthy of such a glittering reward.

The only remaining possibility was the lady de Severies. Obviously she was an embarrassment, but only to her family. Why, then, was Henry Bolingbroke, for his hand was surely behind the offer, willing—no, eager—to confer wealth, position, and land on the lately claimed bastard of a relatively unimportant northern baron?

With his face still stinging from the cold water and closeness of the blade, Hugh returned to the armory. All through the quarters, men stretched and scratched themselves, nonchalantly pissed against the walls, and pulled on their clothing amid grunted conversations, shuffling feet, and the creaking of cots.

Outside, the rain had departed, leaving in its wake a watery grey landscape. On the horizon a bank of low clouds raced eastward across a bruised sky. Hugh walked at an unhurried gait toward the stables. The air of the spring morning was crisply cool, tingling his fingertips and freshly shaved face.

The packed earth of the lower ward had dissolved into a morass of glutinous yellow mud. Near the stables the swampy ground was pooled and pocked with hoofprints. It was yet early, and the stable was silent save for the sounds of the horses. In another section of the vast structure he saw two boys, their faces blank as sleepwalkers, forking manure into a two-wheeled cart.

Hugh found Chewbit in a stall near the end of the aisle. At his approach the tall, sturdy gelding gave a snort of recognition and pricked his ears forward. Hugh gave the outstretched neck a pat. He was fond of the animal, despite its often obstinate turn of mind. It was a handsome horse with a well-shaped head, hinting of Eastern blood, and a powerful conformation, long-legged, but well muscled with prominent withers.

The gelding was a true black, showing no hint of brown points about its muzzle or legs, and unmarked save for a whorl of white hairs on its forehead. Hugh took his time saddling the horse, tinkering with the bridle and its faulty buckle, before he led the black out into the swampy yard and rode toward the village of Windsor.

At the MERRY MAID a number of Hugh's men were already standing about in groups, waiting. Hugh bought a round of ale for all, talking to this man and that, and in a process that was to some degree unconscious, weighed their words, the unspoken language of their actions, deciding which of them could bear the most responsibility.

Presently, Martin arrived with Alyse Watsdoughter in tow. Plump and pink-faced, she was scrupulously clean and dressed in a blue kirtle. In Hugh's estimation she looked more a fresh-faced field laborer than a proper lady's maid, but considering her mistress's derangement and where they were going, her sturdiness might well be an asset.

The remainder of the day was spent in haggling with merchants and purchasing supplies of food, wine, and cloth. As the hours passed the sun returned with a golden vengeance, glaringly bright, sparking off the puddles and baking a crust on the mud of the village streets. By late afternoon it was quite warm.

Hugh settled his entourage—men, beasts, chars and carts— in an open stretch of ground beyond the market. It was evening when he left Martin in charge of the campsite and returned to the palace.

He had scarcely settled Chewbit in his stall when he caught

sight of his father's servant, the fair-haired boy with the pro-
tuberant eyes. The boy had seen him as well and broke into a
trot.

"Lord Canby wishes you to come at once," the boy said,
coming to a halt before the stall. Hugh nodded, noting the
boy's urgent tone. He was becoming thoroughly annoyed with
William Canby's peremptory summons, or perhaps it was the
boy's smirking manner that ruffled him. In any case, Hugh
was not in a mood to be rushed. He took his time unsaddling
the gelding. The boy jigged about impatiently, following Hugh
as he hung his saddle and tack on the wooden rack opposite
the stall.

Had Hugh suspected what was awaiting him, he would have
been even less inclined to hurry. At the suite he was confronted
by his father and three clothiers, a fat man and his two assistants.

Willam Canby greeted him with little explanation, other than
an exuberant slap on the back and the muttered words, "The
saints are with us. The little queen has agreed. She will give
her permission, but only if she approves of you."

"What are you saying? I must go before her?"

"Yes, of course," Canby replied impatiently, hustling Hugh
into a chamber off the foyer, where a number of servants were
industriously filling a wooden tub with pails of steaming water.
The air was stifling, laced with the scents of musk and cypress.
The humid dampness made it difficult to breathe. Hugh felt
as if he were underwater.

All about the room a colorful assortment of doublets, hosen,
boots, all manner of fine clothing lay in piles atop the chests
and cupboards. The clothier and his assistants trailed in after
them, locked in a hushed discussion. It seemed they had been
measuring Hugh by sight as he strode into the room, for no
sooner than they entered, they were babbling fitting sizes back
and forth and set at once to selecting certain items from among
the stacks of clothing.

"When?" Hugh finally managed. "Now?"

"Yes, as soon as possible," Canby remarked, blithely brushing aside his objections. "She is only a child. You should have no trouble turning her head, she is fond of flattery. I dare say you have charmed your share of young ladies. Now off with your clothes and into the bath."

Hugh slowly removed his jacque. His fingers moved haltingly over the closures of his linen shirt. "You don't expect me to wear those?" he stated, clearly opposed to the padded black-and-scarlet brocaded doublet held up by the fat clothier.

The clothier's sparse eyebrows lifted. He turned his fat, shining face to Willam Canby, and in an abashed tone, protested, "It is the latest fashion, my lord!"

"For jongleurs," Hugh grumbled.

"The black and scarlet, yes," Canby agreed, nodding to the clothier. And turning back to Hugh, emphasized, "The little queen judges all men in the image of Richard of Bordeaux. Yes, yes," he agreed, reading the look of disapproval in Hugh's eyes, "by all accounts our Richard was a foppish fool, but all the same we do not wish to disappoint her."

While Hugh bathed, William Canby instructed him on what he must say, how he must conduct himself. Hugh's head was buzzing by the time he stepped from the tub. Servants awaited him with toweling and the fawning clothier doused his damp flesh with more scent.

Dressed in the black-and-scarlet doublet, fine woven hosen, and tall, parti-color boots, Hugh felt foolishly conspicuous. In his estimation, he smelled like a whore and looked like a troubadour. A glance in the clothier's mirror only served to confirm his conclusions.

"Magnificent!" the clothier declared with an air of accomplishment, an opinion immediately seconded by his mawkish assistants.

Canby chuckled, clapping Hugh on the shoulder. "You are an earl now," he said, "and by God, you must dress the part. Keep in mind what I have told you about the queen. Do not speak to her as you might a child. She despises to be treated so. And do not concern yourself about the language. The uncle, de Severies, speaks both French and English with equal ease, and he is eager for the marriage."

A servant came forward with Hugh's sword and scabbard. Close behind the servant the clothier waited, a red velvet bag cap in his hands. Hugh's first impulse was to refuse to wear the hat, but he relented. What did it matter, he told himself. Not even the ridiculous hat could make him appear any more of a fool.

At the queen's suite of rooms a servingwoman with a round, flaccid face, dough-colored in the lamplight, admitted Hugh. He was shown into a small chamber, where a short dapper man, richly attired in a jewel-studded doublet awaited him. He introduced himself as Count Arnaud de Severies, courtier to King Charles of France and uncle to the unfortunate lady de Severies. He was middle-aged, possessed of a somewhat dissipated handsomeness, and with an unctuous manner that Hugh instinctively mistrusted.

De Severies studied him with an appraising eye, then declared, "You are more suitable than I had expected, young, tall, fair-haired and," he said, looking closer, "she is fond of pale eyes; you are certain to please her. However, you must remember to smile graciously. For Madame, appearance is everything. She is but a child, you understand. You do not speak French?"

Hugh admitted he did not. He had only a rudimentary knowledge of the language, what a soldier need know, vulgarities for the most part.

"It is of no importance," de Severies said, dismissing the matter with a flourish of his hand. "I shall convey your words, and hers. Though I must warn you, her ladies-in-waiting will undoubtedly be present. They understand English far better than Madame, so weigh your words well."

The servingwoman who had admitted Hugh appeared at the door arch. De Severies took the lamp from the woman and sent her away. "Come," he said to Hugh, and led off down a shadowy hallway. At its end was a long rectangular hall, whose one entire wall was set with tall graceful windows.

Isabelle, the child queen, swamped in a gown of saffron silk heavily embroidered with gold and sewn with a multitude of seed pearls, was seated on an ornate Florentine chair, her back to the tall lancet windows and flanked by her two ladies-in-waiting. Had it not been for her noble demeanor, Hugh would have thought her comical, a child masquerading as an adult.

Wall sconces had been lit against the purple twilight gathering beyond the windows. Hugh listened as de Severies introduced him. He did not understand most of it.

The queen waited, a small, still figure. De Severies's long-winded speech ended. He bowed slightly and, in a whispered aside, murmured to Hugh in English, "Speak your greeting."

"Madame, God give you good evening." Hugh felt a fool.

"Messire, you are welcome."

"Madame, if it please you. I come before you in good conscience, and with the approval of the holy church to make known my desire to take to wife your fair lady-in-waiting, Dominique de Severies."

Dutifully, the dapper de Severies translated the words.

The little queen, looking particularly solemn, pressed her lips together in preparation to speak, then hesitated as if making a conscious effort not to refer to her favorite lady-in-waiting by her pet name, Sancha. "Dominique," she began in a childlike voice, "is very dear to me. I grieve for her misfortune."

Isabelle's bejeweled hands lay unmoving on her gown. Only her eyes, shining in the lamplight, betrayed any emotion. "I am informed by my father's courtier that you are fully aware of Dominique's affliction. Nevertheless, you have sworn to shelter her and treat her with kindness and affection."

De Severies discreetly cleared his throat, and repeated the words, their equivalents or nearly so, in English.

"Madame, so I have truly sworn before God," Hugh replied.

Her gaze shifted to the courtier, then again to Hugh. She said, "Messire, I am certain you have been told that I am merely a child, and lacking in wisdom, and perhaps it is true. But I am neither so young nor so foolish as to believe you feel any deep affection for my lady de Severies."

There was a moment of flustered silence. De Severies, whose English was heavily accented, stumbled a bit on the first words of his translation. The two girls standing behind the little queen exchanged glances.

Hugh felt the pressure building behind his eyes. What the child said was no more than the truth. How was he to reply? He dragged in a slow breath, attempting to sort through his thoughts. The words he had intended to say, lies mostly, sounded, even to him, insincere, implausible at best. After a moment, he managed, "Madame, I have pretended no unseemly affection, none other than a man might rightly owe his betrothed. I can do no more than faithfully swear before God that I will, till the last of my days, tenderly care for the lady and keep her from harm."

The little queen, her voice sharp, replied, "Messire, as I have learned through sad experience, men often break their oaths, to their king, and yes, even to God. Why should I believe you will not neglect my dear Dominique, keep her in misery, and squander her dowry?"

De Severies sighed with frustration. Nothing was going as he had planned. Smiling, he addressed the queen rapidly in French. The exchange went on for several moments, while behind the queen's chair the two ladies-in-waiting whispered with their heads together. Finally, the fairer of the two leaned forward and murmured something into the queen's ear.

As she did, de Severies turned to Hugh, and in a barely audible voice, repeated the little queen's words.

The muscle in Hugh's jaw tightened and his gaze flicked back to the child awash in the saffron silk dress and the sulky faces of the two ladies-in-waiting. Obviously, the queen considered him as much a traitor to Richard as any member of Henry Bolingbroke's court. Hugh had half expected as much, though it did nothing to lessen his consternation, nor the sinking feeling in the pit of his stomach. Had he come this far, only to have all he had ever dreamed of, the fief, the dowry, slip through his fingers like smoke?

Eight

De Severies looked suddenly pale and quite possibly even more agitated than Hugh. He stepped quickly forward, addressing the child in their native tongue, "Madame, in God's name, I have devoted my energies to the righteous and merciful purpose of arranging a marriage for my beloved niece. You who have not seen her have no notion of the piteous nature of her affliction."

The conversation between them, earnest and argumentative, went on for some time. Hugh understood nothing of what was said, for it was in French, and they spoke in a very low tone. After a time, de Severies raised his head and looked to Hugh, a mysterious smile on his lips. "Messire, come forward if you please."

Ill at ease, Hugh approached. The two young ladies-in-waiting, hovering at the little queen's elbows, glowered at him.

Again the courtier flashed a smile, though this time bright with victory. "Madame has agreed. She will give her permission," he announced. "I have assured her that you shall treat our beloved Dominique with all the care and devotion which so sacred a trust deserves."

Isabelle leveled her gaze on Hugh, and offered her hand, heavy with rings, for him to kiss. Child that she was, there was something distinguished, almost imposing in her manner.

Accordingly, Hugh took the proffered hand and, bowing gallantly, brushed his lips to the cool fingers. He raised his head, and for the briefest instant their gaze collided.

The child blinked, her dark eyes liquid in the lamplight.

Hugh retreated a step, bowing once more before addressing her. "Madame, in that you have graciously entrusted the lady de Severies into my care, I beg you believe that there is no other who would serve his obligation with more honest assurances of care and tenderness than I."

Isabelle's lips twisted bitterly with emotion, and she turned her head away, attempting to hide the tears that glistened in her eyes.

Hugh's words respoken through de Severies, she seemed not to hear. Abruptly she made a slight motion with her hand, indicating for them to withdraw.

Hugh returned to his father's apartment. He felt a fool strutting about in a brocaded doublet, and was anxious to change back into his serviceable leathers.

He found his father alone in the solar, reading a book. Hugh was surprised, not so much by the fact that his father could read, but by the fact that he had never thought of his father on such human terms before.

"Has she agreed to the marriage?" Canby asked, closing the book.

Hugh's reply was a sleek smile. With a flourish, he doffed the foolish hat and tossed it in the direction of a large chest that stood to one side of the door. "So I am told. I understood very little of what was said." Crossing the chamber, he spied an ewer of wine on a sideboard. "May I?" he asked, selecting a goblet from the shelf above.

Canby chuckled. "Providing you pour one for me." He leaned forward, shifted his body in the chair, and set the book aside. "I took the liberty of sending a servant to collect your belongings from the armory."

Hugh returned with the wine. "Why?"

"Swynford has secured an apartment for you," he said, reaching for the goblet.

"Really?" Hugh's brows rose in amazement. "Where?" He slouched into a chair.

Canby sniffed at the wine. " 'Twas no bargain, this malmsey. Rank, don't you think? Strong as owl shit! I've fine Bordeaux at my home in London, from my new wife's estates. Bordeaux, now there is righteously good wine."

Hugh took a mouthful, rinsing it over his tongue before swallowing. He shrugged. "I've tasted worse. Am I to sleep there tonight?"

"Uh, yes. At the end of the passageway." He indicated with a jerk of his goblet. "You can hardly bed a bride in the armory, after all."

Hugh gave a snort of laughter. "I admire the man's confidence." At the time, it did not occur to Hugh that anyone should expect him to consummate such a union. His thoughts were on other matters. He took a long swallow of wine, concluding, "In my opinion, Richard's little queen may yet refuse her permission. She was none too pleased. No date was set."

"It will be tomorrow at prime."

Hugh looked at him. "How can you know that?"

"Swynford has arranged everything, the chapel, a feast, musicians. He was here, sitting where you are, not an hour ago." Canby continued to sip at the wine, smacking his lips. " 'Tis a pity most of the court have already gone," he mused, "followed Bolingbroke off to Westminster. Still, there'll be more than enough to make a drunken noise. Parliament does not convene till the feast of St. George. Time aplenty for them to stagger off to London."

Hugh and his newly found father took a second goblet of wine, then a third. Canby, it seemed, wished to reminisce.

"Do you recall the day I came upon you and your half-brothers fighting over a fox kit they had snared in a trap?"

"Yes," Hugh said. He had not thought of the incident in years.

"I had been out hawking," Canby recounted, leaning back in his chair. "I happened upon the melee and put a halt to it. I think they would have killed you. Perhaps not, though, you were a doughty little churl. They had beaten you bloody, but in the end you carried away the damn fox kit, didn't you?"

Hugh smiled and took a sip of wine. "They had no right to kill it," he said finally.

The elder man chuckled. Eventually he turned the conversation to his new, young wife, the joys of amour, and laughingly suggested to Hugh that what the lady de Severies needed was a good sound mating. Having explored that topic, he went on to speak of the north country, the feud with his sons, and his hatred for his liege lord, the earl of Northumberland.

Hugh listened, stifling an occasional yawn and offering an opinion when called upon. It was just as well, Hugh thought. He would not sleep. He sat there following the conversation, wondering if he had not done a very foolish thing in taking charge of a demented girl and an embattled fief.

In another wing of the palace, the servants of Thomas Swynford were already engaged in preparations for the wedding. The bride's trousseau, trunks, and casques of clothing had arrived from the queen's apartments earlier in the evening and were now stacked in the foyer about to be rerouted to her husband's quarters. Several varlets, chosen for the task, stood about talking, awaiting their instructions.

The constant chatter of women's voices drifted into the foyer from the sick chamber, where as many as eight women collided, bumped, and hustled about the small room, attempting to bathe and array the invalid bride.

A spare little serving girl with yellow braids tightly knotted about her head, burst into the crowded room to report, "There's no rain, St. John be blessed, but the fog is thick as sauce!" The little serving girl's announcement was followed by a chorus of sighs and more chatter. "At least the train of her gown won't be ruined," one woman declared, while another remarked, "All the better not to look like a drowned bird!"

" 'Tis sad," the spare little maid, said, "for as she rides to the chapel, none will see her gown." There was a murmur of agreement, for what a sight the gown was, sapphire velvet in color and delicately embroidered with interlacing silver roses, and set with sparkling brilliants. It dazzled the eye; indeed, the gown seemed to light the corner of the room where it lay in readiness.

The women's conversations swirled about Sancha as she was guided to a copper tub and sat breast deep in the warm, scented water. She was scrubbed, scented, and toweled, tugged one way and then another as the women determinedly arranged her damp hair, colored her face, and laced her into her clothing.

Earlier, Sancha had awakened to a frightening new awareness. The nausea and vertigo had passed away, but the confusion remained. No matter how she tried to concentrate, she could not recall coming to Windsor. Neither did she have the vaguest recollection of her betrothal, nor the man she was to marry.

For the most part, the women exhibited great patience with Sancha's endless questions. They readily consoled her and offered their assurances. Some questions they would answer, but those concerning King Richard and Madame Isabelle, they purposely ignored. The fat woman, Delphine, moved about the room, overseeing everything. More than once Sancha noticed the woman's hard glance directed at a talkative serving girl and how suddenly it silenced her.

While one serving girl knelt to slip the lushly embroidered silken slippers on Sancha's feet, another placed a circular veil of sheerest silk upon her dark head and topped it with a dainty silver circlet.

Perhaps it was the sapphire color of the gown, for Sancha had brought it with her from France, or perhaps it was the whisper softness of the velvet that stirred a memory of her childhood home, and of her leave-taking four long years before. How vividly she recalled her excitement at being chosen to be a demoiselle of the little Isabelle! How odd, she thought, that she could remember a day so long past, and nothing of the present.

The reality of her impending marriage did not strike her

with full force until she was ushered into the courtyard where in the torchlit mist horsemen appeared like figures in a dream. Their voices seemed to come from all directions as they shouted back and forth in high good spirits. "Here is the fair bride!" one loudly announced, raising his voice above the clatter of iron-shod hooves. Sancha swiftly turned her head toward the raucous voice, and saw a fat man raise himself in his stirrups and peer at her through the yellow-tinted fog. She felt suddenly terrified.

"Why did you not tell us she was so lovely, you sly hound?" the fat man boomed. "I would have married her myself."

"What a randy old goat, you are," called a younger man in a purple hat, who was struggling to control his horse amid the darting servants and jostling riders. "You've already a wife and two mistresses," he accused. A fourth man, with a long face and hollow cheeks, nudged his horse from the mist, his every movement accompanied by a tinkling of bells. "Aye, he's searching for one he can satisfy!" the man said, his voice edged with sarcasm.

The fat man howled with indignation, as those about him joined in the hazing. From atop his palfrey, Thomas Swynford laughed and, turning in his saddle, addressed the hollow-cheeked man.

"Piers, I take it your business is completed?" The man did not answer him with words, but with an ugly slant-eyed grin.

"Well and good," Swynford said. It seemed he was about to say more when a horse nearby balked and sidestepped into another. His horse jolted forward, almost unseating him, and he lashed out angrily at the servant. "You ignorant oaf, right that beast. Here! You, you stupid lout, bring the bride's palfrey about. Be quick!"

Bewildered and shaken, Sancha fixed her gaze on the richly caparisoned palfrey being towed toward her. Her breath stopped in her throat for a frightening moment. Voices and laughter rang in her ears. She gulped a mouthful of the raw-tasting fog and prayed the leering fat man was not her intended husband.

Tears stung her eyes and she felt suddenly giddy with disgust. She raised her hand to her face to brush away the wetness. But before she could, the chastised servant halted the palfrey squarely before her, and a burly servant swung her into the saddle.

Only then did she notice several women among the riders. Apparently, they were to be her attendants. In the flaring torchlight their painted faces floated before her eyes like masks. They were strangers to her, not of Richard's court.

Sancha had been promised that she would not be forced to marry. At that moment she felt abandoned by all the world. She prayed her union would not be with a man who was very cruel, very fat, or very old. She knew firsthand of such a tragedy. At ten she had seen her fourteen-year-old sister sent away tearful and pouting to Anjou to be the wife of an aged, three-time widower.

With high good spirits the procession clattered from the courtyard into the fog, Swynford chatting at its lead. Every sound was muffled by the damp, heavy air; even the sharp black shadows of the battlements and towers appeared blurred and indistinct.

Before the chapel, flaring torchlight illumed the splendid columns. The great doors stood open and a small knot of people waited. In the murky darkness of the chapel yard figures groped through the fog, for the most part curious servants and a few beggars who waited patiently to scramble for coins tossed by the wedding party.

William Canby raised his eyes, idly gazing at the chapel's ornate facade. He took a deep breath, his gaze lingering over the stone gargoyles and the posturing saints, only dimly visible in the mist. Incense from the smoking censers mingled with the tarry odor of the torches.

Canby coughed sharply and raised a hand to his mouth. He took a step, turned, and clasped his hands behind his back. Moments passed. Presently he inclined his head toward his son. "Have you the ring?" he asked in a hushed voice. The ring William Canby spoke of was a ruby ring that had belonged to his first wife. He'd given it to Hugh the night before, and said to him, "It should have been your mother's ring." But he was drunk when he said it.

Hugh patted his hand against the breast of his doublet, and nodded. His stomach hurt with excitement, anticipation. A clatter of hooves, a murmur of voices, heralded the approaching cortege. He swiveled his head toward the sounds, staring into the fog.

Fat and officious in his silken robes, the bishop noisily cleared his throat and muttered a few words to one of his servers. In the street the cortege emerged from the mist and began to dismount.

Hugh's gaze seized on the small indistinct figure of a girl surrounded by attendants. Two were required to carry the train of her gown, while two others, one at either elbow, guided her up the terraced steps. Hugh saw at once that his bride was neither fat nor lame, and as her face materialized from the luminous morning fog, he saw also that she was strikingly lovely.

Hugh felt a sudden twinge of uneasiness in his chest. For some reason, unknown even to himself, he found her beauty distressing. For an instant he stared at her in sheer amazement. The sound of the bishop's voice made him start like a man wakened from a dream, and he quickly extended his hand to hers.

Sancha, unaware of him until that moment, shuddered at the alien touch of his hand. Her heart wrenched painfully to a standstill. Blinded by tears, she glimpsed only a shadowy outline, a phantom made larger than life by the fog. All about her there was the rustle and shuffle of people moving into position. Her throat constricted painfully and her hand, imprisoned in his, felt as if it had turned to stone. At first she dare not raise her eyes, fearing what she would see.

Almost against her will, she stole a sidelong glance, and then another. He was a stranger to her, young, tall, and not altogether displeasing, but a stranger. She watched his hand pass over his chest, making the sign of the cross, saw his lips moving in prayer. No, she decided, there was nothing about him that was familiar to her. How could he have come daily to visit her as the physician had claimed? No, she had never seen him before, never.

The bishop's fat, florid face blurred before her eyes and his words ran through her thoughts like water. She could not think beyond the shock of realizing that her innocence, the world she knew, was gone forever. Fear gripped her heart, and when the time came to repeat her vows, the words stumbled from her lips piecemeal. For all intents and purposes she was now the wife of the stranger who stood beside her.

At last the wedding party entered the church, where the Mass would be read, where galaxies of candles illuminated the lofty stained glass windows and the dim figures of saints lined the walls, only half-seen in their niches.

Hugh guided her before the altar, unable to reconcile himself to her feeblemindedness. The cruelty of it stunned him. She was beautiful, soft, and warm, and there was a certain look about her, about her eyes, her lips, that inflamed his body and filled his mind with sensual imaginings.

Once the shuffle of feet and hiss of voices died to silence, the bishop's sonorous voice droned out the solemn Mass of the Trinity. Special blessings were pronounced upon the bridal couple, and soon afterwards came the chanting of the *Agnus Dei*. The Mass ended.

The dull, clangorous tolling of the bells began, and Hugh stepped forward to receive the bishop's kiss of peace. Turning back, he took his lady wife's face between his hands and touched his lips to hers.

There was no response. It seemed to Hugh that she did not

so much as blink, and he was left with the unreal, foolish sensation of having kissed an inanimate object.

The exodus from the chapel began. Hugh led his new bride into the grey morning and the usual congratulatory comments. His bride seemed oblivious to all of it, and to him as well. He was almost relieved to relinquish her to her attendants, who came forward carrying a sapphire velvet cloak to wrap round her shoulders.

The fog, far from dissipating, had thickened. His father, Swynford, and the other members of the wedding party stood about in groups, talking in animated voices as they awaited their horses.

Hugh was joined by his father as he tossed coins to the beggars. "There, but for the grace of God, are we," William Canby remarked, pitching a last fistful of pennies into the mist, where the beggars scrambled on all fours, cursing the fog and dodging the servants as they brought the horses to the foot of the terraced steps in groups of twos and threes.

The sound of the bells vibrating on the damp air followed the cortege through the ward and to the hall, where a feast awaited.

Since it was a Friday, no meat was permitted, and the hall reeked of fish. Entering, Hugh noticed the hall was already half-filled with guests. He imagined them to be Swynford's crowd, for he saw no one he recognized. Most of them appeared drunk.

Hugh took his place at the table. His bride was seated beside him. She moved as if in a trance and sat motionless, staring vacantly at the platters of eel shimmering in jelly, and fish of every description, all sauced, baked, or fried and cleverly arranged amid glazed and spiced vegetables. From the kitchens a constant stream of servants brought custards, doucettes, little sugared cakes dusted with spice, candied figs and pears, and wine, and more wine.

For all Hugh's considerable efforts, his bride could not be

coaxed to eat, not by Hugh, nor by her attendants, who had taken seats close to her.

"Let the women fret with her," William Canby advised his son. "Girls that age are foolish. Who can say what goes on in their heads."

A young man, seated on the other side of Hugh's father, leaned out with his elbows on the table and shouted, "They are like unruly horses, they need to be ridden!"

His remark drew a round of laughter, and a fat man with his cheeks stuffed with food, raised his goblet, saluting Hugh. "Such a pretty, young face and so tender," the fat man sighed. "I envy you this night." A toast was proposed, and afterward still more coarse humor made its way round the table. As the feast continued, broadsides of randy jokes were exchanged, the wine flowed freely, and the guests roared with laughter.

Hugh joined in the revelry, drinking and laughing. It was expected of him. However, time and again his gaze returned to the pale, proud face in the sapphire gown. The old fool was quite correct. She was lovely, slender as girls of that age commonly were, when they were no longer children and not yet women. But there was also in her the unmistakable promise of lushness, evidenced by the soft white tops of her breasts, which peeked coquettishly from the décolleté of the sapphire blue dress. Most appealing of all was the innocent, childish face, the dramatic dark-lashed eyes. Hugh felt suddenly miserable, angry at fate, and perhaps God as well. What was he to do with her? It was an impossible situation, and so he drank.

Musicians trooped into the hall. Two men wearing particolor hosen and flamboyant satin shirts carried a harp between them. A fat woman in a vermilion gown followed, her dagged sleeves fluttering with each sweeping gesture of her plump arms. Others in equally bright garb carried a variety of musical instruments. Tall and short, the musicians entered. Among them was a troubadour with shiny, well-oiled black hair and heavy-lidded eyes. He played a lute and sang in a mellow voice, praising the bride's beauty in poetic verse.

With his half-closed eyes he likened her beauty to a rose, her lips to coral, her eyes to jewels. Hugh's attention shifted to his bride. She appeared unmoved by the slick-haired troubadour's crooning praise. She sat very straight, staring off into nothingness, and wearing the same sad, resigned expression as when Hugh had seen her hours before at the chapel. With the bride properly praised, the musicians set to playing loud and lively music for the noble company's dancing pleasure.

Later in the day the chattering female attendants took Hugh's bride away with them. He assumed they had retreated to the garderobe. Not surprising, for anytime he'd glanced at the elegantly gowned attendants, they had their noses in a wine goblet, and he reasoned they would have to do something with all the wine they'd downed. For the past hour they had giggled incessantly; everything seemed to amuse them. Hugh had discovered that the red-haired attendant, a skinny girl with a long neck, was Swynford's second wife. She was little older than Hugh's bride. The others were also Swynford kin of one degree or another.

By that time most of the guests had abandoned the table to join the line of dancers rhythmically moving about the hall. The music blared, loud and unmelodic. It made Hugh's head hurt—or perhaps it was the wine.

Hugh had drunk more than his share of the fiery burgundy. He stood to one side of the dais, watching the dancers and talking, more accurately listening, to Thomas Swynford, his father, and several other men whose names he had heard and just as quickly forgotten.

One, whom Swynford referred to as Piers, was a tall, unpleasant-looking fellow with deeply pocked skin, hollow cheeks and a ghoulish expression. He wore a golden ornament in one ear and little bells adorned the tops of his fine cordovan boots.

Swynford, whose eyes were bright as embers, hung on the man's shoulder, presumably to keep from falling down.

Another was middle-aged and grossly fat, and the fifth, a

young man in a foppish purple hat. It seemed to Hugh that
someone had said he was the nephew of Archbishop Arundel.
He certainly talked like a rich man, for he bragged, "When I
was last in Calais, I purchased half a dozen new hounds, coursing hounds for taking deer."

"Hare and heron are my pleasure," the fat man remarked.
"I prefer hawking to hounds, but this time of year I've no
birds to put up," he finished, with a sigh of complaint.

Hugh imagined that he was referring to the season, May
through August, when the hawks were mewing and unfit to
fly. Hugh had always considered hawks more trouble than they
were worth. It was true they ate little and carried no fleas, but
neither were they so loving nor loyal as a hound. But he kept
his opinions to himself. In any case, the fat man had monopolized the conversation and was gleefully reciting his entire
arsenal of hunting tales. He was still talking in a loud voice
when Hugh glanced over his shoulder to the dais and noticed
the four giddy attendants leading his bride back to the table.

The fat man saw them as well, particularly the bride, for he
shouted, *"Le voy! Le voy!* See her! See her!" It was a call
used by hunters to signify that a doe has been sighted.

Swynford, much amused by the witticism, gave a hearty
laugh, staggered a bit, and pummeled Hugh on the back. *"Sa
say cy avaunt!* Forward sir, forward!" he shouted, employing
yet another hunting call, and laughing so that his eyes squinted
to slits.

" 'Tis time to put the bride to bed!" William Canby crowed.
The words were hardly off his tongue before they echoed back
from Swynford and the others. In the center of the hall the
music bleated to a halt, the dance ended. The revelers were
quick to take up the call, and the women were as shameless
as the men. " 'Tis time to put the bride to bed!", they called
out, repeating the words at the top of their lungs till all were
chanting, " 'Tis time to put the bride to bed!"

A crowd began to gather, and Hugh was propelled toward
the table on the dais. Amid the laughter and ribald comments,

Swynford was loudly relating the misfortune of a cross-eyed knight who upon his marriage bed surprised both himself and his bride with his faulty aim. The air shook with laughter.

Trapped in the moving tide of revelers, Hugh glimpsed the physician Crowl at the table. He had been unaware of the man's presence until that moment. He looked again through the bobbing heads, and saw Crowl offering a goblet to the lady, apparently coaxing her to drink from it. Hugh saw her turn her head in mute refusal, and Crowl's insistent expression. He drew nearer, his lips moving rapidly. Whatever it was he said caused the lady to relent, and she tipped the goblet to her lips.

The rowdy charivari delivered Hugh to the dais, where his bride's giddy attendants stumbled over the trains of their gowns as they pulled and tugged the unwilling bride to her feet.

Sancha's one, small, white-knuckled hand clung desperately to the table, defeating the determined efforts of the twittering attendants. Finally the redhead, weak with laughing, discovered the problem and set about prying loose the bride's fingers, one by one. Her sudden triumph sent Sancha careening sideways.

At the same instant, someone shoved a wine goblet into Hugh's hand. From the corner of his eye he saw his bride lurch toward him. He flung out an arm to catch her, surely preventing her from falling. Wine sloshed from the goblet, marking the front of her gown from bodice to hem with a great dark stain.

"Kiss her! Kiss her!" the drunken crowd shouted. Hugh pulled her to him with a hand round her waist and planted a chaste kiss on her tightly compressed lips. A chorus of hoots and boos rose from the crowd, accompanied by taunting shouts.

"He doesn't even know how to kiss his bride!" they laughed. The more licentious shouted, "Perhaps he needs tutoring! I'll gladly show him how to tup her!"

Hugh drained the goblet and set it aside. "Enough," he said laughingly. "What do you expect! Another kiss may satisfy you, but it will certainly not satisfy me!"

The crowd's momentary laughter soon turned to shouts,

louder and increasingly lewd, until their chanting became deafening.

Seeing that there was no other way to silence them, Hugh cinched his startled bride in his arms and kissed her, crushing his mouth to hers, passionately. He could feel her struggling against him, sense her terrible confusion as he pressed the kiss. He knew he should release her, but the wine had gone to his head and the feel of her excited him. His heart raced and his pulse pounded wildly. In his hands she was supple as a piece of silk, warm and delicious, so that he was seized by the unreasoning desire to smother her with kisses, caress her, and crush her to him until she became a part of him. It was an impulse so overwhelming that it seemed to jolt his every nerve, from his fingertips to his brain. His head reeled and his blood rushed to buzz in his ears, deafening him to the raucous applause of the crowd.

The invasive, almost barbarous kiss roused Sancha to rebellion. Startled and frightened, she shoved against her drunken husband with all her might.

Hugh, caught unawares, staggered backward a step before regaining his balance. He saw her hand rise, but he was too drunk, too slow to dodge. Her palm collided solidly against his cheek, a sharp crack that rang in his ears and jarred his vision. But what truly amazed him was the loud, lewd obscenity, succinctly English, that tumbled from her pretty French lips.

Where had she learned such a word? His cheek burned as if it had been scalded, but even that could not stop him from laughing. The crowd went wild, roaring, almost bursting with laughter. A flood of talk followed and one among them, shouted, "Not married a day and already they are quarreling!"

Sancha turned swiftly away, convulsed with shame and anger. But there was no escape. She was mobbed by her attendants, who, along with a dozen or more women guests, swept her away toward the bridal suite in a smothering cloud of perfumes and rustling velvets and satins.

Noisy as excited hens, the jabbering women pulled and pushed Sancha through the palace's passageways into the apartment and at last into the bridal chamber. There they stripped away Sancha's last shred of clothing and defeated her every desperate attempt to dally or otherwise delay the inevitable. Added to this was Sancha's increasing mental agitation, which the women, to Sancha's total despair, mistook for pretense or coquetry, and mocked her.

"I'd give my pearl earrings for a night with him!" a fair-haired girl crooned in a dreamy voice.

"I wish I might spend a night with those handsome arms about me!" another giggled.

On and on they went, swooning and sighing until Sancha wanted to scream at them. Only when the women began to depart the chamber did Sancha's humiliation turn to terror, for she recalled with heart-stopping accuracy that only a short time before she had soundly slapped the face of the man who would soon enter the room, handle and touch her, indeed have his way with her. Beyond that vague reference, Sancha knew little of what went on between men and women.

In truth, Sancha had spent nearly four years at Richard's English court, but under unusually strict conditions. Sancha had been barely twelve, a child, when she became a lady-in-waiting. At the time, little Isabelle was of an even more delicate age, and it had been Richard's emphatic directive that the crude realities of life be kept from his child queen at all costs. Oh, it was true that Sancha, Alene, and Marie, in the manner of all young girls, had often gossiped and giggled over such mysteries. Even so, Sancha knew nothing of the sordid realities. She suspected certain things, of course, and it was that half knowledge, the spine-tingling uncertainty, the fear of things only vaguely guessed at which began to fill her thoughts with frightful imaginings. She had heard dreadful tales of girls who had been cruelly misused by men. And now, suddenly abandoned by the women, and left nude on the bed like a lamb offered to a wolf, Sancha was immobilized with terror.

In the hall, surrounded by the men, Hugh was pummeled back and forth, plied with randy tales and fed more wine before he, too, was escorted to the bridal chamber. By the time Hugh reached the apartment his brocaded doublet had been stripped from his back and his linen shirt hung open to the waist.

"I'd wear my spurs to bed, if I were you!" someone shouted. A lanky young noble with a big nose had sent a servant to scrounge a bridle from the stable, and held it before him, jangling the bit as he strode along. "Put this in her mouth," the young noble laughed. "You know what to put 'betwixt her legs!"

Once inside the apartment Hugh was escorted down the short hallway, for all the apartments were laid out in a like fashion. As the boisterous company arrived before the chamber door they ran headlong into a gaggle of chattering, giggling women, who were exiting the chamber. Hugh was jostled through their midst and thrust into the room.

Nine

He pushed the door to and set the latch, leaning his spine against the iron-banded door. He could still hear the revelers on the other side, jesting, laughing.

When he looked at the bed, he saw his bride in all her naked glory. The women had stripped her of her clothing, and the bed of its coverlet. She had only her slender arms to hide behind. She huddled in the center of the bed with downcast eyes, making herself as small as possible, seated more or less on one hip, her legs tucked tightly beneath her.

At the sound of the latch she had swiftly raised her head, and now regarded him with a mingling of terror and contempt.

Hugh stood there dumb as an ox, staring at her through a haze of wine. He felt monstrously foolish, embarrassed somehow, for himself and for her. Several moments passed before he realized he still held a wine goblet in his hand. He looked about for a place to set it down.

Her clothing lay in a disorderly heap atop a long, low chest, which was built into the wall, and whose top served as a bench. The sapphire gown, blue as a twilight sky and sewn with brilliants, winked and glittered in the candlelight. Hugh set the wine goblet beside the clothing. As he did, he noticed the flimsy chemise she had worn beneath the gown lying on the floor.

He stooped, retrieving the circle of whisper-soft silk, crossed to the bed, and held it out to her. Her hand shot out with a spastic motion, baring one small, round breast as she snatched the silken chemise from his fingers.

Hugh turned away. He heard her quick movements, the sound of her weight shifting on the bed, and could imagine her throwing the chemise over her head, the pale arch of her arms, the small, round breasts. The thought moved him with desire. He repressed the urge to turn and look. Instead, he stripped off the fine silver belt and ornate ceremonial dagger. He set them aside and went to fetch the coverlet and, as an afterthought, a pillow.

When at last he turned back she had donned the chemise and was staring at him, wide-eyed, as if he were a wild beast about to devour her. Her eyes were like spots of ink, black and liquid.

The instant their gaze met, she looked swiftly away, retreating behind a sweep of dark lashes. Hugh moved toward the bed with slow steps. He dropped the coverlet at the foot of the bed and the pillow he tossed against the carved headboard. He sat down. The bed creaked beneath his weight. "Do you understand that you are my wife?" he asked her.

Sancha avoided his gaze, fixing her eyes on the bed beneath her. She shook her head. Her heavy, dark hair fell forward like a curtain. "I do not want you," she said in a small, miserable voice.

Hugh took a deep breath and turned to pull off his boots, No sooner than his back was to her, he heard her scramble to grab the coverlet and, glancing over his shoulder, saw her dive beneath it. He said nothing, only stood up and, with a brusque movement, shed the linen shirt, dropping it unceremoniously onto a folding stool which stood beside the bed.

He stood there, eyeing the pitifully small lump beneath the coverlet, immovable except for his broad chest rising and falling. Silent, save for the sound of his deep, regular breaths.

At last he asked, "How old are you?" He had no idea, no one had told him, though he thought her no more than sixteen or seventeen, and perhaps less.

There was a long, tense silence. All at once a terrible sob tore from beneath the coverlet, followed by a storm of weeping. Not the ordinary tears one might expect from an overwrought girl, but a terrible wailing sound, as if her heart were being ripped from her breast.

After he had regained some semblance of his composure, Hugh stretched across the bed and, supporting himself on one elbow, addressed what appeared to be her head beneath the bulky coverlet.

"Shhh," he murmured, in a voice brimming with humor, for he could not help but think that everyone in earshot must believe he was torturing her. "There is no need to cry. No one is going to harm you." His head was spinning from the effects of too much wine, and the more he tried to assure her, to console her, the harder she cried.

His final mistake was in attempting to uncover her, so he might reason with her face-to-face. She resisted, dodging his hands with the agility of a weasel, repulsing his every effort to pull her from beneath the downy coverlet, twisting, squirming, thrashing, and finally bringing her knee up into his groin. It was a glancing blow, but created a momentary diversion, enough to allow her to leap screaming from the bed.

Dragging the coverlet with her, Sancha dashed to the door, where she made a frantic assault on the latch. She pounded against it with her fist, she pulled, she tugged. It was hopeless, the latch would not budge.

Hugh rolled from the bed and bounded across the chamber to where his lady wife, concealed beneath the downy coverlet, screeched and pounded on the door. He grabbed for her, catching only a handful of coverlet. Again, he took aim, again, he captured only an armful of fluff. It was suddenly all too ludicrous, he in his barefeet and she wailing like a fishmonger beneath the bouncing coverlet. He began to laugh, making a sort of breathless panting sound as he grappled to lay hands on her.

At last he seized her, twirled her in the coverlet as neatly as a spider might a moth, swept her into his arms and carried her, howling, back to the bed.

No sooner than she touched the bed, Sancha sprang from the coverlet and scrambled away on her hands and knees. Hugh lunged after her, laughing and clumsily falling across the bed, catching a fistful of silken chemise, before dragging her back and cinching her to him.

Imprisoned in his arms and sensing there was no escape, Sancha gave a heartrending cry of despair and began to weep full force. Hugh folded her in his arms, ignoring the great hiccuping sobs that jarred her slight body with each bruised cry and momentary recovery. One-handed, he propped the pillow behind him and sank back into its downy embrace. "Shhh, shhh," he murmured, drawing her closer. "There is no need for you to cry, I am not going to harm you."

Summoning her last shred of resistance, Sancha attempted to break free, but he held her against him as if she were in a vise.

"Lie still, dammit! Listen to me!" he said. And with his free hand he pressed her cheek against his chest, as if he could force her to listen. "Shhh," he soothed, smoothing back the hair which had fallen forward across her tear-splashed face. Her hair was magnificent, thick and long. The sheer weight of it made him smile with wonder, excited him somehow.

She struggled less and less, and he, holding her captive, continued to stroke her hair, marveling at its feel beneath his fingers. After a time her weeping gave way to a pathetic whimpering sound, and he said to her, "Now, my little beauty, we are going to settle our misunderstanding. A wife should not be frightened of her husband."

"I want nothing of you!" she blubbered, her voice breathless and strangled by hiccups. "I do not wish to be your wife!" She squirmed, attempting to turn her cheek from the crisply curling hair of his chest and the mingled scents of their skin, for the skirmish had left them both clammy, damp with perspiration.

"No, why not? I am young, healthy, reasonably good-natured, and," he added with a touch of humor, "athletic." He smiled down at her, watching for the slightest movement of her long black lashes, before continuing. "Neither am I overgiven to drinking or brawling." He angled his head to better see her, smiled and winked cunningly. "Tonight being an exception, of course. But even the saints, or so we are taught, were not without sin."

His warm breath smelled of wine, fermenty and intoxicating, and his velvety, deep voice sounded like a lullaby in her ear. She struggled less and less, gradually succumbing to the power of the elixir. His voice grew softer, fainter, as if it were coming from a great distance, and soon she could no longer distinguish his words. Her eyelids fluttered, becoming heavier with each beat of her heart, and the dancing yellow light of the candles began to fuzz and blur. She tried valiantly to rally her thoughts, to remain vigilant, but moment to moment her energies failed her and she felt herself slipping into nothingness.

The whimpering ceased. Hugh looked down at her. She appeared to be asleep. It occurred to him that it was another of her deceits. But, no, he determined, lessening his grip, her body was as limp as a rag. He lifted her, easing her down on the bed. His hand beneath her brushed a firm, little, round breast and he could not resist exploring its soft roundness. She did not make a sound. It gave him a queer feeling and he took his hand away to grasp her by the shoulder and with the other hand tug on her hip to better position her. As he did, the silken shift rode up, exposing her legs. It seemed there was no way he could touch her without sending his blood to racing.

How tempting she was, soft and delicate. And he recalled how he had first seen her on the bed, naked, all pink and white with a look of alarmed modesty. His mouth went dry at the thought. He reached out his hand and touched her thigh. It was warm, soft, and satiny. She did not stir, even as his hand moved upward, plowing the shift before it, exposing the sweet curve of her hip, the pale smoothness of her belly, and the little patch of feathery dark curls nestled between her legs.

Hugh was bewitched, without a will of his own. His hand drifted downward, caressing the dark feathery down. The feel of it curling about his fingers, the indescribable sensuality of it, sent a long shiver through his body. The curls were warm and moist, and he could not keep from pushing her pale leg aside and tracing a finger over her, touching her. She did not stir.

An ache of desire throbbed through him. As drunk as he was, he was hard, ready, acutely aware of his erection, and the strict tightness of the parti-color hosen. Dimly, he was aware of the mattress shaking, only to then realize it was him, trembling. With a great effort, he grasped the coverlet and drew it over her.

It was hopeless, he could not do it, even though he was shaking like a stud horse, even though it was expected of him. He could not take her, not like that. She was unconscious, or seemed to be, limp, lifeless as a corpse. It was like having ado with something dead. The thought disgusted him. He lurched up from the bed, feeling clenched and uncomfortable, hardly able to walk, and went to the window and opened it.

The world appeared swallowed in blackness. A single dying torch flickered in the courtyard below, and the faint sound of music, voices, and laughter drifted on the damp air.

Clean sheets, Hugh knew, would please no one. All the same, he could not bring himself to mate her, not like that. For a time, he had no idea how long, he remained before the window, then went in search of the silver-hafted dagger.

There was a reluctant tapping at the door, followed by a furtive female voice. "Sire, the first bell has sounded for prime."

Hugh raised up on his elbows, making the bed creak. The voice had a familiar sound, but he did not recognize it, not at once. The room was dark, the candles reduced to puddles of wax. He threw a long leg over the edge of the bed and sat up.

The slumbering form beside him stirred, but did not wake. Hugh located his boots in the darkness and stuffed his feet into them, then reached for his shirt.

The voice beyond the door, came again. "Sire, shall I bring a candle?" Hugh was on his feet by now, pulling his shirt across his shoulders. He grunted a reply, as he strode across the chamber searching for the leather satchel containing his belongs. He had seen it only hours before, but now, in the dark, could not locate it.

He heard the door open, and the moving light of a candle imprinted itself on his retina. He found the satchel on a bench beneath a shuttered window. It was raining outside. He heard the sluice of water and breathed in the dampness.

When he looked up, he saw Alyse Watsdoughter's face illuminated in the halo of candlelight. "How did you come to be here?" he asked, incredulous, not yet entirely awake. He thrust an arm into the sleeve of his leather jacque and, finding the other sleeve, hiked it onto his shoulders.

"Martin brought me last night," Alyse said, looking flustered, avoiding his gaze.

Hugh continued to rifle the contents of the satchel and at last he found his gloves. "You were here last night?" he mumbled, pulling on the left glove taking care not to disturb the slice on his finger. He did not bother to put on the right, rather clutched it in his gloved hand.

"Yes, my lord. Shall I wake the lady? There's women who've come to dress her. I told them they needn't bother, but the fat one insisted."

"Yes, wake her," Hugh replied. His head was beginning to throb; even his eyelids ached.

Shadowy figures appeared at the doorway. Several more women entered the chamber. One carried an oil lamp, scattering shadows before her. The room bloomed with a yellow light.

Swynford's fat servingwoman, Delphine, followed the others into the chamber, a pewter drinking cup held before her.

Sancha awakened to a circle of faces staring down at her. She gave a startled little cry and jolted up so abruptly that she heard her neck snap.

From above her, a voice said, "It is time for your elixir, my lady." Sancha looked up just as the broad Delphine shoved the pewter cup into her hand, and commanded, in her brusque, decisive manner, "You must drink this at once, my lady!"

Sancha caught only a glimpse of her husband as he strode across the chamber. The mere sight of him caused her to burn with embarrassment, for although her memories of the night were muddled and disjointed, she cringed at recalling the unspeakably lewd kiss he had forced on her before all those assembled in the hall. Equally vivid were her memories of his bare, muscular shoulders, the feel of his hands on her flesh, and the strange tumultuous excitement of his embrace.

Thankfully she was soon distracted from such thoughts. Surrounded by the bustling women and badgered by Delphine, Sancha raised the cup to her lips and drank the foul tasting mixture. A hand seized the empty cup, and someone lifted the chemise over her head, while another doggedly wedged her feet into a pair of slippers.

Someone, perhaps it was the fat Delphine, remarked that the lady's hair should be braided. No one bothered to confer with Sancha. Her head was pulled first one way and then another as her dark hair was rudely twisted into plaits.

Women rushed about the room, their combined voices garbled and unintelligible. Sancha was hardly listening when a stout girl with a round pert face approached her, and said, "My lady, I am called Alyse, and I am to be your maidservant." Sancha had no time to respond to the girl with the dark green gown draped across her arms. She was pulled to her feet just as a sleeved camisa of silk was dropped over her head, followed rapidly by the green gown.

While the gown was being laced, an old woman with grizzled greying hair began stripping the bed of its linen. Innocently, Sancha's gaze fell upon the sheet, and the spatter of rust-colored stains.

Her heart slammed against her ribs. Her face colored with shame and her stomach heaved at the thought of what had befallen her. She felt suddenly weak, dazed. No, she reassured herself, it was not possible! Surely she would have some recollection of such a mating? Frantically, she searched her memory. But she could recall only her tears of frustration, the disturbing sensation of his arms, and the warmth of his embrace.

A cold clamminess enveloped her. She gasped for breath. She could not recall, not with any certainty! Did he? Did she? She could not remember! She was dizzy with panic. Her mouth tasted of violets, her stomach churned. The floor seemed to drop from beneath her feet. She felt all at once too hot, breathless, as if there were not enough air in her lungs, and though she tried to keep down the awful-tasting potion, she brought it back up almost at once.

Women scattered in all directions. Two returned with cleaning rags and pails of water. While the others, hoping to comfort her, patted her hands and tittered among themselves, proclaiming her sudden bout of nausea to be a certain sign that she had conceived. Their well-meaning remarks only served to horrify Sancha, who stood by trembling with tears in her eyes, until she was set on a bench.

Another cup of powders was hastily mixed, and Delphine, ever watchful, stood over her to be certain that she drank it.

Hugh, exiting the garderobe, had heard the commotion, but walked on past the bedchamber, which was now swarming with women.

The hallway was no longer in darkness. Someone had lit a wall sconce, and in the foyer Hugh noticed his father's young servant leaning nonchalantly against the wall.

He had not taken another full stride, when his squire, Martin, entered the apartment's foyer. His cloak was dripping wet and he added more footprints to the watery trail left by the servants. He greeted Hugh and, removing his sopping hat, reported the charette was waiting in the courtyard. The remainder of the carts and horsemen, he said, awaited them on the road. He had sent a servant boy to fetch Hugh's horse from the stable, and asked for further instructions.

"Wait here," Hugh told him. "Escort my lady wife and Alyse to the charette. Oh, yes, there is yet a casque of clothing in the bedchamber, see that it is carried down and stowed." Martin nodded, stepping aside as two servingwomen rushed past, carrying pails of water.

Hugh found his father and Thomas Swynford in the candlelit solar. As Hugh entered, William Canby lurched up from where he sat slumped on a bench. "God's blessings, my son," he said in greeting, and with an immoderate grin inquired, "Your health, how goes it? And your lovely wife's?"

"Well enough," Hugh replied, his gaze sliding to Swynford, who was sprawled on the bench beside the blackened hearth. "You are too modest," Swynford said, laughing softly, saluting Hugh with the wine cup he held, and murmuring between his teeth, "Poor girl."

William Canby continued to chuckle as searched his doublet, patting the richly quilted fabric and fumbling through its inner lining. At last he withdrew a packet of papers. "I have here some letters of introduction. Acquaintances of mine who will gladly shelter you and your lady wife as you journey north." Hugh accepted the packet and tucked it inside his jacque.

"The roads are plagued with all manner of lawlessness," William Canby warned, taking his son by the shoulder, and musing, "I would have been better pleased if you had hired more men to accompany you. The area around Nottingham is infamous," he said, detailing a particularly ugly incident where murder was done to a party of six travelers.

Hugh listened but with only half an ear. He had decided long ago that he was the best judge of his own interests. He showed no open disrespect, but this man's concern for his well-being, this "father" who had until only days before considered him of no more importance than a mote of dust, rather irked him. Did he think him a fool? He had survived without his well-meaning advice for twenty-three years.

The lilt of female voices and the sound of footfalls in the passageway swiveled Hugh's attention to the door arch. He saw his lady wife wrapped in a cloak and Alyse pass by, followed by Martin, two young varlets with the casque of clothing supported between them. Four or five servingwomen trailed after them, their arms laden with cushions and bundles. Swynford and William Canby saw them as well. Swynford's head turned, following their progress, and William Canby quickly summed up his remarks. "You must not keep your lady wife waiting," he said.

"No," Hugh agreed, preparing to go.

At this, Swynford set aside the wine cup and rose to his feet. "I doubt we shall meet again," he said, stepping forward. "At least, not face-to-face." He offered his hand to Hugh. "Good health and good fortune."

"My lord," Hugh replied, thinking Swynford's hand was damp and limp as a fish. Hugh turned to go, then paused and, as an afterthought, asked, "When might I expect your courier, my lord?"

A slow smile crossed Swynford's lips. "Expect the unexpected, for it is there you shall find him."

William Canby laughed, accusing Swynford of sounding like "some prissy fool of a priest with all his parables," and slapped a hand on Hugh's muscular shoulder. "By the rood! I shall miss you!" he exclaimed, and walked with Hugh to the door arch. "When parliament ends, I am bound for Calais. I have interests there, and a new, young wife, quite as pretty as your own. Here! God's protection! Be cautious of your back where Northumberland is concerned. He will set your half brothers against you, and God knows they do not need encouragement."

It seemed to Hugh that his father was going to follow him to his horse, filling his ear with advice, but he went only as far as the apartment's foyer. In the courtyard rain peppered down from a leaden sky.

Hugh walked swiftly toward his waiting horse. By chance he caught a glimpse of his lady wife framed in the charette's window. He saw only the back of her head, before someone, Alyse, he imagined, secured the hide window covering. He walked on. He had no need to see her, for in his mind the image of her ivory-and-rose body, the scent of her skin, the feel of her hair beneath his hands, was as real, as tangible as the rain-slick cobbles beneath his boots. He took Chewbit's reins, mounted, and, with Martin riding at his side, rode toward the peak-roofed gatehouses.

Ten

Where the king's road turned north toward Oxford, the remainder of the entourage, carts and horsemen, waited in the wet, predawn blackness, huddled in their cloaks, their faces turned from the rain. At the approach of the riders and the charette, a cartman came forward, sloshing through the mud, with a lantern swinging in his hand. Hugh wasted no time deploying the company, with guards fore and aft, in the style of a military expedition. Carts were maneuvered into line and riders jostled in the mire.

Their shouts pierced the inky blackness inside the charette, ringing out above the steady drumming of the rain upon its wooden frame. Sancha shut her ears to the sounds. Tears stung her eyes, yet she would not give in to them. She sat stiffly in the red leather-upholstered seat, unyielding, unaware.

In her shame, her mind struggled to make some sense of the bewildering turn of events which had altered her life so dramatically. *If only I could remember,* she grieved silently. A thousand unanswered questions assailed her tortured mind. She felt lost and alone, betrayed, no longer trusting even her most basic instincts. How confused she was, and frightened.

The charette lurched forward, jolting the two young women back in their upholstered seats. "Oh!" Alyse whooped with surprise, as her head was thrown back. "Mother Mary!" she exclaimed. And suddenly remembering her duties, gushed in an urgent voice, "My lady, are you badly shaken?"

"No," Sancha murmured in reply. She could hardly speak

past the lump in her throat. She wanted desperately to grasp the maidservant's plump hand, and spill out her miseries. But how could she tell her, *his* servant, the shameful way in which he had abused her during the night? Much less confess to her own woeful ignorance concerning the relations between men and women. No, she decided, she would remain silent.

" 'Twill soon be daylight, my lady," Alyse piped cheerfully, hoping to lighten her lady's mood. In the darkness she could see little of her mistress, only a hint of her coif, the line of her small shoulders. After a moment of silence, Alyse smiled into the blackness, confessing, "I have no fondness for the dark."

"Nor have I," Sancha finally murmured, her voice small and stifled.

Alyse waited for her mistress to say more, for it seemed she would, but she lapsed again into silence. And a bit later, as the day dawned, Alyse saw she was fast asleep, her dark head lolling with the swaying motion of the charette.

After a time, Alyse raised the hide coverings of the windows, allowing in the grey, watery light of a rainy day, but still her mistress slept.

Beyond the dim and creaking interior of the charette, mist and darkening skies dimmed the emerald green of the countryside. It seemed the dreary numbness of the grey day lay heavy on everything, on the sodden fields, the black-barked trees, the overflowing roadside ditches. Long into the day, the lady slumbered. Alyse thought it queer for one so young to sleep as soundly as the dead.

Eventually, lulled by the sway of the charette, Alyse, herself, fell asleep, only to be awakened in what she fancied was the blinking of an eye when the charette ground to a halt, and the sound of conversations reached her ears.

Poking her head from the window, Alyse saw carters climbing down from their carts, and riders dismounting, leading their horses through the dripping roadside trees toward a swiftly flowing little stream, its waters yellow with silt. A group of carters passed by the charette's window, armed with pails to fetch water for the cart horses. Alyse shouted to them, inquiring, "What place be this?"

A burly fellow with a pail in each hamlike hand, turned and called back, "No place I've ever been!" And nudging the bearded fellow striding at his shoulder, asked, "How 'bout you, Mole?"

"Aye!" The fellow laughed, his pink lips splitting the wiry blackness of his beard. " 'Tis no place I've ever been!" After him, another answered like an echo and soon they all joined in the teasing, their voices carrying back over their shoulders.

"Deptford or thereabouts," a voice said from below the window. Alyse started, and looked down to see Martin Sims looking up at her, his eyes brown as nuts and his sandy hair rumpled as a colt's mane. "A goodly fifteen leagues from Windsor. I doubt the provost's arm is so long as that," he remarked in his dry tone of voice.

Alyse sent him a sour look. Did he think her daft enough to run away? She was about to speak her mind when she saw the young lord walking toward them, leading his horse.

"Where is your mistress?" Hugh asked, passing his horse's reins to Martin, and instructing, "See he's watered."

"She is sleeping, my lord," Alyse said, glancing swiftly back to be certain what she said was so, and seeing that it was, added in a concerned voice, "Soothly, she has slept all the day."

Hugh, stooping his shoulders, climbed inside the charette. He smelled of the outdoors, of rain and grass and horses, and stood there looking too tall for the diminutive interior of the char. "Leave us," he said to Alyse. She shimmied past him, climbing from the charette. Through the fringe of trees she saw Martin leading the master's horse toward the stream.

Inside the charette, Hugh studied for a moment the pale slumbering face, then reached out a hand and gently shook the slight shoulder.

Sancha's eyes jarred open, a little muffled cry of fright escaped her lips.

"I did not mean to startle you," Hugh said apologetically. He smiled at her and, crouching down to balance on the balls of his feet so he might better see her face, took her hand in his. "We have halted to water and rest the horses. Would you care to walk with me and take some air?"

Sancha gave him a look of pure loathing and snatched her hand away. She pushed herself deep in the red-upholstered seat and turned her face toward the window, refusing to see him, hating him with every throb of her pounding heart.

He smiled, half-expecting her hostility. "Something has upset you?" he suggested, his gaze settling on the curve of her forehead, the pink-tinted cheeks, the sweep of lush black lashes. "I hope the journey has not been too uncomfortable. Are you certain you would not like to step outside? The rain has ended . . . it might do you well to straighten your legs."

Outside the charette, Alyse folded her arms across her breasts and waited. After a time, she glanced about and, seeing no one, cocked an ear toward the charette. If she had hoped to overhear their conversation, she was disappointed. She heard only Hugh Canby's voice, and not a word from her mistress. She had edged a bit closer when the door suddenly opened and Hugh Canby swung down from the charette.

"Martin will bring food and wine. See that your mistress takes something."

"Yes, my lord, certainly I will," Alyse said.

Not half an hour passed before Martin tapped on the door of the char and passed a wineskin and a basket containing a slab of cheese and a loaf of bread to Alyse's waiting arms. Alyse made over it as if it were a feast. She was truly hungry. But her mistress would take nothing.

Later as they lurched and swayed down the grass-grown main street of a nameless village, where a sow and piglets rooted in the mud and peasants halted to stare at the passing procession, Sancha asked her maidservant, "Do you know the place we are going?"

The tone of her voice, like that of a lost child, quite touched

Alyse. "Why north, my lady, to Evistone Abbey." She was so
moved by her mistress's melancholy expression that she further
confided, "Soothly, mistress, I know very little of the place."
And then, quite against her better judgment, confessed that
she had only overheard a portion of the master and Martin's
conversation.

Alyse's penchant for gathering information was by no means
limited to eavesdropping, and speaking in sibilant tones she
shared these further tantalizing bits of gossip with her mistress.
"One of the carters told me that a saint is buried there, a holy
man at any rate. He said the abbey's walls are thick as the
Tower of London's, and we'll be safe from heathens there."
Talking was as natural to Alyse as breathing, and she chattered
on endlessly.

In listening to her lively banter, Sancha sensed her maidservant's sympathy, and gradually she warmed to her, if only
a bit. Now and then Sancha offered a word of agreement or
cautiously asked a question.

Heartened by her mistress's budding interest, Alyse tried her
best to be amusing. She told of her life in Surrey, of coming
to Windsor to seek a livelihood, her misfortunes, and how
Hugh Canby had rescued her from a life of hardship and given
her hope for the future. It was not entirely the truth, rather
Alyse's version. She omitted, for instance, that she had survived by luring men to drink and then robbing them. But her
gratitude to the young lord was real and true, and she made
no bones of it.

Sancha listened half in disbelief, half in wonder, as the rosy-
cheeked Alyse praised Hugh Canby to the skies, a man Sancha
knew to be base. Had he not stolen her dowry and ravaged
her? He was a thief, and worse. Worse, because he was young
and handsome and self-possessed, and she had no weapon
against him.

It was all Sancha could manage to keep silent. Even in her
misery she could not deny that her future had always been in
the hands of the king, and many a young lady with a handsome

dowry had been handed off to favorites, as enticement or reward. Just as there was no denying that Richard would have
passed her to a favorite, and long before, had it not been for
little Isabelle's insistence and the king's tenderness where her
wishes were concerned.

But Richard was no longer king. And though there was
much of the recent past Sancha could not recall, she could
bring to mind vividly the day, months before, when a messenger had brought word of the king's arrest. She remembered
the crowds of people gathering in the streets of London, and
the look of pain in the little queen's eyes. Faces and scenes
burst upon her mind's eye, little vignettes, bits and pieces of
the past, and something more, a memory, a thought? Something just beyond her mind's grasp, like an object concealed
in darkness, only half-perceived, that left her feeling oddly
frightened and uneasy.

Alyse continued to talk. She told of her experiences at Windsor, and that once, she had seen King Richard and his little
French queen. " 'Twas when I first came to Windsor. I was a
kitchen laborer, and myself and two others climbed upon a
wall so we could see the little queen walking in the garden
with her ladies. Now that be strange, don't you think? Why I
must have seen you, my lady, though I couldn't say. I hardly
saw the ladies' faces, for their gowns caught my eye. I had
never seen such a sight, silk and satin, sewn all over with
precious stones so that they glittered and sparkled like jewels
in the sunlight. 'Tis sad, though, about the little queen," Alyse
mused. "To be so young and already a widow."

Her words struck Sancha like a hammerblow. "King Richard!" she cried, aware once more of the strange sense of uneasiness, like a shadow creeping over her.

"Yes, my lady, did you not know? They said he died of a
broken heart, because he had lost his crown."

Sancha did not cry aloud. She turned her face to the window
and wept bitter, silent tears. They spilled down her cheeks and
dripped onto her bosom. Occasionally, a sob escaped her trem-

bling lips for vain and foolish Richard, for little Madame, and for herself.

With dusk approaching, the company plodded on toward Oxford. There the road followed a gravel terrace surrounded by marshland, and crossed the river south of the city.

At the St. Aldate gate a long queue of merchants stood waiting in the cool, damp twilight. Customs officials, lanterns swinging from their hands, questioned the merchants as to their goods, poked and peered into carts, and stated the levied tax.

Invariably the merchant protested, and after a period of loud haranguing, the tax was sometimes reduced, though more often not. Success seemed to hinge on the determination and longwindedness of the merchant.

The wait was indescribably tedious. When at last Hugh's retinue of riders, charette, and carts stood before the gates, the customs official demanded the merchant levy from Hugh. He demanded payment of one half denier for each cart, two deniers for the charette, plus five deniers for each salable item and bundle of wares of what sort soever being brought into Oxford.

"I am not a merchant," Hugh explained, quite rationally. "These items are my personal goods; I have no intention of selling them."

The red-nosed official was unmoved. "Sir, you would not be the first merchant to attempt to pass himself off as a traveling noble. In my position one meets all sorts of scoundrels."

Hugh's patience was worn quite thin. He could feel the back of his neck getting hot. "I assure you, sir, I am neither a scoundrel nor a merchant. I am a traveler." And to prove his statement, he produced the first of the missives. "I have here a letter of introduction to Sir Walter Louthe, who I believe is the king's bailiff." Such was the manner in which his father had addressed the letter.

The customs official considered the statement, then shouted to one of his minions, instructing him to bring a lantern. Opening the letter, he tilted the paper to the light and scrutinized the heavy black script. Since the official was, himself, in Sir Walter's service, his attitude changed at once. He apologized several times for any inconvenience, and was only too delighted to instruct Hugh as to the most direct route to the bailiff's residence.

As it turned out, the house was easily located. It stood among the larger and more affluent homes that occupied the church square of St. Ebbe's. Furthermore, the three-storied timber post and beam building was easily identified by the ornate twisted columns which graced its limewashed facade. In the blue twilight, the structure appeared starkly white and resembled some sort of monstrous confection, that once seen could never be forgotten. Entering the courtyard, Hugh noticed sprawling stables and a number of wooden storehouses to the rear of the residence.

A bent and wizened little manservant greeted Hugh at the great house's door. With measured steps he ushered Hugh and his squire into a dimly lit gallery. The only light was that of a wall sconce.

Presently the servant returned with a lamp in his hand. In his wake, came a short, stout, balding man dressed in fashionable velvets. Hugh presumed he was Sir Walter Louthe, and addressed him accordingly.

"God give you good evening, sire. I am Hugh Canby, and I bring you my father's greetings," Hugh announced, offering the letter in his outstretched hand.

"A good evening, indeed, messire," Sir Walter said in a jolly voice, accosting Hugh and embracing him like a long-lost kinsman. "Welcome! Welcome! God's teeth, I should know you are William's son by sight alone. You are the very image of him! How does he fare?" he asked, taking in hand the proffered letter.

His remark brought a smile to Hugh's lips. It seemed everyone saw the resemblance but Hugh himself. "Well enough," he responded. "He is at Westminster for the opening of parliament."

"Ah yes, parliament," Sir Walter drawled, remarking, "We've had 'The good parliament' and 'the bad' . . . though I fancy none could tell the difference!"

Hugh could not help but be amused by the jest, and, in a like manner, he was immediately put at ease by the man's affable nature and the heartiness of his welcome. It occurred to Hugh that Sir Walter Louthe must be greatly obliged to his father, for he did not hesitate in his offer of providing food and lodging for Hugh's sizable retinue.

Once the logistics of finding quarters for nearly three dozen men and stabling forty-four horses were put to rights, Sir Walter trotted out his family and introduced them to Hugh and his shy and strangely silent bride.

The chamber they were given for the night was large, as were the other rooms they had seen, and because of the great expanse of floor, gave the impression of emptiness. Aside from the huge hearth where a servant knelt to set a fire, there were few furnishings. Only a bed, stoutly framed and hung with heavy, musty-smelling, saffron-colored draperies, a tall chest, an upholstered stool, and a long, low, graceful bench adorned with leather pillows. To the far side of the chamber was a doorless arch which led to a narrow passage. At its end was a garderobe, and along its course were several cramped alcoves, servant's quarters, not unlike monk's cells, with space for little more than the straw-filled cot.

With the weariness of their journey washed from their hands and faces, Hugh, his lady wife, his squire Martin, and Alyse Watsdoughter gathered at the long table in the hall. They were joined by their host, Sir Walter, his rather stout, ruddy-complexioned, blond wife, her elder unmarried sister, several other female relatives, and Sir Walter's two youngest sons, boys of twelve and fourteen who ate like wolves.

The fare was plain but plentiful and consisted of black pudding, a puree of lentils, dark bread, cheese, apple tarts, and ale. Invariably a night of drinking and its resultant hangover left Hugh with a raging appetite, and he made the most of the provincial, but warmly gratifying meal.

Sancha sat beside her healthy, broad-shouldered young husband, unmindful of the din of pewter tableware and drone of conversation. She could think only of later, and of the moment when she would once again be alone with him. A thought which inspired her not only with panic, but with a host of never before experienced sensations that she could neither understand nor put into words. She was in despair, and picked disinterestedly at her food, eating only a bit of cheese and a corner of an apple tart. The crumbly cheese and too-sweet pastry lodged midway in her throat, and though she could not abide the taste of ale, she was forced to take a sip to keep from choking.

Sir Walter, with his bulging stomach, three chins, and fat rosy cheeks was hardly the image of a justiciar, but he had been just that, Hugh learned. By his own admission he had been sheriff of Redesdale. "I was captured in a skirmish by Humphrey Douglas, the one known by all as 'Black Douglas' and aptly named for his deeds. Were it not for your father's intervention, my head and parts would have surely graced the walls of his pele."

Sir Walter had much to say on the subject of the brutal mercenary Black Douglas. "He has a foot in each camp; he is loyal to no one, save himself." Sir Walter went on to tell of a countryside locked in perpetual struggle. Where the "raid" was everything, and each warring faction, the English, the Scots, and the broken clans, or "limmer thieves" like Black Douglas, who thought of themselves as neither Scots nor English, lived by the axiom, "Do the enemy three hurts for one!"

" 'Tis a desperate land, without law or mercy, with few comforts and a bleak climate. For myself, I was never so pleased as the day I rode south," Sir Walter admitted.

Servants moved silently about the table, as Sir Walter spoke of his varied and colorful experiences. "Our own barons are no less treacherous," he warned. "They have as few scruples as Black Douglas. Mark my words, there will be grief. There's a civil war a-brewing, and your good sire, God protect him, may find himself caught in the center of it."

"My father?" Hugh remarked, realizing how little he actually knew about the man.

"Aye, 'tis a dangerous game he plays, promising old Northumberland one thing, and Bolingbroke another. 'Tis like a man with two mistresses. In the end he shall have to betray them both. I should not care to be in your father's boots on that day."

"You believe it will come to bloodshed, this quarrel between Northumberland and the king?" Hugh asked.

"Our king Bolingbroke took the crown by conquest. There are others who consider themselves more noble. And they are not alone. Those same barons who betrayed Richard might just as easily betray Bolingbroke."

While Sir Walter and Hugh discussed the current state of the realm, the women spoke of more mundane matters. Sancha sat by mutely, toying with her food and racking her brain for a means of avoiding her husband's attentions.

One foolish scheme after another she discarded, until from her early days at Richard's court, she recalled a certain lady whose husband was a well-known brute. Whenever her husband was at court, the lady took to her sickbed, a complete invalid, requiring the constant attentions of a servingwoman, only to make a full and complete recovery the moment her churlish husband rode away. The more Sancha considered the scheme, she thought it the perfect ruse. After all, there could be no doubt that she was ill.

She had just about summoned enough courage to speak, when she heard Sir Walter say, "Richard lives, or so the rumors have it." Until that moment, Sancha had been too deep in her own thoughts to pay any heed to their conversation. She swiftly turned her head, fixing her stunned gaze on Sir Walter's fat, pink face. Richard, alive! She prayed it was so.

"He is dead and buried," Hugh remarked. Martin, efficiently

sopping up the remains of his porridge with a hunk of black bread, nodded in agreement.

Sir Walter merely shrugged. "All the same there are those who swear they have seen him. I grant you 'tis likely the sort of gossip born of wine and ale. Though I've heard similar tales from more levelheaded men. They say Richard escaped his prison, and Bolingbroke in desperation had his henchmen search out a certain priest who resembled Richard, and 'twas his body they paraded through the countryside."

Hugh took a sip of wine. "I saw Richard's body at Cheapside, lying in a cart."

"And what did you think?" Sir Walter inquired.

"That it was he."

"You had seen him in life, our King Richard?"

"Only once," Hugh was forced to admit. "At a tournament, some years ago."

"You saw the body closely?"

"No, the square was mobbed with people. Though others did, and they were of one accord."

"Not all," Sir Walter suggested. "Some say Richard had a mole on his cheek and the corpse did not." He smiled suddenly, his voice once again affable. "But I must agree, I do not believe he is alive. I do not think even Bolingbroke would dare to propose a marriage between his son and the little French queen, not if Richard still lived."

Sancha was aghast. How dare Bolingbroke! He was a murderer! They were all murderers! At the sound of her sharply indrawn breath, Hugh turned to her.

"I feel unwell," Sancha gasped.

He looked at her curiously, she thought, before announcing, "It seems the rigors of the journey have quite exhausted my lady wife." He looked at her again, as if he were trying to read her thoughts, and said, "So that she asks to be forgiven if she retires to her chamber."

All eyes turned to Sancha, who flustered wordlessly for a moment before finding her voice. Once she had murmured her regrets, she allowed Alyse to lead her from the hall with an arm round her waist.

In the busy passage between the hall and the kitchen, Alyse collared a household varlet and sent him after a lamp. He had already vanished into the kitchen when she recalled she must have a cup of wine in which to mix her lady's medication.

She called to a passing serving girl and asked her to fetch a cup. The harried girl dashed away. Presently she returned with a cup to the foot of the stairs, where Alyse and Sancha waited with the glum-faced varlet.

The instant Alyse's hand closed over the cup, the varlet led off up the wooden stairs and down through the darkened halls. Once inside the chamber, the gangly boy lit a wall sconce and stoked the remains of the smoldering hearth fire until it roared like a demon. Then, not having uttered a word, he departed with his lamp.

After Alyse had helped her mistress to undress and don her night shift, she retrieved the little jewel casket from the luggage and prepared her mistress's medication.

Alyse was determined to prepare the elixir just as the physician had instructed and measured carefully, dipping the tiny silver spoon into the odd-scented purple crystals, leveling the crystals with her finger and slowly stirring it into the wine. As she did, she noticed her mistress kneeling in prayer by the bedside. Her glorious dark hair unloosed from the braids tumbled about her shoulders, starkly dark against her pale cheeks. She had eaten practically nothing all day and Alyse feared for her health.

She waited until her mistress climbed onto the bed, then offered her the pewter cup, remarking, " 'Tis only this you need, mistress . . . 'twil make everything right."

"No," Sancha said turning her face away like an obstinate child and refusing to drink the evil-tasting medication. She feared the cloying sweet elixir as desperately as she did her husband's attentions. For each time she sipped of it, she be-

came confused and ill. "I am sick," she moaned, hoping to
play on the good-natured Alyse's sympathies.

"But my lady, the physician said you must not pass a day
without it." Alyse coaxed and wheedled, but in vain. She could
not move her mistress to raise the cup to her lips and drink.

"No," Sancha said, shaking her dark head. "I will surely
bring up my meal! Feel my head," she cried in a distracted
voice. "I am feverish!"

"Nay, my lady," Alyse said, after placing a plump hand on
her forehead. "You are cool as I, mistress."

"No," Sancha contradicted. "I am burning with fever!" And
realizing her maidservant was unconvinced, gave a sudden con-
vulsive gasp. "Ow!" She swooned, clasping her breast with
one hand, and Alyse's pudgy arm with the other. "Ow! The
pain is killing!"

Alyse's blue eyes widened with alarm. "My lady? Oh . . .
my lady! I will fetch the master!"

"No!" Sancha shrieked, gripping her sturdy arm with renewed strength. "No, do not leave me. Aha, the pain is passing.
It is bearable now. No, do not leave me! You must stay by my
side tonight!"

Within the hour Hugh entered the room to find his lady
wife buried beneath the coverlet, and Alyse, her head nodding,
seated on a stool beside the bed. At the sound of the door,
Alyse bobbed up from her seat, blinking. "My lord, the mistress is ill. She refused to drink her medicine. I feared to leave
her. I did not know what to do."

"Why did you not come to me at once?" Hugh demanded,
berating the serving girl for her lack of good sense. He strode
across the chamber, stripping off the dark wool doublet he had
worn to supper. "Where is the lady's medicine?"

"There," Alyse, pointed, indicating the chest. As she did,
she noticed Martin step inside the chamber. He looked past
her toward his master, as if for permission, then made his way
through the open door arch toward the garderobe and cramped
sleeping quarters.

Beside the bed, Hugh leaned over his lady wife. She had once again buried herself beneath the coverlet. As he peeled back the bedclothes, the tantalizing aroma of rosewater and female tickled his nostrils, filling his mind with sexual images.

Sancha lay very still, hardly breathing, not daring to open her eyes, wishing with all her heart that he would go away and knowing he would not.

"She complained of a fever, sire," Alyse reported.

Hugh gazed down at her. "Do you feel unwell?" She did not answer. He laid a large hand on her forehead. She felt cool to his touch. "You must drink the medicine," he told her.

"No," she responded in a whining voice. "It makes me retch."

Hugh's thoughts were so intent upon the pretty face, the dark puckered brows, that for a moment he said nothing. She did not look to him to be ill. She looked more like a contrary child. And he imagined if he did not put a halt to such behavior before it became a habit, she would make his life miserable. "Go to your bed, Alyse," he said softly.

Sancha sat up swiftly, forgetting her fever, desperate not to be left alone with him. "No! I want her to stay with me! Alyse!"

Alyse hesitated, her plump face lined with uncertainty, but a meaningful glance from Hugh sent her hurrying from the room.

Sancha stared after her with parted lips, then, in defeat, fell back into the pillows.

"Why will you not drink your medicine?" Hugh asked, smoothing her hair caressingly from her face.

Sancha recoiled from his touch, squirming deeper into the pillows. "It is poison!" she cried, sobbing into the pillows.

Hugh gave a weary sigh and settled with one hip on the edge of the bed, thinking perhaps the physician was right. She was hopelessly deranged, mad and would ever be. In a soft voice he asked, "Why should anyone wish to poison you? I was led to believe the elixir may bring about your cure. Certainly it cannot harm you."

"I will not drink it, I will not! No, never, never, never," she wailed, no longer able to swallow the sobs that tore from her lips.

Hugh sat back confusedly, his hands in his lap. He knew of no way to comfort the lonely young exile who lay weeping. His touch, his very presence, seemed only to torment her. "We are strangers, aren't we?" he conceded. "Do you even know my name?" He did not think she was listening, though he noticed she had stopped crying.

Sancha shifted beneath the coverlet and raised her head from the pillows, suddenly startled to realize that, truly, she could not recall his name. She sniffed, giving a slight shake of her dark hair. Someone had told her, Alyse, mayhap? Though now she could not remember either his name or who had told her. Her thoughts tumbled wildly. She wanted only to return to the life she had known before, to Marie and Alene, and Madame.

"A name, at least, is a beginning. I am Hugh Canby, third son—No," he said abruptly, refusing to color the truth. "I am the lately claimed bastard of Lord William Canby." He watched, attempting to read her expression. "Above all, I mean you no hurt. I swore an oath to your queen to care for you, and regardless of my birth, my word is that of a knight." Again he paused to gauge her reaction. "If the elixir will mend your thoughts, surely you must see the value of it?"

Sancha hazarded a glance at him, almost willing to believe the earnest grey eyes, the kind voice.

Hugh saw her silence as a victory. She had not refused, and so he rose slowly from the bed. He took the cup from the chest and looked back, thoughtfully. "If I drink of the elixir," he offered, "will you be satisfied then that it is not poison?"

Eleven

She gave him a wary sidelong glance, but did not reply. Hugh returned to the bed and seated himself as before, his hip brushing against her leg beneath the coverlet. He raised the cup. "Do you see?" he said, and catching her eye, tipped it to his lips. The cloying liquid rolled over his tongue and the taste of it all but pulled a knot in his stomach. Somehow he managed not to grimace. "There, it is not poison."

She met his gaze with great grave eyes.

"Here," he said, offering the cup to her.

She raised herself warily, edging away from him as much as she was able. But when he tried to place the cup in her hand, she refused.

"No," Her voice was barely a whisper. "You will force me . . ." She was too mortified by the crudeness of the words, the thought, to say more.

"Are you afraid I will kiss you again?" he asked ruefully, taking her hand and placing her fingers about the cup.

Sancha's breath caught in her throat, she felt as if she were suffocating with humiliation. The way he was smiling frightened her, and now she could not stop her lip from quivering. Suddenly she was seized by a tumultuous anger, she wanted to shout at him, accuse him so that all in the house would hear, but her exasperation strangled her and the words blubbered from her lips. "You have harmed me . . ."

"I?" His smile deepened. "I would rather to cut off my hand than cause you unhappiness." Laughingly, he confessed,

"In truth, I very nearly did, a finger at any rate." Opening his left hand, he revealed a deep gash at the base of his littlest finger. "I was not expecting a ceremonial dagger with an edge like a Saracen's blade," he explained. "For a moment in the dark, I thought I'd separated my finger from my hand." His grey eyes crinkled in amusement, as he suggested, "If the amount of blood is taken into account, I'm certain Swynford's servingwomen have declared you Christendom's most innocent virgin."

Sancha stared at his handsome young face, unable, at first, to grasp his meaning. When at last the full force of his disclosure dawned on her, she could do no more than stammer, "Your blood? But why? Why did you?"

"I was drunk as a porter and you were dead asleep. 'Twould have been a pity to put so much effort into something neither of us would remember. Besides," he said, "it pleases me more to think of love as a gift to be given. Not something to be taken, like a bath or a hasty meal." And with a smile, he urged, "Here, drink your elixir."

Won over by his words, the velvety voice, the clear grey eyes, Sancha obediently accepted the cup. She swallowed the evil-tasting brew, passed the cup back to him, and lay down. She closed her eyes, but the image of his earnest face, his injured hand remained. Had he truly cut himself to satisfy their crude curiosities? She desperately wished to believe him. She lay there tense as a string stretched to breaking, listening as he moved about the room, and later felt the mattress yield beneath his weight. She had not intended to go to sleep, but as before the elixir triumphed over her nerves.

Lying beside her, Hugh fell asleep almost at once, only to awaken a short time later, his heart panting with delight, still gripped by the sensual excitement of a dream.

He raised up, thinking the dream had ended too soon, only to have the darkened room spin about his head like the firmament. He drug a hand across his eyes, but it did no good. "Jesu," he mumbled. He felt as if his head might float off his shoulders, as if he'd drunk a tun of sweet, purple ozey. No, worse, for when he tried to fix his eyes upon the flickering hearth, he saw not one but three. He lay back heavily, closing his eyes, hoping to halt the dizzy chase-go-round and searching his mind for the cause of his discomfort.

He had taken but a single cup of ale, neither could he lay the blame on his hangover of the day before, and then he recalled the mouthful of sickeningly sweet elixir. She had called it "poison." Mayhap it was. For all at once a cold clamminess came over him, his mouth filled with saliva, his stomach cramped. He lurched up, stumbled down the pitch-black hallway to the garderobe, and retched until his sides ached.

Martin, awakened by the commotion, came groggily from his alcove. "Be that you, sire?" he asked, and then asked a second time before he got an answer.

By then Alyse was peering from her alcove. She could see little in the darkness, indistinct forms, but she heard the sounds, their voices, and in a penetrating whisper, called, "Is my mistress ill?"

"Go back to your bed," someone told her. It seemed to Alyse that it was Martin's voice. She heard them moving about for near half an hour before all fell silent once again.

In the morning when Alyse went to rouse her mistress, she found the master up from bed and dressed. The lady, she noticed, was still sleeping soundly. He was standing by the hearth, a heavy iron poker in his hand, raking up a fire from the embers. She turned to fetch her lady's medicine and saw the jewel casket standing open upon the chest. The powder box, fashioned of carved horn, which held the elixir was gone. A momentary flash, green and iridescent, splashed the room. Alyse whirled about, dumbfounded.

"Your mistress is cured," Hugh told her, casting the empty box into the flames. "She has no need of an elixir."

Alyse stared for a moment in dumb amazement, then nodded dutifully. As soon as he had gone, she woke her mistress and told her in hushed tones how the master had burned the elixir powders in the hearth. Sancha, drowsy and muddled, did not at first comprehend. Only later, when Alyse told her of the commotion during the night, did she grasp its significance and feel somewhat vindicated.

The house was in darkness as Sancha and Alyse made their way down the staircase by the light of a single candle. In the solar which led from the hall, several servants moved about like sleepwalkers and, in the passageway beyond, candles guttered in the draft from the open doors. Outside in the courtyard, stars still winked from between the clouds.

Sir Walter, as bleary-eyed as his servants, had risen to wish his guests "Christ and the saints protection" on their journey. He and Hugh stood talking, standing on the darkened cobbles of the courtyard as the horses and carts assembled.

A servant boy with a lamp in his hand appeared from the darkness of the courtyard, and led Sancha and Alyse down the line of carts to the charette. In the noisy gloom men shouted back and forth above the constant jangle of harness. Unseen in the blackness, a horse gave a brusque shake; others stomped and snorted.

Finally, accompanied by the barking of dogs and the creak of cart wheels, the entourage set out. Beyond Oxford's walls, a blush of pink tinted the eastern horizon. They traveled ever northward into a rare spring day. Sunlight sparked from puddles of standing water and the warm breath of May was scented with the sweetness of grasses and meadow flowers.

Hugh rode at the fore of the procession. His stomach still pained him, and now he was equally troubled by what he had done. In destroying the elixir he feared he might have condemned his young wife to madness or death, or both. The physician had warned him of just such a fate. But as Hugh was well aware, physicians were not always particularly wise, nor even honest. Surely, he argued, if a single swallow of the elixir had so affected him, what havoc would cup after cup of it wreak on her slight body? No, he decided, he had done what he believed to be best. At any rate he hoped it was, since it was now too late to do otherwise. Time and again he dropped back, so he might catch a glimpse of his lady wife.

Sancha's mind was too filled with her own thoughts to notice his scrutiny. From the window of the lurching charette she watched the constantly changing scene of rolling meadows, placidly grazing cattle, and farmsteads. The pleasant countryside reminded her of her home in Gien, and her dear nursemaid, Violetta. Sadly, she did not recall her parents with such fondness. They were forever absent, choosing instead to spend their days at the king's court in Paris. Their infrequent homecomings, however, were occasions of great excitement. Sometimes they would bring an infant with them, a new brother or sister, birthed at court, only to be left in Gien in the care of the nursemaids. Of course, there would be gifts and sweets and much merriment. There was also gossip, scandalous tales brought back from court by her parents' servants.

She particularly remembered the shocking tale of a great baron's daughter, an heiress, who had been abducted by a brash young knight. After his offer of marriage had been rejected as unworthy, the handsome, young knight had boldly carried the heiress off to Brittany, which, as any courtier could tell, was inhabited by barbarians.

At the time Sancha's innocent imagination was stirred by the thought of the beautiful girl and the handsome, brave knight. Indeed, in her mind the tale took on the high romance of a troubadour's fable. *How strange,* Sancha thought, *to think of it now,* and she wondered if the poor girl had felt as helpless and unhappy as she?

Oh, it was true, Sancha conceded, her abductor was not altogether unpleasing, with his muscular physique, clear grey eyes, and engaging smile. Perhaps he was not even the lickerish monster she had at first believed him to be. But without a doubt he was among the traitorous knights who had betrayed Richard, and aided the usurper Henry Bolingbroke. She and her dowry were his reward, payment for his treachery. That she could never forget, nor forgive.

Alyse sought in vain for ways to amuse her mistress as the weary hours dragged by. She told funny tales she had heard, and occasionally commented on some view. But try as she might, she could seldom coax more than a polite, but brief reply from her mistress.

Day by day the pattern was repeated as they journeyed north. At each day's end they prevailed upon the hospitality of another of Lord William Canby's acquaintances, and in a sense became the unwanted and unwelcome guests of a score of merchants, nobles, and abbots.

Between Hugh and Sancha, a tenuous truce existed. Free of the stupefying effects of the elixir, she became a self-assured young woman who returned his admiring grey glances with an unsmiling air. There were no further hysterics. She answered when spoken to, and generally deported herself according to her station. They slept in the same bed, though chastely, and their hosts, ignorant of this, invariably thought them well paired.

For Hugh it was quite different. Sancha made him feel as if he did not exist. Even when she fixed her eyes on him, he had the impression that he was of no more importance to her than a blade of grass. It was a new experience for Hugh. He was accustomed to easy conquests, to tavern girls who were as easily forgotten. But Dominique de Severies, the little queen's much endeared "Sancha," remained elusive, beyond his grasp. His mind dwelt upon her, as did his dreams.

Quite casually, one evening at the table of a wealthy Nottingham alderman, Sancha mentioned that she disliked being closed inside the charette for hours on end.

"Would you prefer to sit a horse?" Hugh asked, pleased at the prospect of having her ride beside him. On the morrow a honey-colored mare, a doe-eyed creature with an abundant flaxen mane and tail was brought out for her, a gift from the alderman's own stable.

"I shall call her Angele," Sancha announced, fairly beaming. It was the first time Hugh had seen her smile, and he wished the smile with all its sweet innocence had been meant for him. How pretty was his young wife. She sat the little mare with perfect grace, her movements lithe as a young willow, and time and again Hugh's gaze went back to her and lingered there.

There was something about her which held him, some allure which he had never encountered before. Something, which fastened onto his soul and would not leave him in peace. He was at war within himself. At one moment resolute, deciding to demand his rights as husband, only to realize in the next breath that his male pride would not allow it.

League by league Hugh and his new household made their way north. The weary pace at times wore on everyone's nerves. It was particularly tiresome for Hugh, who was only now coming to realize the full weight of his responsibilities.

As a soldier he had been accustomed to a relatively carefree existence. His travels had for the most part been with a swift-moving armed column which could easily cover fifty leagues a day. But now, with cumbersome carts and a charette, a mere twenty leagues was all that could be expected. The threat of rain to mire the deeply rutted roads left Hugh fretting at the sight of a cloud. Unsafe bridges which could only be crossed with a prayer and singly, one cart at a time, were yet another concern.

They approached one such bridge near Rawcliffe. It was a rickety span of wood whose rotted planks bowed with the weight of a single horse. Neither did the stone piers on which the planking rested inspire confidence. They had been undermined by many a spring flood so that even the lightest traffic caused the entire conveyance to shake as if taken by a fit of ague. Hugh, along with Martin and Rumald, walked out on the span, inspecting the planks and eyeing the sadly neglected piers. Not satisfied, Hugh crossed the bridge and climbed down the weedy embankment for a closer look at the more unstable of the two piers. Martin and Rumald traipsed after him.

On the opposite bank, many of Hugh's troop had dismounted

and were standing about gawking and idly talking. Sancha and Alyse had also dismounted and, tethering their mounts, walked out to the edge of the embankment above the stream. The distance to the water was intimidating, and the bridge from that perspective appeared an absolute derelict.

"Holy Mary, I pray we are not forced to cross," Alyse whispered, recounting how earlier she had seen a raven swoop down above the road. " 'Tis no good a raven brings, none at all."

Beside her, Sancha suddenly gave a little breathless gasp, clasped a gloved hand over her lips, whirled about, and walked swiftly back to her mare.

Alarmed by her sudden departure, Alyse hurried after her. "Mistress? Are you ill?"

For an instant, Sancha could not reply and made only a slight motion with her hand. "No," she finally managed, her voice sounding strained. Still she could not face Alyse. She pressed her forehead against the mare's satiny neck, speaking softly to the beast, avoiding Alyse's inquiring eyes.

"It is nothing," Sancha assured her maid. For she dare not say what she had felt. Nor could she have explained, even if she had dared, the eerie feeling that had seized her so suddenly, a feeling of weightlessness, of falling and the vision of murky water rushing up to meet her. She turned her face from the mare and smiled at Alyse. "I am weary, nothing more." Again, Sancha smiled bravely, though inside she was trembling, terrified by the thought that she might truly go mad, just as the physician had warned.

Hugh, Martin, and Rumald made their way up the embankment, through the glossy green weeds. Hugh stepped out on the span once more, halted and looked about. He could not decide whether to risk a crossing or turn back and suffer a seventeen-league journey to Beal, where another bridge crossed the river. The trio were deep in a discussion, when a merchant, as fat as the palfrey he was riding, approached the bridge leading two heavily laden packhorses. He halted before them and wished them a hearty good day. "I see you are hesitant to cross our good abbot's bridge," the merchant said. He was sweating profusely, so much so that his shining face resembled a lump of lard melting in the sun. "Not that I find fault with your wisdom, sire," the merchant assured. "I pray aloud to God and his holy mother each time I set foot upon it."

"An abbot is responsible for this bridge?" Hugh was incredulous.

"Indeed, sire. The abbot of St. Michael's."

"Why in Christ's name is it left in such parlous condition?"

"Why," the merchant chuckled, "truly I cannot say. The abbot has collected funds for its repair these many years. I, myself, have bought enough indulgences to enter heaven a dozen times over. But as you see, the bridge is no better for it." And with a jolly laugh, added, "Nor, I dare say, am I. Well, good day to you sire and God's blessings." With that the fat man jiggled his reins and set off across the bridge at a trot. The bridge shuddered; trusses groaned, and planks rattled. Reaching the other side of the span, the merchant raised an arm in salute, then proceeded to weave his way through the crowd of astounded onlookers and clutter of carts and horses.

Hugh, Martin, and Rumald, watching from the far side, exchanged amused glances and started out across the span.

Rumald paused to spit into the water. "I was once apprenticed to a man like that," he remarked.

Martin stepped to one side to avoid a warped plank. "Fat as him?"

"Nay," Rumald remarked, drawing the back of his hand across his mouth. "Stupid as him."

Hugh chuckled. "Ah, but he's on the other side, an' we aren't."

With his faith in the bridge somewhat restored, Hugh escorted his lady wife and her maid across on foot. He then proceed to send riders in pairs, carts singly. The crossing, though nerve-racking, was accomplished without incident.

As midafternoon approached, Hugh halted the procession.

Food was brought out, simple fare, for it was Hugh's intention to reach Barlby Castle by nightfall. As the company gathered in small groups beneath the roadside trees, cloths were laid out and loaves of bread and wineskins appeared.

Alyse went to fetch food and wine. Alone beneath the trees, Sancha was speaking to her little golden mare in dulcet tones. Since childhood she had loved animals, large and small. She loved to pet and caress them, to talk to them, and ofttimes she would go so far as to kiss them. It was just such a scene Hugh happened on as he tethered his horse. "I receive no sweet kisses from your lips," he teased.

Sancha spun about, startled by his sudden appearance. Her cheeks tinted pink. "You are not so pretty as she."

"Perhaps if I grew longer ears and a tail."

She gave a little soundless laugh. "You would look like a jackass."

Hugh grinned. "At least I would amuse you. Come," he coaxed, extending a hand to her. "Sit under a tree with me." He had a wineskin slung over his shoulder and looked at her expectantly,

Sancha had no desire to go anywhere with him. "Why?" she asked.

"Because I have asked you to."

"Where is Alyse?" She looked round searchingly.

"I have sold her to a shepherd," he said in a jesting voice.

Sancha frowned. His handsome, grinning face infuriated her. She gave him a black look and turned to pet her mare.

Hugh walked on a short distance. "She is talking to Martin," he informed his wife. "Sharpening her charms on him. She has an eye for a manly chest." Hugh found a likely spot in the shade of a large rowan tree.

Beneath its dense canopy, only weeds flourished. Hugh kicked down a circle were they might sit in comfort. "Come, before the weeds spring back." He set the wineskin down and removed his belt and sword so he might sit in comfort.

Reluctantly Sancha abandoned the mare. "Alyse is wiser

than that," she said, seating herself and arranging her skirts.
"Do you think that is all women care for?"

"It is a good beginning." He smiled, seating himself beside
her on the ground. Taking the wineskin in hand, he offered
her the first drink.

Sancha drew her dark brows into a frown. "You know very
little of women." It crossed her mind to refuse his wine, but
she was hot and thirsty.

"You must tell me." He leaned back, setting his spine
against the trunk of the tree and watching her.

She aimed the thin stream of wine at her open mouth. "Tell
you?" she said finally, daintily brushing a trickle of wine from
the corner of her lips. "Tell you what?"

"What sort of man would please you, a tall man, a short
man? Better still, a man with a wooden heart?"

Sancha felt herself beginning to blush. "I want no man. If
I were to wish for something, I would wish for my life to be
as it was before."

"At Richard's court, as if nothing had changed? But it would
have, you know. Everything changes, you and I, this moment.
What would have been your fate when one fine day your little
queen got her fluxes and went to Richard's bed?"

"That would never have happened," she said with a flush
of temper. "Richard's love for Madame was pure and without
coarseness."

"Then so much the worse for you, my innocent lamb. Do
you not know there are some men who prefer the caresses of
other men? Think for a moment if you had been passed off
to one of Richard's favorites. What sort of man would he be?"

Her dark eyes flashed in response. "No! We were free to
choose. I would never be forced to marry! Madame promised!"

"Ah, but she gave you to me. So much for the worth of her
promises."

"She had no choice! It was because of the usurper, that
criminal, Henry Bolingbroke! He forced her to do his bid-

ding!" When she raised her eyes, the smile had gone from his lips.

"You must never say that again."

"Why? It is the truth!"

"All the same, you must not say it."

The words he had spoken about Richard still angered her. "Richard was not such a man!" she said hotly.

"Perhaps not, I do not know . . . only what I have heard." A flurry of movement caught his eye. "Ah, here is Alyse."

Sancha was comforted by Alyse's presence, but her good humor did not return. She refused the cheese and would only nibble on a chunk of bread. Her heated conversation with her new husband had quite soured her appetite.

By nightfall they were the guests of the elderly castellan of Barlby Castle. To Sancha's delight his wife was French, the daughter of a minor Burgundian noble. It was a joy for Sancha to speak her native tongue once again, though later she felt more homesick than before.

The lady of the castle, barely out of her teens and married to a man thirty years her senior, was openly envious of Sancha's good fortune.

"Mon Dieu," the lady exclaimed, "he is so handsome and so young. What I would not give to have such a lover."

Sancha smiled and thought her own thoughts. She considered Hugh Canby the worst sort of traitor. For all his kindness toward her, he had betrayed Richard and Sancha's precious little Madame.

She would never forgive him, and as the journey continued, her attentions, rather than being lavished on her young husband's handsome face and muscular physique, were showered on the honey-colored mare, her pet. She secreted away sweets from her host's tables for the beast's greedy delight, and fretted constantly for its well-being. And the little mare, as if she sensed her own importance, was docile as a lamb. She had no vices, save for one.

With the village of Dipton behind them they traveled on

beneath a meltingly warm May sun, through fertile valleys where cattle moved slowly through lush pastures and peasants plowed the fields with oxen, turning over the dark earth, leaving brown ridges in the wake of their plows amid patches of weeds and bobbing wildflowers. The road, more of an overgrown lane, followed the meandering course of a shallow tributary of the Tyne.

Several hours into the trek, a wheel of a heavily loaded cart became mired in a rut. After several unsuccessful attempts to free the cart, Hugh decided to lighten the cart's cargo. But what should have amounted to a simple chore soon turned into a minor catastrophe when a keg of iron nails rolled from the cart's rear gate and broke open on impact, showering the road and weedy berm with its contents.

After the initial round of curses, accusations, and finger-pointing, Hugh put an end to the noisy debate and set the men to searching. Half a dozen men crawled about on their hands and knees scouring the ruts and the matted weed stalks.

Forged by hand, nails were a precious commodity. They were also deadly, for a stray nail picked up in the soft frog of a horse's hoof was certain to lame the animal and was often a death sentence.

Men milled about as the noonday sun beat down unforgivingly on the rutted path. The day was hot despite the breeze that stirred the treetops and billowed the tall grass of the surrounding meadows.

Sancha, too warm in her heavy clothing, shifted uncomfortably in her saddle and gazed longingly across the rolling meadow to the stand of sheltering trees and the sparkling waters of the stream. The scene was cool and inviting, infinitely more exciting than the elbows and backsides of men searching for nails amid the weeds.

Impulsively, Sancha twitched her reins and, alerting Alyse with a toss of her head, cantered toward the sun-dazzled riffles. Alyse followed on her palfrey, though at a much more sedate pace.

At the stream's edge, birds called and shrubs starred with dainty white flowers scented the warm air with their honeyed aroma. Beauty was all around her. Sunlight danced on the shallow riffles, and where the crystal-clear water eddied about her mare's hooves, the sand was studded with little pebbles that shone like gems.

Sancha let the reins go lax. She was transfixed by the scene, so much so that she put aside for the moment her notion to dismount, remove her slippers, and wade in the cool water.

But the mare, immune to such flights of fancy, was hot and itchy. Her head went down. She pawed at the sandy bottom. In a trice her knees had buckled, and down she went.

Sancha, whose experience with horses was limited to riding with the queen's ladies in processions and hawking expeditions, was taken completely unawares. She shrieked with surprise and scampered from the toppling mare, receiving a good dunking in the process.

Mortified by her less-than-graceful descent, but uninjured, Sancha struggled to her feet, water streaming from her clothing, and made for the shore. Staggering beneath the weight of her waterlogged skirt, she slipped, wrenched her ankle, and fell once more into the shallow water.

At that moment, Alyse, astride her palfrey, came plodding from beneath the trees. Seeing the scene all at once, the mare on her back, thrashing the air with all four feet and her mistress floundering to rise from the water, Alyse imagined the worst.

Twelve

Back at the road, moments before, Hugh was directing the placement of a heavy chest inside the charette. The interior was hot as an oven, and it was also narrow, with little room to maneuver. When the chest and the two sweating men became hopelessly wedged, Hugh lent a hand.

The last thing on his mind was the whereabouts of his lady wife. Yet the instant the shrill shriek reached his ears, he knew at once it was Sancha's voice. He bolted up, nearly braining himself on the charette's curved roof.

He had no sooner squeezed past the heavy chest and dropped to the ground, when he heard yet another scream, louder and longer. It was Alyse, and from the direction of the stream.

One of the cartmen rushed up to him. "Sire! Something's amiss! There by the stream!"

"Yes, yes," Hugh said. "I know." Several others dashed up, all talking at once. Hugh pushed past them, shouting, "Martin! Bring the horses!" Martin suddenly appeared from the rear of the mired cart, nodded, and took off at a run.

Rumald, who had been supervising the search for the nails, jogged forward, waving his arms. "I saw them ride off just before! I'll go with you!"

"No," Hugh remarked, reasoning that it could well be the prelude to a bandit attack. "Stay with the carts," he commanded. "All of you, on your guard!" he shouted down the line of carts. There was a clatter of swords and bucklers. A horse whinnied and Hugh swiveled his head to see Martin riding up at a fast trot, leading Chewbit. Martin tossed the reins to him. Hugh stabbed his boot in the stirrup, mounted, and the pair galloped toward the stream.

By the time they arrived on the scene, Alyse had towed her mistress from the water and sat her in the reeds. Her frolicking mare had also splashed from the stream, had a good shake, and was unconcernedly cropping marsh grass.

Hugh was more shaken by the experience than Sancha. He looked her up and down, shoved up her skirt and examined her ankle, which was already blue and expanding before his eyes.

When he was at last satisfied nothing was broken, he began to berate her in a soft furious tone of voice. "You've no damn sense! You're fortunate as hell you weren't kicked or crushed! Didn't you feel the mare's knees buckle? Couldn't you guess what she was going to do? It's your own fault, you've spoiled the damn beast till it's silly as a lapdog, till it's fit for nothing but the hacker!"

Sancha's tearful defense of both the mare and herself availed her nothing. Roundly chastised, she was placed on her wet saddle and led back to the charette, from which she was forbidden to set foot. Her shouts of protest, her angry accusations, many of them spoken in her native tongue, since she could muster no sufficiently colorful equivalent in English, fell on deaf ears. She was condemned to ride in the charette with her swollen foot propped on a pillow.

On the seventeenth day of their journey, they sighted the city of Hexham. It was a milestone of sorts, for their final destination, Evistone Abbey, lay but several days' journey to the north. In the fiery twilight, the city's massive walls took on a reddish tint. Alyse, leaning from the charette's window, was so impressed by the cast of the dying sunlight upon the walls that she murmured, "Bejesu," and hastily crossed herself.

"What is it?" Sancha's movements were still hampered by her swollen ankle, and she moved awkwardly to see.

"Oh, look, mistress, 'tis the light, 'tis red as hellfire."

Sancha twisted her body in the leather seat so she might view the fantastic cast of light and shade upon the great stone walls. The sight of it caused her to draw in her breath in a little voiceless "ohhh." The last dying rays of a fiery sunset spilled across the distant hills, bathing the rugged landscape, each tree, each clump of turf, in a spectacular ruby glow. The air shimmered, red to gold, and before her eyes shadows deepened, and the hills seemed to step forward in dark relief against the fading sky.

Twilight was falling as the entourage halted before the abbey of St. Andrew. Their entry coincided with the deep throaty voice of the angelus bells.

"I am Brother Jacob," the fat young cleric who greeted them said. He appeared to be scarcely more than a teenager, for his skin was white as a lily and too smooth ever to have known a blade. "Our holy bishop sends his blessings and extends his abbey's hospitality. I will escort you to the stables and guesthouse." The young priest, leading the way, trotted beside Hugh's horse.

"I should like an audience with your bishop," Hugh called down from the saddle.

"Our holy bishop rarely entertains, though he does make exceptions for endowments," the priest puffed. "Do you wish to make a gift to the altar?"

"It is unlikely, since I am now the prebend of Evistone Abbey."

The young cleric turned an astonished face to him and remarked, "In that case, my lord, I am certain the bishop will desire an audience with you."

At the stable yard grooms appeared, mostly young boys under the direction of an elderly lay brother. While the carts were being unhitched and the horses led away, Hugh arranged for his men to be sheltered in the lay brothers' dormitories and fed from the kitchens.

Again the young priest let it be known that although the bishop's hospitality was extended to one and all, wealthy guests were expected to purchase indulgences.

Hugh had the distinct feeling that he would not get off cheaply, and he could not help but wonder how many bridges were in the bishop's dioceses.

It was well-nigh dark by the time Hugh, his lady wife, Alyse, and Martin, bearing a minimum of luggage, followed the priest. Hugh, carrying Sancha, hoped it was not too long a walk. She was slight, it was true, but even the lightest burden becomes tiresome after a distance.

The priest led them beneath an ivy-covered arcade and through a garden, fragrant with herbs in the evening stillness. Along the route the young cleric pointed out the dormitories set aside for pilgrims and the abbey's infirmary. The guest-house, he assured Hugh, was reserved for more notable personages.

The interior, like most monastic structures, was without adornment. Inside their chamber, Sancha insisted on being set down. She disliked being carried; above all, she disliked her husband's hands on her. His touch left her feeling confused, ashamed.

She shook out her skirts, and limped about, finally perching on one of the cots. Alyse crossed the room with an armful of cushions carried from the charette.

"Poverty, obedience, and chastity," Hugh murmured, glancing about the bare chamber, taking in the limewashed walls, the narrow cots, and whistling a little as he undid the latch on the shuttered window. He opened it fully, allowing a draft of cool air to circulate in the stuffy room. "I wonder what I shall see in the abbot's residence?" he mused aloud. "Upholstered chaises and Saracen rugs, no doubt." When he turned from the window, he saw Alyse bent over his lady wife, the two of them speaking in soft, secretive tones.

While Alyse arranged the small cushions behind Sancha's back and beneath her injured ankle, Hugh sent Martin to see to settling the men and horses.

Martin had just gone out the door, when Sancha announced, "I will ride tomorrow." She raised her head and tossed a challenging glance at Hugh.

"Not until you are able to walk," he told her.

"I am perfectly able to walk." She leaned forward to take another of the cushions from Alyse's hand. "It was you who insisted I should be carried," Sancha reminded him.

A sound from the courtyard drew Hugh's attention back to the window. It was a lay brother with a collection of empty wooden pails. He stooped to retrieve the one he had dropped, and in turn two more tumbled away. "Go and fetch some water, Alyse."

"There is water, my lord. A lay broth—" She paused midword as she realized his meaning, sheepishly closed her mouth, and slipped from the room.

Sancha looked up nervously. "Why did you send Alyse away?"

"Because I wish to talk to you."

"Her presence did not prevent you from speaking to me earlier."

He laughed softly and sat down on the bed. "No, but what I have to say to you now is quite different."

Sancha lowered her eyes, tracing her fingers over the cushion's brocaded design. "In what way?" she asked breathlessly. His nearness panicked her. Each day she knew, instinctively perhaps, that it would be soon. She felt suddenly clammy, unable to dispel the thoughts of the final moment, a bed, moist flesh, and the obscure act of which she knew too little truth and too many whispered tales, so that the thought of him left her frightened, squeamish, and yet, infinitely curious.

"It concerns only you. Because you are my wife, and . . ."

Her voice cut across his words. "I have no wish to be your wife!" she blurted out. She would not look at him and clutched

the cushion to her bosom like a shield. Her cheeks burned
with resentment. The silence between them was unbearable.
She felt his weight lift from the bed, heard his footsteps as he
crossed the chamber, and the sound of the oaken door meeting
the frame. Voices drifted back to her from the passageway,
first his, then Alyse's. The door opened and Alyse entered, a
scowl upon her face. "Does your ankle pain you, my lady?"

"No." Sancha said, miserably, thinking, *It is my heart.* She
could hardly say that, not to Alyse, who would surely repeat
it.

Hugh walked out into the purple dusk. The first stars twin-
kled overhead. A haze of smoke rose from the kitchens and
the cool air was spiced with the aroma of roasting meat. Hugh
had no appetite. He walked through the garden, toward the
arcade, feeling powerless, impatient, and angry, unable to understand why the foolish young woman he had married did
not see fit to care for him. All his kindness and patience were
wasted on her. She divined none of it, comprehended nothing,
not his admiring glances, his tenderness toward her. She rejected him. He did not understand her. Such a thing had never
happened to him before.

Beneath the ivy-covered arcade the darkness was broken by
a series of stone lanterns, carved in the likenesses of gargoyles,
that smoked and stank of tallow. Hugh walked on through the
pools of light, his footsteps ringing hollowly on the paving
stones. He had not gone far when he met a man coming from
the opposite direction.

Hugh, distracted by his own thoughts, had not heard the
man's approach. He was totally unaware of his presence until
the man suddenly materialized before him, with a tinkling of
bells.

Hugh quickly stepped to one side, avoiding a collision. After
a moment of mutual confusion they exchanged civilities. To
Hugh's complete surprise, the man declared, "By the Holy
Rood! Are you not William Canby's son?"

"I am," Hugh admitted. "Though I confess, sir, you have

me at a disadvantage." In the sickly wash of lanternlight, the
man's features took on a grotesque slant. He was ungainly tall
and, whether from habit or nature, stood with his shoulders
slightly hunched.

"Ah, forgive me. Allow me to introduce myself. My name
is Exton. I am a wool merchant by trade. I was present at your
wedding celebration. I trust you and your lovely bride have
had a pleasant journey?"

"As pleasant as the king's roads allow. You are a resident
of the north country, sir?"

"Not really. My dealings take me all about the realm. Well,
I must not delay you. Good evening to you, sir, and safe journey."

Hugh nodded and continued on along the arcade. The man's
face stirred a vague memory. Curiously, it seemed to remind
Hugh of something unpleasant. The name, though, meant nothing to him. "Exton," he mumbled as he strode along. But he
was too aggravated to think. The image of his wife would not
let him be. He pushed the name from his thoughts. He'd had
more than enough annoyances that day without racking his
mind for more. There was still the matter of an audience with
the bishop. As prebend of Evistone Abbey, Hugh could hardly
ignore the man. Even so, he did not intend to sit at St. Andrew's and await the bishop's convenience.

At the stables, Hugh walked around, checking the carts and
talking to the men, to Martin and to Rumald. He had nothing
better to do. The familiar smell of horses, the subtle mingling
of hay and manure, seemed to have a soothing effect on him.
He was still there when the young priest, Jacob, brought him
an invitation from the bishop to dine at his table that evening.

In the bishop's hall, where the honored guests gathered at
the high table, Hugh and Martin joined the others. There were
ten guests, aside from himself and Martin, all prosperous merchants judging from their lavish clothing. They stood about on
the dais, waiting to be seated. The man Hugh had met unex-

pectedly in the arcade was present. Hugh acknowledged him with a slight inclination of his head.

Long lines of black-robed brethren filed into the cavernous chamber, taking up their positions at the lower tables. Several clergymen and two novitiates emerged from a door arch to the rear of the dais. The more senior of the group, a heavy man with wiry eyebrows and not a hair on his head, introduced himself as the bishop's chancellor. "His Grace sends his regrets. He is at prayer this evening." That said, the chancellor stepped to the fore of the dais and led the assembled monks in prayer.

As the Benedictus ended, the childish novitiates, neither of whom was older than eight or nine, came forward, one carrying a golden bowl filled with water, the other a towel of silk, heavily embroidered with gold thread.

The youthful novitiate holding the water bowl sank to his knees, whereupon the chancellor washed his hands with dramatic gestures and held them out to be dried by the second novitiate, who did so with much bowing and kissing. Following the ceremony, Hugh, Martin, and the other guests were seated, and the monks at the lower table sank down on their benches.

A bell sounded and an army of servants poured from the kitchens with a multitude of heavily laden platters. Steam rose from the piping hot trays of fish and eel, fowl, venison, and pork. The variety of meats was astounding, roasted, stuffed, boiled, and fried, many served with sauces and dusted lavishly with spices. For all the tempting dishes, the meal was a dreary affair. Open speech was prohibited.

Hugh noticed the food served to the lower tables where the main body of monks sat was less grand, and he wondered what sort of fare had been offered his lady wife and her maid. Because of the order's vows, women were forced to remain sequestered in the guesthouse and take their meals in their quarters.

As the meal progressed, the chancellor, through discreet signals to his servants, would send gifts of the more-splendid meat dishes to the lower tables, where the monks, forbidden to speak openly, sent up a constant chorus of hissing and whispering, and punctuated their voiceless conversations with gesticulations of their fingers and hands. They put Hugh in mind of a company of buffoons rather than holy men, and he watched half-amused as each successive gift of meat was greeted with an even greater display of hissing, exaggerated head bobbing, and flapping hands.

The ale served at the meal was also memorable. It was sweetened and flavored with a fruit, whose true nature remained a mystery. Martin was the first to taste it. He looked as if he'd swallowed a bug.

Occasionally Hugh would glance down the table past the sauced partridges, the tarts of spiced pork liver, the flampoyntes and pottages to the wool merchant he had met in the arcade. He was, Hugh decided, possessed of a face not easily forgotten. Hugh was certain he had seen him before, though he could not say where or when. Perhaps it was just as the man said. Even so, the thought nagged at him.

Later at the guest quarters as he lay in his cot, Hugh again tried to place the man's face. Unsuccessful, he drifted off to sleep. He spent a restless night, tossing, turning, lost in a dream of long ago.

It was not a dream at all. He was no longer asleep, no longer a child wandering alone in the forest. The gnarled tree had altered and become a man's form framed in a yellow wedge of light. Hugh narrowed his eyes against the glare and raised himself on one elbow. He could see plainly now that it was Martin, bare-chested with his cropped hair standing on end. He was speaking in hushed, but urgent tones with someone on the other side of the half-opened door. Someone holding a lantern.

"What is it?" Hugh asked, his voice sounding slurred, too loud in the silent room.

Sancha, whose cot was nearest her husband's, bolted up

from her coverlet at the sound of his voice. Alyse, nearby, roused and lifted her head.

Martin stepped to one side and opened the door. Rumald entered. Light flooded the chamber, and Rumald, peering from the yellow halo of lamplight, reported, " 'Tis a large company of riders at the abbey's gates, fifty horsemen, maybe more. The gateward said they be Northumberland's forces."

"Rumald and I could have a look?" Martin suggested, crossing the chamber. He located his shirt and tugged it across his shoulders.

Hugh grunted affirmatively and lay back in the cot. His first thought had been to roll over and fall back to sleep. But by now he was fully awake. He asked the hour.

Rumald shrugged. "Nearly lauds, I ken. There were candles lit in the chapel when I passed."

"Northumberland has ridden all night," Hugh surmised, mumbling to himself. Why? he wondered. It was true, Hugh had heard reports of border raids from his various hosts, but he doubted that a few insignificant skirmishes would send the mightiest of the Percys scurrying north. He was curious. "Wait," he said, throwing aside the coverlet and dragging himself from the comfortable hollow his body had made in the straw-filled mattress. He pulled on his hosen, his boots, and grabbed his shirt.

Sancha's inquiring gaze followed her husband's every movement. "Is this man your enemy?" she whispered, a note of alarm creeping into her voice.

Hugh glanced at his wife. In the harsh slant of the lantern-light her eyes appeared almond-shaped, very dark, very appealing. "No," he said, running a hand through his tousled hair. "It is nothing. Go back to sleep."

Sancha waited only until the echo of their footfalls had died away before she climbed from her cot and hobbled across the darkened room toward the window. Alyse fumbled through the darkness to join her at the embrasure. From their vantage point the young women could see a portion of the abbey's lengthy forecourt. Torches and lanterns bobbed to and fro in the blackness, voices rang out, and dogs barked amid a crush of milling horsemen. The chaotic sounds and the little that Sancha could discern from the dark distance frightened her. Even with Alyse beside her, she felt alone, helpless as a leaf in the wind.

In the courtyard below, the swarm of horses and men, and the jangle of mail and brutish monosyllabic commands raised such a din as to confound the senses. Hugh pressed into the throng, dodging horses, making little headway. Halfway across the courtyard, the sea of riders parted momentarily and he saw lanterns appear before the chapel. He struck out toward them, changing direction once again. When he glanced back, he no longer saw Martin and Rumald.

Figures converged before the chapel, moving in silhouette. A group of brethren came from the open doors to confer with the riders, and a pair of horses with a litter slung between was led forward. Hugh advanced by stops and starts. All about him riders dismounted, jangling with weapons and jesting aloud. Conversations and laughter erupted.

Behind his back, Hugh heard a loud burst of obscenities, and a hand caught his arm. He jolted round to see his half brother Gilbert. "By Satan's rotten terse! How have you come to be at St. Andrew's?" he demanded.

"I might well ask the same of you," Hugh responded, freeing his arm with a hostile shrug. As he did he saw Walter, the younger brother, lurking in the shadows, talking with a small group of men. It did not surprise Hugh that Gilbert and Walter were together. Even as children one never strayed far from the other.

Walter eyed Hugh, then made a comment to his companions. Hugh did not hear what he said, only the laughter. His attention was diverted by a soldier, who bumped past him in the shoulder-to-shoulder crowd.

"My lord Northumberland," the soldier called out, and reached to grasp the reins of a large grey that crab-stepped from the swarm of horses, men, and confusion. Alighting from

the horse, Northumberland stepped into their midst. He was
not at all what Hugh imagined, this mighty patriarch of the
Percys. And though his legend was larger than life, he was a
slight man, wiry, with a drooping moustache and a huge beak
of a nose that protruded from beneath his helmet. He turned
to Hugh abruptly, fixing him in a formulated stare and queried,
"You are William's bastard?"

"I am, my lord," Hugh acknowledged.

"He is dead," Northumberland remarked in a brusque voice.
"Eight days past at Wallingford." He directed his next words
to Hugh's half brothers, something concerning the bishop.

For a moment Hugh could not think beyond the words "He
is dead." The litter, of course. But it had not occurred to him
that it contained a corpse. Why should it? He stared, his eyes
unfocused, as three men, soldiers, struggled to remove a large
humped form from the litter. Several more men rushed up to
lend a hand with the awkward burden that had been wrapped
in cloth and lashed to a plank. Figures moved to and fro across
Hugh's line of vision. Another group of clergy emerged from
the chapel, among them the chancellor and a fat man, wrapped
in a gold cloth robe, whom they addressed as "Your Grace."

Dead, as simply as that. No, Hugh did not believe them.
Perhaps he spoke aloud, for when he walked toward the litter,
Gilbert called after him. "Oh, the old fool is dead well enough,
though I should have preferred it was before he took leave of
his senses!"

"Enough," Northumberland rebuked sharply. "The subject
is threadbare. I've no time for petty quarrels." There was a
certain timbre in the man's voice, his prowling gait, that demanded obedience. He elbowed past his sons-in-law, and with
decisive steps went to greet the bishop.

From over his shoulder Hugh saw Gilbert and Walter trail
after him. Presently the group walked off in the direction of
the chapter house. Hugh made no attempt to join them. They
had not asked him to.

Martin, mired in the crowd, at last located Hugh as he was

about to follow the litter into the chapel. "Go back to the guest quarters," Hugh told him. "Keep watch over my lady wife." After Martin had gone, Hugh wondered if he had sounded foolish. Dazed and still in shock, he had reacted as he had as a child, rushing to guard what he held dear, fearful of his half brothers. Little had changed. He had grown older, but the fear remained.

A priest in dust-laden robes and a lay brother with a lantern led the strange procession through the nave. Braces of candles burned on either side of the altar, and before the waxen image of St. Mary the Virgin.

The dead man's stench filled the chapel. A coffin had been sent for, but in the meantime the body was laid on the floor by the altar rail. Hugh could not imagine his father dead, and would not be satisfied until the shroud had been laid back and he had seen the corpse. The priest, who had accompanied the body from the south, first dismissed the soldiers, then instructed the elderly lay brother to unwind the stained linen. The man moved slowly, arthritically, setting the lantern aside, then fumbling to locate the end of the linen wrap.

At first, Hugh could not recognize the hideously blackened and distorted features. The hulk that lay on the chapel floor bore little resemblance to the man with whom he had talked and laughed little more than a fortnight before. The body appeared hideously misshapen. Upon his sunken chest a huge gout of blood had pooled and caked upon the silken tunic. "Is that a wound?" Hugh questioned, his eyes afire with suspicion.

"No, not at all, my lord," the priest responded. "Rather the mark of a surgeon. The heart was removed." And he indicated a small ornately carved box on the altar, explaining, "It was Lord Canby's wish that his body be interred here in the crypt below the altar he endowed, and that his heart be placed with his first wife at St. Mies."

The thought of his father's heart, shriveled in a wooden box, the stinging stench of decay, all of it, sickened Hugh. A wave of nausea swept over him. He turned away, feeling cold and clammy beneath his clothes. He could not bear to look at his father's corpse. "How did he die?" he asked in a feeble voice.

"Alas, I was not present." The priest made a motion for the lay brother to rewrap the corpse. "I was told he was stricken at a feast, seized by a painful spasm in his chest, collapsed and died within moments. It is not uncommon in older men, those who are fond of rich food and wine."

Hugh knew something of his father's appetites, if only by reputation. He recalled the wine, the new young wife of which his father had bragged. "Yes," he muttered, hoping his father had enjoyed them while he still could. As Hugh walked back through the nave, three sturdy lay brethren were maneuvering a coffin in through the doors. He waited for them to pass by. Outside the May day had dawned clear and sunlit.

In the shaded arcade it was yet dim and cool. Hugh had transversed half its length when he heard the pumping sound of running footfalls. He halted and turned to see a young novitiate with a tonsured head jogging toward him on sandaled feet. He paused, waiting for the boy to draw even with him.

"His Grace," the boy panted, "wishes to inform you that the funeral mass will be sung promptly at midday, my lord." Hugh nodded and walked on. Behind him the boy mopped the perspiration from his face with the sleeve of his robe, and began slowly walking back the way he had come.

Hugh entered the guest quarters and climbed the wooden staircase. Odd, he thought, that so little time had passed, and yet so much had changed. He still had not come to terms with his father's death, the realization that it was too late to form any true judgment of the man who had sired him. He felt resentful, angry, and a little frightened at this new and disturbing turn of events.

Topping the stairs, he caught sight of Martin standing in the passageway, lounging with his shoulder to the wall. The moment Martin saw him, he pulled himself from his slouch and walked toward him. "I talked with Rumald," he informed his master, in a confidential tone. "He spent the morning chat-

ting with some soldiers at the stable. They said Northumberland and his knights are riding on today, after the old lord's
put under the ground."

Under the ground. The phrase stuck in Hugh's mind. Of
course, it wasn't the case at all. His father was to be placed
in a crypt beneath the chapel, but he said nothing. It didn't
really seem to make any difference. He and Martin talked for
a few moments. Rumald had learned a wealth of information
from the soldiers. Hugh listened to Martin's retelling, and afterward sent him to fetch his set of finer clothing from the
leather-bound trunk in the charette. Hugh did not wish to appear at the mass in leathers, like some common yeoman.

Inside the chamber, Alyse was plaiting Sancha's hair. At the
sound of the door, both young women looked up. Martin had
told them of the unexpected death, and Sancha, seeing her
husband's stricken expression, felt compelled to say, "The
death of a father is very sad. My heart grieves for you."

Alyse, working a plait of heavy, dark hair, paused to murmur
a word of condolence.

"Will you escort his body home?" Sancha asked.

The note of genuine sympathy in her voice surprised Hugh.
"No, he is to be laid to rest here, at midday."

"Then I shall accompany you."

"The mass will be long, and you would have to stand."

"My ankle is much improved," she pointed out. But receiving no satisfaction from Hugh, she turned to Alyse. "Would
you not agree that it was, Alyse?"

Alyse concurred with a quick bob of her head. "Tis true,
sire, the swelling's all but gone."

Hugh's gaze swept past them. "There is no need for you to
suffer through the mass." He recalled the stench of the corpse,
the gloating look on Gilbert's face.

"It is my duty," Sancha reminded him, and in the same
breath went on to ask if the clothing she was wearing was
appropriate. The fitted gown of watchlet-shaded velvet and its
matching silk-lined hooded cloak were simply cut, and had

been pressed into service after her dousing in the stream. At Richard's extravagant court the ensemble would have been suitable for nothing more formal than a hawking expedition, but she was far from Richard's court. In fact, her days at court seemed a lifetime ago.

Hugh did not hear half of what Sancha said. His mind was elsewhere. He had decided to scrape away several days' growth of stubble from his jaw and went to get the blade from his leather satchel. When Sancha repeated her question, Hugh, intent on positioning the polished metal disc he used as a mirror, made a politely vague reply.

In the excitement of the moment Alyse had miscalculated. And now, suddenly aware of the lopsided braid, she clucked to herself, raked her fingers through her mistress's heavy tress, and quickly reworked it, twisting and plaiting the thick, dark hair. She was putting the finishing touches on the gleaming braids, when Martin arrived with the master's wedding clothing.

"Shall I wear a coif?" Sancha asked her husband. She had a moment before sent Alyse to search out the crispine of gold net from among the items in the small casque. When no reply was forthcoming from across the chamber, Sancha glanced to her husband. He was naked to the waist. She felt her cheeks pink and averted her eyes. "Yes, bring it to me, Alyse," she said, raising her voice above the sound of Martin shaking the creases from his master's brocaded doublet. She would wear it, she thought, out of respect.

The bells were tolling as Hugh, with Sancha leaning heavily on his arm, Martin, and Alyse went out into the warm, windy, spring afternoon. At the chapel a crowd of mourners, clergy for the most part, had already gathered. Hugh's father's coffin stood before the altar. The surrounding candles guttered and flared in the draft. The doors of the chapel had been propped open, but even so, the noisome odor of decay was impossible to ignore. Thankfully, the coffin's lid had been secured. Hugh was grateful for that at least. Scanning the crowd, he saw Northumberland and his entourage standing off to the left of the altar.

Conversations had broken out and the drone of voices drifted through the chapel. At first, Hugh did not notice his half brothers; their backs were to him. Then, one among the group of men must have told them of Hugh's arrival, for they shifted and looked back over their shoulders. Hugh glanced away, debating where he should stand.

A priest, the one who had greeted them on their arrival at St. Andrews, appeared from the press of brethren and indicated for Hugh to follow him. Martin stepped aside and, taking Alyse by the elbow, guided her past the font, to the right of the open doors, where the squires and pages stood.

By the time Hugh and Sancha threaded their way through the crowd of monks, Gilbert and Walter had taken up positions at the head of the coffin. Hugh and Sancha were directed to stand beside them.

Gilbert made do with a contemptuous stare, but Walter, his lips moving viciously over his teeth, turned on Hugh. "Whoreson!" He all but spit out the word. "You have no right to be here!" Gilbert, between them, seized his younger brother by the shoulder and shook him.

Everyone in the chapel heard. Heads turned, conversations came to a halt, the shuffling of feet died to a strained silence. After a moment someone coughed, and the buzz of voices resumed.

Sancha was aghast. She could hardly believe her ears. Her eyes darted from the clenched face of her husband to those of his half brothers, and then to the stone floor of the chapel. She did not know how to react to the boorish behavior of her brothers-in-law, and was at first more bewildered than outraged by the repulse.

A hush came over the mourners as the bishop, immense in his jewel-encrusted robes, entered from the vestry door. Six priests and twice as many servers followed in procession. Their Latin chants resounded through the chapel. Incense puffed from the swaying censers, mingling with the stench of decay.

From memory, Sancha recited the latin prayers with the others. Hugh's voice droned in her ear, deep and earnest. For as much as she had not wished to be his wife, she could not deny that there was in him a certain decency, a goodness of character. She looked toward the altar and in sidelong glances she saw Hugh's half brothers, their heads dropped on their chests in an attitude of prayer. The bishop's voice intruded on her thoughts. He spoke of God's infinite mercy and forgiveness. His bejeweled sleeve winked and glittered in the candlelight. Sancha understood almost nothing about her husband, and even less about his half brothers' anger. She glanced up at Hugh. Tears glistened in his eyes. She was overcome with a desire to comfort him, but not knowing how, simply pressed her fingers into his hand. As the Credo was being said, a draft of air swept through the chapel, extinguishing many of the candles. A door slammed, and curls of bitter-smelling white smoke hung in the air.

Though emotions ran high, there were no further incidents as the mourners departed the chapel. Outside in the blustery sunshine of the courtyard, the priest again hailed Hugh. Groups of mourners walked slowly past as the priest informed Hugh of his father's will, which was to be read by the bishop that very hour at the chapter house. According to the priest, the document, drawn up years before, had been amended shortly before William Canby's death. Hugh was about to decline the invitation when the priest added, "His Grace, the bishop, strongly desires your presence."

Hugh was left with little choice in the matter; he could hardly ignore the bishop's summons. Sancha, leaning on his arm, scowled in the sunlight. "What of your brothers?" she asked in a fretful undertone. "They are certain to be present?"

"They are half brothers," Hugh corrected her with a smile. "And I am not in fear of them. Now go with Martin and Alyse. All will be well."

Thirteen

At the chapter house, Hugh was shown into the accountancy room with its litter of parchment rolls, leather-bound volumes and ink pots. The bishop, who had abandoned his jeweled vestments for more serviceable attire, was seated on an ornate chair, his fat arms resting on the table where he conducted his accounts. There was a wine goblet before him, and a packet of papers sealed with scarlet wax. At the other end of the table sat a pale, round-faced man dressed in the robes of a priest.

Hugh bowed and said something appropriate. He was aware of Northumberland, the patriarch of the Percy clan; he had commandeered the room's only other chair. Hugh's half brothers, Gilbert and Walter, were sprawled on a bench against the opposite wall.

Entering, Hugh had noticed there were several other men scattered about the chamber. One he recognized as Simon de Lacey. Hugh had seen him on the lists at York during the last tournament. The other two he did not know. All had wine goblets in their hands.

"Come join us, Evistone," Northumberland said, purposely choosing to call Hugh by the name of his fief. It was less confusing than Canby, since there were now no less than three of them in the room. "I think you could probably do with a mizier of wine."

A servant approached Hugh with a goblet. Hugh lifted it from the tray and touched it to his lips.

Without rising from his chair, Northumberland quickly dispensed with the introductions. "Hugh of Evistone . . . Bishop Guerney, Father Antonio, Simon de Lacey, William Mowbray, Edward Prescott." He paused, perhaps for effect, or perhaps merely to catch his breath, though his lips quirked in amusement as he remarked, "And of course, you are acquainted with your half brothers. Sit down, Evistone." He watched as Hugh sank down on a bench near the hearth, the only one not occupied. "I should like to dispense with our business as quickly as possible, so that Bishop Guerney may proceed with the reading of the will. You are aware that your father, William Canby, was my vassal?"

"Yes, my lord" Hugh answered slowly. "It was brought to my attention." His father had touched on the subject briefly the night before the wedding. Later, in Oxford, Sir Walter Louthe had provided him with an even more disturbing insight into the arrangement. Hugh sipped at the wine. It was too sweet and he did not care for it.

"Was it also brought to your notice that through William Canby's claim of blood, you, his heir, on agreement became my vassal? And that although the fief and abbey came to you as an escheat, land granted by the crown, you are nevertheless bound by oath to pay fealty to me, both in revenue and force of arms?"

Hugh understood perfectly. He was being soundly warned. All the while he had the uncomfortable suspicion that Northumberland knew of his father's involvement with Thomas Swynford. When their eyes met, Northumberland grinned slightly, in a way that made Hugh feel as if he'd been caught stealing something.

"I shall expect to see you among my barons at Warkworth castle on Michaelmas. What say you to that?"

"The only words I might with honor, my lord, that I am your liege."

A chuckling sound came from deep in Northumberland's throat. "You take to solemn vows as eagerly as a tavern maid to a troubadour." Laughter rippled through the chamber. Hugh

could feel the heat rising from his collar. All eyes turned to
him and the expectant, amused expressions on their faces set
a muscle in his jaw to twitching.

With a flick of his hand Northumberland silenced them. But
when he again turned his gaze on Hugh, all the humor had
gone from his features. "I do not believe you truly appreciate
your position, Evistone. On one hand you have sworn loyalty
to Henry of Bolingbroke, Henry IV, king of England, since he
has so proclaimed himself. And on the other, you have sworn
fealty to me, your liege lord. I am reasonably curious as to
how you will rally to my summons, while at the same time
defending the king's banner."

"Much would depend on the circumstances, my lord," Hugh
replied, but with considerably less suavity than he had intended. "Are we not all of us vassals of the king?"

Northumberland smiled grimly. "To which king do you refer? The usurper Henry of Bolingbroke, or Richard?"

"Richard is dead, my lord." Hugh could see his answer did
not please Northumberland.

"Yes, and if you are to believe Henry's lies," Northumberland said with a snort of mockery, "Richard starved himself,
out of obstinacy or remorse. It is by far more reasonable to
believe that murder was committed, and if that is the case, the
Holy Father may yet place Henry of Bolingbroke under inter-
dict."

Hugh wondered to which pope Northumberland referred. He
had heard there were two Holy Fathers, rivals, and that they
spent their days not in prayer, but in denouncing one another.
With such riches at stake it seemed unlikely they would halt
their quarrel, even to excommunicate the king of England.

Northumberland hammered on. "Only a fool refuses to look
to the future," he said. "And regardless of Henry Bolingbroke's
outrageous claims of heredity, his grasp on the crown is pre-
carious. He has seized it by force, and only by force shall he
manage to keep it." Northumberland's voice grated. He was
angry, and as the bitter discourse continued, he took no efforts

to conceal his naked hatred of Henry Bolingbroke, nor his motives.

Hugh was beginning to understand why his father had chosen a post in Calais, preferring to battle the French rather than return to Redesdale and the inevitable confrontation with Northumberland. For despite Northumberland's age, fifty at least, and unimpressive stature, there was something inexpressibly savage about him. Perhaps it was the pale calculating eyes, or the mouth, loose and curiously cruel beneath the drooping moustache. He was not a man to be trifled with, or one to trust, Hugh thought.

"I wonder," Northumberland postured, arching a brow in Hugh's direction, "have you deliberately placed yourself in this awkward position in order to profit from a handsome payment? Simply put, my young hound, a man cannot serve two masters. And since all that you have has come to you through Henry Bolingbroke, it is only reasonable to assume that you would serve his interests above mine. And that would be a mistake. For if you dare to oppose me, be it no more than a missaid word, you will lose considerably more than a fief and an abbey. I trust I have made my position clear?"

The knuckles of Hugh's hand, gripping the goblet, were white. Anger and fear boiled up in his throat. Somehow, he forced himself to remain calm. "Perfectly clear, my lord," he managed, though his voice was stilted.

"I'm glad to see that you are not a fool, Evistone. I detest fools." Looking about, Northumberland showed a jovial smile to his barons. "Here, here, how has this happened?" he said, turning his wine goblet upside down and shaking it. "It is empty as air!" Making much of it, he turned a roguish eye on the bishop, and demanded, "What sort of host allows such a thing!"

Laughter and idle talk followed. Servants hastened to bring more wine. Presently, the bishop took charge of the assembly and the seal on the will was broken.

The document was lengthy. The bishop's voice droned on,

dull and monotonous as a wheel in motion. "A silver and gilt reliquary box, suitable in workmanship and weight to grace the altar of St. Andrew's Abbey of Hexham. As well as a silver fretwork censer, two cruets for water and wine."

After the lengthy list of endowments, the bishop paused to lubricate his throat with several deep draughts of wine. Next on the list was the large and lucrative fief of Redesdale which passed to Gilbert, the eldest son. To the second son, Walter, came a bequest of £5000, along with rental property in the city of Hexham.

It was the will's codicil, drawn up shortly before William Canby's death, that brought Hugh out of his dark and brooding thoughts. Loving mention was made of his second wife along with a bequest of £6000. She was also to retain control of her dowered properties. The revelation did not sit well with Hugh's half brothers, who grumbled to each other.

There were a number of other bequests to churches, monasteries, and chapels, among them St. Mies, where William Canby's heart was to be laid to rest within the coffin of his first wife. Lastly, there was a provision for his bastard, Hugh Loxton. Obviously, the codicil had been drawn shortly after William Canby's recent second marriage, but well before he had considered claiming his illegitimate son.

Hugh was taken by complete surprise, particularly when he heard the bishop pronounce, "In the sum of £5000 as well as the tract of land, known as Aubry and its village, both having previously been included within the boundaries of Redesdale."

A growl of protest came from Gilbert. But Walter, seated beside him, reacted like cannon powder touched with a spark and leapt to his feet with a thunder of outrage. "No, before God, no!" he bellowed. "He is the son of a harlot, he is filth, he has right to nothing!"

Gilbert, who by the look on his face was in complete agreement, grasped his brother's arm and pulled him back onto the bench. It did not silence him and, as he attempted to shake off his brother's grasp, he continued to shout abuse. Walter probably would have done so until he was hoarse, had it not been for a searing glance from his father-in-law, the earl of Northumberland.

"Apologize," Northumberland's harsh, loud voice rang out. "I will not have this. Do it at once! Either that, or you will apologize to me and then to him, too!"

"Yes, apologize. Apologize," the others added one by one.

Walter sputtered, half-choking, and glared at Hugh as if he would like nothing better than to slit his throat. Finally, the words were forced from his lips. "I ask your pardon."

Hugh stared at him, his every muscle tensed, fully aware that for the first time in years he had come within a heartbeat of a complete and violent loss of temper. He drew in a deep breath. But there was still an edge to his voice when at last he answered, "I have put it from my mind. As they say, evil to him who recalls the past."

Northumberland leaned back in his chair and smiled broadly, disclosing a row of long, uneven yellow teeth. "Well spoken, Evistone, well spoken."

The reluctant apology, Hugh was soon to discover, did not in any way lessen the ill will of his half brothers. Within the hour the terms of the document were settled, and those in the chamber filed into the passageway. Hugh found himself shoulder to shoulder with the elder of his half brothers.

"You miserable streak of piss!" Gilbert muttered, keeping his voice low. "You will never claim Aubry!"

Hugh met his half brother's gaze challengingly. His mouth straightened to a rebellious line and his jaw took on an angry, determined set. "Take yourself to the devil!" he told him, also in a low tone.

They walked on in the midst of the others, their eyes locked like two ferocious beasts about to do battle. Neither broke stride. In another ten paces they reached the door.

Northumberland, de Lacey, and the several others who had preceded them down the dim passageway, were waiting there, talking. They looked up when they saw Gilbert, and hailed him. He strode toward them.

Hugh sauntered on into the white glare of the stone-paved courtyard. Echoes of their conversations followed him. The breeze gusted past, fitfully. Above the horizon long, swirling clouds streamed across a blazing blue sky.

The sight of the swiftly moving clouds brought to mind the image of his grandfather. What had he called such clouds? Hugh searched his memory. *Mares' tails,* he reflected, yes, and he realized he had not thought of the old man in years.

He felt suddenly exhausted, conscious now of the tight, hollow sensation in his chest, the quick pounding of his heart, the tenseness draining from his muscles.

It occurred to him that he would have taken great pleasure in bashing Gilbert's skull against the flagstones. Doing so, however, would not have solved his predicament. He had learned long ago that there was little to be gained from conflict. And quite frankly, his half brothers, although thoroughly disagreeable, were at the moment the least of his problems.

As he walked, he began to consider calmly, rationally, how he might keep Swynford convinced of his usefulness as a spy, while at the same time manage to appear a loyal vassal of Northumberland. At best it would be challenging, at the worst, deadly.

Martin, having snapped a branch from one of the abbey's trees as he returned to the guest quarters, had settled down with his knife to whittle away the time while he waited for his master's return.

His mistress and Alyse were seated nearby, amusing themselves with a board game brought from the charette. Every so often he would hear them remark on the game and giggle a little. At times his mistress's English, which was heavily accented and often sprinkled with unheard of words, brought a smile to Martin's lips.

The two were laughing, when Martin, quite distinctly, heard the sound of bells, little jingling bells, in the passageway. He thought nothing of it, for it was the fashion among merchants. But when he looked again at his mistress, she had left off smiling and her pretty face was suddenly pale as death. She was so upset that Martin, to appease her, went to the door and looked down the passage, and reported, " 'Twas naught but a merchant and his assistant."

When Hugh arrived at the guest quarters, Sancha and Alyse were still sitting on one of the cots playing the board game. They looked up swiftly at the sound of the door. Martin, seated on the bench, had nearly succeeded in reducing the last of the stick to shavings. The click of the latch sent him lurching to his feet, scattering wood chips onto the floor. "Is it settled?" he asked, relieved to see it was his master.

"To the bishop's satisfaction, at least," Hugh said with a grin as he entered the room. The look he gave Martin indicated, however, that there was more to tell and he would be told it later.

Hugh removed his doublet. His shirt was damp with perspiration. As he dropped the brocaded doublet on his cot, he saw that a meal had been laid out on the sideboard, a platter containing a wedge of hard cheese, a loaf of bread, a wine ewer, and a stack of wooden cups. "Who was it brought the food?" he questioned.

"A lay brother," Martin replied, scooping up the wood shavings and walking to the window. "Near an hour ago," he added, dusting off his hands.

Since he had entered the room, Sancha had watched her husband expectantly. Now she lowered her eyes in an expression of modesty, and smoothed an imaginary crease from her gown. "I am glad you have returned," she said. Only then did she recall that her swollen foot was propped on a cushion, and quickly spread her skirt to conceal it. "We have waited to take our meal, so you might join us," she said, her dark eyes watchful. "I was afraid for you. Your brothers frightened me with all their ugly words."

"Aye, they were loud enough in the chapel," Alyse remarked in an undertone, as she gathered up the game pieces.

"They are beasts," Sancha concluded, "to behave so vilely before God. I do not like them."

Hugh smiled, took a wooden cup from the stack, and filled it with wine. "There is common ground. I do not like them either."

The prospect of food didn't really appeal to Hugh, but after the strong wine collided with his empty stomach, he thought better of it. There was not a table in the room and since Hugh was opposed to the notion of eating standing up, he and Martin moved the only bench before the sideboard. Alyse busied herself breaking the bread into chunks, while Martin put his knife to good use on the wedge of cheese. Sancha, bored with her role of helpless invalid, wished to be useful and poured the wine.

The four young people sat down to their meal. Since they were all of them hungrier than they had admitted, there was little conversation. After a time Hugh made known his intention to leave Hexham on the morrow. He spoke of the journey, the route to Evistone.

Sancha sat listening, pleased at the prospect of their departure, as if by simply fleeing she could escape the demons that bedeviled her mind. At that moment it did not seem to matter that every league brought her closer to a mysterious home far to the north and life with a stranger, equally mysterious.

Indeed, she had never really considered Hugh, not until that morning in the chapel, when she had seen him standing before his father's coffin with his soul laid bare and tears glistening in his eyes. Suddenly, everything about him held a fascination for her. She found herself watching him, listening closely to his every word. It was as if she had never seen him before, and in a way, perhaps she had not.

The afternoon heat hung in the room and their youthful

faces glistened with a sheen of perspiration. All during their leisurely meal they had been aware of the activity in St. Andrew's forecourt, where Northumberland's forces gathered. After a while, Hugh walked to the window, a wine cup in his hand, and watched.

Several sharp raps on the chamber door jolted Hugh from his thoughts. Everyone started. Martin scrambled up from the bench, snatching up his knife. Hugh, moving quickly, set aside his cup, reached beneath the cot for his sword, and drew it from the scabbard. As he approached the door, he motioned Martin to take up a position to the left of the threshold. When at last Hugh lifted the latch, he found only a novitiate with a frightened expression waiting on the other side, a plump boy who spoke with a lisp and said he had been sent to deliver a summons from the bishop. "He asks that you appear promptly at evensong, my lord."

Hugh stared at the boy a moment. "Tell him I accept his invitation," he replied, and shut the door. He felt ridiculous standing there with a sword in his hand, half-believing Gilbert and Walter had come to kill him. He was beginning to jump at shadows.

It was well after dark when Hugh left the bishop's solar. At the stable, he spoke again to Rumald. Martin had spent the evening there talking, watching a dice game, and waiting for Hugh's return. They strolled back to the guest quarters together.

As they walked, Hugh remarked on his conversation with the bishop. "Apparently, he thinks me not altogether devout. He shall be sending one of his priests every few weeks, to review my accounts." Hugh smiled, and in a jesting voice, remarked, "To be certain I have not run off with the reliquary box."

Martin snorted. "If it's sin he's searching for, he should try looking in his own monastery. You know young Donel? Rumald says one of the monks lured him into the smokehouse with the promise of a ham, kissed him on the neck, and scared the wits half out of him. Donel fought him off, but now he's afraid to go take a piss by himself."

Hugh laughed. Donel was sixteen, a tall boy, and solid as a steel buckler, well able to take care of himself. "At least he shall know better the next time. Did he break the man's bones?"

As he walked along, Martin, chuckling, shook his head. "Nay," he said, and as an afterthought added, "but he should have."

The first floor dormitory of the guest quarters appeared deserted. No lights were visible. The staircase was steeped in blackness. Above, a single sconce lit the dreary passageway.

Even before they entered the room, they heard the lilt of feminine voices and laughter. Sancha and Alyse, both dressed for bed, were again seated on a cot playing merles with the colorful game board situated between them.

The rose color of Sancha's chemise was like a magnet. Hugh could not take his eyes from her.

"Is it true then, my lord?" Sancha asked, a smile still on her lips. "Shall we leave tomorrow?" She spoke slowly, carefully pronouncing the English words.

Her glorious dark hair hung down loosely, tumbling over her shoulders, as if she, or probably Alyse, had just shaken it out and brushed it. It was beautiful hair, Hugh thought, recalling the sheer weight of it, the cool silken texture.

"Yes, at first light. I have told Rumald to saddle your mare, and a horse for Alyse."

Sancha did not go so far as to thank him, but she did smile, a pert little smile of victory, as she leaned forward to help Alyse gather up the game pieces.

Hugh shed the brocaded doublet. In the morning he would exchange his finery for leathers.

From across the room, Martin, stripped to the waist for bed, came to fold his master's clothing.

"You can do it on the morrow," Hugh told him, noticing Alyse in her chemise cross the room and place the board game with the luggage. He also noticed Martin's ardent gaze as it followed her.

Stripping off his own shirt, Hugh laid it aside, and recounted for his lady wife some of what had transpired during his meeting with the bishop. He searched his thoughts for some news that might please her. Finally he said, "He is sending his representative, a priest called Antonio. He will be calling at Evistone every few weeks. He seems learned. I am told he speaks your language. Perhaps his visits will break the monotony."

Sancha aimlessly arranged the covers of her cot. Perplexed by the odd word, she raised her face and looked at him directly. She did not understand. "Monotony," she repeated, investing it with a certain coquettish charm of which only she was capable.

Hugh was unable to repress the smile that tugged at the corners of his lips. Somehow he managed not to laugh as he attempted to explain. He thought her priceless. In the soft glow of the candle she appeared smaller, fragile, incredibly soft and desirable.

The comical conversation went on until Sancha, more confused than before, finally uttered the word, "Oh," smiled, and lay back on her cot.

Hugh sat down to remove his boots. Time and again his gaze went back to her, to the curve of her lithe young body beneath the coverlet, the way her hair gleamed in the candlelight. At times it was difficult for him to believe that she was truly his wife. He glanced over the room one last time and, seeing Martin and Alyse were in their cots, snuffed out the candle's flame. He could not so easily rid himself of his wife's image. She remained in his mind, her delicate prettiness, the swell of her small breasts beneath the rose-hued chemise. Lying there in the dark, the intensity with which he suddenly desired her was torture.

On the morrow they resumed their journey just as the eastern sky colored with a pastel blush of pinks and yellows. Beyond the monastery's gates, the clatter and clomp of their carts and horses echoed through the deserted streets of Hexham. The city's walls faded into the distance as league by league they pressed northward. Sunlight flooded over the hills and the May day unfurled before them like a beautiful blue banner.

Soon the road deteriorated, slowing their pace. Its eroded course narrowed to little more than a lonely and sequestered path through the piney woods. Hardly a road, it twisted through wasteland abloom with buttercups, led them into the foothills, through sun-dazzled upland meadows, and across barren ridges of rock. At midday they halted to rest their horses and eat a bite.

Rumald sought Hugh out. He came from the line of horses and carts, squinting in the sunlight, his forehead furrowed as deeply as a plowed field. He was eager to tell the young lord what he had seen earlier in the day, or at least what he believed he'd seen. "It looked to be a man. I saw him on a hillside, above the road. Could be it was a deer I saw, and not a man at all. The trees was thick, and the form I glimpsed was no more than a shadow. Still it gave me a bad feeling."

"Could be outlaws," Martin suggested. "The lay of the land would be to their liking."

Hugh knew the habits of outlaws better than most. He had spent much of his youth in the service of Ralph Neville, who hunted outlaws with the same passion that other men reserve for the hart and the wild boar. Rumald's sighting only confirmed the uneasiness Hugh had felt for hours, the strained, tense sensation of being watched.

During the years spent in Neville's service, Hugh had grown accustomed to danger, to the tight fluttering in his chest, the knot in his stomach, and the prickling of his spine. In a queer perverted way it had been exciting. But this day he explained it away, setting the cause on his nerves. Foolishly perhaps, for there among the hollows and thick woods was a haven for murderers and thieves.

"You know what action to take if we are attacked," Hugh reminded him. He had talked with Rumald and his men the night before, and only that morning repeated his orders.

Hugh was most concerned for his wife's safety, and his gaze shifted to where she sat beneath the shade of a tree with her maid. Their voices carried back to him, mingling with the song of birds and the sounds of men and horses. Hugh's attention returned to the conversation. When he looked again a few moments later he saw his wife and her maid hurrying toward the charette.

He was still talking to Rumald and Martin, when Alyse in her blue kirtle, come tromping back through the tall grass.

"What is it, Alyse?" Hugh called. "Where is your mistress?"

"She wishes to ride in the charette, my lord."

Hugh was mystified. "Why?" he asked, quite naturally, since she had badgered him for days to allow her to ride the mare.

"She does not feel well," Alyse said, lowering her voice appreciably. Martin and Rumald stood by, taking it all in.

"Is she ill?" Hugh questioned, a look of alarm spreading across his features. For his deepest fear was that she would suffer a relapse. He would have only himself to blame; it was he who had foolishly destroyed the elixir.

"Oh, no, sire," Alyse was quick to reassure. "At least, not in the normal way."

When questioned, Alyse hemmed and hawed, unwilling to say more. Hugh could drag no sense from her, and in frustration strode off to speak to his wife. He tapped lightly on the charette's door. "My lady," he called, "are you ill?"

"No!" came her tart reply.

Sounds of rapid movement came from within the charette. He opened the door. She whirled about to face him. "Alyse tells me you do not feel well," he said to her.

"It is nothing," she insisted, looking very pale and very embarrassed. "I am fine," she said obstinately, before at last, pleading, "Please, go away!"

As a result Hugh was more determined than ever to discover what was wrong with her. Poised to enter, he noticed a length of linen strip lying atop a clothing casque. Only then did it dawn on him that her mysterious complaint was a monthly one. It was as simple as that. The crisis he had constructed in his mind did not exist. He said no more, closed the door, and walked back, unable to decide if he was annoyed or amused.

Horsemen and carters milled about, preparing to get under way. Sancha's and Alyse's mares were unsaddled and added to the string of spare horses, and the travelers set out once more. They passed an anxious afternoon, following the rutted, twisting road. In places the course led through wooded valleys where the tops of close-set trees met, forming graceful arches. Little sunlight filtered through the canopy of leaves, and the deep shadows that pooled upon the dirt track provided a cool, though fleeting, respite from the heat of the day. In other places the forest's lush undergrowth verged out, threatening to swallow the path, sending branches and brambles to scrape against the sides of the carts as they passed.

Toward evening the humid air grew stifling. The clouds thickened and in the distance an enormous purple cloud rose slowly above the hills, eclipsing the dying sun and tinting the woods with a murky light.

Martin drew his horse close to his master's and, pointing to the boiling clouds in the distance, said, "There's a storm coming."

"Yes," Hugh agreed, shifting in his saddle to look back over the weary line of carts and horsemen. "We shall all get wet," he said with a touch of grim humor.

A sudden gust of wind tossed the treetops. Its chill humid breath roared past, shaking the roadside brambles to life and causing the horses to shy. Shadows deepened. A brilliant flash of lightning forked across the blackened sky, and huge raindrops pattered down, slapping the leaves, pecking at the faces of the riders and darkening the hides of their horses.

From inside the charette Sancha watched the approaching

storm. The spectacle had revived her lagging spirits, and taken her mind off her miseries, the nagging ache low in her back, and her painful cramping, a condition that had been made worse by the sway of the jouncing charette. Beyond her window, a blinding flash, white and iridescent, lit the sky, followed by a crackling peal of thunder. "Oh, Alyse, look, see how beautiful it is!" But Alyse could not be coaxed from where she cowered in the rear of the charette.

Sancha watched spellbound, reveling in the fury of the storm. Raindrops splashed against her face. "Once," Sancha told her maid in a scandalous voice, "Madame Isabelle's mother was nearly struck by lightning. Imagine, the queen of France!" she said, excitedly. "Her pavilion was rent from top to bottom! The draperies of her bed were scorched! Afterward, Madame said that her sinful mother became very devout, but only for a short time." She was in the midst of telling an incident from her childhood, when suddenly, by the glare of a lightning flash, she fancied she saw figures of men among the trees. They seemed to spring up out of the ground. Wild, hideous figures that charged forward with distorted mouths and howling cries. Sancha was not conscious of her own scream, only of Alyse's sweaty hands dragging her backward, away from the window.

Fourteen

In the lashing rain, Hugh and his men met the onslaught with glinting steel. Few had been trained as soldiers. They were the most of them failed tradesmen and apprentices. Albeit, well armed, and imbued with the last-ditch hope of making a life for themselves in the north. Even so, Hugh was impressed by their resolve, the raw courage they displayed in the face of death.

The attack for all its savagery ended as suddenly as it had begun. In the driving rain it was impossible to judge their enemy's numbers. They were simply gone, as if they had melted into the forest.

In the eerie aftermath, Hugh's horsemen milled about, shouting back and forth above the voice of the rain and the rumbling thunder. One of the carts had lost a wheel to the swampy verge. Horses stumbled and slid in the mire of the road. Occasionally, a lightning flash revealed a crumpled corpse.

Bringing his horse even with the charette, Hugh called in through the window. "My lady, are you harmed?" He heard his wife's voice, then Alyse's, and from their tones judged them to be shaken but unhurt. He was about to call out once more when Rumald's horse slid into his with a grunt. Chewbit jolted forward a step. Hugh snatched at the reins.

Rain streamed down Rumald's face. "Do we go on? Or hold our ground? They may not yet have had their fill of us."

Hugh steadied his mount. "We hold. Where is Martin? How many have we lost?"

"Here, my lord." Martin drew his horse to one side. "None lost, three wounded," he reported, blinking in the downpour.

"Badly?" A blaze of lightning lit the air, thunder crashed. Hugh felt Chewbit shudder beneath him.

Martin's horse shied. He turned the animal, and called out, "No, they will all of them survive!"

Men on foot slogged past, leading their horses. Hugh called to one of the men, dismounted, and passed his reins to him. Martin and Rumald clambered from their saddles and sloshed after their master. They found eight dead outlaws.

The travelers spent an uneasy night, listening, grasping for sounds, hearing only the drubbing of the rain and the low growl of thunder as the storm slowly retreated.

Sancha would not allow Hugh from her sight, and later insisted he sleep in the charette, before the door, so that the hideous creatures who had attacked them might not steal back in the darkness and murder her and Alyse.

By the grey light of a drenched morning they counted only six sodden corpses. Apparently two were not quite so dead as they had appeared, and had limped or dragged themselves away to rejoin their clansmen, or to die elsewhere.

All that day they came upon smoldering farmsteads. Time and again they halted to offer what aid they could. The stunned and bloody survivors spoke of "limmer thieves," border raiders, who considered themselves neither Scots nor English and warred against both.

After hearing the peasants' grisly accounts of murder and rape, Hugh suspected that he and his entourage had blundered into a small group of stragglers, heading north with their booty. Thanks be to God, for had they met the main body of raiders, they might well have suffered the same terrible fate as the peasants.

Sancha's willingness to help the survivors, to wade through the mud and comfort the women and children, did not go unnoticed. Her horror and disbelief soon turned to compassion which knew no language barrier and was an inspiration to all, particularly Hugh. At one farmstead he lost sight of his wife, only to find her kneeling in the mud beside a peasant woman, praying over the woman's son. There was nothing more to be done for him.

Wearily the travelers journeyed north into a wild, barren countryside. Wide wastes of moor stretched away as far as the eye could see, and even with spring upon the land there was a sense of pervasive loneliness. The following day they entered the foothills where the Roman legions of Hadrian once had trod.

Sancha's first view of the manor house and adjoining abbey left her more forlorn than she imagined was possible. It was isolated, surrounded by forest, and she could only guess at the lonely solitude of the winters.

Her unease was only heightened by the sight of its inhabitants. The old men and boys who scrambled from the stone and earthen ramparts were unkempt and coarsely garbed. In appearance they were more like rabble than villeins, and despite their initial cheers, no less fearsome to Sancha than the howling outlaws of the forest.

The abbey's monks, seven in all, came out to greet the young lord, their new administrator, in point of fact, their abbot. They, like the men who had come from the ramparts, were either very old or very young.

One of the brethren, a round-shouldered old man of at least seventy with squinty eyes and a big reddish blue nose, came forward through the sparse grass starred with dandelions to greet Hugh. "I am Brother Malcolm," he said. The fringe of hair that encircled his bald pate was white as snow, and he wore the rough brown robes and sandals of his order.

"Since I am the eldest," the old man announced, "I have been chosen to speak for my brethren. We welcome you with prayers. For many long months our abbey, indeed this fief, has been without a master's hand, as a ship without a sail. Thanks be to Christ and the saints who have brought you safely into our midst." Aside from Brother Malcolm's welcoming words, little else was said. The men and boys, who had come in from the fields at the approach of the travelers and taken up defensive positions on the ramparts, were as loath to converse as the brethren and watched the newcomers in wary silence.

The household servants, who numbered eleven, not counting the half dozen or so children, were much the same, with their suspicious stares and stoic demeanors. The women were even less talkative than the men. And the children, according to their ages, either hid behind their mothers' skirts or stood staring, as reticent as their elders.

The manor house was of ancient construction, moldering and miserable, whose chambers were small and ill lit. A stout servingwoman, taciturn and glum-faced, led Sancha and her maid through the house.

Sancha, too, was silent. She was near to tears, so sharp was her disappointment. She had never believed she would be forced to live in a place so wretched. The least of her father's villeins, she thought with conviction, lived in finer means.

The house's few windows, mere slits in the walls, had no glass. Some were fitted with heavy shutters, others with hide coverings. The air smelled of dust, and an odd, peculiar mustiness. Built of stone, post and beam, the house was in essence a large rectangle that, excluding the hall, was divided by passageways onto which a multitude of rooms opened.

By way of a wide wooden staircase they mounted to the second floor. There the windows were larger and all fitted with shutters, though the rooms, save for the solar, were laid out in similar fashion. Above this was a crude cast third story, more of a loft, inhabited only by mice and spiders. The living quarters—the dreary solar through which the master's bedchamber could be reached, a garderobe, and perhaps seven or eight smaller rooms—were all equally drab and colorless.

It was hours before the travelers were settled, at least to some extent, in what was to be their new home. After Sancha's clothing casques and banded trunk had been hauled up the wooden staircase and into the bedchamber, she and Alyse unpacked.

Later they sent a servant for water, stripped off their mud-died clothing, and washed. Alyse had no other kirtle to change into, and donned her night shift. As much as it would have pleased Sancha to give Alyse one of her own gowns, none would fit. Alyse was much too plump.

For Hugh, the remains of the day left scarce enough time to accomplish all he had planned. He did manage to walk through the abbey with Brother Malcolm, view the stables, the orchards, and in the distance the fields and forests.

As they walked back toward the abbey, the old clergyman showed signs of tiring. He plodded along, short of breath, but stubbornly determined to tell the young man beside him of the former prebend and master of Evistone.

"His name was John Lumley," the old monk said. "I am told he was a favorite of King Richard's. But when Richard lost his crown, John Lumley lost his head and all his lands."

Brother Malcolm halted, paused for breath, then moved on again. "As far as I know," he said, "John Lumley never once laid eyes upon Evistone. Oh, I expect he held many more prof-itable fiefs. I heard he lived at court. It was his steward, a vile man, unpleasing even to God, who loves all sinners, that was master of Evistone. When word reached him of Lumley's death, the steward gathered up all that was of value and ran off to God only knows where."

The old monk halted once more. "There!" he said, raising an arm and pointing to the perimeter of the abbey's graveyard. "Follow me, I will show you evidence of the steward's evil deeds." Leading the way, Brother Malcolm stomped through the tangled grass. "Someone told him that the Roman soldiers buried here were laid in their graves wearing golden helmets. You see what he did?"

As Hugh drew nearer, he noticed the ground was littered with human bones. Fragments of skulls and ribs. Bits of pel-vises washed clean by the elements. A leg bone, starkly white amid the tall grass.

"I told him there was no gold, but he would not believe me."

Hugh surveyed the scene, the mounded earth overgrown with grass and weeds. "Why have you left the bones uncovered?"

"Alas, they should be buried," the old monk readily agreed. "But I have no way to know if these Romans were truly Christians. Twice I have sent word to the bishop asking for his permission to bury them, but as yet he has given me no reply." The old monk went on about the Romans. It seemed a subject of which he was inordinately fond. His wrinkled face took on a glow of almost-religious fervor when he spoke of them. He was telling Hugh of a coin he had found. "It was lying on the ground, just as if someone had dropped it the day before," he said, motioning to a strip of wasteland just beyond the orchard where he had found it.

They continued on, walking past the graves of the faithful. The tops of weathered stones jutted from the spring green grass. In the distance, a handful of sheep moved slowly across a grassy knoll and the sound of a lamb bawling for its dam carried on the evening air. They paused once more beneath the scrolled iron lych-gate.

Brother Malcolm, squinting his eyes in the dying light, gazed back over the grave lot, the sweeping expanse of hillocks and woods. Perhaps it was the sight of the sheep, the bawling lamb, that gave voice to his thoughts. "In the midst of death there is life," he reflected. And turning to Hugh, asked, "Or is it the other way round? I can never recall."

Hugh did not know, he confessed with a smile, as he walked along with Brother Malcolm, up the earthen path toward the abbey's garden. A dozen ancient yews, like sentinels, lined the pathway.

"Here are the apostles," the old monk said, smiling fondly, reaching out to each as he spoke. "Here is John, Peter, Paul," he said, giving each its name.

Coming from beneath the trees Hugh saw a broad, square-faced man seated on a stone bench amid the overgrown herbs and tangled rose canes of the garden. The man, roughly garbed and clutching a filthy lambskin cap in his callused hands, leapt to his feet at their approach, and rushed to greet the old monk.

"Brother Malcolm," the man cried. "Is it true what I have heard? Is there a new master come to Evistone?" But before the monk could reply, the man blurted out. "The boy who came to fetch me swore it was so. You must come with me, before the new lord, Brother Malcolm. Else't wise I am certain to be punished for the steward's deeds. You must come with me and tell the new master I am an honest man!"

"I am your new master. I am lord of Evistone," Hugh said to the man's startled face. "And if you are as honest as you claim, you have no need to be in fear of me."

The man made a little bow, bobbing his head. "I'll not fail you, my lord. Me and my lads, we have not lost a single lamb this spring. As Christ is my witness I am an honest man. The missing wool, 'twas not my thievery but the steward's."

Hugh saw a half-grown boy and an older man standing a ways from the garden, but watching attentively. They, too, were coarsely dressed and wore hats similar to the one the shepherd kneaded as he spoke.

"What he says is true," Brother Malcolm sighed, easing his old bones onto the stone bench. "Euan is a good man, a Christian. Your flocks will be safe in his keeping. He and his men are not to blame. This season the wool shall bring profit to the abbey and fief, and not to that weasel of a steward."

After profusely thanking the young lord and the monk, Euan the shepherd took his leave. Beyond the lady garden's stone gate, the half-grown boy and the man who had been watching fell into step with him.

Sunlight slanted low on the horizon, casting a lavender haze over the wild, weed-filled garden. Brother Malcolm rose stiffly from the bench, promising, "Tomorrow, my lord, I will lay out the abbey's accounts for you. They are yours now. I have kept them badly, I am afraid. My eyes are no longer sharp and my hands, well, I have no talent for the stylus, my script is poor. But you will see."

The throaty iron clangor of the chapel bells shook the air, announcing the angelus. Hugh was not looking forward to poring over the accounts, which he knew would be all in Latin. He bade the monk good evening, and left him there in the garden.

The manor house teemed with life. Hugh's men gathered round the long table in the hall to sup with their young lord and discuss the future. Since a meal of such proportions had not been served in the manor's hall for more than a year, there was much confusion in the kitchen that evening. What was finally brought out by the servants was the selfsame meager fare on which they had survived the lean months, that of barley in mutton broth, oat cakes, cheese, and cider that had sat too long.

Above in the solar, Sancha had a tray brought to her and Alyse. Sancha wrinkled her nose at the food, and even Alyse, who was easily pleased, remarked, "Back in Surrey, pigs eat better than this!" After the two young women had commiserated over the food and maligned the cooks, they went back to their game of merles.

Darkness fell, and they lit a second candle so they might better see the game board. Long after they had both begun to yawn, they could still hear the noisy conversation and laughter of the men in the hall.

Seated on pillows before the vast, empty hearth, they played on. They had nodded off for the umpteenth time, when Hugh entered the solar, an oil lamp in his hand. He was naked to the waist, his hair still damp from where he had availed himself of the well house. He, Martin, and a number of the other men had washed off the dirt of the road in the stone chamber adjacent to the kitchen, much to the enjoyment of the women servants, the majority of whom were widows.

In the fantastic play of shadows, he looked larger to Sancha, somehow threatening. "Could Alyse not sleep here on a pallet?" Sancha asked, conscious of his eyes on her, of her own racing pulse.

He remained at the door, obviously waiting for Alyse to leave. "She has a bed in which to lie."

Sancha looked forlornly to her maidservant. "But if I should have need of her during the night?"

"You can call out for her, she will not be far."

Clearly he had made up his mind. Sancha could only watch as Alyse obediently got to her feet, took a candle, and crossed to the door arch.

The sound of the door closing made Sancha's heart beat faster. She heard her husband's footfalls on the planked floor as he went toward the bedchamber. Alone with only the stub of a candle, she pushed the game pieces to the center of the board, one by one. For weeks, all throughout their journey, Alyse, even Martin, had always been near, if not asleep in the same room, then mere steps away.

Now, Sancha thought, for the first time since the night of her wedding, she would be alone with her husband. The thought suddenly filled her with the fear of her own imaginings.

Every sound was intensified. She heard him moving about in the bedchamber, heard the sound of a shutter being opened, then another, the rusty protest of the hinges. Her gaze slid from the gaudy painted design of the game board, to the stub of the candle which would soon sputter out and leave her in darkness.

She was near to desperation. Surely, she thought, her husband must realize that her monthly flux had not yet completely ended. Sancha had always been squeamish about such things, reluctant to discuss her body even with Marie and Alene. For the briefest of instances she considered how she might tell her husband. No, she decided, she would rather be burned as witch than suffer such an embarrassment.

A dozen other panic-stricken thoughts flittered through her mind, before she realized that she no longer heard him. Something, an instinct perhaps, caused her to raise her eyes. He was standing in the door arch, watching her, looking tall as a tower with the lamplight at his back.

"It is a sorry place I've brought you to, a home hardly fit for peasants."

The timbre of his voice sent a strange thrill up her spine, and for a moment her lips moved mutely. Words escaped her. Earlier she had walked in the little lady garden with its wooden shrine to the Virgin, riot of weeds, and overgrown sundial. And since she could think of nothing else about the miserable outpost to commend, she said, "The lady garden, if tended, would be truly beautiful, and even the house could be made more comfortable with effort." She said so confusedly, realizing that in his own proud way he was apologizing to her.

Her words hung in the warm air of the room. At last he said, "Why did you not open the shutter? It is stifling in here."

"I think it must be broken." She did not bother to say that she and Alyse had tugged and pried, all to no avail. Instead, she watched in silence as he crossed to the window and stood tinkering with the latch. The shutter creaked open, and a breath of cool air touched her skin.

He came and stood above her. "You look as weary as I. Come to bed."

Just then the candle, reduced to a puddle of wax, flickered and sputtered out. The time had come and there was nothing to do but go with him into the lamplit room. She settled in the large square bed, catching only a glimpse of his naked body before she drew herself into a tight little knot, and stared at the shadowy, smoke-darkened wall, the black void of the empty hearth.

Fifteen

Her fears were unfounded. In the darkness he did no more than lie down beside her, and sooner than she believed was possible he was slumbering soundly. For a time she listened to his breathing, deep, even, peaceful. Eventually, she, too, fell asleep, only to lose herself in tortured dreams.

Through the eye of her sleeping mind she chased Touffu, the curly-coated little dog, down a labyrinth of darkened corridors. Her heart pounded in her ears and her body ached with exertion. A single desperate thought drove her forward. She must catch the little dog, capture him. But her feet dragged, heavy as lead, sticking to the ground, and each time she drew near, the little dog evaded her grasp. On and on she pursued the curly-coated little beast until he scampered through a door arch into a boudoir hung deep with scarlet cloth.

Sancha recognized at once Madame Isabelle's chamber, the monstrous bed, the scarlet drapes. Helpless to prevent it, she watched the little dog wriggle beneath the draperies and leap onto the bed. "No!" she shrieked, lunging after him, throwing aside the draperies, only to be paralyzed by the sight of a great black thing, half man, half beast with gleaming fangs and blood streaming from its slavering jaws. The beast's slitted yellow eyes glittered wickedly, and to her horror, she saw it gather on its thick haunches and hurl its fearsome weight at her.

Her chilling scream brought Hugh to wakefulness with a violent jerk. For a moment he struggled with the thrashing

girl. In his groggy state it was all he could manage to restrain
her flailing arms and keep her from tumbling onto the floor.

"A beast! There is a beast!" Sancha babbled. Her eyes roved
wildly over the darkened room as she struggled to awaken
from the dream in which reality and some other unknown
world were horribly intermingled. "I felt its breath on my face!
It had such teeth, like a wolf's, and . . . ohhh!"

"Shhh, a dream, only a dream." Hugh drew her close. To
his surprise, she did not resist, but grasped his arm and buried
her face in his shoulder.

"Do you not see?" she cried, trembling.

"Shhh, there is naught to look upon, it was only a dream."

She gave a slight movement of her dark head. "No," she
moaned, "it is true. The sickness is returning, just as the physician warned. I am going mad."

"No." Hugh gave her a gentle shake. "Because of a dream?
Everyone dreams." He felt Sancha's head toss more vehe-
mently, and in a tortured voice, she cried, "They are horrible
and evil dreams!"

He stroked her hair. "Lie back with me, and I will tell you
of a dream that I had as a child, a dream I sometimes wake
to yet." Absently, he pushed the tangled waves of dark, silky
hair back from the frightened, pale face and in a lazy voice,
said, "My grandfather was a woodward and as a small child
I lived with him in his hut. Often I went with him and his
men when they would go into the forest to cut wood. I loved
being in the forest and I would find excuses to slip away."
Smiling down at her, he added, "Deceit is strong in children.
Sometimes I would watch the birds. That they could fly fascinated me. I would study them for hours, so that often in my
dreams I would find that I, too, could fly. I would soar above
the forest, wheeling higher and higher. Then suddenly, to my
dismay, my miraculous talent would desert me and I would
plunge downward, falling, falling. I would never strike the
earth, but awaken, terrified and trembling. There," he said,
"what do you make of that?"

"Are you not in fear of heights?"

"Heights? No, there is no need, I have not yet learned to fly."

A faint smile touched Sancha's lips. She did not believe him, at least not that his grandfather was a woodward. "The grandsons of peasants do not become nobles. If truly your grandfather was a woodward, how then could you be a knight?"

"An earl," he reminded her with a touch of humor. "And only because of him who fathered me." His words raised in his mind the day, weeks before at Windsor, when he had glared back at his father as an equal. He felt a twinge of regret perhaps, that they had not been worthy to know each other better. "Why do you ask? Am I not noble enough for a demoiselle of the queen?"

"No— I mean, yes! Oh! I did not mean to say . . . you have been kind to me. It is only that . . . I—"

"Yes, I know, I was not your choice. Now, close your eyes. Go to sleep and dream of pleasanter things."

For the first few days in her new home, Sancha brooded over her dream. To add to her unhappiness, she unexpectedly saw Martin and Alyse coming down from the rough-cast upper story, which was little more than a deserted loft. The look on their faces left no doubt in Sancha's mind as to what they had been doing. She was left feeling hurt and somehow betrayed, unable to understand how such a thing could have happened before her very eyes and she be completely unaware of it.

The lovers, blind to all but each other, had not noticed her. They were far too busy looking into each other's eyes. Sancha did not mention it to Alyse, but afterward she did not feel the same toward her, and was more lonely than ever.

Left to explore the rambling manor house alone, Sancha discovered storerooms filled with sacks of goose down, woolen cloth, and linen, heavy and cold, woven by the old women for bedding and household use. An entire room was given over to the making of candles, stocked with sealed jugs of tallow, coils of wicking, and wooden molds.

Sancha walked through the little lady garden, prayed in the chapel, saw the stables where her mare, along with the other horses and cows, ate its fill of hay and oats.

She explored her surroundings wearing a large straw hat of peasant origin that she had discovered in one of the store-rooms. One day she wandered despondently through the orchards, hardly speaking to Alyse, who had accompanied her. On other days she viewed the fields, peeked into the outbuildings where butter was churned and cheese was produced, and where at harvest, apples were pressed for cider and the ale was brewed.

But always she was forced to return to the house where she was subjected to the malignant glances of the servingwomen, their shrill voices and impossible brogue. Sancha felt their stares on her back and heard their whispered comments, which seemed to rise and fall in accordance with her approach or departure. Even the children shied from her smiles.

The inhabitants of Evistone were hard-bitten northerners, wary and suspicious of strangers. But to those they claimed as their own, they were kindness itself and fiercely loyal. Hugh Canby they had accepted readily. He was one of them, born not ten leagues distant. Even the men who had accompanied him from the south were gradually gaining the people's trust and goodwill. Those with trades were making a place for themselves in the nearby village, while others reclaimed long-deserted farmsteads. The lack of men of marriageable age in Evistone made them all the more attractive.

Alyse, too, was making inroads. She had worn down the ill will of the reigning kitchen matron, Morah, the mother of fourteen children, who by blood or marriage claimed relationship to most of the population of Evistone. She was a large, authoritative woman, near to sixty years of age, sturdy as a centenarian oak and about as broad.

Only Sancha, despite her best efforts to win over the servants, remained an outcast. Ever since her arrival she had been an object of curiosity. She was a foreigner, and an inquisitive one at that, asking questions that they could hardly understand, and sounding like she was talking through her pert little nose.

More than once Sancha had seen them mocking her behind her back. Pinching their noses with a thumb and forefinger and giggling like idiots, as they gobbled back and forth at one another.

Day in and day out, they watched her movements as avidly as the Londoners had watched King Richard. At times Sancha found the servants' constant prying funny, at others, irksome. Through it all she smiled, believing that soon the women would lose interest and she would no longer be the cynosure of every eye.

Life at Evistone took on a routine. Every morning Sancha awoke to an empty bed. Hugh, as was his custom, rose early and went off with Martin and a few of his men. He spent the days tending to the business of his fief or hunting. He would seldom return until evening, and then, smelling of the outdoors and of horses.

Normally the sun had just begun to creep over the window embrasure when Alyse came into the bedchamber to help her mistress dress. In all honesty, Sancha needed no assistance. The kirtles she wore were simple garments which laced either in front or on the sides, and little different from those worn by the servants save for the quality and color of the cloth.

But Sancha, in spite of everything, enjoyed Alyse's company. Alyse, by nature, was always cheerful and, as a rule, full of gossip about the servants. Consequently, Sancha had learned the names of most of the servants, their children, and their relationships.

On that particular morning, Alyse braided her mistress's hair and they went down the stairs together. The kitchen was noisy, crowded with women, and the day's oat bread not yet in the oven. There was cold mutton broth and nothing else. Sancha paled at the suggestion. She could not tolerate mutton of any sort. There was something about it, a smell perhaps, that reminded her of a wet wool blanket. She would have sooner eaten one of her slippers.

She elected to have bread and honey and, while the bread baked, she waited. A breeze wafted in through the windows and through the open door that June morning, but it did little to cool the stifling air of the kitchen.

Sancha remained, idly stroking the grey-striped cat that came importantly in from the garth, tail held high, to mew and rub against her legs. Looking down, Sancha saw one of the tabby's kittens had followed her inside, a skinny little white creature, soft as a moth with a tiny pink nose. It was irresistible to Sancha and she scooped it up and cuddled it. "This little one is so beautiful, but so tiny," she cooed. And turning to one of the girls loitering near the oven, one of Morah's granddaughters, she said, "Fetch some milk and a bowl."

Sancha had to repeat herself twice, speaking slowly, before the girl, a hefty buck-toothed lass called Jenn, at last understood. It was only when old Morah realized the milk was for the kitten that her face turned the color of a ripe plum.

Alyse held her breath, but the old woman did no more than glare at her granddaughter's retreating back, grumble, and peer into the hearth, where she was rendering down a huge kettle of lard. Still grumbling like an approaching storm, old Morah clunked the spoon against the rim of the kettle and, from a willow basket to one side of the hearth, took a handful of wood chips and flung them into the fire, which leapt up with a renewed voice.

Four little girls came in from the mellow summer morning to crowd around Sancha, each with a kitten to show her. Sancha spoke sweetly to the little girls and cooed over the kittens. It was the first time any of the children had approached her and she was pleased, nearly ecstatic, to have won their trust.

One little girl, with dark hair and darker eyes, shyer than the others, hung back. She held out her kitten with outstretched arms for Sancha to take, but she would not come nearer. She reminded Sancha of her littlest sister. The thought tugged at her heart, and she wondered forlornly what had become of her. She prayed that the youngest of her sisters would not be forced into marriage and sent off, as she and her elder sister had been, to live out her life with a stranger.

When Sancha raised her eyes, she saw the bread being removed from the oven with a long-handled wooden paddle. At one of the worktables, Alyse, knife in hand, halved a honeycomb. The girl named Jenn came back, carrying the milk. And Sancha, waiting, saw Morah toss another handful of chips onto the fire, causing it to flare, crackle, and spit.

Sancha gently placed the white kitten on the floor, and rose to her feet. For the briefest of instances she could not guess what had distorted the face of the girl with the bowl in her hands, for no sound came from her throat. Only when the girl screamed and Sancha saw the bowl of milk leap into the air, did she realize.

The bowl crashed to the floor and the bloodcurdling cry became a chorus of shrieks. Sancha whipped around to see the shy little girl blazing like a candle, her mouth agape, squalling loudly as flames greedily raced up her kirtle.

Morah swooned, the others screamed and clutched each other. The child, squalling and panic-stricken, thrashed her skinny arms and leapt about.

Perhaps the shy little girl had backed too near the hearth, or an exploding ember had ignited her skirt. No matter how it had happened. Horrified by the scene before her, Sancha grabbed the child and threw her skirts around her, smothering the flames. When the little girl was calmed enough to be stripped of her scorched clothing, they discovered she had suffered no serious burns.

As swiftly and as surely as Sancha's quick actions had saved the little girl from serious injury or death, from that day forward "the foreign lady" was accepted by one and all.

That evening when Hugh returned, he heard of the incident.

The story was on everyone's lips. Later, before the meal was served in the hall, Hugh praised his lady wife and all present drank a toast to her.

His words embarrassed Sancha, and she murmured, abashed, "I did not want for praise, only to spare a little child from harm."

"All the same it was brave of you, and since I am your husband, I may say so if it pleases me to."

"Yes." Alyse leaned toward her mistress, and speaking softly said, " 'Tis true, no one else knew what to do. If the child had run away, well, she'd surely have been burned to the bone."

When late that night Sancha awoke, trembling and terrified from yet another of her tortured dreams, Hugh blamed it on the excitement of the day.

With all her heart Sancha wished to believe him, but she could not. For in her dream she had again chased the curly-coated dog, running, running. Again she found herself before the scarlet-draped bed.

But there the dream altered like a rippling image on a quiet pool and the beast became a man crouching above a lifeless body, a man's body. Its hands moved rapidly over the corpse in some ghoulish pantomime. Suddenly, as if the cloaked figure sensed her presence, it turned swiftly on its haunches and, raising its head, revealed an evil, leering face.

Paralyzed with fear, Sancha watched as slowly, from beneath the cowl, a dark and shriveled hand beckoned her to come closer.

The trilling sound of her own screams awakened her, and no amount of comforting words could dispel the horror of the dream, the fear of lurking madness.

Several weeks passed and between Sancha and Hugh little had changed. He made no attempt to force himself on her, and perhaps for that reason she had come to feel more at ease in his presence. To please her he had put men to work replastering the walls of the solar. And on a grey summer day when he found her crying, wasted with loneliness, he sat and talked to her for hours of foolish things, and to amuse her played a game of merles, which he despised to do.

Several times, when she had been awakened by disturbing dreams, he had held her in his arms and comforted her, so that she came to trust him more and more, to feel secure with the scent of his skin in her nostrils and the sound of his heart beating in her ear.

One day not long afterward, Sancha spent the morning in the lady garden. She had made ambitious plans to restore the neglected beds and walkways. Several sprawling, shaggy roses all abloom were the first to receive her attentions. Alyse worked by her side, but not in silence. Each time she pricked her finger on a thorn, she complained.

Locked in a struggle with an errant rose cane, Alyse grumbled. Back and forth she wrestled the thorny fugitive, her plump neck wet with perspiration. When, with the sound of a springing snare, the rose cane sprang back, speared her straw hat, and whipped it from her head, Alyse came to the end of her endurance, and her patience. She swore an oath. "Roses!" she hissed in a vexed tone. "They're naught but the devil's walking sticks, and worse than weeds!"

It was near to midday when a tinkling sound, not unlike the sound of little bells, raised Sancha's head with a jolt. She listened. The distant jingle put a cat's paw on her neck. Her arms went prickly as from a chill, and she turned her head toward the yew trees, for the sound seemed to be coming from their depths. Just then she saw a figure break from the shadows of the trees and come striding through the tall grass.

" 'Tis a peddler!" Alyse said. "And oh, look, he has a wee monkey with him!" Sancha saw, but made no reply.

Children chasing in the garth had also sighted the peddler, and, shouting and laughing, they sprinted barefoot along the path to mob around him. Soon, trailing after them in groups of twos and threes, the servingwomen came from the kitchen, stretching their necks to see. A curious boy from the stables came out to look, then called excitedly to his friends.

And what a queer sight the peddler was, with his foolish hat and parti-color trappings. It seemed all he possessed he carried on his person, including a little brown monkey that perched on his shoulder like a gargoyle. The peddler was nearly as curious as his pet, for he was an odd-shaped, stubby little man sewn end to end with gaily colored buttons. All manner of gaudy beads hung round his neck, and wherever one looked straps and belts crisscrossed his body, more than could be counted. An assortment of metal buckles and amulets dangled from the straps, jingling and winking in the sunlight, and on his arm he carried a basket filled with ribbons that fluttered merrily.

He came into the lady garden in his odd, skimming gait. He did not look to be a cripple, yet he dipped with each step, giving the impression that he somehow went on one leg at a gallop while walking on the other. Grinning ear to ear, the peddler lifted his enormous feathered hat, made a ceremonious bow, and greeted one and all.

The little brown monkey went back and forth across his shoulders, chattering noisily, causing all the children to squeal with delight. In the meantime the peddler produced a flute from among his many treasures and, calling down the monkey, began to play and jig about. At the sound of the music the monkey began to dance. Round and round it went like a little withered old man, hopping and pirouetting. Everyone laughed and clapped their hands, including Sancha, who had quite forgotten the sound of the jingling trinkets and the eerie sensation it had given her.

His tune at an end, the peddler tucked the flute among his beads and straps. He then burst into rhyme, reciting little ditties

for the amusement of lady and her maids, praising their love-
liness and feigning to read the future in their hands. He offered
advice on securing a husband, predicting the weather, and cur-
ing illnesses. At last the peddler spouted out his inventory of
goods for all to hear. "Charms and gaudies!" he cried. "Amulets, buckles, and ribbons!" His list went on without an end,
and he seemed never to take a breath.

Across the garden in the abbey's sacristy, Hugh was sifting
through the fief's accounts. Brother Malcolm sat nearby,
wringing his hands as he attempted to recall his entries. The
old monk's scribing was even worse than he had admitted to,
and Hugh wondered if he would ever be able to make sense
of it. Line by line Hugh worked on doggedly. But unable to
resist the sound of music and laughter, he put down his stylus
and walked out into the garden.

As if on cue the monkey leapt upon the peddler's shoulders
and snatched the hat from his head. With a podgy hand the
peddler grabbed furiously after the feathered creation, swore
loudly at the monkey, and, with a tug, reclaimed his foolish
hat. He flourished it, and bowing low, asked, "Have I the great
pleasure of addressing the noble lord and good master of Evistone?"

"That you have, my colorful friend," Hugh replied, laughing
at the monkey's antics.

The peddler babbled off a litany of voluble compliments,
before entreating, "Allow me to present you with a gift, my
lord. 'Tis a buckle of great quality, one well suited to a virile,
young man like yourself." From a pouch at his waist, the peddler took a bright metallic buckle and, entrusting it to the monkey, sent the creature ambling across the stones.

Hugh crouched down to take the proffered gift. But the wizened little beast would not release it until Hugh had taken a
penny from his belt and offered it as a bribe. Once Hugh held
the gleaming buckle he was indeed surprised by its quality. It
was silver, finely chased, and not likely to be found among a
mountebank peddler's goods. Surprised, yes, though not nearly

so profoundly shocked as when he turned it over in his hand and noticed a shred of paper on which someone had scrawled a cryptic message. "Did I not warn you to expect the unexpected?"

Hugh's thoughtful gaze followed the monkey as it scampered off, balancing itself with its tail and dragging its tether. With a hop, it leapt onto its master's shoulder.

Hugh held up the buckle and nodded to the peddler. A score of thoughts crossed his mind, not the least of which was a new respect for Thomas Swynford.

Hugh waited, fingering the buckle and observing the peddler as he made his sales, taking a penny here, a penny there, selling buttons, ribbons, and beads among the noisy children and gabbling servingwomen.

Having completed his business, the peddler called to Hugh. "My lord!" he shouted, and struck out toward the sacristy. The monkey followed like a demented child. "Might an honest merchant call in your garth from time to time? A poor peddler's life is hard. 'Tis all I can manage to keep the wolf from my door." The peddler's piercing black eyes met Hugh's, and the glance that passed between them was filled with meaning.

"I'll grant you that," Hugh agreed, crouching down to observe the monkey. "What manner of ape have you there?" he inquired of the peddler.

The man shrugged and buffed his humped nose with a forefinger. "I know not, my lord, only that it was brought from across the seas. It came to me by barter. 'Tis an evil little beast, but useful."

Hugh took another coin from his belt and held it out to the monkey, whose eyebrows rose and lowered like a wasp's feelers. Hugh gripped the coin tightly. The frustrated beast chattered, scolding him, and tugged with all its considerable strength. Finally, it pried the coin from Hugh's grasp. " 'Tis a consummate thief, your pet."

"Aye," the peddler grinned, " 'tis almost human."

People milled about in the garden and the children watched

from a distance. Before he spoke, the peddler glanced warily over his shoulder to be certain he would not be overheard. "Have you nothing for me?"

"No, when you return," Hugh promised.

"Where shall I seek it?"

It seemed reasonable enough to Hugh that they should not be seen together. The fewer who knew, the safer for both of them. And thinking quickly, Hugh remarked in a low tone, "Came you through the grave plot?" Earlier Hugh had glimpsed a horse cropping grass amid the tilted stones. The peddler nodded, and Hugh continued. "On the plot's boundary is a tumbled wall. A young rowan stands halfway along its length. The message will be there, beside the tree, in a crevice in the rocks. You will see it."

The peddler's expression did not change, only his eyelids twitched with comprehension at the young lord's words. Bowing, he took up his basket filled with ribbons. "I thank you, my lord, for your generosity." He held out his arm and the monkey leapt onto his shoulder. "Ah, the sun hurries down the hill," he sighed. "I must be off. I've a long route to take afore I come this way again on St. Swithin's Day. God keep you, sire."

Days dragged past. During this time Sancha was visited by no further dreams. She was, in fact, more troubled by her own awakening desires. She would often catch herself daydreaming about her husband, who was not really a husband to her, but who lately stirred her emotions so that she thought of him in the most ardent and embarrassing ways.

The sight of his muscular body, which had at first inspired only fear in her, now left her smothered with blushes. It was as if she was drawn toward him by some great impulse of mind and body, so that no more than the thought him, of his smile, his voice, served to both excite and annoy her. As much as she desired it, it also plagued her every waking moment.

She could not rid herself of the impulse, and it remained like the sound of a buzzing gnat trapped inside a room.

Idleness was her greatest enemy. With nothing to occupy her time, she would sometimes fall prey to a helpless, haunted feeling. It would *descend* on her—there was no other way to describe the sudden stifling fear—and, if only for the briefest of instances, fill her mind with confusing images, dark and foreboding. Gigantic figures fluttered in her mind's eye, coming together and then jerking apart, like a clutch of ravens squabbling over a dead hare. She could not say what it was they sought, for the object of their greed remained unseen. In the blink of an eye, the sensation would pass, leaving in its wake a terrible feeling of dread.

One day in the hot sunshine of the lady garden, Sancha was pulling weeds from among the pinks at the base of the Virgin's shrine. She raised up to straighten her back, and, looking from beneath her straw hat, saw her husband and his squire, Martin, return with their horses.

Sancha said nothing to Alyse, who was still busily pinching weeds. She did so purposely, imagining that once Alyse knew Martin had returned, she would contrive some errand so she might be alone with him, if only to talk.

The lazy drone of bees hummed in Sancha's ears as she blotted the perspiration from her forehead with the back of her hand. She watched the pair, dusty and hot from one of their excursions, stop by the stone trough to water their horses and cool them down.

Her husband stripped off his shirt, baring his muscular shoulders, plunged the shirt in the trough, and soused himself down to his waist with cold water. Leading the mounts from beneath the elm tree, Martin let the horses drink. Afterward he took a pail from beside the trough, skimmed it across the water, and poured it over himself, then shook like a dog. As she looked on, Rumald and several other men came from the direction of the stables. Soon their loud, jesting voices carried to the garden.

"I see they've returned."

The sound of the voice startled Sancha, who only then realized Alyse was standing beside her, squinting from beneath her straw hat at the figures under the elm tree.

"Yes," she responded, even more surprised when Alyse went immediately back to pulling weeds. Sancha continued to watch her husband, admiring his healthy, young body, and at the same time sensing some inexpressible need, a need she was so suddenly, piercingly, aware of that she felt herself blush.

It was only the heat of the day she felt, she told herself, and went back to dispatching weeds. Alyse, having finished with the small bed of pinks and chives, soon found an excuse to leave the garden. "I should go harry the kitchen servants; otherwise, they will spend the day gossiping. They've no sense of time. It's all the same to them if we go to our beds with naught but cheese and bread for our supper."

"Yes, go," Sancha said, pausing to run her hand across her forehead once more. There was, she thought, at least some truth to what Alyse said. In any case, she wished to be alone with her thoughts.

She worked on for a short time, determined to rout the cocklebur plants from the camomile bed. When the invaders all lay withering on the flagged path, she gathered them up in her linen apron and, with a great sense of accomplishment, carted them off to the end of the garden. There, hidden behind a clump of juniper shrubs, the refuse pile sweltered in the sunlight, scenting the air with the sweet green odor of decay.

Returning to the manor house, Sancha found the hall empty and silent, save for the discordant cackling of the women in the kitchen. Above, in the solar, several men were still at work on the walls, and an old woman with a broom was driving clouds of dust before her. Sancha went into her bedchamber, shut the door, and set the bar.

The sun had gone from the windows. Even so, the afternoon

heat saturated the chamber. Sancha undressed and, filling the basin with water from the ewer, washed her face and hands, and all the places ladies must. Afterward she slipped on a silken camisa. She brushed out her long hair, applied a few daubs of rose-scented perfume, and debated which gown she would take from the banded trunk that had traveled north with her. After much thought she chose a violet-hued frock of Brabant linen, trimmed in silver braid.

All the while she prepared herself, she was thinking of the past, of the grand world of the French and English courts, of days spent in luxuriant and vast chambers. She had been surrounded by gold and the glitter of jewels, by great courtiers, beautifully gowned ladies, poets, and musicians. Then she had been a pretty, innocent girl, a pampered daughter of the nobility, a demoiselle to Madame Isabelle, the eldest daughter of the king and queen of France who was soon to be the queen of England.

Sancha mourned the past. Her heart ached to have her life return as it was then, but she was wise enough to know it could never be. She knew also that she would have eventually gone to a man's bed, and she doubted that a great baron would have acted with as much kind restraint as her lowborn earl.

Perhaps, she thought, *in time I will come to love him.* She could not deny a certain softness in her heart for him, and more—desires which shamed her and ofttimes left her flustered, breathless, in his presence. Even as she glanced one last time into the mirror of Florentine silver, a present from her little queen, she still had not come to a decision.

The solar was empty when she emerged from the bedchamber. Motes of dust hung in the air and the odor of the damp plaster followed her into the passageway. She went down the staircase in search of her husband. The hall was as deserted as before. She did not find Hugh. Neither could she locate Alyse or Martin, though that did not particularly surprise her.

Sancha's search finally led her into the kitchen garth, where she met Donel, sitting with one hip propped on the stone wall, flirting with two girls from the kitchen. The blond girl's dimpled smiles, meant for Donel, vanished at Sancha's approach. Sighting his mistress, Donel lurched to his feet and gave a respectful nod of his head.

"Do you know where I might find my husband?"

"No, my lady, Though earlier I saw him by the abbey with the old monk."

Sancha passed back through the kitchen, where two old women were plucking partridges and the yeasty odor of bread wafted from the ovens. In one corner of the smoke-blackened room, three little girls were playing on the earthen floor, and a boy seated by the hearth was turning a leg of mutton on a spit.

Retracing her steps through the low-beamed hall, Sancha turned down the passageway, opened the narrow door, and went out into the slanting sunlight. With quick steps she walked toward the lady garden. Halfway along the garden's flagged path, she halted.

There at her feet was her pristine bed of camomile. She stood gazing down at the dainty flowers, as if she might find the answer to her dilemma hidden amid the misty foliage. She stooped down and with great care broke off a single sprig, held it to her nose, then plucked another and another until she had gathered a small bouquet. Then on she went along the flagged path, enveloped in a sweet, fragrant cloud of camomile, but still undecided.

As she approached the sacristy door, she caught sight of her husband. He was seated at the accountancy table, wearing the white linen shirt he had dipped in the horse trough earlier in the day. His pose was one of deep concentration. He had rolled up the shirt's broad sleeves several laps, but not bothered to tuck the tail of it into his hosen. And the crumpled shirt hung loosely from his shoulders, gaping open in a disheveled fashion. On the table before him a number of leather-bound ledgers were scattered about, and in one hand he held a stylus.

Sancha paused before the scarred oaken door, suddenly suffocated by fear. She nearly fled back across the garden path. But mastering her resolve, she raised her hand and tapped on the door's worn surface.

"Come," Hugh called out, his tone abstract, his thoughts centered on the sheet of paper before him.

The last rays of sunlight followed her inside, tinting the stagnant air with a queer orange light.

On seeing her in the doorway, Hugh's features lit with surprise and with pleasure. He laid the stylus aside and rose to his feet. "Welcome, my lady."

Sancha returned his smile. "You are alone?" she asked, gazing about to be certain. In the unreal light the room and all within appeared encased in amber.

"Yes, certainly," Hugh said, raking a hand through his tousled hair, preening, "until now, of course." There was something different in her manner, and though he could not say what it was, it made his heart beat faster.

She pushed the door to, severing the golden ramp of sunlight. "Where is Brother Malcolm?"

Hugh came quietly from behind the table. "Praying for our souls, I expect. I am certain mine is in need of redemption. I have spent the last hour swearing oaths and attempting to compose a letter to our holy bishop."

She held out the flowers for him to admire. "I have brought you a bouquet."

He leaned toward her. "They are sweet-smelling, though not nearly so sweet and lovely as you. Daisies are they not?"

"Camomile," she corrected with the air of an elder sister. "Is this your letter?" she asked, evading him with ease and going round the table, to glance down with a sweep of dark lashes. A sudden smile teased at her lips. "The paper is blank."

"Yes," he conceded, a note of amusement in his exhaled breath. "My command of Latin is limited to psalms and ledgers, to things I understand, like sin, and hides and wool."

She looked up swiftly, her dark eyes sparkling, and, laying

down her bouquet, arranged her skirts and seated herself on the stool. "I will write your letter, if you like."

"You are learned in Latin?" It seemed not a day passed without his pretty little bride managing to surprise or amaze him. At that moment she appeared as businesslike as a Lombard banker seated among the ledgers. He nearly laughed. It was not that he doubted her talents—well, not entirely. It was something his grandfather had once said about taming a fox, that it was no different than educating a woman, for the end result was to make them both more cunning.

"Of course," she asserted, with a flicker of velvety black lashes. "It was King Richard's wish that Madame and her demoiselles be tutored in languages. Latin was by far the more simple, English, nearly impossible. Now to begin," she murmured, taking up the stylus and tipping it in the ink pot, "I think you should flatter His Grace. Men love flattery far more than women, and since a bishop is surely more pompous than an ordinary man, the words must be very grand indeed."

"Why yes," Hugh said, so amused he thought he might burst from the effort of trying not to laugh, and thinking he would not trade her for all the treasures of Christendom.

The abbey's dogs were the first to sound a warning. Their baying cries alerted a group of men gathering up their tools after a day's labor on the earthen ramparts. The men, sighting only two riders, did not sound a general alarm. A boy among them, farther-sighted than the others, made the pair of wayfarers to be clergymen astride mules.

Approaching the abbey, Antonio, the bishop's diocesan representative, raised a hand to shade his eyes from the dying sunlight and, turning to the lay brother riding at his side, commented, "Thanks be to the Lord God, Evistone Abbey has been spared." Antonio, having viewed the destruction left in the wake of the raiders, feared he would find the abbey in ruins. He had no desire to be the one to carry such news back to the bishop. Ill tidings were not to His Grace's liking and oft as not he exacted his displeasure on the messenger.

For all his trepidation, the abbey appeared unscathed. Inside its earthen ramparts normalcy was everywhere, in the sight of men and women returning from their chores, in the voices of children at play. Chickens scattered before their mules, cattle lowed from the stone and wattled enclosures, and the summer dusk was heady with the aroma of roasting meat. There was also evidence of new construction, stacks of logs and fresh-cut lumber.

As Antonio expected, the monks were at their evening devotions. Their rhythmic Latin chant echoed from the chapel. Workmen gathered round to stare. A smith came from his forge, shouting to several boys who were forking manure from the stalls.

"Where might I find your master?" Antonio inquired. He was not accustomed to be kept waiting.

"He is at the manor house, I expect," the smith advised, an opinion seconded by one of the boys, who took the reins of the priest's mule.

In the storeroom, Martin heard Rumald shouting to the stable lads.

"It is nothing," Alyse giggled.

But Martin raised up, freeing himself from her arms, and looked from the window. " 'Tis a priest. The bishop's man I'll wager. I have to go."

"Nooo," Alyse teased, reaching after him.

"Yes, stop it now," he scolded, "no more foolishness!" Holding her at bay with one hand, he struggled into his hosen. At the threshold, he looked both ways, then slipped from the room. He was still adjusting his clothing as he came at a jog trot down the passageway. He greeted the priest in the hall, called for a servant to fetch wine, and sent the lay brother off to the kitchen to be fed.

When asked directly where his master could be found, Martin, flustered as a maid with grass stains on her back, responded that he had last seen him conferring with Brother Malcolm at the abbey. "I will send a boy to inquire of him."

This Martin did. The son of a kitchen worker, a boy of seven or eight with a shock of white-blond hair, went skipping out through the garth, hopping and leaping like a young calf, along the earthen path that led roundabout toward the rear of the abbey.

Before the sacristy door, the boy heard laughter. The deep voice of a man, and the clear, musical notes of a woman. It was certainly not what he had expected, for the monks were a dour lot, and for a moment he did not know what to do. Then, recalling his instructions, he tapped, a bit timidly, on the door.

Hugh appeared at the threshold. The boy started, and stood openmouthed like a mute. Eyeing the lady seated at the monk's table, he repeated the message he was given. "A priest has come, my lord. He is waiting in the hall."

"A priest, you say?"

The boy nodded, looking round the edge of the door to better see the lady.

"Run back and tell our visitor that I will greet him presently," Hugh directed, and, turning the boy with a large hand on his shoulder, said, "There's a good lad, now hurry on." Hugh remained a moment a the door, watching as the boy darted down the path.

Carefully, Sancha drew out the last dark, sweeping curve. Stylus in hand, she looked up from the letter. "Who has come?"

"The bishop's representative, most likely. The priest I told you of, from Hexham, Father Antonio."

"To inspect the abbey?"

"Yes, and to settle matters with my half brother."

Sancha frowned at the thought. She hoped it would not mean yet another confrontation between Hugh and his half brothers. It would, she imagined, take more than the presence of a priest to breach the ill will that existed between them. "Your letter

to His Grace the bishop is complete, save for your signature."
Sliding the paper across the table, she offered Hugh the stylus.

The sun had retreated from the window and moment to moment the light in the room grew increasingly dim. Sancha rose
from the stool and shook out her skirts. Laying the stylus aside,
Hugh hastily closed his rumpled shirt and stuffed it into his
hosen.

Outside in the twilight, Hugh caught her hand and guided
her toward the path. By way of objection, she asked, "Is it not
a nearer distance across the lady garden?"

Hugh assured her that it was not, though he was smiling as
he said it. Where the path curved and dipped behind a stand
of hazel shrubs and young blackthorns, he halted, drew her
into his arms, and said to her, "I cannot endure this any
longer."

Sixteen

Sancha regarded him wide-eyed, with a look of innocent surprise. "What can you not endure?" she asked in a voice hushed and nervous with excitement, even though she knew exactly what he meant. For the mere touch of his hands had sent an involuntary tremor of delight coursing through her body, from the tips of her breasts to somewhere much, much deeper, urging her to twine her arms about his neck and press against him. She was suddenly aware of his height, his hard-muscled body, and the tantalizing pressure of his belt buckle against her soft flesh.

Hugh's heart beat wildly. His hands slid downward to caress the curve of her hips, and bringing his face close to hers, answered in a low tone, almost speaking into her mouth, "That you are the subject of my every thought. I think of you every moment of the day, only you and nothing else."

"What then is the remedy?" Her voice caught in her throat with a choking sensation.

"Either I must have you, or I must make a bed for myself in the abbey."

"Would you not prefer to lie in your own bed?"

"Only if I might have you."

Sancha stared into his eyes, blue-grey and smoky with desire. *He is asking me,* she thought, and recognized the restraint in which he had held himself for her sake. However, at the moment her gratitude and her powers of reasoning went no farther than the primal feel of his strong, young body against hers, and the answering throb of her own passion. It was only as nature intended that she should touch her parted lips to his, inviting him to take possession of her mouth.

Hugh needed no more inducement than the cool, shy brush of her lips. The sweet torment of the unattainable now suddenly within his grasp left him light-headed with anticipation. He was trembling as he covered her mouth and sent his tongue to twine and dance with hers in a deep reckless kiss that filled her mouth and stole her breath away. Tasting her, he wanted more. His hot breath fanned against her ear and his lips swept down the warm hollow of her throat. "Tonight," he mumbled, his voice no more than a deep rustling whisper, as his hands drifted possessively down her back to cup and caress the curve of her rump.

For an instant it seemed to Sancha that he could crush her. The animal heat of his body, the hump of his arousal hard against her belly made her weak. "Yes." Her breath came in gasps, so that she could hardly speak. "Tonight."

His reply was a deep grumbling sound, and with a suddenness that stunned her, he set her back away from him. "We must go," he rasped, releasing her, gulping for air. "The priest is waiting."

In the absence of his support, Sancha thought her knees would buckle. But when she tried to return to his arms, he held her away, watching her with dazed eyes, an unfamiliar smile flickering on his lips. "Enough," he told her. "I will not be able to walk."

Hugh and Sancha entered the hall, their faces flushed with color. If the priest, Antonio, did not recognize the look of passion, the women in the kitchen had, and tittering, nudged one another and whispered as they passed through.

Father Antonio introduced himself to Hugh. He bowed majestically to Sancha, which made her smile. He did indeed speak French. But it was so heavily accented with his native Lombard that it was almost unintelligible to her. Thankfully, he soon reverted back to English, which she could better understand.

As for the man himself, Sancha could not decide if she liked him or not. His hands were soft and white as a lady's and his voice smooth as oil. In appearance he was very ordinary, neither tall nor short. He reminded her of a pig, though she could not say why. For although he was plump and his face a little flabby, he was not fat. Perhaps, she reasoned, it was his eyes, which were small, muddy brown in color, and imbued with a sort of porcine determination, the full extent of which she was about to learn.

Alyse came from the kitchen as the hall table was being set for supper. Soon Hugh's men arrived at the hall, all those who had not settled themselves into a farmstead or the village. Among them were Rumald, Donel, Martin, of course, and Alyse, who took a seat beside her mistress.

During the meal, Father Antonio monopolized the conversation. He first described, in great detail, the years of his youth, which were spent in the warring city-states of his native land. When more wine was brought, he spoke of his days in Avignon and of the grandeur of the papal palace. It was clear from what he said, and from what he left unsaid, that at the time he had been a spy of the Roman cardinals.

Any attempt by Hugh to steer the conversation toward the affairs of Evistone Abbey Antonio deftly turned into another of his reminiscences. Time passed, and the priest talked on and on.

Martin, Alyse, Rumald, and the others remained at the table, leaning on their hands and elbows. From the glances they exchanged it was clear they longed to escape. Though none longed to do so more fervently than Hugh, whose mind, indeed his whole being, was inflamed with a single desire, to be alone with his wife. And for a third time, he said to the priest, "I would enjoy nothing more than to continue our conversation, but you must be weary after your long day's ride."

"No, no, not at all," Antonio quickly responded. "You cannot know how it pleases me to converse with men of intelligence. In my diocesan inspections I am often thrown into the company of louts, tailless apes who pass themselves off as clergymen. These days most clergy are dumb as stones, clerks and country priests who know little or no Latin, not even the true meaning of the church services they recite.

"Oh, yes, I have seen it all," the priest said with a wag of his flabby cheeks. "Allow me to tell you of the scandalous diocese of Hereford," he said, glancing down the table as he gathered his wind. "Of the 212 clergymen, only forty-one have not been accused of some lewd or dishonest infraction. Some have set themselves up as tradesmen, others forge wills, sell the sacraments, and seduce women in church. It is no wonder the peasants consider it bad fortune to meet a priest on the road. I, myself, have heard a peasant say that he would rather greet a toad than a priest. Oh yes, it is all too clear, the church is falling into disrespect. One longs for the days of old . . ."

The priest droned on. Oil lamps smoked. Hugh fingered his wine cup. His patience was at an end, his nerves in shreds. His eyes met Sancha's.

She pursed her rosebud lips and surreptitiously rolled her eyes. All along the table the glum faces of the captive audience stared back with dazed expressions. Of the servants, two young boys had fallen asleep in the corner amid the rushes that were scattered over the floor, an old woman sat dozing on a stool by the kitchen entryway, and the young girl who had been serving wine leaned against the wall, her head fallen onto her breast.

At the table, Sancha shifted on the bench uncomfortably. When Hugh's hand found hers beneath the table, she smiled wanly, rallied a bit, and stifled a yawn. Her tingling excitement, the heart-stopping anticipation, like the sharp edge of her desire, had been dulled by hours of boredom. She was so sleepy it was all she could manage to keep her eyes open. She scarcely heard a word of the priest's discourse on theology, and his recounting of the martyrdom of St. Peter.

"Peter, in fear of his life, fled Rome," Father Antonio said dramatically. "As he walked, it is said he envisioned that he met Jesus making his way into the city. 'Lord, where are you going?' Peter called out to Him. 'I am going to be crucified for a second time,' Jesus answered. And from his words, Peter realized it was his own death that was in question and he returned, giving himself up to be crucified."

It would, Hugh imagined, have been a far less painful death. For by now he was beginning to think of the priest as a personal enemy, one who was determined to keep him from enjoying the corporeal delights of his wife's young and lovely body.

The torture continued. Suddenly a loud, resounding crash rocked the hall, halting the priest mid-word and rousing everyone from their stupor. The old woman staggered up from her stool, the boys raised their heads from the rushes, looking about like owls, and the girl who had been leaning against the wall now scrambled on her hands and knees trying vainly to raise the heavy iron candle standard that she had inadvertently toppled when she dozed off. It had narrowly missed the priest. Fortunately, its candles had not been lit; otherwise, they should have all been stamping out a fire.

"It is entirely my fault," Father Antonio insisted apologetically, rising to his feet as Donel and Martin and several others leapt past him to right the weighty iron furnishing.

The priest looked on ruefully. "I am afraid I have put the child to sleep with my musings. In truth, I too am feeling a bit weary. I know how you must long for conversation. Life in so remote an outpost is tiresome, I've no doubt. But there is always tomorrow."

"Yes," Hugh said glumly, "tomorrow."

Doors closed along the passageway of the darkened second story. "I thought he would talk until morning," Hugh said in an undertone, as he guided Sancha through the door arch of the solar. The candle lantern he carried sent shadows leaping along the freshly limewashed walls.

"You directed her to overturn the candle standard?" Sancha

accused, her voice brimming with suspicion, believing he had
and giggling softly as she recalled the look on the priest's face.

Hugh denied it. "Had I thought to, I would not have waited
so long, nor had it done with such poor aim."

Once inside their bedchamber, Hugh pushed the door to with
his shoulder, set the lantern aside, and went to open the shuttered windows.

Sancha began to disrobe. Her slow-burning fatigue had been
replaced by a sense of tingling expectation, and yes, fear. Her
fingers fumbled a bit over the laces of her gown. All she knew
of the act between men and women was what she had overheard from servants at Richard's court. Their outspoken words,
blunt and crude, had shocked her, left her feeling credulous
and terrified. Her first flux had come to her that summer, and,
frightened by their tales, she had brooded for weeks over her
dawning femininity. She glanced across the room and saw
Hugh before the window. It was clear what he was doing. She
looked away, back to her gown, which she folded and laid on
the iron banded chest.

"There is no moon tonight," Hugh observed, positioned as
he was before the long, narrow window, legs apart and braced.
He refused to use chamber pots, they were awkward, suitable
only for women and old men. And that night, above all others,
he had preferred not to take the long trek down the passageway
to the garderobe.

Completing the ritual, he stepped away from the window,
and began to shed his clothing. Every so often he glanced at
his wife as she removed the pins from her braids, or rather at
her budding nipples which jutted impertinently against the
filmy camisa. One, then the other of the dark braids fell, still
plaited, unfurling halfway to her waist.

The sight of her lithe body, golden in the candlelight, beneath the transparent camisa, left Hugh feeling clenched, rigid
as a fist. He tore his gaze from her and sat down on the bed
to remove his boots. At that moment his feelings for her were
more sensual than tender.

He wanted her with an aching desire, wanted her that moment without fuss or bother. However, she was not a tavern girl, accustomed to coarseness and indecency, nor an adulterous wife. If he was to have her affection and trust, he knew he must proceed slowly.

Because of her nervousness Sancha began to chatter senselessly about the evening spent as a captive to Father Antonio's reminiscences. Occasionally, she would cast a secretive glance at her husband, who was now naked to the waist. His lean, powerful form appeared sculptured in the candlelight. He looked taller, and the corded muscles of his broad shoulders appeared like those of an animal, one who might easily crush her.

"Did you notice that Rumald fell asleep?" she said. "How is it possible that even a priest could talk for so long a time without stopping? I have never seen a person eat so many tarts. His appetite is as inexhaustible as his store of words."

Finally, when she could think of nothing more to say, she slipped behind the wooden privacy screen with its cloth-covered panels to use the chamber pot. It was maddening. She could do no more than tensely balance herself over the crockery pot, her legs trembling. All at once she heard the sound of Hugh softly whistling to himself, like a man about to set to work. The melody followed him about the room, further stifling her urge. Succeeding at last, she shimmied from her camisa and donned her night shift. He had stopped whistling. She experienced a moment of sheer terror, then shivering with excitement, or perhaps mortal fear, she ventured from behind the screen.

For one terrible instant she thought the room empty, that he had gone. She blinked with confusion, then saw him half in shadow lying in the curtained bed, awaiting her. She needn't have worried. Nothing, save an army of attacking Scots, would have dragged him from his bedchamber that night. He lay there like a wolf in sheep's clothing, having covered himself to the waist with the light coverlet, a concession to her modesty. The only hint of his intent was the bulge beneath the bedclothes, which twitched and rose seemingly with a will of its own.

Nearing the bed, she heard the rustle of bed clothing. A cool breeze from the open windows, noisy with the song of crickets and scented with new-cut hay, brushed her face and sent a rash of gooseflesh racing up her arms. The candle flame flickered in the darkness, causing movement on all sides, dazzling her eyes. When Hugh reached out and caught her wrist, she gave a sudden voiceless start.

"I did not mean to frighten you." His soft laughter was so spontaneous, she stared at him. "Are you better now?"

"Yes," she managed. "It was the candlelight."

His undeceived grey eyes searched her expression. "Are you afraid? I would never harm you. You believe me, don't you?" he asked, drawing her down to lie with him.

Sancha slid beneath the cool sheets, trembling, hoping he did not notice. Her mind swarmed with thoughts. It was such a powerful feeling, to want him, his body touching hers, and at the same time wishing to be anywhere but in his bed. For it seemed suddenly strange to lie with him, even though she had for weeks. He had even held her in his arms, but not as he would tonight.

Tonight was different, frightening to her, honing her every sense, magnifying her every feeling a thousandfold. She felt his skin touching hers, warm and moist, and knew beyond a doubt that he was perfectly naked.

"I have been waiting for tonight," he said to her, "since first I saw you." His hands moved about her head, gently raking his fingers through her plaits, setting her dark hair free to cascade over her soft shoulders. "That night in Windsor," he continued, his voice a deep rich purr. "I was very drunk. You were so tempting, so beautiful." He paused, breathing in the scent of her hair, as he carefully rearranged it, smoothed it between his fingers.

When he had finished, he lowered his head close to hers, and planted damp, nibbling kisses on her ear. "I could have had you then," he whispered. "At least, I like to think I might have. I had drunk enough to blind a horse. You went limp in my arms, lifeless as a little dead rabbit. I could not bring myself to take you. I would not have hurt you. I will not hurt you now, I swear to you." Between his kisses were more endearing words, half of which she did not understand, but sensed in deep exquisite shudders that made her heart thud against her ribs.

His lips brushed her jaw, her throat. His strong hands, stroking her, gathered up her shift. Only when his fingers smoothed over her thighs, and slipped between to touch her, did she lose her courage. The tips of his fingers grazed her, made her tremble with a hot, hungry ache deep inside, and frightened her. Slowly, his hands pushed the shift up over her head and away. She cried out, a sudden helpless, breathy sound, a moment blinded, smothered by the shift before it floated from her vision.

"Please!" she bleated, turning her face from his kiss. "There is something I must tell you." She did not know how to make him listen, and struggled with his hands to distance herself from the touch of his fingers. "I do not know how . . ." she pleaded miserably, pressing against his chest.

Humiliated, she began anew. "I do not know the way to . . ." But she could not say the words, and tried once more. "I cannot, I do not know how . . ."

Hugh shifted full-length beneath the coverlet, drawing her with him. She felt his chest expand, the furry hair prickle against her bare breasts, and that part of him as yet unseen, and only guessed at, nudge against her thigh.

"There is nothing you need know," he told her softly. "Save that I love you." There was more he said, but his voice was lost to the softness of her tender breasts, her nipples hard and pink as knots. She was not listening, she could no longer think beyond the sensation of his lips on her, his hand caressing the sensitive skin of her thighs.

She moaned softly, a protest, as his fingers brushed the

feathery triangle of curls, and pressed inside, rubbing back
and forth, teasing. Instinctively, she arched against his touch,
seeking more, knowing now what she must have, and accepting
him when at last he moved between her legs and clasped her
hips to his.

She gasped and stiffened at the touch of him, the stretching
prod of his entry. His panting voice seemed inside her head,
insistent, grunting, coaxing. A searing pain tore through her,
a sweet agonizing ache that lessened with each successive tug
and rhythmic thrust.

As much as he had promised not to, he had hurt her, frightened her with his panting, growling whispers, his dumbstruck
look of ecstasy and greed. She clung to his heaving body,
seeing only the line of his broad shoulders, helpless against
his strength, the urgent, rapid pumping of his loins. A surge
of liquid heat blazed up in her, sweet and wild and terrible,
consuming her, as if a whirlwind had seized her up, borne her
to the heights, then flung her back to earth, dazed and aching,
with the feel of him still inside her, and reality dribbling from
between her legs.

Cradled in his arms, praised and kissed, she forgot the pain,
recalling only the pleasure, the wild excitement of his body
moving against hers. They passed the few remaining hours till
dawn, sleepless, lost in each other's intimate embrace. The sun
was just touching the window embrasure when they rose from
the rumpled, love-marked bed. Sancha, thoroughly corrupted,
was no longer the innocent demoiselle. No mysteries remained,
either of the obscure act, or of her husband's young and healthy
body.

In the abbey's forecourt, Martin, Donel, and Father Antonio
along with his clerics were waiting to depart.

The village of Aubry, ceded to Hugh in his father's will,
was larger than Hugh's present holding of Evistone, but appeared no more prosperous. There was but a single wide dirt

road, from which half a dozen rutted lanes radiated. Shops and houses lined the thoroughfare, which ended at a stone church of Saxon construction, surrounded by hovels, huts of wood and thatch.

In the church's forecourt, several servants loitered. Hugh noticed they wore his half brother's livery. Neither did the palfreys tethered nearby escape Hugh's appraising eye. They were blooded animals, handsome as the saddles on their backs.

Entering the dim interior of the church, Hugh was prepared to face his half brother Gilbert, and probably Walter as well. It was not the case. Gilbert had chosen not to appear. Instead, he had sent his cleric and his steward.

"How am I to assure His Grace of Gilbert Canby's goodwill, when he has not seen fit to show his face?" Father Antonio demanded of the cleric, who was also a priest.

The cleric made several rambling excuses. Plainly, he had no talent for telling lies, and seemed miserable in the part he had been cast to play. "My lord Canby does not refuse to comply. No, no, not at all," the cleric hastened to assure. "It is simply that in his grief, he wishes more time so that—"

"So that he might devise a means to deny me what is rightfully mine!" Hugh said, his voice, impatient and angry, cutting across the cleric's words.

"Assuredly not! Nothing could be farther from the truth," the cleric responded, the timbre of his voice rising appreciably. "As lord Gilbert's confessor I can attest to his good faith. As a servant of God—"

"How casually you invoke the name of God! You, cleric, are a liar, with or without a cowl!"

"Dare you to slander a priest of the Holy Church!" the cleric retorted. The shouting match between Hugh and the cleric went back and forth.

Finally, Father Antonio slammed the leather-bound document to the table with such force that the surrounding objects leapt into the air. "You have wasted my time," he accused the cleric. "What is more important, you have wasted the bishop's time, not to mention squandering his patience. And that, I promise you, will not be to either you or your lord's benefit! Tell your master he will appear here, two months hence, on the feast of St. Simon. He will appear, or he shall suffer the loss of the sacraments!"

Hugh doubted that Gilbert would be much concerned for his soul. In the end, Hugh suspected, he would be forced to fight for Aubry. There would be no other course for him and his half brother. One of them would live and one would die.

On the return to Evistone, the threat of rain dogged them all afternoon. Time and again they heard rumbling thunder, like a low, muffled drumroll echoing through the heavy air. By the time they had wound their way through the hills and dales, damp and darkness enveloped them. It was sunset when they arrived at the abbey, and the mist, beginning to lift, grew luminous with the last rays of golden light.

There was no less food in the hall that evening, but noticeably fewer faces, fewer ears to suffer another of Father Antonio's lengthy dissertations on nearly every subject.

Brother Malcolm, who shunned the eating of flesh and subsisted mainly on oats, joined the others at the table that night, and won a victory of sorts. For he, unaided and without force, managed to wrest the conversation from Father Antonio long enough to learn that the bishop had approved his request to bury the Roman bones which lay scattered over the hillside beyond the grave plot.

One of Father Antonio's many topics was an interminable account of the life of St. Anselm. Hugh heard not a word of it. His thoughts were centered entirely on his young wife.

Sancha, well aware of the power of her attraction, delighted in her husband's flirting glances. She felt his burning glance touch her skin, her eyes, her very heart. Beneath the table, their fingers touched and their hands met in a warm clasp.

Having lived all evening, indeed all day, with the expectation of love, once they were shut up in their bedchamber, they fell into each other's arms. With long, lingering kisses and caressing hands, they shed their clothing. Hugh carried Sancha to bed and lay down with her, taking her in his arms and pressing his lips to the curves of her flesh, to her cool little breasts, her milk white belly, the little black mole above her mons, the dark feathery tuft of curls.

Sancha was his entirely, the greedy recipient of his love. In the warm pleasure of their coupling, his husky voice teased her. "Tell me what it is you want?"

"No," she pleaded, still new to a man's love and bashful, wanting him, but not wanting to say the words.

"Yes." His deep voice tickled her ear. He flexed, probing, continuing the labored, breathless exchange of coaxing and contradiction. "Tell me that you are mine, mine with all your heart. Say the words to me."

Soft and breathy little mewing sounds escaped her parted lips. Her hands tugged at him distractedly, his back, his buttocks, seeking a means to draw him closer.

Heat flamed through his loins. He could not hold it back. A final sinuous, supple movement of her hips destroyed the last vestige of his concentration. He was lost, dumbstruck by the force of his coming. His face took on a masklike quality, and his breath whistled through his teeth in ragged gasps. Anchoring his hands on her hips, he urged, "Tell me!"

"Yes," she cried, tortured. "I am yours, yours, with all my heart!" The words burst from her lips like sobs. She heaved against him, lifting her hips to meet his pumping thrusts, craving the full measure of him.

She had expected only the pulsing thrill of his erection inside her, the wild excitement of his body moving against hers. She was not prepared for the sudden, intense spasm, the moment of joyous, mindless gratification, that left her clinging to him, shaken and trembling with astonishment.

Lying together they talked about many things, hopes and dreams, the life they would have. Eventually they fell asleep, only to awaken and repeat the process, to the point of weariness.

* * *

On the morrow, Hugh came down to the hall early in order to wish Father Antonio a safe journey for his return to Hexham.

"Do not trouble your sleep over Aubry," Antonio advised. "The bishop will deal with your half brother. Northumberland cannot afford to displease the Holy Church." At the door, Antonio turned to Hugh and, clasping the young man's muscular shoulder, said, "You look exhausted, my son," and with a chuckle added, "I fear I have kept you too late in the hall with my ramblings."

"Not at all, Father," Hugh answered. "The pleasure has been mine."

As Sancha's interest in her new home grew, she learned from Brother Malcolm of the long-ago past and the Roman legions who had once ruled the north country, indeed, much of England.

"In this very place," Brother Malcolm informed her, "stood a Roman villa. The stonework of the abbey and the manor house are near as old as the great Roman wall."

Brother Malcolm delighted in describing the glories of the past to her in glowing words. But it was the wall that truly fascinated her. She was determined she must view it. She had no difficulty whatever in convincing Hugh, for it was summer and he was in love; in his eyes there was nothing prettier, more tempting than the sight of his young wife riding across a moor, or picking wildflowers in a meadow.

They set out one morning, early, when the air was yet cool and shimmering with adventure, and rode for hours. At last, nearing their destination, they set their horses at a walk up the slope of a dry meadow. The wasteland along its fringe had been taken over by a stand of tall mullein with its long candlelike spikes of golden blooms and broad sea-green foliage.

The afternoon was warm and fair and the distant fields of nodding rye and thatch-roofed farmsteads they had passed appeared as perfect as a scene from a breviary. Coming from a dim green glade, they saw the moorland rolled before them, clothed with heather, gorse, and yellow broom. After a time they dismounted and led their horses.

Until then their conversation had been no more than comments on a hare that bounded out before their horses, a bird's nest in a patch of gorse and brambles that contained four eggs, and the butterflies that drifted in clouds, fluttering above the flowering broom.

Of late Sancha had thought little of the past and of her little Madame. But on that morning she had encountered a hefty, redheaded kitchen girl, one of Morah's sturdy granddaughters, bemoaning loudly that Donel had tossed her aside for another, her cousin. The girl ranted, telling all who would listen that she would have no other man for St. Agnes had told her so.

The mention of St. Agnes brought the past vividly to Sancha, and afterward she had not been able to push it from her thoughts. "Do you know the story of St. Agnes?" she asked Hugh as they waded through the broom. The sunlight in his hair turned it to gold.

"No, I confess, I do not."

"She was a beautiful noble who preferred death to a marriage against her will."

He smiled at her. A look of uncertainty darkened his eyes, but his tone gave no hint of it. "Thankfully your convictions were less extreme."

"Madame's were not," Sancha said, head down as she walked. A butterfly with orange-tipped wings brushed past her face. She looked at Hugh, her dark brows drawn together in a frown. "A year past, on St. Agnes's Eve, we were at Sonning Hill. King Richard was seldom there, and Madame, well, she was coming of an age . . ." Sancha paused to search for a word.

"To realize what it meant to be a man's wife," Hugh supplied.

"Yes, I think. She longed to be with Richard more and more. But he seldom came. When I would see them together, I sometimes thought he was embarrassed by her little affections. The few times he journeyed to Sonning Hill, he brought with him such a menagerie of favorites, actors and musicians, that everything was thrown into confusion. It was like a carnival. Oh, it was exciting, with all the foolery and music. But such pastimes no longer amused Madame. She wanted Richard to herself."

For a moment, Sancha walked before her mare, wordlessly. "She was afraid, I think, for Richard and for herself. And on St. Agnes's day we fasted, taking not even a sip of wine. Then on that night of nights we went to the chapel to pray. It was there Madame vowed that she would have no husband but Richard. She would, like St. Agnes, prefer to go to her grave. And afterward she swore to us, to myself, Marie, and Alene, that we should never be married against our will. That is why I could not believe she had abandoned me."

"Perhaps she believed she was doing what was best for you? You were very ill when your friends, the demoiselles, came to see you."

"Marie and Alene? They came to visit me as I lay sick?"

"You do not remember?"

"No, not at all."

"Yes, they talked to you, tried to coax you to speak. You did not seem to recognize them."

"And you, you were there?"

"Yes."

"Do you think I am still ill?"

"To my eyes you are as fine and fair as the day."

"But you cannot see inside my head."

"Ah, but if I could," he teased, "what might I find, feathers or gingerbread?"

Her face dimpled to a smile. "You had best pray it is nothing versed in Latin, else you would be sorely tested."

At that, he laughed. "I see I shall be forever in your debt." In another few strides they topped the crest of the hill. "There, do you see it?" Hugh pointed to a line of grey stones snaking away across the moorland. "There is the Roman wall."

He boosted her into the saddle, then, taking his horse's reins, slid his boot into the stirrup. They set off at a canter toward the crumbling wall.

Sancha rode her little mare a short distance along the moldering grey stones, turned, and rode back. Hugh had already dismounted. He caught the mare's reins and, taking Sancha by the waist, set her on the ground.

Sancha frowned into the distance, sighting along the wall's serpentine course, and slowly drew her eyes back to the section of stones before her. "It is not very grand," she concluded, after inspecting the project with a critical eye.

"Well," Hugh conceded, "it's not the tallest of walls, I suppose, and no longer the stoutest. But when you consider that it stretches for leagues, near to seventy, I am told, and has since the time of the Caesars, well now, that is impressive."

"But it is not at all what I expected. I thought it would be very big." She held out her hands to indicate size. When she looked at him, he was laughing soundlessly. "What have I said to amuse you?" she asked, sending him a peeved glance, and also a smile.

He lent down and plucked a dandelion clock. "Here." He handed it to her. "Make a wish. Hold the clock before your lips and blow briskly. If you succeed in blowing away every seedlet, your wish will be granted."

Sancha, expecting a trick, was at first reluctant. Finally, she took a deep breath and pursed her lips. "Aha, a word of warning," he cautioned. "If you fail, you must pay a ransom."

Taking in a deep breath, she puffed mightily. And seeing she had failed, giggled, pleading, "No, another! There is a trick."

He reached out swiftly to catch her hand. "One blow is all you are permitted!"

"Phoo, it is impossible!"

"All the same, you must pay a ransom."

Encircled by his strong, young arms, she looked up at him, laughingly. "Alas, I am at your mercy, monseigneur, I have no coin."

"Ah, but you have lips sweet enough to poison a heart," he said, brushing her cheek with a kiss.

"Poison! Have I poisoned you?"

"How else might I explain my lack of interest in comely girls? I lie abed all night, sleepless."

She laughed. " 'Tis not my doing!"

" 'Tis," he contradicted, bringing his lips to hers and thoroughly kissing her.

His hand moved possessively to cover the soft rise of her mons. Scandalized, but nevertheless laughing, she pushed at him. " 'Tis not my lips!"

" 'Tis heavenly, that patch of fur," he murmured in her ear, undaunted. "I swear if the ground were not so hard, I'd take my ransom here."

Seventeen

Midsummer's day came, and at the abbey the nativity of St. John the Baptist was celebrated. Through that night bonfires could be seen in the long meadows, glowing through the dark like great orange eyes. All the next day the evidence of the peasants' "nied fyrs" smoldered and smoked. Brother Malcolm was furious and denounced the "pagan deed." For weeks afterward he reproached the peasants who crossed his path, troubled their consciences and threatened them with mysterious punishments. Euan, the shepherd, avoided him like a pox, as did many of the servants.

As the summer bloomed with the heady scent of roses and fresh-scythed hay, Sancha often accompanied her husband about the fief, riding on her honey-colored mare. She saw the lush grass fall before the farmsteaders' scythes. And later, on a dry warm day, she watched as the haycocks were constructed. The huge shocks of hay, built tall to withstand the soaking rains, intrigued Sancha. With childlike enthusiasm she joined the farmsteaders' womenfolk, laughing and lending a hand to raise one of the golden masterpieces.

Above all Sancha loved to watch the sheep. She rode out with Hugh and Martin the day the flocks were driven to the pens. All morning she sat her mare, observing the unfolding drama in the meadow, as shepherds' dogs streaked across the grass like shadows in pursuit of the scattering sheep. The skillful dogs darted among the swarm, tireless, turning, checking, sending the obstinate sheep hurtling toward the enclosures, where they bawled mournfully and waited to be clipped.

At month's end Sancha busied herself in the lady garden. She was working alone one morning, planting a clump of daisies she had discovered growing wild in the grave plot, when the most astounding thing happened. The morning had been quiet, broken only by the occasional call of a bird. All at once the air of the garden seemed to come alive with sound, a whirring, droning sound, as if a multitude of angels hovered overhead.

It was not angels, but a cloud of bees, who descended, wings vibrating the air, and settled on the Blessed Virgin's shrine. Oswald, the abbey's cook, and also its beekeeper, came as swiftly as his old legs would carry him. It was a great event and within moments of hearing the news, everyone, stable boys, servants, and wide-eyed children, gathered in the lady garden to view the miracle.

The dusky, swarming mass of bees encased the shrine like a living shroud so that the statue seemed to quiver to life. Among the spectators, some sank to their knees to pray, and constant murmurs of awe rippled through the crowd.

Brother Malcolm took it as a sign and began to pray. "Let us with loving hearts offer our voices in fervent praise of the Blessed Virgin Mary," he called to one and all. "That through her intercession we may be freed from the sinful past and renew in grace our thoughts and words and deeds." Raising his hands, his eyes heavenward, he cried, "Blessed are you, Mary, for in your soul dwelt the Holy Spirit of whom David sang. Blessed are you who were deemed worthy . . ."

Even old Morah, flanked by her granddaughters, waddled from the kitchen, smelling of oat flour and yeast, to hear Brother Malcolm's prayer. Later, Brother Oswald collected the swarm. He moved, hardly visible beneath the teeming mass, his arms draped with long living beards of bees as he trod softly toward the orchard and the coiled straw skeps.

* * *

Two days of steady rain made Sancha a prisoner of the solar. It was there, while sitting in the lamplight with Alyse, that Sancha raised her eyes from her needlework and glimpsed a table draped with a cloth. It was an ordinary table, one she saw daily, but on this occasion the cloth had been draped over it diagonally. With a frightening suddenness she again experienced the inexplicable stab of panic, the same icy fear that had clutched her heart that day in the lady garden when she had heard the sound of bells. All day she was haunted by a sense of dread.

But if at times Sancha's thoughts were dark and troubled, she did not lack for affection. Hugh doted on her, wanting her near him and sharing his thoughts and decisions with her. In all her life Sancha had never felt so precious, or so completely trusted by another.

In the privacy of their bedchamber he behaved with her like a bear with a honeycomb, greedy and caressing. She became his in every sense of the word, abandoning her modesty, and becoming strangely at ease in his presence. Actions and words that several months before would have caused her to glow with mortification, now came as easily as the air she breathed. Her every perception had undergone a glorious metamorphosis. She was like a caterpillar suddenly transformed into a magnificent butterfly, or a scholar who at last discovers the answer to some great enduring riddle. She was exalted. Quite simply, she was in love.

Summer came full force. The meadows were perfumed with clover and in the fields the oats nodded in the breeze, yellowing to the sheaf. For Sancha, the hot summer days filled with new emotion left her with no wish to recall the past.

Hugh was fond of saying to her, "You are the most beautiful girl in the world." To which she would softly laugh, and as if to flaunt the truth, give a shake of her abundant dark hair. "How can you know? You have not seen every girl."

To which he would invariably reply, "I have no need to, because you are mine." It seemed to Hugh that he had loved

Sancha from the moment he had first laid eyes on her. And now, having tasted the intimate joys of possession, he delighted in handling her, stroking her, kissing her. He would often bury his lips in her hair, planting little seductive kisses at the nape of her neck, while murmuring the most outrageous, at times hilarious, statements. Until Sancha, weak with giggling, would give in to him once more.

One sultry night when they lay together, too damp with perspiration to fall asleep, Hugh spoke of the life he had known as a child, how he had lived with his grandfather, who was a woodward, and roamed the forest, free as any wild creature.

"And when you became a squire?" Sancha asked.

"They taught me belief in God, and to know He rose in flesh and blood—and how to kill men as well." He lay back, watching her through partially closed eyes. "Strange, now that I think back, for it was the priests who were in charge of us. The discipline was harsh. I remember that as well. I was nearly nine when I was sent off to the Nevilles' stronghold. There were five of us," he recalled, and smiled. All sons of local nobles, by one route or another. Many a night I spent kneeling in the chapel chanting psalms for the good of my soul. The priests taught us Latin, to read and scribe, and accountancy. If we went astray, they beat us with a rod."

"Truly? Did they beat you often?"

"Often enough."

"Why? For sinfulness?"

"For using my English tongue too readily." As Hugh spoke, he idly curled a lock of Sancha's thick, dark hair about his finger. "Perhaps if I had been more diligent in my verse, I might have spared myself a few beatings." With an audacious wink he added, "I might even have become more cunning in my Latin grammar."

Sancha giggled, assuring him that the bishop, after reading his letter, must by now believe him very cunning. And, of course, it was all because of her. They teased and spoke as lovers do and then fell silent. When Sancha spoke again, she asked, "Why do you never speak of your mother?"

"She is dead."

"Had she no other children?"

"No, she was very young. She died of a fever. I cannot recall her, not her face."

"And your grandfather?"

"Dead also."

"Did Brother Malcolm tell you that he discovered me searching the stones in the abbey's grave plot, one day?"

"No, he said nothing to me. My kin are not there."

"Yes, he told me."

"What did he say to you?"

"Very little. He was concerned I would see the Roman bones and that they would distress me. He said only that he did not know of your kin. Where are they buried?"

"In the forest, beside my grandfather's hut." And with a note of regret, Hugh added, "I should have gone long ago to say an Ave for their souls."

"Might I go with you?"

Hugh looked at her and smiled. In the dim light her eyes were dark and deep as wells. "Yes, I would like that."

For a week, Hugh's time was devoted to matters in the nearby village, of which he was lord. Several structures were nearing completion, as were the stalls of the market ground. All week he, Martin, and Rumald had not returned to the hall until late, always in very good spirits and smelling faintly of ale.

One warm, breezy morning, Hugh made a pilgrimage to his grandfather's hut. Sancha, riding along beside him, took note of everything, the trees heavy with summer foliage, the dazzling blue sky, and the low-lying meadows dense with tiny blue flowers.

The sun was directly overhead as Hugh halted amid a stand

of ancient oaks. He looked around, lost to time. "I know this place. I came here as a child. The trees are taller, perhaps, but little else has changed." He urged Chewbit on a short distance, reining him in before the mightiest of primeval oaks.

Sancha jiggled her mare's reins and followed. "Here, this is my tree," he said dismounting, leaving his reins to trail, and searching the tree's gnarled girth for the cross he had carved there years before. At last he found it.

Sancha climbed from the mare to see. After a moment, she asked, "Is your grandfather's house close by?"

"Yes, just there, atop the knoll."

Once again in their saddles, they left the oaks behind and clambered up the brushy hillock. At its crest a young forest had risen with the passage of time. Thick brush and brambles blocked their path, forcing them to seek another route. At last sighting what he believed to be the hut, Hugh and Sancha dismounted, tethered their horses to a bush, and walked.

Little remained of the humble structure, no more than a tumble of stones and rotting logs. Mats of blackened and moldering thatch, long fallen to the ground, peeked through the tangle of vines and brush. Kicking a path through the undergrowth, Hugh led Sancha into what had been the hut's single large room. There, a stagnant dampness enveloped them and the air was cool and humid, as if they had stepped into a cellar.

Beneath their feet, the hut's earthen floor was grown thick with lichens and moss. Sancha found an abandoned bird's nest in an overhanging bush, and started with alarm when she saw a shrewmouse scurry under a rotting beam.

A pell-mell of grey stones entombed one corner of the derelict. Where the hearth had been, Hugh discovered a rusted tangle of iron implements, and a pot, half-filled with earth, in which a fern had taken root.

The unmarked graves of his mother and grandfather, Hugh could not locate. He and Sancha searched for a time through the trailing vines, the brambles, and windfalls of branches. In defeat, they said their Aves before the ruin, and rode slowly back the way they had come.

That night, after they had loved and fallen asleep, Sancha awoke and lay listening to her husband's deep and peaceful breathing. She thought of the ruined hut, of a little boy without a mother, and recalled from long ago the words to a lullaby, taught her by her nursemaid. In the silvery light from the window, she studied her husband's slumbering face, smashed against the pillow. She saw the boy that had been, the tousled hair, ashen in the moonlight, and could not help but wonder if one day she would bear his child.

The rain returned with heavy showers that left the sky dulled and filled with spongy clouds. It was on such a day that a group of pilgrims came to Evistone Abbey. Merchants were a common enough sight, but not so pilgrims. According to Brother Malcolm, they were the first in nearly a year.

The group consisted of four men, two younger, who had been paid by wealthy patrons to make the trek on their behalf, and two older men, soldiers, they claimed, who had led sinful lives and now wished to make amends before they were called to judgment.

Hugh offered the pilgrims the hospitality of his table that evening. They accepted gladly, as they did Brother Malcolm's offer of a place to sleep in the abbey's dormitory.

The men ate like wolves and, between stuffing their mouths, related what they had seen during their travels. They had begun their journey in Newcastle, one of the younger men said, remarking, "There's a revolt brewing in the north. When I reach Carlisle, I'll not return."

" 'Tis true," the other youth attested. "There's talk of it everywhere you go. Some say old Northumberland has made a pact with the heathen Scots and the Welsh."

"Aye, its always the same, there's no pleasing people," the square-faced soldier snorted. "When Richard was king, they wanted him gone, and now that Henry's king, well, they want the same for him."

Hugh listened to what they had to say, just as he listened to passing merchants' tales. Some were fables, some were not. Even so, Hugh could not conceive of Northumberland allying himself with Scots or Welshmen.

The talk of politics, of Richard's death, and of the usurper Henry Bolingbroke, distressed Sancha. She had found a measure of peace and happiness at Evistone, and she did not wish to be reminded of the past.

The evening ended with Brother Malcolm's history of the abbey and its Roman past. Sancha suspected the holy man often invented what he did not know, or could not recall. His recollections were never twice the same, nor was the saint's relic, which allegedly reposed in the abbey's reliquary box. On that occasion, Brother Malcolm, with a smile as guileless as a child, claimed to possess a finger bone of St. Dunstan, the saint reputed to have tweaked the Devil's nose with a blacksmith's tweezers.

Sancha attempted to hide her amusement. Only a week before Brother Malcolm had told her and Alyse, quite distinctly, that it was a lock of the venerable saint's beard.

On hearing his tale, Alyse, who had been pale and listless all day, revived enough to nudge her mistress and smile.

On St. Swithin's Day the warm air held a heavy dullness. Beyond the open kitchen door the garth shimmered liquid and rippling in the glare. Sancha had enlisted Alyse and several of the little girls to help her bind bunches of herbs to hang and dry. The little girls' chatter mingled with the clatter of pots and gabbling voices of the servingwomen kneading bread.

Two boys, whose childishly round faces were streaked with dirt, burst into the kitchen, shouting, " 'Tis the monkey! He's coming up the path to the lady garden!"

" 'Tis the monkey and the peddler," the other boy shouted,

not to be outdone. "Hurry, come and see!" At that they both
bounded out the door, hopping and chirping in imitation of
the little beast.

All work came to a halt. The bread was hastily covered with
cloths, the herbs put aside. Sancha and Alyse followed the
women into the garden where the little monkey twirled round
and round and the children squealed and danced to the peddler's tune.

Before the bed of pot marigolds, Sancha saw the white kitten, sleek and now half-grown, stalking a butterfly. She took
the young tabby in her arms, stroking her soft white fur.

Ending his merry tune, the peddler's attention turned to the
lady of the manor. "The Virgin's blessings on you, my lady,"
the peddler said, with a flourish of his garish hat. "If it pleases
you, my lady, your kitten be near as lovely as yourself. For
such a pretty pet would you not spare two shillings for a velvet
collar and a shiny bell?"

Morah crowded in to see. "Harrumph!" she snorted, loud
as a horse. "Whoever heard of such a daft thing!"

More than likely she was referring to the cost and not the
precept. But the peddler, unaware of the old dame's tightfist-
edness, hastily defended his merchandise.

"I'll have you know, my good housewoman, the nuns at
Chalford Priory place collars on their beasts."

"Nuns may not keep beasts!" piped Gusti, one of Morah's
buxom granddaughters.

"Say you, and perhaps the Holy Father, but them at Chalford
Priory do. Cats they have, and dogs, and one has a pet squirrel.
I swear upon the Trinity! They take them into church with
them sometimes. I have seen it with my own eyes. I tell you,
those worldly nuns do not deny themselves the pleasures of
life. They wear trinkets and gaudies, and that is not the half
of it." Silencing his opposition, he whisked another collar from
his pouch and again turned to Sancha. "See here, my lady, a
nice collar of Lincoln green tricked in golden thread, and the

bell's a different note." As if to prove his words, he jingled it before her eyes. "Hear its little tune?"

The peddler's leering grin and the tinkling bell sent a faint creeping chill up Sancha's spine. She set the kitten down, and, when she raised her face, her smile had gone. "I do not like the sound of bells," she said, drawing back a step. Then she turned and hurried off toward the garth.

The thistles were in bloom when Sancha again rode out with Hugh. On his most recent hunting expedition he had seen a large group of deer, and knowing well Sancha's love of animals, wished for her to see the graceful creatures. He and his men had taken two large harts, but wisely left the does to tend their fawns.

The route Hugh chose led deep into the hills, where the woods were dark, smudged with fog and mist. As the sun rose higher, the leaden fog slowly lifted, affording them a breathtaking view of the vastness of the land, of the hills rolling away like emerald waves, blue in the distance and lost in mist.

They halted high above a narrow dale. Below, a little stream broadened to a sparkling shallows. Reeds and sedge grass grew rampant along its banks, smothering out all but their own kind. But away from the marshy ground, the long, weedy meadowland was splashed with color, the unexpected purple hue of the thistles and scarlet-fruited berry bushes.

After securing the horses, Hugh returned to the spot he had chosen as a lookout. Sancha, while waiting for his return, had discovered a multitude of tiny yellow wildflowers growing beneath the trees. At Hugh's approach, she looked up and smiled. "Look, are they not lovely?" She held out a blossom to him.

Hugh took it and held it to his nose. "Not much of a scent, has it?" Then, dropping his hand to scrutinize it, he commented, "Pretty bit of work, though."

"Do you know what they are called?" Sancha asked, reclaiming the blossom.

Hugh shook his head, admitting ignorance on the subject. "I know as much of flowers as my left heel knows. Brother Malcolm might," he suggested. "If you like, I'll pull up a clump of them before we go. You can take them back to the abbey with you. You might coax them to grow in your lady garden."

"Yes, I would like that," Sancha said, beaming, already deciding which clump she would choose and how she would carry them. When she looked again at Hugh she noticed something in the meadow below had captured his attention. "What is it?"

His swift glance came back to her. "Only birds, feeding in the reeds by the stream." At times the depth of his feelings for her swept every other thought from his mind. His gaze lingered over her as she moved among the flowers. She was very like a flower, he thought, bright and delicate.

"Do you want to see the deer?" he finally asked.

"Have they come?"

An amused glint came into his eyes. "Not yet. We have to sit and watch for them."

From their lookout on the outcropping, they could see the entire dale. "Eight does and as many fawns. Both days they came this way," Hugh told her, directing her gaze to the route he'd seen them take through the brushy meadow. "They will take the same path," he said with the canny foresight of a poacher's grandson. "If we are patient," he murmured close to her ear, "we will see them. It is a beautiful sight."

They sat talking in low whispers, about everything and nothing. Sancha's English was gradually improving, but when Hugh teased her over a word for which there were several meanings, she looked at him nonplussed and declared that in English there were too many words. Which was, she observed with a giggle, "Why the English are never able to say what they mean, and never mean what they say." From there the conversation deteriorated into playful teasing and kisses, ending only when Hugh, laughing soundlessly, declared that they would frighten off the deer.

They lay together in the sparse grass, watching. For over an hour they saw absolutely nothing cross the dale, not so much as a bird. Casually, Hugh mentioned, "Martin has asked my permission to take Alyse for a wife."

Sancha gave him a profound look. She could not have been more shocked if he had told her the sun was falling from the sky.

"Alyse hasn't told you?"

"No. I have seen them together," Sancha remarked with pursed lips.

"When this matter with my half brother is settled," Hugh went on, "I will need a steward for Aubry. I had thought to name Martin. Do you disagree?"

"No, of course I do not. He is loyal, but I shall be lonely without Alyse."

"There is Gusti?" Hugh said, suggesting Morah's yellow-haired granddaughter.

Sancha's dark eyes narrowed. "You know her name?"

Hugh could not keep from grinning. It amused him to think his lady wife was jealous, particularly of Gusti, who was a big girl with a large bosom, red cheeks, and bulging eyes. There was, however, a certain animal attractiveness about her. At least Donel seemed to be smitten. "A man should know his servants' names. Do you object to the marriage?"

Sancha fixed her eyes on the ground before her. "No, I would not deny Alyse her happiness." She saw an ant foraging in the dry grass, going hither and thither. She looked up suddenly meeting her husband's clear grey gaze. "Could they not wait for a time?"

Hugh hesitated, a bit bewildered. "Has Alyse not told you of the babe?"

"Alyse! She is *enceinte!*" Sancha was more hurt than shocked by the news. She could think only of how cruel Alyse had been not to confide in her. She was about to say as much when Hugh signed for her to be silent. Leading her gaze with his, he sighted across the dale.

From deep in the hillside thicket a dozen or more moorcocks sprang into the air on whirring wings. And in the silence left behind, Hugh and Sancha heard the distant crack of brush. With each passing moment it grew louder.

Sancha fixed her eyes expectantly on the spot. But a horseman, not a deer, broke cover from the thicket. A second followed close behind.

"Outriders," Hugh whispered. Several moments elapsed. Voices carried across the dale and more riders appeared. They came by pairs, endlessly it seemed, slipping from the deeply wooded slope into the weedy meadow to slosh through the shallows and vanish once again into the forest.

By their clothing and their shields, Hugh made them out to be Welsh. What was even more amazing was that the English riding with them bore Northumberland's device upon their shields. Hugh watched, intent, thinking there had been more than rumor in the pilgrims' tales. It seemed Northumberland might truly be plotting against King Henry.

An hour after Hugh and Sancha had seen the last of the soldiers' backs, they began their return journey. Sancha could not fathom Hugh's excitement. Her day had been spoiled. She had not seen the deer as he promised. She had learned her servingwoman, whom she had come to love as a sister, did not feel she could confide in her, and, as a further disappointment, she had forgotten her flowers.

In the hall that evening, Sancha could hardly bear to look at Alyse. And though Sancha tried not to let her wounded feelings show, later she wondered if she had been cool to Alyse and felt a twinge of remorse.

Toward morning, Sancha was awakened by a terrifyingly familiar dream. She lay back, her heart pounding, as she recalled the ghoulish, cloaked figure with the shriveled, beckoning hand. For the first time, she sensed the creature had something concealed in its cloak, something round and smooth. To think of it made her flesh crawl, and she tried to put it from her mind.

There was a mist that morning, but the sun soon burned it away. Sancha was in her lady garden when the rattle and creak of cart wheels pivoted her attention from the rose shrub, where she was gathering petals, to the abbey's forecourt. A merchant's cart and a number of heavily laden pack mules halted amid a cloud of dust. One of the younger monks came out to greet the merchant. Their voices carried into the garden, and if Sancha was not very much mistaken, the merchant had just proclaimed himself a purveyor of fine and sturdy cloth.

Sancha whisked the bowl of petals into her arms and with rapid steps hurried toward the manor house. The heels of her slippers clicked a tattoo as she swiftly crossed the hall and mounted the stairs. She paused in the solar only long enough to deposit the bowl of petals on a large square-topped chest and disappeared into the bedchamber.

From the water ewer she filled a basin and quickly washed her grimy hands and shining face. Peering into the polished mirror, she repaired her braids, which lately she wore coiled over her ears, and wiggled her perspiring body into a fresh kirtle. With all haste, she took the small jewel casket from her clothing casque and, rifling it, located the sack containing her allowance, all that remained from when she had been a demoiselle of the queen.

Down the stairs she flew, and into the stifling heat of the kitchen, where she found Alyse sitting, pale and silent, at one of the long tables. Before her on the table's rough surface was a bowl of soured milk, Morah's much-touted cure for all that ailed a person. The thought of the sour milk combined with the heat of the kitchen all but turned Sancha's stomach. "Oh, Alyse, come with me!" Sancha cried. "I need your advice!" She swept past and out into the garth, giving Alyse no choice but to follow. Alyse did so, but only with great effort.

Halfway along the path, Sancha glanced back over her shoulder. Clearly, Alyse was miserably ill. It is heartless of me, Sancha thought, to drag her out into such heat. She hesitated, then walked on, resolved to see the matter through.

At the abbey, Sancha immediately sought out the merchant. She found him to be a podgy man of middle age with thinning, slick black hair and a haughty manner. He boldly proclaimed, "I sell only the finest cloth," intimating that the cost was in keeping with the quality, and not for country folk.

Once he realized that he was speaking to the lady of the manor, his demeanor altered to one of complete complaisance. Sancha, however, was not so easily duped. For if the merchant's shrewd, glaring eyes were the mirror of his soul, she thought it very likely that he was every bit as greedy and grasping as she had first suspected.

She was no amateur where merchants were concerned. As one of the queen's demoiselles, she had often had to deal with the hordes of jewelers, dressmakers, and assorted merchants who constantly vied for the queen's favors. Of the three young demoiselles, Alene had possessed no talent for haggling, and Marie had too often lost her temper. Only Sancha had gained the proper combination of wit and tenacity needed to defeat even the oiliest of scoundrels.

The merchant perhaps perceived this when Sancha insisted on seeing the cloth right from the cart, and at one point scaled the cart's rear gate to inspect a bolt of fine heavy silk.

"These are not vivid enough," Sancha complained. "And see! Here? Is this not a flaw? You spoke to me of quality!"

The merchant, beginning to sweat, dragged out more cloth. Sancha carefully inspected it. "What do you think of this shade, Alyse?" Sancha inquired of her wilted maidservant. Between negotiations with the merchant, Sancha discussed each length of cloth with Alyse. The merchant, whose face was growing red from the heat of the day or frustration, stood first on one foot and then the other.

By the time Sancha had paid for and collected her cloth, the merchant was mopping his brow with his sleeve. Once in the hall, Sancha led the way up the stairs. At the landing she halted and smiled at Alyse, whose arms were as laden with cloth as her own. Instead of entering the solar, Sancha turned directly into Alyse's chamber.

"Where shall I put your marriage gown?" she asked.

Alyse, exhausted and at the end of her self-control, came a few steps into the room, sat down with her burden of cloth and began to weep.

"Alyse, what is it?" Sancha asked, placing the cloth on a bench.

Alyse, her fair skin blotched with emotion, covered her face with her hands and whined like a whipped child. "I am so ashamed. I was afraid to tell you," she wailed. "Afraid you would think me a whore and send me away!"

At the sound of her weeping, Sancha took the cloth from Alyse's lap, set it aside, and embraced her. "Shh, *minet chérie,* you must not cry. There is no need for it. All is well."

"But why?" she sobbed, tearfully indicating the cloth, "It is more than enough for three frocks, and I am not deserving of one!"

"That is untrue; your kindness has meant everything to me. And, well, you must have some sort of dowry. Are you not soon to be the wife of my husband's steward? Above all, you have been my very dear friend, and I hope you shall always be."

"Soothly, I will ever be that," Alyse promised. The young women, reunited again, sat and talked for a long while, about the marriage gown, the baby, and the future.

Martin and Alyse's wedding was celebrated at mid-month on a scorchingly hot day. A feast was set in the hall and afterward several rustic musicians, five men from the nearby farmsteads, armed with lute, bagpipes, and drums struck up a loud if not melodious chorus.

Hugh, who had downed more than his share of wine, presided over the festivities with the air of an indulgent father. As lord of the manor, he was expected to lead off the first dance. Taking Sancha by the arm, and with the caterwauling of bagpipes in his ears, Hugh propelled her across the hall in a boisterous jig. Around and around they went, while she, giddy with laughter, hung on for dear life.

One dance was quite enough, and afterward Sancha was content to sit safely at the table and watch the others, red-faced and disheveled, their clothing dark with perspiration, as they capered and lunged about the hall.

Blond Gusti pranced about victoriously, brandishing Donel on her arm, while her red-haired cousin, Jenn, fumed on the sidelines. Presently Rumald took pity and asked her to dance. Even old Morah romped to the music, jerking Euan the shepherd about the hall like a dog with a rat.

The ribald jokes and riotous laughter that passed up and down the table had no effect on Alyse, whose shining face was wreathed with smiles. But Martin colored with a continual blush and wore a silly grin all evening.

The musicians gave out one by one, as did the revelers. Some collapsed to sleep in the rushes, while others trailed off laughing and shouting, barely able to hold themselves upright.

It was nearly dawn when Hugh and Sancha fell into bed. Hugh wanted only to close his eyes. Sancha wanted to talk. She discussed the day's events, predicted Alyse's baby would be a boy, and laughed again over Morah dancing with the shepherd. Finally, she remarked in a wistful voice, "I shall always remember tonight." But when she looked at Hugh, he was sound asleep.

The village of Evistone, if indeed it could be called such, was scarcely three leagues from the abbey. Sancha had ridden through it on only one occasion. It had but a single street and a handful of houses, and at least a quarter of the village's population had come north with Hugh.

On the hot August afternoon when Sancha again rode into the village it was for the St. Bartholomew's Day celebration. Riding alongside Hugh, Martin, and Alyse, Sancha surveyed the scene. She noted six new structures, half-timbered houses, whose first floors were given over to shops. But the largest and most prestigious of the new buildings was the tavern.

She suspected it was destined to be the village's gathering place. Beside it a small market had evolved, and on that day the stalls and weedy grounds were crowded with people—farmsteaders from the surrounding countryside, villagers, and those from the manor and abbey. Sancha noticed Morah and her clan among the throng, Brother Malcolm, several of the monks, and the young men from the manor's stable. She saw Rumald standing before the tavern, and later, by a stall selling leather goods, she spied Donel holding hands with Gusti and talking earnestly.

Hugh pointed out each of the new buildings to his lady wife, obviously pleased with what he had accomplished in the village. Additional land had been cleared; wisps of smoke still drifted from the mounds of smoldering tree stumps. And in several locations, stacks of freshly dressed posts and trusses dotted the trampled earth. Once they dismounted near the market grounds, Hugh and Martin disappeared into the crowd, talking to this man and that.

Sancha and Alyse strolled leisurely through the market, looking at everything. At some stalls brightly woven shawls were being sold; others offered iron pots, clay pots, and wood bowls. Belts and saddles were being sold beside a lace merchant's stall, and the blacksmith, who had come north with Hugh, was shoeing a horse behind the tavern.

Cookfires had been lit and strips of mutton and plump little game birds were slowly being roasted, perfuming the air with their aroma. Alyse, now continually hungry, eyed the roasting birds. "I hope it will not be too much longer before we eat."

Stepping away from the market stall, Sancha rose on her tiptoes, and craned her neck to see over the crowd. Beside the tavern the last of the tables were being set up in the grass. "We should go take our seats," Sancha suggested. She, too, was hungry, and because of the heavy linen gown she wore, beginning to feel the heat of the day.

They arrived at the tables in time to witness the tapping of the first barrel of ale. Sancha at last caught sight of Hugh amid the crowd. Martin was with him, as was the village's first tavern keeper. Sancha recalled him from the journey north. A great noisy mob of men, old and young, had gathered to see the lord take the first hearty quaff of ale, and declare it fit to drink. A cheer went up as Hugh gave the brew his loud approval. Afterward there was ale for all.

A solemn prayer led by Brother Malcolm and a blessing preceded the food. Throughout the afternoon the discordant, ear-piercing notes of bagpipes, lute, and drums throbbed through the market. Shouts of glee split the air and dancers cavorted through the dust with more exuberance than grace.

Sitting at a table in the shade, Sancha and Alyse watched the antics of the dancers, laughed and talked and sipped on ale. Knots of people drifted past where they sat. A chase of children swarmed by, shouting and tussling. One fell and skinned his knees. Flies, black and biting, tormented everyone, and at a moment when the musicians halted to restore themselves with ale, Sancha and Alyse heard someone in the weeds beside their table retching. Finally, bees came to crawl over the tabletop, attacking the remains of food and seemingly intent upon drowning themselves in half-empty cups of ale. Sometime later, Sancha could have sworn she saw Donel and Gusti slip behind the tavern. When Sancha mentioned it to Alyse, she laughed and patted her swollen belly.

The celebration wound to a close at sundown. Slowly the crowd began to thin. Sancha spotted her husband standing near the now-empty ale barrels, engaged in an animated conversation with a group of men. She had hardly seen Hugh all day. He had given her no more than a hasty smile, a brush of his fingers on her shoulder as he passed by the table. Martin and Rumald separated from the group. As they passed the tables,

Martin shouted to Alyse that they were going to fetch the horses.

Sancha stood up and shook out her skirts. Alyse dumped the dregs of her ale beneath the table and got to her feet.

A loud carping voice rose above the babble of noise. Sancha, always inquisitive, observed a confrontation between Gusti and her grandmother, the formidable Morah. The subject seemed to be Donel, who had spent the day with Gusti on his arm. He looked drunk, swaying a bit as he led his horse.

Just then, Alyse turned and looked inquiringly to Sancha. In reply, Sancha said, "He wants her to ride his horse."

"What, again!" Alyse jested, rolling her eyes and giggling along with Sancha.

Back and forth the words flew. Morah was having none of Gusti's temper. "You'll get in the cart with your kin!" the old matriarch shouted. Sancha did not hear Gusti's retort, but she saw the old woman box the girl's ears, grab her by the arm, and jerk her backward. "You! Get in the cart!" Morah yelled. "You little scum!" Everyone heard that.

Donel, pleading with the grandmother, was following at a safe distance when several of the young men from the stable, also full of ale, sauntered up, most notably, a broad, square-faced boy of Donel's age, called Jerem.

"They'll be trouble now," Alyse predicted. "Jerem's hot after Gusti. He's always grabbing her."

Apparently it was the truth, for Jerem and his friends moved in on Donel, jostling and bumping into him.

"Hoy, Gusti!" Jerem swaggered to the blond-headed girl. "I've a finer horse than that!"

"Aye," one of Jerem's friends added, " 'tis a prettier color, too!" The comment evoked a burst of laughter from the other boys, and from the onlookers who had gathered. Moment to moment, the raillery escalated. Sancha saw Jerem come from around the rear of Donel's horse, though she did not see him stealthily raise Donel's saddle and slip something beneath it.

Just when it seemed there would be a scuffle, Jerem and

his friends exchanged a few parting insults and staggered on, stopping a short distance away, jabbing each other in the arms and laughing.

With mulish reluctance, Gusti climbed into the cart, taking a seat beside her redheaded cousin, Jenn, whose face fairly glowed with satisfaction.

Donel took up his horse's reins and put his foot in the stirrup. The instant his backside met with the saddle, the horse squealed, reared up, and bolted forward at a gallop. People screamed and darted from the horse's path, scattering right and left, while Jerem and his friends doubled over laughing.

"Oh sweet Jesu! The fools!" Alyse shrieked. "Martin! Martin!" she called frantically.

Galvanized to action, Sancha dashed away in a desperate search for Hugh, certain that Donel was about to be killed. Somehow, in the confusion, she located him. He was having a last ale with the tavern keeper and the blacksmith.

The commotion had halted their conversation. Sancha arrived just in time to see Donel sail from the horse's back into a brace of bearberry shrubs. Hugh and the men were already in motion.

"Hurry! You must do something!" Sancha shouted at their backs as they sprinted toward the shrubs. Martin dashed after them. A mob of people stampeded past, including Gusti, screaming at the top of her lungs, and Jerem and his friends, still choking with laughter.

Across the market plot, Sancha watched as Hugh and Martin pulled Donel from the shrubs. Rumald sent someone to catch the horse. All agreed it a miracle that Donel had not been killed. His face was scratched and bleeding, his ear gory, and his bloodstained shirt in shreds.

Jerem appeared, grinning and unrepentant, flanked by his friends, to hurl one last taunt at his rival. It took no more. Donel threw off Martin's steadying hand and charged into Jerem headfirst. The pair went down tumbling, rolling on the ground, swearing and battering each other with their fists. If

Jerem's friends thought to join in, the stony look Hugh sent them changed their minds.

Near to hysteria, Sancha shouted at Hugh. "Stop them!"

A ring of spectators had gathered, cheering wildly as the combatants knuckled, gouged, grunted, and kicked. It was horrible to watch, and Sancha, determined to put an end to it, dragged at Hugh's sleeve and screamed in a shrill voice, "Make them stop!"

Hugh gave her a cool smile. "He deserves a beating," he told her.

For a moment Sancha sputtered in complete bewilderment, then squalled, "They are going to be killed! Stop them!" she demanded. "Stop them, now!"

But Hugh only laughed. "They'll not hurt each other," he told her, shifting his attention from her, back to the vicious grunts and knuckles cracking against solid flesh.

His refusal put Sancha in a fury beyond words. Color rushed to her cheeks. She was about to shout abuse at her husband and would have done so, if she had not seen Donel's fist smash into his rival's nose with a sickening thud and loose a great geyser of blood. She winced, suddenly sickened by the sight, and dashed off toward the tavern.

Her mare was there with the others. She slowed her steps as she approached so as not to frighten the horses, and reached out for her mare's reins. She heard footsteps behind her, and Hugh's hand caught her by the elbow.

"Where are you going?" There was a chuckling sound in his voice. "You are acting like a child," he said to her.

Sancha glared at him wordlessly, attempting to twist from his grasp.

"What is the matter with you?" he asked, holding her fast and regarding her with a smile that seemed to imply ignorance on her part.

Her eyes flashed with anger. "I do not wish to see them kill each other! And you! You are worse than they! You are a beast!"

His chuckle became a soft laugh, and he tugged her toward him. "Walk back with me."

"No!" she refused, fighting against his grasp.

All at once Martin appeared. "It's over," he said, coming toward the horses. And Alyse, walking beside him, remarked matter-of-factly, "Donel beat him good and proper. No more'n Jerem deserved for putting a burr under a man's saddle."

Sancha was so angry, she was trembling. From atop her mare she looked back toward the market and saw Jerem's friends dragging him away, bloody and beaten. Only a few knots of people remained, and Donel, leaning on Rumald, limped toward his horse. The sound of women's voices, shrill and strident, came from out of her range of vision, though it sounded very like Morah and her granddaughters arguing.

In the twilight, the party returned to the abbey. Sancha rode all the way tight-lipped with annoyance, and staring straight ahead.

Eighteen

Later as Sancha, Alyse, and several of the women sat sewing in the solar, they were subjected to the sounds of laughter and loud talk rising from the hall where the men were discussing the day's events. The fight was retold several times, accompanied by hoots of laughter, thumps, thuds, and crude remarks.

With each stitch of her embroidery, it became clearer to Sancha that she had been blind where Hugh Canby was concerned. To her infatuated eyes he had appeared perfect, without a flaw, kind, decent, and good. Now she saw him for what he truly was—a man possessed of a streak of pure obstinacy, arrogant and smug as any other man. Because he had opposed her, he had lost all charm for her. The more she thought about his words, the tone of his voice, the more annoyed she became.

Laughter sounded from the hall. She looked up with a vexed expression. "Jenn, push the door to," she commanded. Hearing her name called, Jenn's attention snapped from the voices drifting up the stairs to her mistress. Slow and balky, she set her needlework aside and closed the door.

Hugh came into their bedchamber that night, smiling and affectionate as a little boy who had misbehaved. Sancha did not want his kisses. "How can you be so cruel?" she accused. "To you it is sport. You nearly let them kill each other!"

"Me?" he said with mock surprise. "How else were they to settle it? Besides, no one was hurt, nothing more than a bloodied nose and skinned knuckles. It was best for them to have it out, there, without weapons. Now it is ended."

"Ended!" she cried. "You are as much a beast as all the other English!"

He caught her by the shoulders. "Why am I now a beast?" he asked her, softly smiling. "Because I would not do as you asked?"

The truth infuriated her, and she pushed against him with all her might. Nothing he could say improved her mood, and so he undressed in silence. By candlelight Sancha sat brushing her hair with furious strokes, and later refused even to say goodnight to him.

She was no more pleased with her husband the following morning. She scarcely spoke to him as he dressed. After he had gone, Alyse came and, together, they went down to the kitchen.

Jam was being cooked and the air of the low-beamed room was redolent of blackberries and baking tarts. As always, the kitchen was crowded and noisy. Morah, in fine voice, carped at the sticky-fingered children, shooing them from underfoot. And before the hearth, the chastised Gusti stood stirring the jam and pouting, not raising her eyes from the pot. As soon as Sancha entered the room, her tabby leapt from the window embrasure and came to greet her. She saved a bit of her milk for the cat, who rubbed lovingly against her skirts and purred.

Since they had nothing better to do, Sancha and Alyse helped Jenn and several other women fold tarts. When their handiwork came from the oven, Sancha and Alyse each selected a still-warm tart and went out in the garth to sit beneath the plum tree.

Sancha's mention of the fight the day before only elicited a shrug from Alyse, who licked the jam from her fingers and remarked with a philosophical air, " 'Tis what men do."

It seemed no one but Sancha was in the least concerned about Jerem's and Donel's injuries, with the possible exception of Gusti. When Sancha mentioned it to Alyse, she made a droll face and pointed toward the stable yard. From where she sat, Sancha could not see. She stood up, looked, her jaw dropped open. There were Donel and Jerem with blackened eyes, swollen faces, and battered knuckles, working side by side, talking and jesting like the best of friends as they sat in the dirt oiling the cart horses' harnesses.

The revelation was too much for Sancha. After finishing the tart, she put on her straw hat and went into the garden. The overflowing bed of pungent, blue-green mint with its myriad of pink-spired blossoms had invaded a little nook of harebells with intent to smother them. Savoring the scent of the mint, Sancha plucked and pinched.

Earlier, she had seen her husband enter the abbey. She remained by the mint, watchful as a cat. Every so often she would look from beneath her large hat and sight across the lady garden to see if he was still in the sacristy, seated at the table working on the fief's accounts. She deliberated for some time in the noonday heat. At long last she returned to the manor to wash her hands and face, repair her braids, and touch some rose-scented oil to her skin.

In the abbey, Brother Francis approached the altar. Sunlight pouring through the stained glass panes cast odd-shaped ruby, blue, and yellow reflections onto the tiles and on his hands as he paused to light the candles for the afternoon devotions. A draft, smelling of dust and summer heat, swept into the chapel with a robust man, wearing tall boots and a mail shirt beneath his surcoat. A noble, for Brother Francis saw he wore a knight's sword on his hip and his silver spurs gleamed in the blaze of sunlight from the open door. Brother Francis, abandoning the candles, came forward, chink-eyed as a mole in the bright glare. "Might I be of assistance, my lord?"

"Where might I find your prebend, Hugh Canby, master of Evistone?"

Brother Francis, whose normal countenance was one of startled surprise, batted his eyes and said, "Here, sir, in the sacristy," and indicated a door arch to the right beside the Virgin's altar. Only then did Brother Francis notice three horsemen, dismounting in the forecourt, lean, hard-looking men and well armed. He was about to scurry after the man, when Brother Malcolm and the other brethren entered the chapel.

A loud battering at the door of the sacristy brought Hugh to full attention. "Come!" he shouted, expecting Euan, the shepherd, with an accounting of the young wethers to be driven to the meat market in Hexham. The sight of his half brother Gilbert left Hugh bereft of words. He tossed down his stylus and rose to his feet, not knowing what to expect.

"God's greetings, brother," Gilbert said with a portentous smile.

The fact that Gilbert had called him "brother" was warning enough, and not wasted on Hugh, nor was the thought that misfortunes always come in pairs. "Where is Walter?" Hugh queried, feeling the hairs on the back of his neck prickle. His rapid sidelong glance raked the lady garden door, fully expecting to see Walter burst through it, sword in hand.

"Bedding a whore, most likely," Gilbert remarked, coming into the room. "He is not with me."

"Why are you here?" Hugh's every nerve was keyed for combat.

"I come in the spirit of largesse," Gilbert said with a show of upturned palms. He drew up before a large dark-stained wooden cupboard which contained several covered pottery ewers, a line of small pottery drinking bowls, one of which held a collection of styli. "Wine?" he inquired, taking up one of the ewers and inspecting it.

"On the left," Hugh directed. "That is ink."

"One for you?"

Hugh turned the sheet of paper before him facedown and came from around the table. "No. You have not answered my question."

Wine overflowed the bowl. "First, come with me into the chapel," Gilbert said, setting aside the ewer. He downed the wine and noisily cleared his throat. "Damn the dust! It is chok-

ing today! Let us go before God, together, so you know I speak
the truth. Then I will tell you why I have come."

Hugh gave a tentative nod of his head. He doubted Gilbert
would murder him there in the chapel, not with the entire assembly of monks to witness the deed. Still he was wary. He
opened the door for Gilbert and closed it after them, entering
the chapel a step behind his half brother.

In the gloom of the nave, the brethren stood silent and immovable, gazing with reverence at the altar, where Brother
Malcolm invoked, *"O salutaris hostia, quae caeli panddis
ostium."* O sacred host, O bread of life.

In the garden, Sancha paused by the blossoming privet
hedge, where the strong, honeyed scent perfumed the air. She
breathed in deeply, then set out once more, walking thoughtfully along the heat-soaked stone pathways, selecting with
great care a bouquet, a peace offering to take to her husband.
She plucked some daisies, white and vain, a handful of pretty
blue harebells, and a trio of scarlet poppies. As she walked
toward the abbey, she noticed some men and horses in the
forecourt, but thought them travelers. More truthfully, she
thought nothing of them. Her mind was on other matters.

She tapped lightly at the sacristy door. There was no answer,
save for the Latin chant floating on the humid air. She pushed
into the chamber and found it was deserted. Odd, she thought,
for she had seen her husband earlier through the window. She
crossed to the table, wondering where Hugh had gone. Not far
surely. A stylus lay precariously close to the edge of the table.
She picked it up and placed it beside a sheaf of accounts,
stacked upon a ledger book. It was then she saw the single
square of paper, turned on its face. There was something
scribed on it, for she could make out the shadow of the letters.

She did not know why she looked at it, beyond simple curiosity. The dark curving script sprang up at her like a viper.
For there, as best she could discern the English words, was

the scene they had viewed across the dale, the Welshmen riding with Northumberland's knights. She laid down her bouquet, her hands were trembling. The pilgrims words were there as well, and the phrase, "the king should be advised." Sancha knew of only one king, the usurper, Henry Bolingbroke!

She felt suddenly cold, sick to her heart to realize that the man she loved with all her soul, was a spy, a traitor, and had always been. She, and everything else he possessed was paid for by treachery. He was just like all the others who had betrayed Richard, set Henry on the throne, and called him king.

Voices just beyond the door sent an instant flutter of panic through her. *He must not find me here,* she thought desperately. She would never reach the lady garden without his seeing her. She was trapped! Her eyes roved wildly over the room. It was then she noticed a narrow door not three strides from where she stood. She had no notion of its existence before that moment, and no notion of what lay behind it. She lunged toward the door, praying it was not barred. "The flowers," she gasped. She darted back, snatched them up, and slipped through the door.

After a moment, Sancha heard an unfamiliar man's voice say, "You are certain we cannot be overheard?"

"Of course. What have you come to say?" That, she knew, was her husband's voice, and edged with impatience. She raised her eyes to the sliver of light which remained between the door and frame. She dare not close the door completely now, for fear they would hear. When at last she glimpsed Hugh's visitor, the sight of his half brother Gilbert stunned her. She did not understand. She stood there in the dimness almost afraid to breathe, her heart thundering in her breast.

Within the chamber, Gilbert poured himself another bowl of wine. "I took a great risk in coming here. I would not want it known." He sank down on a bench by the wall. "I have come directly from Warkworth."

Hugh moved to the table, crossed his arms, and stood resting his hip on it, waiting to hear what Gilbert would say next.

"My wife is there, visiting, awaiting the birth of our second child. She prefers the comforts of her father's castle." He sucked in a mouthful of wine, and swallowed slowly. "What do you know of Owen Glendower?"

Hugh was intrigued. "That he calls himself a prince of the Welsh people, and that he is an enemy of King Henry."

"He sits this very day at Warkworth, discussing an alliance with my father-in-law, Lord Northumberland, and his eldest son, Hotspur," Gilbert announced, waiting for Hugh's reaction.

The nickname amused Hugh. All the Percys had them simply because there were as many Percys as fleas on a dog, and most were christened Henry. "You have ridden all this way to tell me that?"

Gilbert's heavy lips quirked. "I would not have troubled myself. You would soon hear it in rumors. Just as you have surely heard tales of Richard alive and roaming the north country."

"Tales of Richard's ghost," Hugh suggested with a grin.

"Richard in the living flesh. Tales only, for which your father-in-law is no doubt responsible. No one believes them."

"Save for Richard's little queen." Gilbert sucked again at the wine. "If my father-in-law has his way, he will use her to spark a rebellion."

"His arm is longer than I thought. Is she not at Windsor, or near abouts?"

"No longer," Gilbert assured him. "Your foolish King Henry has tucked her away at Chalford Priory, north of York, in an attempt to force her into a marriage with his son, young Harry. Better that than be forced to return her dowry.

"Apparently, word of Henry's plan reached the French king, who at the moment is in a period of sanity, or at least what passes for sanity. He is sending an emissary to hear his daughter's decision. Either she will wed King Henry's son or return to France.

"Unless, of course, Northumberland succeeds in spiriting

er away to ride beside the actor he has hired to play the part
f Richard. You did not know that, did you?

"Sure as whores have pox, Northumberland means to take
er from the priory. He had hoped to win her trust. But now,
here is little time. If she cannot be convinced to come will-
ngly, he will take her by force. Though I doubt it will be
ecessary. I am told she despises King Henry and his sons
with as much venom as my father-in-law."

"Why have you told me all this?" Hugh asked, even though
e had already guessed. Gilbert had only to prove his disloyalty
o Northumberland to be rid of him forever, and in the process,
spare himself the loss of Aubry.

"Because you are Swynford's spy," Gilbert told him. "King
Henry Bolingbroke's man, just as our father was."

"That is an ugly accusation. I am as loyal to Northumber-
and as you. More so, for I have not betrayed his trust."

"He is a vainglorious old shit!" Gilbert spit, jerking himself
from the bench and crossing the room to pour himself another
cup of wine. "The man means to rule England by one means
or another. This rebellion of his is doomed to failure, and when
it is put down, all those involved will lose their lands—if not
their heads." He took a gulp of wine and walked back. "I do
not intend to lose Redesdale. I've waited too long to gain it.
Before our father died, all I possessed came through my father-in-law. Now matters are quite different."

"You've only to send a message south," Hugh suggested.
"The king cannot be that difficult to find."

"Goddammit!" Gilbert growled, "Northumberland is my father-in-law! My wife is his . . . If he were to discover my
perfidy . . ."

"Yes, and you would much prefer it was my head that fell!
And as an added incentive, you would keep Aubry. What of
Walter? He has ever been your lackey. Send him with your
message!"

"Walter is not so much a fool as that. He will not bite the

hand that feeds him. Besides, his mind is too slow for such subtleties."

"Then you have ridden too far in the sun, Gilbert. I am no man's spy. If you wish to warn Henry Bolingbroke, you must do it yourself!"

Behind the door, Sancha remained transfixed, only vaguely aware of the small, shadowy, vaulted chamber in which she had concealed herself. The walls, hung deep with vestments, altar cloths and dorsers, seemed to close in on her, and the stagnant air reeked of sweat and frankincense.

From where she hung at the door's edge, she could have reached out and touched her husband. She saw the side of his head, the determined line of his jaw, the small white scar behind his ear that shone through his closely cropped fair hair.

She listened. She had no choice but to hear. His every damning word seemed to drive a spike into her heart. The voice that had sworn to love her, whispered sweet obscenities in her ears, and groaned over her in pleasure, was faithless. Tears burned her eyes, spilled down her face, threatening to suffocate her. She could not bear to listen, yet feared to go, to make a sound that would betray her. She glanced again at the confined little chamber's outer door, at the thread of daylight glowing beneath it.

Gilbert was about to speak when a thunderous knell surged through the air of the chamber, followed by the rolling, iron rumble of the abbey's bells. He hesitated, setting aside the bowl, waiting to place his words between the mournful ebb and swell of the clanging bells. "I am offering you Aubry."

The bait, Hugh concluded. No trap was complete without it. "I will have Aubry in any case," he told his half brother, raising his voice. What did he care who heard?

Gilbert's face blanched with anger. "Not without bloodshed."

They stared at one another for a moment. Finally, Gilbert swore an oath and strode to the door. "Do as you will!" He grabbed the iron handle, paused, looking as if he were about

o utter another curse, but too enraged for speech, flung open
he door and stormed into the chapel, pursued by the clanging
f the bells.

Moments before, when the first deafening peal had sounded,
Sancha had edged slowly away from the door, then whirled
about, frantically brushing past the silken cloths and vestments
hat fluttered back to cling to her clammy face like spider's
vebs.

Out of the shadows, the image of a little white-haired boy
ook shape. At first, Sancha thought him a dog with his furry
white hair, sitting on the floor, half-hidden by the robes and
cloths. A muffled cry escaped her lips. Had he been there all
he while, watching her?

His chirpy voice came from the gloom. "I'm waiting for
Brother Malcolm," he exclaimed, shifting nervously, and showing her the parcel that he clutched. "I found it over the hill,"
he said, and as if to prove his words, plunged his hand into
he soiled cloth and proudly drew out a gleaming skull. " 'Tis
a Roman's I ken!"

The boy's swift, triumphant gesture, and the skull with its
grisly unhinged jaw, loosed an avalanche of crushing memories—the curly-coated dog; the torchlit chamber; the men; the
grimy sack; and Richard's severed head with jaw agape and
sightless, half-closed eyes.

Sancha gasped and threw herself at the door. She burst into
he sunlight, and was blinded by the glare. Running mindlessly,
she cast aside her wilted bouquet and fled toward the yews,
through the banded shadows that lay across the dusty path,
down toward the grave plot, thrashing through the tall grass.
On she ran, her lungs afire, the calves of her legs aching with
exertion, until she collapsed against the lych-gate, spent and
sobbing. She slid slowly to the ground, the whole green world
before her dissolving in a blur of tears.

What had been lost to her memory now returned with vivid
horror. Richard's blood-smeared head, his golden hair matted
with gore; a man's boots shimmering with bells; shouts and

curses, and hands snatching after her. One man, tall and evil
looking, seizing her, and shaking her like a rag. "Let me take
her back to Pontrefact and toss her down the midden with her
pretty Richard of Bordeaux." The bestiality of the words recalled made her sick with disgust.

The man's long face was one of ghoulish ugliness, as if the
evil he had done had stamped itself upon his features. It was
the face of the cloaked figure of her nightmares. He had
wanted to kill her. Perhaps he would have, had someone not
swore at him and told him no. Had it been Henry Bolingbroke?
Or another, for someone had said, "We've enough noble
corpses to hide from the French." She recalled screaming,
struggling, breaking free, and then the stairs tumbling before
her, and nothing more at all.

For a long while Sancha lay in the dusty weeds, huddled
against the lych-gate, silently sobbing, choking on her misery.

Inside the abbey's walls, Brother Malcolm, after exchanging
his fine woolen robe for his threadbare work robe, entered the
sacristy to find the young lord hard at work on his accounts.
"Blessings on you this day, my lord," he said in greeting.

Hugh grunted a reply, then looked up from the ledger to
see the old monk raise the lid of a large iron-banded chest.
He had a bundle under one arm, and Hugh asked, "What have
you got there?"

The white-fringed head turned to him. " 'Tis but another
Roman skull. One of the children found it on the hill. Animals
must have carried it away. Brother Alewin will bury it on the
morrow." He bent to tuck the skull into the roomy chest. "Curious," he said, closing the lid with a bang. "In their vaults,
the bones remained unchanged for centuries. But above the
earth, left to the sun and wind and rain, they begin to crumble,
return to dust, as one day we all shall."

Hugh repressed a smile. "A sobering thought."

"Indeed, my lord. That poor soul who once was filled with

life, as robust as you or I, is now reduced to mouldering decay. And so we, too, shall be in time." He clasped his hands before him and padded to the door. "O 'tis true," he mused. "Scripture tells us that our days are numbered, as surely as the leaves of the trees. Shall I send Euan to you?" he asked from the threshold.

"Yes," Hugh replied, and raising his eyes from the ledger spied the decapitated head of a daisy, lying atop another of the leather-bound books. It was fresh, soft, and he wondered how it had come to be there. Euan came into the room and Hugh set the blossom aside.

The hall that evening was again host to travelers, pilgrims who, having been to Carlisle, were returning to Warkworth. They were merchants who dealt in wool and cloth and Hugh was particularly interested in what they had to say.

Between courses, Hugh's gaze settled on his wife's delicate profile, the sweet curve of her cheek, her upturned nose. Her pink prettiness, made exotic by the sultry darkness of her hair, her brows and lush black lashes, filled his mind with a stream of sensual images. He laid his hand over hers on the table and leaned toward her. "I looked for you today, and could not find you," he whispered, lifting her hand and pressing it to his lips.

Sancha stiffened at his touch, and with an icy glance withdrew her hand. She could not look at him without thinking of Richard's gory head, his golden hair matted with blood, and her grief-stricken little Madame Isabelle.

Sancha left the men to talk. Alyse came with her to the bedchamber to help her undress. "There is naught amiss!"

Alyse threw the words back at her mistress. "Is surely! Your eyes are red as if you've sat a month before a smoky fire." She quickly folded the citrine-colored gown, and recalling her mistress's temper of the day before, suggested delicately, " 'Tis something the master has said to you?"

"No, Alyse, 'tis nothing." And she held out the comb to her

maidservant. "Comb my hair for me; it is tangled and it pulls so."

Alyse, not having been able to discover the cause of her mistress's distress, unbound her magnificent long hair and let it fall, tumbling with its own weight halfway down her back. Slowly, gently, Alyse ran the comb through her thick lustrous curls.

Sancha had a childish love of having her hair combed, and brightening, she said to Alyse, "Tell me of your baby." It was a game they played. For Sancha was looking forward to the birth almost as much as Alyse, hence the silliness between them, each guessing, a boy or a girl and then describing how fair and tall and wonderful he or she would grow to be, and even imagining future mates.

When Hugh came to undress for bed, he was in a jovial mood, much improved by wine, and repeated what he'd gleaned from the pilgrims. Several, he noted, were members of the wool guild, returning to Warkworth in time for the yearly sales.

"Warkworth has a sea trade," Hugh told her, stripping off his shirt, and sitting on the bed to remove his boots. "You will see a very different place than Hexham. 'Tis more like London with all manner of goods, and some from as far as the Orient."

From time to time he glanced at Sancha, seated on the upholstered stool before the little table that held her silver polished mirror. Her distant look had bothered him all evening, and now seeing her toying with the comb, he thought her still angry from the night before. He was about to unfasten his hosen when he saw her rise and go on bare feet to the window, open the shutter, and lean out, looking into the warm night.

He came up behind her and took her shoulders in his hands. "What do you see?" he asked. And not waiting for a reply, brushed aside her hair and placed a series of nibbling kisses on her neck, whispering, "Let me love you?"

"I am weary tonight." She sighed and tried to pull away. But he countered by anchoring his hands on her waist. "You have tortured me awhile; isn't it enough?" he asked, his voice icklish and warm on her ear, his hands gliding upward to caress her breasts.

"I am weary," she repeated, annoyed that he would not leave her be. From over her shoulder she sent him a significant glance. "Do you not understand?" She frowned when he persisted, and with a swift motion captured his hands. Even so he would not let her pull them away, nor could she stop him from brushing his thumbs back and forth provocatively over her nipples, teasing them until they hardened and rose in points, dark against the silken cloth.

"What have I done that you must be so heartless?" he said to her, his voice deep and seductive, while his hand, veiled in the silk of her shift, dropped to stroke between her thighs, massaging her through the material.

A throb of desire thrilled through her, raising a pulsing ache low in her abdomen. *No,* she thought, struggling against her own passion. "I do not want to," she told him.

His soft laughter hot against her neck. "Liar, you have made my finger wet."

She pushed against him suddenly, obstinate and angry, and twisted to face him, only to have him cinch his arms about her.

"What have you to complain about?" he murmured, teasingly, cupping her rump with his hands and pressing her against his hardness.

She opened her mouth to object, to make him stop, but her words were lost to his lips, to his invading tongue, and to his breath stealing hers. All evening she had wished for arms to hold and comfort her, to take away the hurtful memories. Now with his kisses, his velvet voice, and hands that knew too well how to bring her pleasure, she was overwhelmed. Later she might regret it, but at that moment nothing else in the world mattered to her.

She went with him, shedding her silken shift, accepting his naked body, letting him stroke her, fondle and caress her, so that when he took her by the waist and eased her down to

straddle his erection, she was eager for the driven pressure o
his thrusts, the probing feel of him inside her, the sudden floo
of warmth.

She swayed over him, her long hair sweeping forward like
a curtain, trembling as his hardness stretched her soft flesh
Poised atop him, the muscles of her hips and thighs quivering
as she tried to spread her legs still wider. Once he caught a
handful of long dark hair and pulled her down to kiss her, kiss
her breasts. His coaxing voice urged her on. She rode him
thrusting her hips forward, driving him deep inside her.

Suddenly, Hugh fell silent. His face lost all expression, his
hands dropped to her hips and braced her to him. The sof
groaning of their voices mingled.

She felt his coming flame up inside her and arched against
him, bearing down, matching his heaving strokes, shamelessly
pursuing the moment of mindless ecstasy that would set her
free and make her cry with pleasure. She was not cheated. The
sweetness that had grown with every moment left her dazed
with its wonder.

Afterward lying in his arms, her thighs slick with his seed
Sancha was overcome with shame. She almost hated him. And
later, when he reached to snuff the candle flame, the sight o
his hairy armpit filled her with disgust.

Later, in the darkness, Hugh awoke and finding her, drew
her near to pet, and stroke, and tease, until she spread her
thighs for him and yielded to his strong, young body. She fel
the bump of his erection against her belly, the stinging proo
of his entry, and submitted once more to his hard rhythmic
thrusts. Rocked in his arms, she gasped with pleasure, wrapped
her slender legs about him and felt again, the sudden pumping
rapture of release.

In the afterglow of their coupling, he held her to him, un
willing for a moment to separate himself from her. "Do you
know that you are the most beautiful girl in the world," he
said to her, his breath warm on her face. "And you are mine."

For a long while after Sancha heard his deep, peaceful

breathing, she lay awake, thinking of poor, proud Richard, and
her tragic little Madame. Little Isabelle, who had suffered so
much, was not to be spared, even now. They would lie to her,
fill her wounded heart with false hopes, tell her that her Richard still lived, and use her to the last drop of her blood. The
English were all beasts, mad dogs, and the one lying beside
her was no less guilty than the rest. No matter what the cost,
Sancha vowed, she must find a way to warn her little Madame
Isabelle.

Nineteen

Rain fell on the morning, soft showers that filled the air with a grey, watery, mist. Sancha was kept a prisoner of the manor house. She spent her time in the solar, sewing, with Alyse and several of the women.

Alyse noticed that her mistress was very quiet of late, which was unlike her. She seemed to Alyse to be struggling under the weight of some terrible burden. However, when Alyse again attempted to discover the cause of her unhappiness, Sancha became evasive and quickly turned the course of the conversation.

The priest, Antonio, and a lay brother arrived near to noon. One of the young men at the stable sighted them through the mist, their mules splashing through the puddled ruts of the road. Father Antonio brought with him several documents to be signed, all concerning the finances of the prebendry, most notably, Hugh's dispensation for the postponement of his consecration. There was also the matter of his age, the fact he was below the canonical age of twenty-five. The cost of such preferments amounted to fully a third of the fief's income, and were payable to the bishop.

Watching from a window in the solar, Sancha saw her husband and the priest cross the lady garden in the rain and enter the sacristy. It all seemed very clear to her now, the priest's comings and goings, Hugh's letter. She was now convinced that the true purpose of Father Antonio's visit was to collect the damnable letter and carry it south to the usurper King

Henry's court. What a fool she had been, she thought, not to have seen it before.

Sometime later, Hugh and Father Antonio returned from the sacristy. Martin and Rumald were waiting for Hugh in the hall. Initially, Hugh had planned to ride out and view several deserted farmsteads. He had hoped to resettle the plots with his own men. But with the better part of the day past, Hugh decided to postpone his inspection.

Wine was brought out, and not long afterward a party of riders, fifteen strong and armed for battle, drew up before the manor. The noble who led them introduced himself as Jerome de Umframville, Evistone's neighbor to the west.

"There's been murder done and cattle driven off," de Umframville explained. He laid the blame on "limmer thieves," Scots from the broken clans, and explained the raid had been carried out against his farmsteads and several which he believed to be on Evistone land.

"I can but ask for your help," de Umframville said frankly. "You are not obliged, though 'tis my belief that if we are united against these wolves, we can bring them down."

The sight of horsemen in the forecourt and the loud conversation in the hall brought Sancha and her women down the stairs. Once she had been introduced to de Umframville, Sancha did not know what to make of him. He was a huge man, a bit older than her husband, with a paunchy stomach that hung over his belt, a broad mastifflike face, and a booming voice that was almost frightening. There was, however, a certain blustery bonhomie about him that made him quite impossible to dislike.

Despite the waning daylight, Hugh, Martin, the priest Antonio, and eight armed men left with de Umframville and his villeins.

Alyse was frantic with worry over Martin. Sancha tried to soothe her. "They are simply bored," she told Alyse. "They will go tear about the countryside until they are tired and hungry and then they will return. 'Tis what men do," she jested.

In all honesty, Sancha did not think them to be in any danger, and quite frankly saw their leaving as an answer to her prayers. Not only was she spared an evening of Father Antonio's dissertations, but with Hugh gone she would be able to make her plans.

All day she had debated what she might do. Realistically, she had no hope of finding her way over leagues of unfamiliar countryside. Chalford Priory might as well have been on the other side of the moon. She would surely lose her way and the roads were dangerous, particularly for a woman alone. She would be easy prey for thieves and desperate men, and of no use to her little Madame Isabelle if she lay dead in a ditch. It was a dilemma, one for which Sancha could find no solution.

Two days passed and the rain remained. In the hall the trails of damp footprints seemed never to dry, and one evening to ward off the damp Sancha had the servants light a fire in the solar's hearth. Sitting with her embroidery on her lap, Sancha considered stitch by stitch how she would take her mare, slip away, and brave the journey south, praying to God to deliver her to Chalford Priory. *I am a coward,* she thought, for she was not altogether sure she could bring herself to do it.

"Our peddler should be coming soon," Alyse offered from the bench nearby. "I've a mind to get a piece of lace from him for the baby's gown. The tiny lace what the nuns make at that priory."

Sancha's hand, armed with the needle, came to an abrupt halt. She looked up with an expression of astoundment. "Was it not Chalford Priory?"

Alyse nodded, rapidly piercing the material with her needle and leaving a wake of neatly chained stitches. "Aye, that's what its called, where the nuns keep dogs and cats."

A murmur of "Ayes" rippled through the solar as several of the women spoke up in agreement. And Gusti, sewing the hem of a dorser, added smartly, "A pet squirrel, too, if you believe the like!"

While the women talked on of this and that, Sancha said a silent prayer of thanks. Surely it was divine intervention that had revealed the peddler to her. He was her only hope. She would send a missive, a letter to Madame. She was certain the peddler could be bribed, but then recalled that she had spent her coins. She did, however, possess some jewelry, brooches mostly, and earrings.

Sancha rose early the next morning. The rain had ended, but a milky white fog had drifted in from the meadows and hollows, shrouding everything with a dull stillness. During the night she had lain awake deciding how she would steal into the sacristy during the morning devotions and write the missive.

Only Morah, Gusti, and a few children moved about the kitchen. Sancha had fetched herself an oatcake and a cup of cider and was watching out the window. Lights appeared in the chapel, but the fog was so thick, she could see little else. While she waited, she composed the letter in her mind. She had already done so at least a dozen times, trying to fit all she must say into but a few words. Even so, she was not satisfied with her efforts. Finally, she saw a light appear in the sacristy.

Three more women straggled into the kitchen, among them, Jenn. She and Gusti were again on speaking terms, but only barely. That morning Jenn hardly spoke at all, except to complain that she was sick with cramping. " 'Tis the curse," she moaned, and went and stood by the oven.

Her words reminded Sancha that her own flux was weeks overdue. It was something she did not want to think about, not then, and she pushed it from her mind.

At last, the throaty iron summons of the bells pierced the foggy morning. Sancha waited, giving the brothers time to assemble in the chapel. Then, casually, she went through the hall, down the passageway, crossed the lady garden and slipped into the sacristy. Save for the faint, ethereal, chanting voices from the chapel, a deathly silence filled the chamber. She lit a candle from the wall sconce and set at once to writing. Every sound had a startling tonality; even the scratching of the stylus upon the paper sounded shockingly loud to her ears.

MOST GRACIOUS AND NOBLE MADAME,

I commend myself to you and beg your kind indulgence. I must write in great haste and have not time to write near as much as I might say to you were I in your presence.

I pray you be warned of Henry Bolingbroke and his treacherous countrymen. They who have so foully murdered their true sovereign, our most beloved King Richard, shall receive no forgiveness in this world nor in the hereafter.

I beg you also do not place your faith in the tidings carried to you by those in league with the earl of Northumberland. For these faithless men are doubly evil to offer your grieving heart hope when none exists. This I know to be cruelly true, and would so willingly give witness before our Saviour.

Madame, you are ever in my prayers. I share your sorrows, and if I might have had my will, I should have come to you. Truly I shall not know heart's ease until I hear of your deliverance from this barbarous realm.

May the Holy Trinity hold you in their keeping. Be consoled that I am well and comfortably kept at Evistone Abbey on this second Monday after St. Aubin's Day.

With deepest affection, your devoted demoiselle, your ever faithful, Sancha.

Sunshine and fair, breezy skies returned the following day. Sancha was in the lady garden clipping sprigs of thyme, when she heard children playing atop the earthen walls shout that the men were returning. The news, carried by the nimble-footed boys, spread throughout the complex of buildings and stables long before the line of riders came into full view.

Sancha had hoped her husband would not return before the peddler came. Her plans were dashed. Many of the men had already dismounted by the time Sancha came to the lady garden's gate.

She was horrified to see two humped bundles, dead men, wrapped in blankets and lashed over the backs of their horses. She darted into the forecourt, assailed by a host of contradictory emotions, at once wishing Hugh Canby dead and at the same time certain she would die of a broken heart if it were true. Dodging horses and threading her way through the crowd, she searched frantically.

When she found Hugh, he was unshaven, stiff-legged, and limping from too many days spent in the saddle. Spattered with mud, he grabbed her and hugged her to him. There were so many people talking she could not hear what he said to her.

He lifted her off her feet and held her to him for a long moment, his whiskers scratching her ear. People milled all around them.

Alyse, with tears in her eyes, had found Martin and lunged into his arms. Rumald, enlisting the aid of Donel and Jerem, began to unload the bodies, and Father Antonio was speaking with Brother Malcolm and Brother Francis.

Standing in the sunshine, Sancha brushed back the hair that had escaped from her braids, and waited as Hugh gave instructions concerning the dead men.

Horses, heads drooping and looking as weary as the men, were led toward the stable.

Time and again Hugh was detained, talking with this man and that. Finally, he steered Sancha through the press of men and women toward the manor house.

His leather jacque smelled of sweat and horses and smoky fires, and his face looked drawn, somehow older. Once in the hall, he took off his sword and belt, laid them on the table, and eased himself down upon the bench. "Fetch me a cup of wine," he told her. When Sancha brought it to him, he caught her hand and pressed her fingers to his lips. "I'm glad to be home," he told her.

While he savored the wine he recounted some of what had happened, not the particulars. Those she overheard later in grisly vignettes, as the exhausted men trooped into the hall and crowded in at the table.

Hugh's attention was soon drawn elsewhere, and seeing an opportunity, Sancha edged away from the tempest of voices. She thought again of the peddler, guiltily, and hoped he would not choose to arrive that day.

There was more confusion in the kitchen, where she found a servingwoman in tears and Morah and the others attempting to console her. Sancha learned that the sobbing woman and one of the men killed had been living together.

Both of the dead men had come north with Hugh to make a new life for themselves. Sancha was touched by the bitter irony of it, by the poor woman's tears and her words, which were broken by sobs. Sancha spoke to the woman, a few words of sympathy, and discovered that she was the mother of the little dark-eyed girl whose clothing had caught fire that day in the kitchen. At least, Sancha thought, she would still have the child to comfort her.

As Sancha stood there holding the woman's hand, Jenn and Gusti brushed past on their way to the hall with ewers of wine. After a moment Sancha followed them. She met Alyse in the short passageway between the hall and kitchen, and taking her aside, said softly, "I have asked them to bring out bread and cheese, and whatever meat there is," and then, lowering her voice still further, mentioned the poor woman crying.

"I'll see they do," Alyse promised, and, giving her mistress's cool hand a squeeze, continued on her way.

Not finding Hugh in the hall, Sancha climbed the stairs to the solar. There at last she discovered him, sleeping soundly, sprawled on the bed, his mouth half-open like a child's. He had not even removed his boots and one silver spur was tangled in the coverlet.

It was late evening before a proper meal was served, and later still before Hugh and the men had their baths. Alyse was helping Sancha to undress when Hugh came into the bedchamber, walking on stockinged feet and carrying his boots.

The scent of soap followed him, his damp hair was slicked back, and his clean clothing looked as if he had thrown it on a moment before, and carelessly, for his open shirt billowed out behind him as he walked.

He set his boots by the bed, jesting that he now smelled sweet as a rose at Maytime, and teased Alyse good-naturedly about Martin having holes in his socks.

Sancha watched his reflected image in the mirror as he stripped off his shirt and slung it over the tall chest beside the bed. She sensed Alyse's eagerness to be gone. Martin was surely waiting for her. "I will finish combing my hair," she told Alyse, taking the comb from her hand. Sancha heard the sound of the door as it closed and in the mirror saw her husband cross the room.

"You are quiet this evening. What is the matter?" Hugh asked, coming to where she sat and taking the weight of her dark hair in his hands. He loved the feel of it, and aimlessly twined it, folded it, buried his fingers in its cool depths.

Sancha looked up swiftly, wide-eyed, her well-guarded secret glittering in the depths of her dark eyes. "Nothing."

Blade grey and inquisitive, his eyes met hers, lifting at the corners as he smiled. "Come to bed," he coaxed.

"I must change into my night shift," she flustered, her dark glance fleeing in all directions as she leapt up in nervous energy.

He moved to block her way, his hands already drawing her into his arms.

"I cannot go to bed in my camisa." What else was there for her to say?

"No," he said in total agreement, bringing his mouth down

on hers, licking his tongue across her lips, and pressing inside while his marauding hands stroked the sweet curves of her body.

It shamed Sancha to know how easily his lips filled her with desire. How quickly the feel of his hard young body kindled a hot restlessness between her thighs. All evening she had dreaded the thought of lying with him, but now, enfolded in his arms and heated by his touch, she did not even pause to wonder at the subtle insidiousness of love, only slid her arms around his neck and rubbed against him.

He made a low sound deep in chest, and wrenched his lips from hers to gasp for breath. "You cannot know how much I want you." The words gusted from his mouth. "I have thought of you for days, of you and nothing else." Nuzzling her, breathing in the fragrance of her long hair, Hugh brushed his lips over her over her jaw, the soft, warm flesh of her throat, while his hands tenderly ravished her, slipped the ties of her camisa and let it fall about her feet with a silken whisper.

His eyes drank in her nakedness, and with his hands on her slim waist, he held her a little apart from him, admiring the suppleness of her slender body, the firm pink-nippled breasts, and that most intriguing part of her, dark as a stain. "Sometimes when I first wake," he said to her, "I lie there watching you. I cannot believe that you are really mine, mine to love forever."

"I will always be yours," she promised, her lips touching his. It was not a lie, she thought, for in spite of everything, all that he was—spy, traitor—he had been her first true love, and would always be. Even now, knowing the truth, she was his to do with as he liked.

She went with him eagerly, stepped from the circle of crumpled silk, and let him lead her off to bed and lay her down. Her nipples slid from his lips, wet and glistening. And when he pushed her thighs apart and lapped her with his head between her legs, she arched up in ecstasy, begging him to come to her. He had not time to shed his hosen, nor did it matter.

He knew he would not last, his seed was spilling even as he thrust inside her.

Afterward, lying on the bed, he wrestled his way free of the clinging hosen and tossed them at the chest. Rolling onto his side, he took her in his arms and settled back with her, gently arranging her silky mass of tangled hair, cuddling her, satisfied for a time just to feel her bare flesh touching his.

In a quiet voice, he told her finally of the raid, what he had seen, and the outlaws' deadly ambush. "I did not fear losing my life half so much as the thought of losing you."

As he murmured to her in the dark, his hand stroked first one, and then the other of her small, round breasts. White and tender, they were like a lure to him, and eventually he leaned to suckle them, to tease out the rosy nipples.

In the shadowy candlelight they came together to love again. She clung to him, completely swallowed up by his strength, his scent, the feel of him boring into her. He wooed her slowly this time, with agonizing patience. "I will love you all my life," he said to her, before his words were lost to silent panting labor and the sudden jarring blaze of passion that they shared.

Beyond the shuttered window the sky was turning light. Sancha awoke in Hugh's arms. In his sleep, his grip had loosened, but his muscular arm still lay across her waist. Moving stealthily she lifted the deadweight of his arm and slid from beneath it.

She grabbed her clothing and hurriedly, silently dressed. Normally she did not rise so early, but she feared if she remained, he would awaken and keep her abed. Her first movements told her that she was tender from his lovemaking. She did not think she could tolerate any more amour that morning. There was also the matter of the peddler. She had no notion when he would make his appearance, but knew she must remain vigilant if her plan was to be successful.

Father Antonio departed for Hexham. Oddly, he had little

to say. It was as if the fierce brutality of their battle with the outlaws had left him speechless, unprepared in the face of death, the face of God. He and the lay brother trotted from the forecourt on their mules just as the summons bell rang for the afternoon devotions.

Several hours earlier, Sancha had observed Father Antonio and Hugh walking through the dewy grass of the orchard, engaged in a serious discussion. At least, it seemed so. She could not hear their words from where she toiled over her roses in the lady garden. It was obvious to Sancha that they had not wished to be overheard, for several times they walked to the boundary of the orchard, faced about, and walked back again.

The full moon brought the beginning of what Morah called "gerst monath," so called for it was then the barley and oats were harvested. The old woman delighted in repeating such kernels of wisdom, particularly to her young foreign mistress. The more mysterious and malignant the tale, the more it was to Morah's liking, and it was with particular relish that she announced to her dark-eyed French mistress, " 'Tis the time of the year when wells dry up, an' dogs go mad, and the bridges all break down!"

The tragedy of the two men's deaths was quite enough for Sancha. Owing to the lack of coffins, they had yet to be buried. It was not until the third day after they had been brought back across their horses that they were finally laid to rest.

The moon, pale as a ghost, still wandered above as the people of the manor gathered in the chapel.

Brother Malcolm said the solemn mass for the dead, and the bells tolled slowly in passing. As the pallbearers assembled, wisps of blue smoke from the still-smoldering candles spiraled toward the vaulted ceiling. Sancha stood beside her husband at the fore of the chapel. The two coffins, hastily made and unstained, sat nearby, and the pungent odor of decay and the resiny scent of the wood blended with that of candle smoke and the tarry spice of incense.

The combined stench made Sancha dizzy, half-nauseous, and she longed to be outside in the fresh air.

The pallbearers, straining with their burden through the misty morning, halted, setting the coffins down twice to rest their arms on the journey to the grave plot. Eventually, the line of mourners followed the coffins through the lych-gate and to the mounds of upturned earth.

Brother Malcolm said the Latin prayers above the sound of women's weeping. As the mourners turned to leave, the sound of soil thudding onto the coffins echoed up the path.

Scarcely had the routine of the day resumed when word of the peddler's coming was carried to the kitchen, where the women were preparing apples to dry. Sancha and Alyse, for lack of anything else to do, had been helping, carving apples and eating their fill. The children's excited cries brought an end to all work in the kitchen and a mass exodus began.

The news that Sancha had waited for so impatiently now threw her into a panic. Her careful plans seemed to her suddenly foolish and useless. How would she manage to speak to the peddler alone, prevail upon him to accept her bribe and carry the letter to the priory? In her imaginings everything had proceeded in perfect accordance, but in the face of stark reality she was less sure of herself, frightened, and disoriented.

"Come with us," Alyse called to her mistress from the garth. "Yes, do come along," several of the other women added.

"No, not today," Sancha replied, gathering the apple peels from her apron. Once the women and skirmishing children had trooped down through the garth, Sancha wiped her stained hands on her apron, removed it, tossed it on the table, and hurried off to her bedchamber.

In the dimness of the shuttered room, she took out her little jewel casket and dumped the contents on the bed. Then she retrieved the letter from where she had wedged it at the bottom of the rectangular, wooden casket. Quickly she plucked up the opal and sapphire brooch, her most valuable piece of jewelry, and secreted it and the letter in the pocket of her skirt. *Now,* she thought, *I must manage to speak to him alone.*

Thankfully, Hugh had gone off with Martin and Rumald to oversee the grain harvest. She assumed they would be gone the entire day, and heartened by the thought, hurried down the stairs.

Cautious as a cat, she made her way from the manor house. The circumventous route she had chosen led through a fallow field, lush with summer vegetation, past a line of trees, and eventually to an islet of woods near the grave plot.

Grasshoppers leapt before her and the sound of serenading insects sounded from the sun-baked grass. Sancha halted at the edge of the trees. From where she stood she could see the peddler's sorrel mare contentedly cropping grass, her sparse tail switching at flies.

Sancha waited, not daring to step away from the concealing shadows of the woods. Mumbling to herself, she went over again for the one hundredth time the words she would say to the awful little man with the monkey. Time passed. Beneath the trees it was shaded, though the day was hot and the still air, warm. Even so Sancha felt chilled. She wrapped her arms around herself and watched the path, frowning into the white glare.

An hour or longer passed before she saw his garish-feathered hat bobbing over the crest of the knoll. Gradually, his head and shoulders appeared, and he came skimming along in his strange gait with the monkey perched on his shoulder.

When she judged him near enough, she raised a hand and waved to him. At first he did not see her, but when she waved again, she saw his head go up in recognition.

The peddler advanced toward her, and with a hand tipped his feathered hat. "The sweet Virgin's blessings on you, my lady. Would you be interested to buy some fine lace or some needles?" From under the monstrous hat his piercing black eyes fixed on her face with a queer, staring look.

"No," Sancha said, her voice high and faint. She felt more unsure of herself with every passing moment.

"Mayhap a charm to secure your young lord's fidelity?"

Sancha shook her head.

"Ah, then 'tis the fine collar you've decided for, for your pretty white kit?"

"No, nothing. I—" she stammered, and began anew. "I recall that you spoke of Chalford Priory, of the nuns?"

He nodded, silent.

"You will be returning to Chalford soon?"

"Aye, I make my rounds, I do."

"Then I wish for you to carry a message for me." The words stumbled from her lips. "I will pay you."

"A message, my lady?" The monkey scampered down from his shoulder and began to chatter, making a high-pitched chirruping sound.

Sancha nodded. "Yes." And raising her voice to speak above the racket, she said, "I am told that King Richard's queen, Isabelle of France, is within the priory's walls. My words are for her alone; no other's eyes must see the message."

"A queen, you say? Well now, that may not be so simple. What have you to offer?"

Fumbling through the pocket of her skirt, Sancha found the brooch and held it out to him. In the harsh light of day it did not look so grand.

Narrowing his eyes, the peddler turned the heart-shaped brooch over in his callused hands. " 'Tis a nice piece," he muttered. "But I will need something more if I am to bribe a nun to carry the missive to your queen. They'd not be letting a poor peddler near a queen, not even near the likes of her what's not a queen anymore."

Sancha's eyes flashed with offense, but she held her tongue. To her, Madame would always be a queen. "I have nothing more to offer," she told him.

The monkey's chirruping grew to a deafening howl. "A pox on you, you filthy beast!" the peddler swore, kicking at the little ape and giving the tether a vicious jerk. The monkey lurched backward, growled, but at least quit howling. "Well now, my lady," the man said, coming nearer, "I see you have on your lovely hand a ruby of some value. Now that, together with the brooch, well that I would accept and gladly carry your message to Chalford."

Sancha's gaze fell to the ruby ring winking in the sunlight. It was her wedding ring. Sounds and voices from the garth reached her ears. She must decide and quickly. There was, she thought, a strange irony about it. How just that a traitor's ring should be the means by which to warn her little queen. Without a twinge of regret, she twisted the ring from her finger and put it in the peddler's callused hand. "No one but the queen must see the words," Sancha warned him, and made him swear to it, before she placed the missive in his hand.

In backward glances from along the path, Sancha watched the peddler lead his horse along the tumbled wall and, after a bit, ride off. On she hurried, head down, her rippling skirts cutting a swath through the tall grass.

The jingle and chink of harness and the brusque snort of a horse brought her head up with a jolt. She whirled about, her startled eyes focusing on a black horse halted amid the trees. It was Chewbit, and with her husband in the saddle! She gaped openmouthed, paralyzed with guilt.

"Where have you been?" Hugh called, inquisitive. Ducking his head and raising an arm to shield his face, he moved the horse from beneath the trees.

Sancha's tongue felt as if it had turned to stone. "My kitten," she explained, saying the first thought that came into her mind. She forced her lips into a smile. "I was looking for her. I could not find her this morning." She glanced up to him, all the while praying that he would not notice the ring was missing, notice her finger which was now marked by a distinct pale band. Her thoughts tumbled wildly. If he mentioned its absence, she would tell him she had taken it off to work in the flowers, or that she had lost it. Her heart sank when she saw him dismount.

"I'll walk along with you," he offered, leading the horse. "You shouldn't wander so far from the house alone," he reproached her, though gently and with a smile. "There are all manner of louts roaming the countryside."

"Yes," she conceded. And recalling that he had gone to check on the grain harvest, asked, "Why have you returned? I did not expect you until evening."

"I forgot my ledger, left it in the sacristy, most likely." As they walked, he spoke candidly to her about his intention to go to a three-field system and also mentioned a strip of lowland pasture he planned to open up for plowing in the spring. He was fond of discussing his thoughts with her, his decisions, as if he were always courting her approval.

In her nervousness Sancha hardly listened to his talk of fields, and seeds, and ways to improve the grain harvest. It was only with great effort that she managed to reply at all. Her foremost thought was to escape into the manor house.

Passing through the colonnade of towering yews, they approached the abbey. In the rear of the building, Hugh tethered Chewbit to a bush and loosened the girth. There was a clump of daisies blooming nearby. He picked a single flower and offered it to Sancha. "In lieu of my heart," he told her, "which you already possess."

His smile was disarming, as was the hint of mischief in his humorous grey eyes, but Sancha, suffocated with guilt, could think only of escape. She smiled, for a brief moment touched by his gallantry, then turned to go.

Hugh, moved by a vague, voiceless desire to touch her, kiss her, caught her wrist. "Come into the sacristy with me."

"Why?" Her lashes fluttered. She balked, intent on keeping her left hand out of sight.

His smile deepened. "Only to please me."

"But I must return," she insisted. "The apples are being

prepared." And hoping to at last effect her escape, quickly invented several additional reasons. It was all to no avail.

Hugh opened the door and followed her inside, into the chamber's cool, dim, mustiness. The mystical echoing chant of the brethren at their devotions drifted from the chapel. Hugh walked to the desk and picked up the small, leather-bound book. "You see, here it is," he said, stowing it in the inside pocket of his open jacque.

Sancha breathed an inward sigh of relief. He had found the ledger; hopefully, now he would leave. She took a step away from the table. He caught her hand, her left hand, the hand without the daisy—the hand without the ring! She felt suddenly giddy. She dropped the daisy, nearly frantic.

But he did not notice the ring's absence, only lifted her hand to his lips and pressed a kiss to her fingertips. "You are very tempting," he said, drawing her near, and in the same breath, whispering, "I may die of desire before tonight."

The warm tickle of his breath against her ear, his casual possessive touch, sent an all too familiar sensation coursing through her body. A quick flush came to her cheeks. "Surely not," she said clumsily, half-smiling, unprepared for his kiss, the clinging touch of his lips, cool and moist on hers.

She felt scandalized by his boldness. That he would kiss her there within the abbey's walls. She tried vainly to protest, but her parted lips merely provided an open invitation for his tongue to brazenly slip inside and twine about hers.

She squirmed against him, unable to halt his hands, which smoothed upward, encircling the swell of her breasts, massaging them through the material of her bodice. Emerging breathless from his kiss, she tried to shove his hands away.

"Undo your laces," he whispered, trailing his lips over her cheek, which shone through the sheen of perspiration red as an apple.

"We are in a holy place!" she scolded hotly. She was both indignant and angry, and was about to tell him how sinful he was, when she felt his hands abandon her breasts and begin to loosen the ties of her kirtle. Panic jarred through her, she pushed against his chest. "Stop it! Hugh! No!" she said in a loud whisper. And for lack of anything else with which to threaten him, blurted out, "You will go to hell!"

He buried his face in her throat, kissing her, sucking in her soft flesh. "I have a dispensation," he mumbled, his voice thick, slurred with amusement. Ignoring her protests, he slid his hand through the open laces of her kirtle and caressed a soft, pale breast, squeezing, tweaking the hardened nipple between his fingers.

Sancha gasped, shaken by desire and shame. "Brother Malcolm, one of the others, they will find us together!" she pleaded, mortified, becoming more frantic as she felt the bodice of her kirtle slide from her shoulders. The cool air touched the heated skin of her bared breasts, sending a shiver of goose-flesh over her arms. "Do you not hear! They will find us!"

"No," he breathed. "They are praying, for wicked men like me." His moist lips swept down her throat, planting a fiery trail of kisses, claiming a rosy nipple, licking it, drawing it into his mouth.

Sancha went weak with desire, a flood of warmth swirled through her. Only the sight of his hands gathering up her skirt roused her, and she hissed, "No!" begging him to release her. His reply was to stop her mouth with an indecent kiss, and continue on with his sweet ravishment. She pushed against him, wiggling to free herself, and the little that remained of her dignity.

But he simply moved closer, making her aware of the strength and heat of his body, backing her against the edge of the table, gathering up her skirt, wadding it behind her, and running his hand up the inside of her thigh.

The edge of the table bit into her lower back, and with her arms trapped against him, she was powerless to keep his hand from finding its way into her camisa. Once he had, the sensuous caress of his finger drawn back and forth made her gasp with pleasure. She was torn between the aching throb deep in her belly and the fear of discovery.

"A little sin is good for our souls," he whispered hoarsely, sliding a finger inside her, probing the velvety warmth and feeling her body yield to his touch.

Sancha moaned and, spreading her legs, pushed toward his hand. The driving motion of his finger flamed through her like wildfire. A soft mewing sound came from deep in her throat, and when he stepped back to unloose the ties of his hosen, she nearly fell against him.

Hugh reached out a hand to steady her. A continual shudder ran through his body. With trembling fingers he tugged at the ties of his hosen. At last freed from the bind of his clothing, his erection bobbed up between them, thick and moist with desire. He moved against her, taking her hand and placing her fingers around its girth, directing her.

She was shivering with anticipation, beyond refusing him, and shamelessly she tried to find a way to satisfy the raging need building inside her. It required both her hands, one to pull her camisa aside, the other working feverishly to end her agony.

His hot whispers rasped against her ear. The feel of his damp flesh, the moist reddened knob working between her legs, left her dizzy with emotion.

Finally, in a fury of frustration Hugh grasped her by the waist and lifted her onto the table, jarring her teeth together. He shoved her skirt aside and pushed between her legs. Their fingers bumped and tangled in their frenzied haste to join themselves. After a moment of breathless panting, Hugh launched himself full into her. She cried out, digging her fingers into the cool leather shoulders of his jacque.

Her sensual animal sound, surprisingly loud, startled him. He brought his mouth down hard on hers, sucking in her lips, sending his tongue to plumb the depths of her silken mouth, attempting to forestall the ever-escalating spiral of his passion.

With a viselike grip he clasped her hips and dragged her forward to fit against him.

Sancha arched toward him, meeting each demanding stroke, teetering on the edge of the table, and sobbing with pleasure into his mouth as his thrusts quickened, harder, faster.

All at once he wrenched his lips from hers, whispered her name, urging her on in explosive gasps that pounded against her ear. She clung to him, hugging her face to his chest, his damp linen shirt, while the edge of his leather jacque slapped against her ear. He stretched her, filled her. Nothing mattered to her now, only the feel of him deep inside her and the exquisite, burning pleasure that she felt. She was lost to everything but the impact of his sudden furious pumping and the coming storm of her passion. Locked in his grip, she felt the spurting shudder of his release, and then her own rippling waves of passion.

The grating groan of the abbey's iron bells drowned out their mingled cries of release.

No one came to disturb them, not even in the moments of further affection, of whispered endearments and kisses. No one saw Hugh lift her from the table, or sacrifice a pristine sheet of carefully trimmed, soft linen paper for her needs. He had time to tie the laces of her bodice, and to brush the creases from her skirts. Still, no one came, though shortly after the bells had sounded they heard the shuffle of feet and murmur of voices from the antechamber as the brethren exchanged their robes.

Hugh and Sancha left as they had come, through the dismal room, now empty, with its depressing smell of incense and unwashed bodies.

After the coolness of the abbey's walls, the heat met Sancha like a blast from an oven. Her footsteps faltered, a cold prickling chill washed over her, and inside her ears a loud metallic roaring made her deaf.

The ground seemed to sway beneath her. She raised her head and in the blaze of sunlight, saw the black horse, the glittering leaves as through a murky glass, all wavering strangely beneath a putrid-colored sky.

Hugh caught her as she fell and carried her limp as a rag to a spot of shade. When she regained herself, she was supported in his arms. "Are you better?" he asked, sharp-eyed with concern.

"Yes, I don't know what came over me, the heat perhaps."

"Are you certain? Would you like me to carry you back into the abbey?"

"No," she said, determinedly. "I am fine."

"You do not look to be." Hugh's eyes dwelt on her. He drew a hand across her forehead, and as her color returned he became gradually reassured. Deciding after all that it was the heat, he began gently to tease her. "Then it is settled. After this, you may have only half a measure."

Sancha sent him a look quick as a sting. Pale and offended, she watched from the shade as he, still chuckling, tightened Chewbit's girth. He would not allow her to walk back to the manor house, and set her on horse's back. Outside the kitchen door he lifted her down, and in parting squeezed her hand, the hand now without his ring. Then he gathered up his reins, swung into the saddle, and cantered off to view the harvest.

Sancha went into the kitchen, to Alyse and the others. Even Alyse did not notice that the ruby ring was missing from her mistress's finger.

Twenty

Days later and many leagues east, banners fluttered atop the towers of Warkworth Castle. Below its massive walls, the prosperous market town of the same name, with its torturous streets, thick walls, and narrow, crowding houses, bustled with industry.

There was a chill in the air that evening, though it was not the brisk weather that hastened Piers Exton's stride down the close, winding street which housed butcher shops, poulterers, and fishmongers. Rather, it was the raker's cart, creaking along the street behind him. Knife-thin and lanky, Exton set a careful course, avoiding the offal that lay rotting and stinking, in the gully that ran through the center of the street. He glanced back with a look of alarm and quickened his steps.

The cart, steadily gaining ground, overflowed with garbage, discarded straw from homes and stables, feathers from the poulterers, and refuse of every sort. Dressed as he was in elegant black velvets, Exton had no wish to run afoul of the chaff and feathers that swirled off the rear of the raker's cart like a snowstorm.

At the street's end, he darted into the square occupied by the wool hall, where weavers, fullers, dyers, and wool merchants plied their trades. Exton hurried past the wool hall, closed at that hour, and continued on toward his lodgings, a tavern at the end of the square. By name, it was called the Trumpet, and was a favorite of the wool guild's members.

Most days Exton spent a brief time at the wool hall, rubbing elbows with buyers from the south and foreigners with their letters of orders. Occasionally, he even transacted a deal. He preferred, however, the atmosphere and milling crowds of the Trumpet, where deals of all sorts were made with none the wiser.

The doors of the tavern stood open in the autumn evening. A good many people loitered before the building, soldiers and prostitutes mostly. Exton pushed his way through the crowd and into the noise of the tavern's main hall. He had only begun to work his way through the crowd when he was met by his assistant, Gui Lantin.

A Gascon by birth, Gui, not yet twenty, was attired in equal elegance. He was a handsome youth, sturdy, though not particularly tall, whose wavy dark hair and heavy-lidded eyes lent him the suave look of a troubadour.

"Morris is here," the young Gui said, pronouncing it "Maurice," with a decided French accent.

"He's taken his sweet time," Exton remarked, regarding the young man with a momentary look of intimacy, as a man might his lover.

Gui returned the smile, and said, "He claims to have brought you something special." Raking the room with his dark gaze, Gui searched out the man dressed as a peddler. "There," he exclaimed, catching sight of the monkey as it jigged atop a table occupied by a group of drunken merchants.

"Go and fetch him," Exton directed, before continuing on. Music blared and there was a constant roar of loud talk and laughter. Making his way past the entrance to a room where a number of dice games were in progress, Exton took a seat at a smaller, less crowded table deep in a shadowy corner, where the only light was from the blazing hearth. He ordered an ale.

Exton's ale reached the table as Gui returned with Morris, carrying the monkey on his arm. "Well?" Exton said. "Gui tells me you have a boon for me?"

Morris shooed the monkey onto his shoulder and dropped

the handful of coins he had cadged from the merchants into his purse. "A boon or mayhap a bane. I've brought the young lord's letter, an' I got gossip that'll set your ears afire. An' then, I've something here you might find more interesting than all the rest." Pushing the monkey away from the table with his arm, he drew a missive from his padded doublet.

Exton cocked an eyebrow and reached out for the letter with its red wax seal. "What's this?"

" 'Twas given me by the young lord's lady."

"From Evistone?" Exton questioned, not believing him. "She's mad as a hare!"

"Not the one I spoke to. She was sane as you or me. Lively little thing, an' pretty as a pearl button. She wanted me to carry the message to Chalford and give it to Richard's queen. She gave me this as a bribe," he said, drawing an object from the pouch at his waist, and after a dramatic pause, laid the ruby ring on the table.

Exton thoughtfully turned the ruby ring in his fingers, then tucked it inside his doublet. Taking a silver-hafted knife from his belt, he slit the letter's wax seal and leaned toward the hearth, angling the letter so he might read it.

Gui Lantin watched Exton's face expectantly. Glancing back to the table, he saw the monkey was about to dip its paw in his wine tankard. He batted at the beast and snatched up the tankard. Morris laughed, and the monkey scrabbled away down the bench, leaping onto the floor, where it began picking through the rushes. Gui swore at Morris and the monkey in French, and shifting his attention back to Exton, noted his stony expression. "Something is wrong?"

Exton made no reply, only leaned down to the hearth, touched the letter to the flames, and, slowly turning it, let it fall. As he stood watching the paper curl and blacken, he took a small pouch from his belt. It jangled with coins, and he dropped it onto the table. "There is your money," Exton said, addressing Morris, as he took his seat once more. "I will not be needing you for a while."

"Don't you want the young lord's letter?"

"Yes, of course, hand it here." Exton extended his hand. "You can go now."

"What about the rest of what I heard?"

"Later."

"Will you be having more work for me, then?"

"Yes, later. Now go."

When Morris, with his feathered hat and the monkey on his shoulder, had disappeared into the crowd, Exton exclaimed, "I wanted to put an end to the nosy little bitch that night. Damn Swynford! This time he will have no say in the matter."

"Shall I take the information south tomorrow?" Gui inquired, indicating Hugh Canby's letter.

"No, I have something far more important for you to do. Within the week Northumberland's earls will be arriving to pay fealty. Our young lord Evistone will be present, that is a certainty. We can only hope he will have brought his wife with him. If not, you will be journeying to Evistone."

"And if she accompanies him?"

"That is what we are going to discuss."

"What about the young lord's letter?"

"Burn it."

Sunlight poured into the bedchamber through the open shutters. Outside the sky was tinted the pale, mild blue of a September morning. On the bed Sancha sat cross-legged in her night shift, clasping handfuls of her luxuriant hair and mindlessly combing, preening the very ends. She paused, and looked up at her husband, naked to the waist and shaving the stubble from his jaw.

He was talking to her, but she was not listening. At times, she was stunned by the beauty of his lean, muscular body. It was, she decided, the sort of beauty one admired in a sleek, powerful beast. But the thought was only a fleeting one, come too soon, perhaps, after the tormented pleasure of their lovemaking. Too soon after she had experienced his tender kisses, his hard-muscled weight, his hands on her hips fitting her to him, the driving cadence of his loins, the final stretching thrust, and the feel of him pumping life deep inside her.

Since the day in the abbey when she had seen and heard proof of his treachery, her feelings for him wavered constantly from hate to love, from feeling misused, soiled by his touch, to feeling secure and precious in his arms. It was a terrible knowledge, to know he had betrayed her youthful trust, worse still, to feel at once love and hate, and both so profoundly.

He stood there gazing at her with the razor in his hand. "You look as though you are suffering. What is the matter?"

Startled, Sancha raised her head. She had not heard him cross the room, silent as a poacher. "Nothing," she said, blushing under his smoke grey gaze.

"Yes. I can tell."

"How do you mean?" Her eyes widened.

"You have that look. Your eyes get big and your lips droop." He pulled a comic face, thrusting out his lower lip.

"No." She glanced away, escaping the gimlet eyes.

"Yes," he concluded, "but you look pretty when you do it." He went back to finish shaving. From across the room, he noted, "You weren't listening to what I said, were you?"

"Of course."

He turned his head to her. "What did I say?"

"I cannot remember all of it."

"If you had been listening," he said, gazing into the mirror and angling his hand, "you would have heard me say we will be journeying to Warkworth with de Umframville and his kin. You'll have his wife and several of her sisters to ride with."

"I would rather Alyse was able to come with me."

"Gusti will do as well."

"Did Donel beg you choose her for my servingwoman?"

"No. Choose Jenn, if you like."

"No," she mumbled, taking up a handful of hair and running the comb through it. Her thoughts were already far away, wondering if the peddler had reached Chalford, and, desperately, if Madame had received her letter.

She felt the bed give under his weight. She had been expecting him to come to her again, even wanting him.

Hugh caught her hand, took the comb away. "You will wear out your hair combing it."

She turned her dark eyes on him. "Will you grow tired of me?" she asked, without a hint of warning.

He laughed. "Before or after I wear you out?" And grinning, he lifted her hand and planted a kiss on her palm. "I don't think there is hope of either happening." He paused, and, turning her hand in his, asked, "Where is your ring?"

"Safe away in my jewel casket," she lied, amazed at how convincing she sounded, so that she went further, adding, "I feared I would lose it among the flowers. It sometimes turns on my finger."

"Wear it when we leave for Warkworth. I would want all the men to know that you are mine."

"Yes, of course."

In the moments before dawn, when all objects appeared deepest blue, blurred and dewy, the forecourt at Evistone churned with activity. Horses and mules, balking and stomping, were hastily hitched to carts; servingwomen dashed about screeching to one another as last-minute chores were attended to. Men shouted and cursed and dogs barked, while through the gauzy mist the riding horses, high-spirited in the cool air, were led from the stables. The first hint of daylight glowed above the horizon when Hugh, Sancha, their servants, and carts loaded with sacks of wool, trundled from the forecourt to join the de Umframville cavalcade for the trek to Warkworth.

By afternoon it was quite warm and Sancha, in her finest velvet travel attire, a gown with cape and hood of deepest russet edged with gold-and-silver braid and matching velvet coif, suffered from the heat. In front and behind her charettes, carts, and tumbrels of all sizes moved in the same direction. Ladies and men on horseback rode on either side.

Baron de Umframville's brother, who resembled him greatly, was clad in yellow-and-green velvets, and looked to Sancha more like a jongleur than a nobleman. Hugh, in black and grey, and wearing a black velvet bag cap pinned with a silver brooch, rode in the midst of the de Umframville men. While Sancha, riding her mare, kept company with the prosperously attired and well-satisfied de Umframville women.

Two of the older women had been members of Richard's court during the time of his childless first marriage to Anne of Bohemia. "She was plain in face and in dress, but the kindness of her heart was rare indeed," the eldest de Umframville stated, her double chin aquiver.

"I wondered of his second marriage," a younger, thinner sister commented from atop a grey palfrey. "He could not have been thinking of an heir." She clicked her tongue. "To marry a fickle child."

Sancha wanted so badly to speak up in defense of her little Madame, to tell them that Isabelle had loved Richard with all her child's heart. But Hugh had forbidden her to speak of it. "The past can only cause you harm," he had told her, and made her promise on the blood of her Redeemer to say nothing. Though she had sulked at the time, she kept her vow now and said not a word on the subject. She listened, only occasionally making a pleasant comment on some triviality and smiling.

Angele, her honey-colored mare, her pet, behaved beautifully among the unfamiliar horses, and Sancha was free to view the distant hills, now touched with shades of red and bronze and yellow. As the day drew out the dusty road passed heathered heaths, downland pastures, and islands of cultivated fields where the stubble of the newly reaped rye against the backdrop of the dark woods was burnished and golden as her husband's fair hair.

At evening, when the shadows at the base of the hills turned to purple, de Umframville called a halt to the procession, and settled the company on the skirts of a woods. Jewel-bright, parti-color pavilions were raised, while overhead in the tall top cover of the trees, flocks of migrating birds set up a chorus. The chill of autumn was in the air, and as evening closed a damp cool seemed to spread from the forest, tingling hands and noses. Cookfires and braziers were lit and soon the odor of woodsmoke drifted through the encampment.

The lengthy ride in the fresh, cool air had given Sancha a monstrous appetite. As she greedily devoured a third glistening game hen breast, succulent with some of its own jelly still clinging to it, and reached for fourth, Hugh smiled at her and puffed out his cheeks, teasingly.

"You are heartless," she whispered to him. And with a gleam of mischief in her eyes, discreetly alluded to the de Umframville women's gaily chewing mouths.

Later, as the fires glowed orange against the chill black night, more wine was brought out. Long after Sancha and her maidservant, Gusti, retired to the charette, Hugh remained drinking and talking with the de Umframville men. Their conversation ranged from the weather, to politics, and the sale of wool. De Umframville spoke of their liege lord Northumberland and of his love of luxury, his greed, and of the celebration that awaited them at Warkworth, particularly the tournament. "I won three horses last year and a stack of armor," de Umframville stated proudly.

Their first full view of Warkworth town, with its massive fortress and walls, was from the arched stone bridge which spanned the slow-moving brown waters of the river Coquet. De Umframville directed Hugh's attention to the docks and storage buildings along the river's edge. "The sea is not two leagues distant. 'Tis a prize, Warkworth, and but one of the jewels in our liege lord's crown.

"He has done much renovation on his fortress," de Umframville confided. "Robert, here, says it is near as grand as Windsor, eh Robert?"

The one called Robert laughed. "Aye, with a new wife he need offer her something to console her lower half, even if it be only be a gold chair on which to sit her arse!"

The wool wagons were diverted to the storehouses, where the bulk of it was unloaded. There the sacks of wool would remain, save for the samplings that would make the journey to the sales which were held daily. De Umframville suggested waiting for a few days before selling. "So we might get a feel for the prices," he said.

The town and all about was teeming with crowds. There were merchants come for the wool sales, some from as far as Genoa and the distant Hansa ports; there were all manner of tradesmen, those who gather at tournaments, armorers, leather merchants, and the like; and there were also troupes of jongleurs, boatmen, and prostitutes.

A city of tents and throngs of carts and vehicles of every description cluttered the commons about the town and castle walls. Martin remained with the carts and wainsmen, making a camp close by the de Umframville wagons, near the river where the town's tanneries and bell foundry were located.

At the castle, the de Umframville cavalcade was hardly noted, such was the general confusion and crowding as the assembling nobles and hordes of servants vied for suites and stable space.

The castle, according to de Umframville, had undergone a vast renovation since he had last visited. He pointed out an entire new wing and splendid tower, intimating, "I hear he brought craftsmen from as far as Venice and Florence, and that there are reservoirs on the roof to supply water to all the garderobes and kitchens." As they made their way to their quarters, they viewed some of the new construction. In places they were forced to track through the dust and debris. Many of the passageways were in the process of being paneled, while in the long galleries, large, colorful frescoes, as yet incomplete, adorned the plaster walls.

It was several hours before Hugh, Donel, Sancha, and her serving girl, Gusti, were settled in their small suite in the guest quarters and began to make preparations for the night's celebration.

Gusti was not nearly so clever as Alyse at arranging hair. Sancha suspected it was because whenever Donel was about, Gusti's expressionless blue eyes followed him constantly. As a result Sancha's hair was jerked, pulled, and twisted. She was spared from losing her temper when, after the last of the luggage was carried to the suite, Hugh sent Donel to spend the night with Martin and the others at the camp, close by the foundry.

After Donel's departure Gusti's talents improved markedly, and with her usual look of grim determination she finally succeeded in affixing the delicate golden caul with its tiny seed pearls to her mistress's luxuriant braids.

Lounging in the window seat, Hugh, dressed and waiting, manicured his fingernails with the ornamental dagger he wore at his belt. He watched, only a little impatiently. At last he pulled himself from the embrace of the pillows, silently crossed the room, and leaned over Sancha's shoulder.

"You are the most beautiful girl in the world," he told her with a smile. His eyes were on the soft cleft of her breasts, and not the elaborate coif.

Together, Sancha and Hugh joined the crush of nobles in the great hall. In its immense size and with its richly attired guests, the hall was as grandiose as anything Sancha had seen at Richard's court. Truly, if Northumberland wished all to know that he was "king of the north," he had succeeded. For the cavernous hall, with its carved panels, and imposing manteled chimneys at either end, was impressive. As were the number of torchbearers, surely a hundred or more, who stood about the hall's perimeters like living candles.

Northumberland's appearance before his liege men seemed

purposely dramatic. He came onto the dais heralded by trumpet blasts, and with his young wife on his arm. He was dressed in a padded doublet of scarlet velvet embroidered in gold, and sparkling with jewels, and all beneath a mantle trimmed in ermine. His wife, much younger, was a tall girl with an extraordinarily long neck and unsympathetic face. She was, however, magnificently dressed in an ivory-colored gown of check-la-toun, an elegant silk, embroidered with a multitude of seed pearls and sparkling with brilliants. With her every movement, the gown shimmered with a dance of sparkling light.

Each of Northumberland's barons made the long trek through the hall to kneel before him and swear fealty. Hugh, less rich and powerful than many, was among the last to be announced. Following the ceremony, the feast began. Swarms of servants dressed in scarlet-and-white livery awaited the guests. So numerous were the servants that the high tables and low were both served at once.

Cloth of gold and tapestries adorned the walls, and such a number of courses and dishes came from the castle's kitchens that a person could not begin to sample all of them. With the sea nearby, many of the dishes were fish, lampreys, and other marine delicacies, served in aspics and pastries. Black puddings and pork pâtés marbled with rivers of lard were also served, as well as sausages, roasted duck, swan, and stork. Stuffed piglets, vermilion and glistening with cherry glacé, glided by on platters, and roasts of venison, racks of hares, rissoles, and pork pies were offered along with huge salmon, baked and gilded with a paste of powdered egg yolks, flour, and flakes of gold leaf, pickled ox tongues, galantines, and mélanges of vegetables. The constant drone of conversations and the clatter of silver plate accompanied the horde of servants as they hovered about the tables refilling goblets and offering new and unusual delights.

Hugh had seen his half brothers take their seats at the high table. At the time he had been engaged in conversation, but now, surrounded by people eating, he observed them at his leisure. Both sat with their wives. At least Hugh imagined the young women seated beside Gilbert and Walter to be Northumberland's daughters. For they favored him somewhat, if only in their expressions of hauteur. Walter's hand moved incessantly to his mouth; he paused only to suck at his wine goblet. Seated to the right, Gilbert was talking to the eldest of the Percy sons, the one called Hotspur. It was then Hugh noticed Simon de Lacey's avid stare, directed not at him, but at Sancha.

As the meal drew to a close and fruit, sugared cakes, comfits, and peeled nuts were offered to the guests, Hugh noticed quite by chance that the ruby ring was absent from Sancha's hand. "Why have you not worn your ring?" he asked, quietly.

"Oh! I have forgotten it!" Sancha exclaimed, feigning an expression of surprise and regret, and suggesting she could go fetch it from their suite once the meal had ended. But Hugh told her, "No, that would be foolish."

He had not the opportunity to say more, for they had been seated with the de Umframvilles, and there was much jolly conversation up and down the table. While the servants were still collecting the silver plate, musicians began to troop into the hall, forty, perhaps more, with every sort of instrument. Then mummers and acrobats performed, and afterward troubadours sang. When the last of them had crooned of love and chivalry, it was announced that the musicians would give play for the guests' dancing pleasure.

The elder de Umframville women, both with scarlet faces and feeling uncomfortable after such a meal, rose to make the trip to the garderobes. The others followed their example. Sancha accompanied them. She was eager to escape any further questions, and needed time to think. The luxury of the garderobe was completely unexpected. She and the others found it to be a marvel of innovation, with mirrors and statuary and running water that at the turn of a silver handle streamed from the wall by way of carved stone lotus blossoms. There were even servingwomen to pass out dampened squares of cloth scented with perfume.

As the women, much refreshed, returned, Lady de Umfram-ville and her sisters met a lady with whom they were all acquainted. Sancha smiled politely as she was introduced and remained for a respectable length of time before continuing on through the jostle of silk and velvet clad guests. Making her way slowly, she skirted the edge of the dancers. She was making some progress when a man bumped into her, soundly, and nearly knocked her off her feet.

Strong arms caught her. "I am a criminal!" exclaimed a sultry voice, speaking in French. "I beg your indulgence, demoiselle, allow me to apologize."

Sancha raised her eyes to see a handsome young man, olive-skinned with dark curly hair and heavy-lidded eyes. He was gorgeously attired and his French was that of the Parisian court. Sancha was enchanted. "Please, your apologies are not needed, I am quite unharmed." It was wonderful to again speak her native tongue, though it struck a faint chord of homesickness in her heart.

The young man smiled, showing a flash of white teeth. "You are a daughter of France, surely, for you speak like an angel." And lowering his voice to a conspiratorial tone, he murmured, "An angel of mercy, my dearest Sancha." With that he slipped an object into her hand.

It was her ruby ring! Sancha was dumbfounded. She looked first, unbelievingly, at the winking red stone, then at the handsome, dark-eyed young man who could not have been much older than herself.

"I am sent by Madame Isabelle." As he spoke the musicians struck up a lovely "carole" and dancers began to move around them. Sancha was so taken aback by his announcement that she followed him into the dancers, moving with him to the music. "Madame desires you hasten to her. It is a matter of life and death. I may tell you no more than that. I pray you do not refuse."

"No," Sancha replied, "I would never refuse Madame." Her mind reeled from his words, French words, true words, which only confirmed her worst fears. But how was she to answer such a summons? Hugh would never agree, never allow it. He had forbidden her to even speak of Isabelle and Richard. Moving gracefully with her partner, Sancha explained her dilemma. As they danced on to the bittersweet and haunting melody, the young man, introducing himself only as Gui, advised her as to what she must do.

On the lower dais, de Umframville nudged Hugh, who was discussing the merits of long bows with Umframville's drunken brother and several young Percy cousins. "Your wife has attracted another admirer," de Umframville said in a hoarse whisper.

Hugh sent a searching glance among the dancers, expecting to see Simon de Lacey, who had spent the entire meal staring at his wife. Instead, he saw an unknown young man of medium height, well built, and near as pretty as a girl. Hugh's eyes burned on him. "So it seems," he replied, smiling despite the sudden push of jealous anger that stiffened his muscles.

"Who was your companion?" Hugh asked when she returned to the table.

"A Frenchman," Sancha said with a glittery smile. The ruby ring secreted in her bosom pressed against her breast like a stone, reminding her to be cautious. "It was delightful to speak my language once again, if only for a brief moment."

"Who is he? Did he introduce himself properly?"

"Oh, yes, he was perfectly chivalrous."

"What is his name?"

Sancha regarded her husband with a pretty air of bewilderment, and with an elegant little shrug of her shoulders, replied, "I do not recall. You are not angry, are you?"

Hugh returned her smile. "I thought you were dancing with one of the troubadours."

"He is a nobleman," she said with a disparaging flash of

her dark eyes, as if it were clear for anyone to see. "He is a graceful dancer. Did you notice?"

Hugh's smile deepened, and brushing her cheek with the back of his fingers, whispered close to her ear, "I would like to break both of his legs."

"You are very cruel to tease me." Sancha forced a little laugh, though her heart was beating furiously.

"Yes," he agreed. "All the same, I did not care for him, for the way he regarded you."

Hours passed before Hugh and Sancha made their way to their suite. Gusti was waiting for them. When asked, she told of eating in the servants' hall and of a fat man who annoyed her and was the reason she had returned early. While Gusti told her tale, Sancha, through a bit of nervous sleight of hand, managed to "find" her ruby ring exactly where she had said it was, in her jewel casket. She slipped it on her finger.

Owing to the vast number of guest suites, the chambers were small. The beds were set into the walls and curtained, the largest niche reserved for the noble guest, the smaller spaces for servants.

Despite its larger size Hugh found the bed confining, too short. However, it was the first time in several days he had lain with Sancha, and his inventive mind soon found a solution to both problems. He was gentle and persistent. The still, warm air behind the curtain was scented with their passion. Sancha clung to him, longing to be held, wanting to forget if only for a time the terrible decision she must make. Moving blindly in the dark she lifted her slender legs, opened herself to his probing heat, and matched his rhythmic thrusts.

Across the blackened chamber in her niche, Gusti heard their intimate whispers, their movements, the unmistakable sounds of their mating. The subtle, soft noises inflamed her senses. Gusti had longed for Donel to content her that night, and since he could not, she quietly contented herself. But even that did not help her to fall asleep. The excitement of the trip, the strangeness of the castle, and the constant shuffle of foot traffic past the chamber door all conspired to keep her restless.

It seemed to Gusti that she had not slept at all when a loud hammering brought her up from her bed, dazed and disheveled to stagger to the door. De Umframville, dressed in leathers, barged in like a bull. With his booming voice, height and girth, he all but filled the small chamber. "By the saints, don't tell me your still abed!" he exclaimed with a hoot.

Hugh's muscular arm appeared first. He pulled himself from the bed, quickly closing the curtain, for the sake of Sancha's modesty, though not before de Umframville caught a glimpse of soft, white shoulder. "Had I no intent to ride today, I should have spent my night so fondly!" His laughter rocked the room. "Christ!" he snorted. "Have you any fire left in that belly of yours?"

Hugh grinned, raking a hand through his rumpled hair. "Enough. What had you in mind?" Gusti handed him his hosen. Hugh leaned his shoulder against the wall and hiked into them.

"Ride with us in the melee today."

Hugh settled himself and secured the ties. "I haven't any mail or plate armor," he said, yawning audibly. "And I've not a tournament horse to my name," he added, crossing the room to the basin, splashing his face and blinking the water from his eyes.

"I've all you need. Ride in my brother's place. 'Tis Robert, damn him! He's so drunk he can't piss straight! If we're a man short, those filthy swine, the de Laceys, will trounce us, and we'll be the butt of their jokes for all eternity."

Hugh agreed to ride. It was the only way to get rid of him.

"Why must you?" Sancha asked as he finished dressing. She had spoken from her heart, without thinking. For if he was riding she would have a chance to speak with Gui. She did not, however, know how Gui would locate her. Particularly when Hugh said, "Come down to the lists with the de Umframville women and watch the melee."

"I do not think I want to," Sancha said from where she lay on the bed. "What if you are hurt?"

"It would please me if you came."

In the end, Sancha promised, and as he leaned in past the curtain to kiss her, she offered her lips for an affectionate peck.

After Hugh had gone, Sancha scampered from the bed. The moment her bare feet touched the floor her head spun with vertigo. She was trembly, too sick for words. Gusti rushed for the chamber pot, held it for her mistress, and was herself almost ill. Sancha heaved and choked, retching until her stomach ached. Only afterward did she feel embarrassed by Gusti's presence, the girl's knowing look. She felt suddenly exposed beyond her nakedness, by her puffy little breasts with their darkened swollen nipples and her rounded protruding belly, which seemed, to her horror, to have expanded overnight.

Sancha, having denied the truth for months, was suddenly overwhelmed by the enormity of her condition. While Gusti looked on stupidly, she fell down on the bed, hid her face in her hands, and began to sob. It was not that she did not want his child; at one time she had prayed that she might conceive.

But at that moment she could not allow herself to think beyond the vow she had made to her little Madame. She could not abandon her, no matter what the cost. With great force of will Sancha pulled herself together and made Gusti promise, swear on God's name, to tell no one. For all her rawboned size Gusti was timid, not at all feisty like short, round Alyse.

The de Umframville women were very amiable toward Sancha and their pleasant conversation eased her troubled mind. As a group they plunged into the milling crowds of the castle grounds, and walked at a saunter toward the lists. On the way they passed the fair, with its multitude of goods and curiosities, and a comment was made that they should take a turn through its aisles on the morrow.

Crowds were tenfold near the lists, where banners fluttered and the fresh-cut lumber of newly constructed stands gleamed in the sunlight.

Between events, a number of young squires tilted at quintains. Galloping their horses toward a pivoting wooden figure armed with a blunted sword, they attempted to strike it on the mark. If they failed, and they often did, the wooden form swiveled round and smote them on the back, knocking them from their saddles, much to the amusement of the crowd.

The eldest de Umframville woman refused to climb into the stands. "It is too high! My word, it looks as flimsy as a market booth," she sneered.

Sancha and one of the younger de Umframvilles remained with her, taking a seat on the first tier of the stand.

"At least my feet are on the ground," the older woman said, smiling with satisfaction.

A copper-colored sun rose above the flying clouds of the September day. By afternoon it was uncomfortably warm, and the dust driven into the air by the horses' hooves blew into the stands in suffocating clouds.

Sancha's stomach still felt uneasy, and the ear-splitting shouts and cheers of the mobs of spectators had given her a headache. As the individual combats progressed, Sancha raised a hand to shade her eyes from the glancing sunlight.

On the lists, two combatants collided in a bone-splintering crash of flesh and metal. One mail-clad rider was catapulted from his saddle and lay motionless in the dust. Men dashed onto the field, and all in the stands rose to their feet. Just then Sancha felt a hand brush her shoulder. When she glanced back, she saw Gui. Their eyes met only for an instant. He walked on, halting beside a booth selling roasted nuts, and waited. Sancha soon made an excuse and joined him.

"Tomorrow at noon," Gui advised. "I will be waiting near the west gate. I will have a horse for you. Do not be late." He squeezed her hand and was gone.

Deafened by the roars of the crowd, Sancha returned to the stands to find the melee had begun. She was unable to locate Hugh among the jostling riders, the flail and din of blunted weapons and thick, rolling fog of dust. Only afterward did she learn that the de Umframvilles had been victorious.

At the de Umframvilles' pavilions, the men, dust-covered and battered, gathered for a wild celebration. Shouts of jubilation rang out as the victors pummeled each other and loudly proclaimed their prowess over the de Laceys.

Divested of his mail and plate armor, Hugh went behind the tent where the horses were tethered to relieve himself. A page, a frail-looking boy, of ten or twelve, dodged from between the horses, and in a prepubescent voice, croaked, "Be at the mews when the angelus bells sounds," then darted away.

Hugh completed the ritual, certain that Gilbert had sent him. He had half a notion not to go. When he returned, several of the de Umframvilles had wrestled a keg of wine from somewhere and there was much bragging and toasting until it was emptied.

Twenty-one

The crashing peal of the angelus bells drove a flock of pigeons, wings beating, into the rose-tinted evening sky, as Hugh made his way past the chapel.

From the pavilions near the lists he had no trouble locating the mews. He had passed the trio of towerlike structures earlier in the day, when those riding in the tournament had been blessed before the chapel. The route they had taken led through the maze of alleyways, past the castle's storehouses. By that hour the passages were deserted. Sunlight still touched the steeply slanted roofs, but all below was deep in shadows and silent, save for his own footfalls, which echoed back from the sheer stone walls.

Reaching his destination, Hugh looked about, and seeing no one, glanced inside the mews. The close, peculiar odor of feathers and droppings met his nostrils. In the semidarkness he could make out a number of large birds roosting motionless on perches of various heights, but he saw neither a falconer, nor his half brother.

"Over here," a voice said from behind Hugh's shoulder. Startled, he leapt forward and whirled about with his hand on the hilt of his knife to see his half brother standing in the shadows of an arched entryway. "You scared hell out of me," Hugh said, ducking into the shadows.

"I was beginning to think you weren't coming."

"I nearly didn't. What is it you want?"

"Peace, prosperity, the things all men want." And before

Hugh could respond, Gilbert, speaking quickly, said, "No, listen, brother, to what I have to say. The French have sent the count de Severies to escort Richard's queen back to France. They are at the moment installed at St. Baldwin's Abbey, close by the priory. But two days hence, Thomas Swynford will hand the French king's daughter into their keeping. They will travel south with only an escort of twenty of Bolingbroke's soldiers and half a dozen French knights. Where the humpbacked bridge at Harewood crosses the Tyne, a company of forty of my father-in-law's soldiers will be waiting in ambush."

"No, I will not do it!" Hugh took a step backward as if to go.

Gilbert caught his arm. "Have you any notion what will happen when the French learn that their precious, and very marriageable, princess has been kidnapped? Not to mention the slaughter of their courtiers and knights?"

Hugh shook off his grip. "It would mean war. Not even Northumberland would risk . . ."

"Oh, yes. He means to put an end to Henry Bolingbroke, by one fashion or another."

"Even risk a war with France?" Hugh said, incredulous.

"What better way? Henry would find it very hard to hold his crown with the might of France before him and a rebellion led by Northumberland at his back. Oh, there'll be civil war here; Henry will not go down without a fight. He may lose Calais. But if he holds England, Henry will crush Northumberland and those of us who do not die in battle will be hanged or beheaded."

"What of the Welsh? Of Owen Gendower?"

"The Welsh," Gilbert scoffed. "They will be no help to Northumberland, no more than they were to Richard. They are like a snake hacked in a dozen pieces; they will not fight as one. Think of it, brother. You may not fare any better than the rest of us. Northumberland will call you to take up arms for him. You'll be forced to choose, to fight or die. Think on that."

"It will never come to pass!"

"Yes, oh yes!

"Then why do you not warn Swynford? Why do you hesitate? It is you who wishes to betray Northumberland."

"Do you really believe Swynford would take my words to heart, his enemy's son-in-law? You've a weaker mind than Walter's!"

"I will not be your messenger!

Gilbert thrust out his closed fist. "Here then!"

"What is that?"

"The keys to Aubry's keep. Take them! Well go on, dammit, take them! Aubry is yours, I give it to you! If I am to be sent to judgment, at least I will not have that to weigh upon my soul. God knows there is enough!" He turned to go and, looking back, said, "A word of warning, brother. Do not ride in tomorrow's melee. De Lacey has his mouth set for Evistone, and judging from his words, for your widow as well."

Hugh was left standing in the shadows. He waited fully ten minutes, watching to see if Gilbert had been followed, then walked back to the castle. His half brother's words troubled him, but he had made up his mind to do nothing. It was too dangerous a game.

Later in the guest wing of the castle, as he and Sancha dressed for another night of feasting, Sancha noticed his side was marked with a large blue-black bruise. When she touched her fingers to his ribs, Hugh winced with pain. Still, he passed it off lightly. "It is naught but a broken rib, I think."

"You are fortunate it was not your head," Sancha remarked with a severe look. She had been waiting for him to return for hours. She sat waiting again, occasionally glancing at him, as he washed and scraped the stubble from his jaw. He seemed preoccupied and had not much to say. It worried Sancha. She wondered if someone had seen her talking to Gui and had told him of it.

The constant stream of platters passing through the hall and the mingled odors of fish and meat thoroughly nauseated

Sancha. She could not bring herself to raise a morsel to her mouth.

After the musicians began to play, Hugh led her out to dance, and asked, "What is the matter?" She replied, as he expected, "Nothing," and he whispered, "I have just the cure for 'nothing.' "

"You are too hurt for that," she reminded him. Her flash of annoyance only seemed to encourage him and, with his lips brushing her ear, he murmured, "It is only my ribs that are broken."

But at the table he was drawn into another de Umframville victory celebration. And later, despite all his amorous talk, he was asleep no sooner than his head touched the pillow.

Hugh rode out from Warkworth Castle early on the morrow, and in the company of the de Umframville men. In the town he met Martin at the wool hall. The market closed at noon. Hugh had sold only half of Evistone's wool. He received several offers from Flemish merchants for the remaining sacks, but the prices they offered were not to Hugh's liking.

The de Umframvilles also had a portion of wool left unsold. "Come along with us; we're headed for the Trumpet. You'll get a decent price there," de Umframville insisted. "I've been selling wool since I was twelve. You'll learn a trick or two."

When Hugh and Martin entered the tavern with the de Umframvilles, it was yet early. The large central room of the establishment, with its long tables set in rows, was nearly empty.

"The merchants don't usually come in till later," the tavern keeper advised the group.

"Piers Exton does," a fat tavern maid, no longer in her prime, disputed.

"An' do you see him, Loll, do you?" The tavern keeper's sarcasm seemed to have no effect on her.

"Nah," she said glancing about. "But he's usual here."

Hugh's curiosity was piqued. "Exton, you say? Does he buy wool then?"

"Not that I ever knew," the tavern keeper remarked. "Mostly

he had to do with jongleurs and the like. Besides he's paid and gone, gone this morning afore first light."

"He was a lodger here?" Hugh inquired.

"Aye, an' I was glad to see his back. He paid well enough, but he'd have that damn beastie in here, stealing things and biting people."

The tavern maid, rolled her eyes in agreement. "They's ornery things, apes. Why he'd grab his little willie-lillie and piss at the girls sometimes. An' he proper bit the goldsmith."

"Go sell some ale," the tavern keeper grumbled, and, turning back to the men, advised, "Now if you're wanting the best prices for your wool, there's Robert Paxton from London; he'll be here later for a certainty."

At the moment, Hugh was more interested in learning more about the monkey. "This ape," Hugh asked, "did it belong to a peddler?"

The tavern maid, still lingering, answered, "Aye, it did. The French lad said he hated it!" Just then someone shouted at the woman to fetch them an ale, and she scurried off across the room.

"A young Frenchman?" Hugh put the question to the tavern keeper.

"Aye, Exton's assistant, or so he called himself," the tavern keeper said with a broad wink. "Pretty as a May queen he was!"

Hugh waited with the de Umframvilles, and did indeed make a sale on his wool, but his thoughts were elsewhere. The idea that Exton, the peddler, and the French lad, as the tavern maid called him, might all be involved in Swynford's schemes disturbed Hugh more with each passing moment.

If Exton was indeed Swynford's spy, then the peddler had merely been a courier. No doubt there were others in his pay, and all Exton need do was to sit in Warkworth, right under Northumberland's nose, like a spider on a web and wait. Then he could send his information south by the peddler or the boy. They had not far to go, Chalford Priory, if Hugh's half brother

Gilbert was to be believed. Still it did not explain why Exton had sent the boy to seek out Sancha. Perhaps he hadn't? None of it made a great deal of sense to Hugh, save for the uneasy feeling that Sancha was somehow threatened by it.

In spite of his concerns, Hugh was unable to return at once to Warkworth Castle. After parting company with the de Umframvilles before the Trumpet, he and Martin rode to the encampment. Hugh paid his men their wages, warned them about squandering it in taverns, and within an hour, departed for the castle.

All sorts of fantastic scenarios wisped through Hugh's thoughts as he rode along the river. What did he truly know about his lady wife? Clearly she was not afflicted with brain fever as he had first been told. Why then had the physician treated her with poppy juice or God knows what? The easier course was to suppose the man a fool. Or was there something more sinister behind his malpractice? She had fallen ill about the time of Richard's death. But he had died leagues away in Pontrefact. Or had he?

"I saw Richard's body lying in a cart at Cheapside," Hugh argued against his own reasoning. Though in examining his memory of the event, what had he actually seen beyond a blackened corpse whose features were distorted by death? In truth it might have been the corpse of any fair-haired man of Richard's height.

There were also Sancha's terrifying dreams to be considered. Had they been born of poppy juice or some horror of flesh and blood? Gradually the dreams had faded. She had been happy or so he had believed. Lately, though, she had acted strangely troubled, and thinking back it seemed to him that it had begun near the time of his half brother's visit to Evistone. The very day he had found the flower lying by his ledger. He could not help but wonder, now as then, if she had read his missive to Swynford or overheard his and Gilbert's conversation? Would she have attempted to warn her queen? He knew well enough her loyalty to her little Madame. From there, the possibilities of what she might have done frightened him.

As Hugh rode on, the day which had dawned grey and overcast grew darker. A drizzle of rain greeted him as he entered Warkworth. Pressing into the crowds, he made his way toward the stables. He quickly settled his horse, and with rapid stride struck out for the guest suites, determined to have the truth from Sancha.

Near the kitchens, the damp air was smeared with grease and the odors of yet another feast, and the passages of the castle were jammed with nobles dressed in silks and velvet and hordes of scurrying servants.

As he approached his suite, he saw Gusti hanging at the door, as if she had been watching for him. Her face was white and anxious. "I cannot find the mistress," she said to Hugh as he stepped into the chamber. "I've looked everywhere for her."

"What are you saying?" he demanded. "Did she not go to the fair with the de Umframville women?"

Gusti shook her blond head distractedly. "She sent me to say she was sick. An' she was, but when I came back she was not here. I thought she had gone to the garderobe. I waited and when she did not return, I went to look for her. I have looked everywhere!" she repeated again, almost in tears.

Hugh circled the room. "What clothes was she wearing?"

"Only her camisa."

"Use your brain, girl, she did not leave here in her camisa. Go and look," he growled.

Gusti rushed to the leather trunk and threw open the lid and began to search. At last she cried, "Her russet velvets, her riding clothes! Why should she wear those?" But when she looked, she caught only a glimpse of her master's back as he vanished into the crowded passageway.

Hugh had no idea where his wife had gone, but he suspected if he found her she would be with the young Frenchman. He had not long to wonder. At the stable he resaddled Chewba

who was none too pleased with the change of plans, and rode
to the gatehouses. There were three at Warkworth. At the third,
a gateward with long stringy hair and a beard like a goat's,
recalled a lady in russet velvets and a young man. "A Frenchie,
he was, an' asking about the road south. How should I know?
I tells him, damn foreigner!"

Hugh tossed the man a coin and rode off toward Warkworth
town. He galloped Chewbit across the field above the foundry,
reining him in as he approached the encampment with the line
of tethered horses and row of carts.

Martin was settling down to eat when Donel came charging
into the tent. "The master's here, something's happened!"

Martin stepped out into the drizzle just as Hugh brought
the black horse to a halt before the tent. He told Martin quickly
what had happened.

"Gone?" Martin puzzled. "I don't understand?"

"Nor do I," Hugh said. "Have the wagons packed, collect
Gusti and the trunks, then go yourself to de Umframville. Tell
him your mistress was taken ill, and that I am returning to
Evistone with her. Once you've the wagons under way, ride
after me as far south as Chalford."

"Where will I find you?"

"I don't know. Quickly, Martin!"

"Yes, my lord."

Riding through the misting rain, Hugh cantered across
Warkworth's stone bridge and turned his horse south.

Earlier that day, when Sancha arrived breathless at the west
gate, she found the handsome Gui awaiting her. He stood a
little back from the traffic, beside an ironsmith's enclosure,
where the forge glowed with a red heat.

Gui was true to his word. He had brought a horse for her,
a bay, rather coarse, but with an easy gait. They were scarcely
away from Warkworth when Sancha entreated Gui to tell her
what news he had of Madame Isabelle.

"There is no particular reason why I may not tell you now,"
Gui said with a mysterious smile. "Madame is unwell. She is
subject to fits of nervousness. Her mother, Queen Ysabeau,
fears for her mind, and wishes her to return at once to France
where there are abler physicians to treat her."

His words both shocked and frightened Sancha. She thought
at once of the physician who had treated her, Bolingbroke's
physician, and drawing from her own experiences, she warned,
"It could be the English are poisoning Madame?" Sancha
knew firsthand of such treatment. Hoping to spare her little
queen the terrifying feelings of madness that she, herself, had
suffered, Sancha readily told Gui how she had been fed an
elixir that took her senses away. As she spoke, Gui occasionally
glanced away, a strange fixed smile on his lips. Sancha found
his smile somehow disturbing, almost repellent, despite his
handsomeness.

However, any misgivings she had were quickly dispelled by
his sympathetic words and manner. Later in the afternoon,
when they were kept waiting by a drunken ferryman for hours,
Sancha asked, "Will you take me directly to Madame?"

That would be impossible he told her. "The English guard
her like a prisoner. You must arrive at the priory with the
courtiers; otherwise, you would surely be noticed."

But when Sancha attempted to learn more of the plot, Gui
refused to disclose any further information. He did not do so
in an ill-bred way, rather, evasively. Though even at that, his
evasion was performed in so charming and lighthearted a fashion that Sancha could not take offense.

Once across the river she had no chance to pursue her questions. It began to rain, a slow persistent drizzle that soon turned
the track to mud, and scented the late afternoon with the smell
of damp earth and crushed leaves.

Sancha's thoughts, which had been centered wholly on the
fate of her little Madame, now turned to Hugh. What must he
think? What must he feel? It tortured Sancha to realize that
she might never see him again, or feel the warmth of his em-

brace. Most of all she feared he would curse her name when he discovered her treachery. She could not blame him. Though what was she to do? She had made a vow and now she must keep it.

She thought also of the child growing inside her and promised silently to always love him. "Him," for she fancied it was a boy lying beneath her heart. The realization that her son would never know his father brought tears to sting her eyes. And as she rode on through the rain, the thought grieved her more and more.

No further conversation passed between Sancha and the young nobleman until they reached a large wood, where several paths led away from the even course of the king's road.

"My instructions were to wait for the count de Severies. There, in the ruins of an abbey." He pointed an arm toward the darkening woods, saying, "It is he who will escort you to the queen."

"Count de Severies." Sancha knew the name, for the man was her uncle, though she had no chance to make it known for Gui immediately reined his horse toward a narrow forest path and led away. Sancha followed. She was perplexed by the necessity of now waiting, when before, all haste had been required. Neither could she picture her fastidious uncle de Severies racing through the mud of a rainy night when he might more easily wait in warmth and safety for Gui to deliver her to him.

Her emotions, however, were in such a state that her suspicions were not alerted. Even the thought that Gui may have intended some sort of romantic interlude did not occur to her.

The path grew progressively fainter, narrower, and overgrown. At last they arrived at a clearing of sorts, and there Sancha beheld a ruined abbey overtaken by ivy, wild shrubs, and brambles. Its shattered facade, gaping windows, and tumbled walls over which vines and brushy limbs twined and tangled, roused in her a vague sense of foreboding. Riding past the tower and its rubble of grey stones, she glanced at the high-set windows of the chapel and the steep angle of the shattered roof.

The rain had ceased to fall, though water dripped from every leaf and its sound filled the silence. As they dismounted their horses, Sancha experienced the unpleasant sensation of being watched. Several times her gaze swept anxiously over the ancient ruins but, seeing nothing, she decided it must be the queer loneliness of the place playing upon her nerves.

Twenty-two

Shivering in her wet clothing, Sancha followed Gui into the deep twilight of a passageway. The route was smothered with brambles, some still lustrous green; others, beneath the roof, were lifeless, brown, and brittle, and sprang back at their passage with a dry rattle.

"We can await the count de Severies in here," Gui said, showing her into a large chamber to the right of the chapel. "It is dry and, if you feel a chill, I will light a fire for you."

Sancha hesitated at the chamber's threshold, imagining for a moment that she had seen Gui's dark glance shift slyly toward another door arch along the murky passageway. "Shall we have long to wait?" she asked.

"No, not long at all."

"Then there is no need to light a fire," she told him, and, peering into the gloom, entered warily. "Do you not fear outlaws in such a place? I would think it very much to their liking." He seemed amused by her suggestion, and so she said no more.

After a time he began to move about the room restlessly. "You do look chilled," he said. "I will gather an armful of branches and light a fire."

"Do not go far," Sancha called. The place unnerved her.

Left alone in the gloom of the chamber, Sancha began to look more closely at her surroundings. It was rapidly growing dark, but enough light fell from the windows to make out footprints in the layer of dust and debris that had accumulated during the long years of neglect. She saw a set of large footprints, neither hers nor Gui's. She raised her eyes, trying t blot the thought from her mind, telling herself that the foo prints might have been made weeks before, by shepherds, o passing pilgrims—or outlaws.

Moment to moment the room grew darker. She waited an waited. Where was he, she wondered? She crossed the roon to a circle of stones. Inside the stones was a bed of ashe where long ago someone had lit a fire for warmth. She stoope down and, illogically, thinking she perceived some heat risin from the ash, reached out to touch a stone. It was warm. Sh jerked back as if she had been burned.

She was frightened now, truly frightened. And then she far cied she heard a faint jingling sound. Her head went up, in stantly alert. It was the horses' bridles, she told herself, thoug she did not really believe it.

Again she heard a tinkling sound, like the sound of litt bells. She stiffened. The sound came once more, louder, close She lurched to her feet, her heart hammering, her eyes frant cally searching the gloom, her ears straining to locate th source of the bells. Yes, bells, she was certain it was bells!

She stood there unmoving, listening. Silence, only wate dripping. She fought back the desperate urge to call out t Gui. Where was he? Instead she moved slowly, silently, feelin her way toward the door arch and the passageway beyon Open to the sky, the passageway shone light against the ink blackness of the chamber.

A silver shimmy of bells. Suddenly, a black form filled th door arch. Sancha screamed and stumbled backward. Whe she looked again, it had vanished. A thrill of terror course through her body and she stared, paralyzed, at the place whe the form had been.

It is he! she thought, wildly, madly. The man with the bell boots, the man who had plucked Richard's bloody, dismembere head from a sack and brandished it like a trophy. The man wh had wanted to silence her that night at Windsor Castle.

Where was Gui? Had he not heard her scream? Why d

he not come to her? And then, with a horrible certainty, she knew why. Why he had lured her away. Why he had insisted they must wait there. She thought of the ring and the peddler. Oh God, she had been so wrong!

A sob rose in her throat, choking her. She tried to gather her wits, but in her panic she could think only of the ghoulish face, the cloaked figure of her nightmares. The silvery sound of bells jingled in her ears. In the vaulted chamber, the sound seemed to come from all directions.

She bolted. Her only thought was to reach the door arch and escape down the passageway. From the far edge of her vision she saw him, his cloak fluttering like the wings of a bat.

"Nooo!" she screeched, loud and piercing, as his hands seized her, pinned her arms to her sides. She opened her mouth to scream, but a hand clamped over her face. Fingers dug into her cheek. She bit down. He cursed at her, enraged.

She threw herself against him, bucking, kicking. Something hard hit her head and swirls of light flashed before her eyes. Afterward, she was only dimly aware of being dragged backward, for a long distance, of her feet bumping over the ground, and of voices. One of them was Gui's.

"The fall would kill her," the young Frenchman predicted. Raising the lantern once more, he gazed down the steep angle of the stone steps which descended from the floor of the chapel into the black void of the crypt, far below. He glanced to Exton. "Why bother slitting her throat?" he said, impatiently. "She cannot escape once we close the crypt."

"No bother, I shall enjoy it. The little whore bit me!" Exton ground out as he shuffled forward, dragging Sancha with him through the drifts of wet leaves that cluttered the floor. "She'll not be causing me any more grief, not after tonight. This time I'll cut her damn windpipe, 'an Swynford won't be here to stop me!" With only one free hand he fumbled to draw the silver-hafted dagger from his belt.

A horse whickered, another answered. The eerie notes carried on the damp air. Exton cocked his head toward the sounds. "I hear the horses. Go and have a look."

Gui had also heard. He set the lantern down and, drawing his knife, bounded into the passageway.

Sancha's reasoning returned. She felt her body shift in his arms. Her eyes, no longer unfocused, fixed on his hand and the metallic glint of a blade. In a fury of panic she lunged against his arms, breaking free.

Her sudden violent movement caught Exton off guard. He stumbled forward, careened into the lantern, and sent it clattering down into the crypt.

Sancha lunged away, but not quickly enough. Exton's heavy hand struck her down. Scrambling on all fours through the wet leaves, she pulled herself up, only to fall again. Springing to her feet, she slid, and fell once more. At last she lurched up on wobbling legs and ran, darting first one way, then another, frantic in the blackness to find the passageway, and unable to in her terror.

Pursued by the mad jingling of bells, she darted away, screaming at the top of her lungs. Something, a hand, hit her shoulder, hurt her. She twisted, bolted sideways, and screamed again.

He was all around her, grabbing, grasping. His fingers gripped her cloak. Sancha flung herself forward, panicked, but like a dog come to the end of its chain, she was jolted to a halt. The brooch securing her cloak, blunt and hard, slammed into her throat. She fell backward, strangling.

Hands groped her and jerked her upward. She flailed her arms, and battered him with her feet. One of her slippers flew off. She kicked and screamed, until a hand closed on her throat, choking her. She could not breathe. She felt herself being dragged backward again. She gagged. Her feet kicked out into empty air. Bursts of light exploded in her eyes and a loud rushing noise inside her head grew louder and louder.

As if from a long distance, she heard a man's voice, a short brutal shout. Then a jolting blow flung her sideways. She hit he floor, barely conscious, but aware of her throat opening, ragging in greedy gulps of damp air.

Two figures, blacker than the black of the chapel, tore at ne another. She could hear their heavy breathing, the animal grunts and vicious grappling sounds.

The momentum of Hugh's cannoning body had sent Exton prawling across the leaf-strewn floor, Hugh atop him.

A bellow came from deep in Exton's chest, and, snarling with age, he countered. His hand, locked on his knife, slashed out.

Hugh wrenched away, felt the push of wind as the blade cleaved the air before his face. Exton flung himself sideways, and came at Hugh again. The glint of steel flashed in Hugh's eyes. He threw up an arm, defensively, and struck out with his knife hand.

A stunning blow shuddered Hugh's forearm and it went numb. At the same time he felt his blade rip cloth, flesh, heard Exton yelp, and retreat, scurrying, crablike, kicking up leaves.

In the next instant, Exton had gathered his lank body into a crouch. He sprang.

Hugh lashed out with his feet, catching Exton solidly in the chest and hurling him backward. Hugh lunged after him. They crashed together, legs thrashing, arms locked in a brutal struggle for supremacy. Hugh's forearm felt dead, and using it as a club, he crushed an elbow down on Exton's throat, trying to pin him.

Exton's fingers clawed at Hugh's mouth, gouged at his eyes. His hand clutching the silver-hafted knife flashed savagely, once, deep.

Hugh felt only the impact of the blade as it drove into his shoulder. It took his breath away. He lost all reason, was blind and deaf to everything. Instinct drove Hugh's right hand upward, his thumb hard against his knife's disc-shaped guard, guiding it as he plunged the blade into Exton's left side, again and again. Noises came from Exton's mouth, a gurgling sound. He struggled on, weakly, until his spine stiffened, and then he was still.

Hugh rolled off him and lay there for a moment, unmoving.

He hadn't had the strength to reclaim his knife, its stag horn hilt protruding from Exton's side.

Slowly the sounds of the living came back to him—rain drops pecking at the leaves, a faint whimpering sound somewhere off to his right. He crawled toward it, at first on his belly, then pulled himself painfully to a crouch.

"Sancha," he called out in a sharp whisper. He coughed, his throat dry as dust. He called her name again.

Sancha clambered up and fell into his arms. Hugh swayed, nearly going over backward before he could brace his legs. He pressed her in his arms and an ecstasy of relief flooded through him. Neither of them spoke; they simply clung to each other with trembling hands.

With a startled movement Sancha raised her head, her eyes rounded, white with fear. "There is another one!" she gasped.

"Out there," Hugh mumbled. "He is dead, I think."

Sancha sagged back against him, only then noticing the queer, slippery warmth of the blood soaking through his shirt. "You are hurt!" she cried, trying to see, trying to feel, to somehow gauge the extent of the wound.

Hugh captured her hands. "No. It will not kill me," he told her and took her face in his one hand. Her chin was trembling. "Are you harmed?"

She shook her head and forcing her way back into his arms, began to cry.

At first she would not answer his questions. Then, as if a dam had burst inside her, the words spilled from her lips in torrents. She told him all of it, sobbing. She confessed to having found his letter in the sacristy, of overhearing the conversation with his half brother. "You refused to warn them of the danger to Madame! You would have let Northumberland take her, break her heart again!" She began to say that she had believed Father Antonio to be Bolingbroke's spy, but she did not complete the thought. On and on she talked and at last she said, "I bribed the peddler to carry my message to Madame."

"Your wedding ring?" Hugh guessed.

She nodded, miserably. And as if in defense of her action, aid tearfully, "I could not allow Madame to be harmed." She egan to cough. When she had breath enough, she added, When Gui came to me in the hall, he put the ring into my and. He told me that he had been sent by Madame. That she yould not believe. That she must hear the words from my lips." ancha coughed again. "He!" she managed, pointing toward ie lifeless black form. "He is the man who murdered Richard! Ie cut off Richard's head! His head! And put it in a filthy sack!"

Hugh held her, listening to her cry, listening to her talk, until e had heard enough. He knew the rest. He was thinking now, onsidering what he must do. There was yet time to put things right, return to Evistone, and leave Northumberland and Swyn-ord to battle over Richard's child queen. First he must retrieve is knife from where it was wedged in Exton's chest. Eventually, e reasoned, the bodies would be found, but even if they were, vho but Northumberland would have cause to want them dead?

He was still considering all this when he lifted Sancha's rms from his shoulders and staggered to his feet. He stood ver Exton's body a moment before crouching to pry the knife ree, wiped the blade on the dead man's sleeve, and slid the nife into the scabbard on his belt. He glanced one last time t the ghoulish pockmarked face, openmouthed in death, then ;ot up and walked back to Sancha. She was standing in the lark with her arms wrapped around herself, shivering. "I have ost one of my slippers," she said.

"Where?" And he began to look in the blackness. He did ıot find it. Presently he came up to her and took her by the houlders. "A slipper is easily replaced. We have to be away rom here, back to Evistone. I have you, that is all that matters o me." But in the midst of his assurances to love and protect ıer, she suddenly pulled away from him and said, "I cannot ;o with you! I must warn Madame! Oh, do you not see! She nust not fall into Northumberland's hands!"

Her words affected Hugh like a dousing. How could she ay such a thing? Did she not realize what was at stake? That

Swynford would kill her if he thought her sane, and that he,
for his treachery, would suffer a like fate, at the very least lose
Evistone? All the emotions boiling inside him, burst to the
surface. "Be quiet," he told her, harshly. "You do not know
what you are saying."

"Yes," she said obstinately, searching in the darkness for
her missing slipper. "I am going to warn Madame!"

He caught her arm and jerked her backward to make her
stand where he wanted. "You little idiot! Do you suppose
Swynford will allow you to speak to her?"

"No. I will go to my uncle de Severies! He will listen to
me. He will find a way!"

"You are going back to Evistone."

"No! I made a vow!"

"What? To be a demoiselle!" He could not keep the scorn
from his voice.

"Yes! A vow made before God. Do you think because I am
a female, my vow is of less value? That it means nothing?"

"You are not going to die for it, I will not let you."

She tried to evade his hand. He took her by the sleeve, and
all but shouted at her, "Can you not understand, I love you!"

"It is not me you love! No! Not nearly so much as Evistone!" she shouted back, her voice filled with spite. "Does it
mean so much to you to be an earl, that you would let innocent
people die?" For a moment she thought he would hit her, and
when he did not, she told him, "I am going to warn Madame
and you cannot stop me."

"Yes, yes I can."

"No! Not unless you kill me! Is that what you are going to
do?"

"You believe that I would kill you?" He was amazed. "I
would die for you—I nearly did!" he sputtered angrily. At last
he shouted a single furious obscenity, drew his knife, and unexpectedly thrust the stag horn hilt into her hand. "Here," he
said, thumping his chest. "If I am so offensive to you, finish
me! I have no desire to live without you!"

Facing him in the dark, Sancha's lips began to quiver. She let out a tearing sob, dropped the knife, and, covering her face with her hands, turned away, weeping, defeated.

Hugh stooped to reclaim his knife from the leaves. At a sound from the door arch, he leapt to his feet.

"My lord?" Martin called, hesitant, seeing the crumpled form lying on the floor. "Are you all right?"

"Yes," Hugh answered. He returned the knife to his belt and glanced toward Sancha. She was still crying.

Martin heard her, but could see only the rise and fall of her small shoulders. He looked at Hugh, searchingly.

Hugh shrugged.

Martin understood. He paused, eyed the corpse, straining to see in the darkness. "There's another one outside." He reported. "He's dead." He took another step, halted, bent down and lifted something from the leaves, exclaiming, " 'Tis a lady's slipper."

Hugh took it from him. "How did you find me?" he asked.

"The ferryman. There's not much that man misses. I followed along an', where the path left the road, I saw fresh prints."

"Good man. Go and bring the horses around. And Martin, run theirs off."

Alone again, Sancha snatched the slipper from Hugh. "You will have to lock me away," she said with a cold fury, as she pressed her foot into the damp slipper. "Otherwise, I will leave! Even if I have to walk I will return to France! I will tell the truth! I will tell the whole world what evil the English have done!"

"Then I will lock you away," Hugh said, propelling her into the passageway with a hand on her shoulder. She whipped round at his words, tugged the ruby ring from her finger, and threw it at him. "I am not your wife! I have ever been your prisoner!" He searched for it in the dark, in deadly silence. Finally he found it, tucked it inside his jacque, and shoved her forward.

When Martin came leading the horses, Hugh boosted her into the saddle. They set off toward the road.

When they came to the end of the close, dense path, Hugh reined his horse to the right. Martin hesitated. "My lord," he called, "that be south."

"And where we'll find St. Baldwin's Abbey," Hugh replied, his mouth set in a grim line.

Sancha's eyes widened with surprise. She said nothing, but in her heart she knew she had won. She knew also how much it must have cost Hugh Canby to throw his pride and ambition in the dust.

They rode out the remaining leagues, each to their own thoughts. Another shower of rain drenched them. The wind came afterward, humming sadly through the branches overhead, sweeping away the clouds and polishing the sky.

Cold and wet through, they arrived at St. Baldwin's Abbey. A lay brother roused from the gatehouse carried Hugh's message into the abbey.

Hugh had said to him, "I have not leave to give the lady's name, save that she is a kinswoman of the count de Severies, and the matter is one of desperate urgency."

The man returned with remarkable swiftness and they rode into St. Baldwin's darkened forecourt. Another lay brother with a lantern in his hand awaited them before the bishop's residence.

Hugh took Sancha by the waist as she dismounted, set her on the ground. Standing there between the horses, he took her shoulders in his hands and spoke to her in a rapid, hushed voice, as if he feared he may not have another chance. "I have loved you more than I might say. I would only ask of you that you do not recall the worst of me."

His words of love, the ardent violence of his voice, made Sancha shudder as if her heart had just been torn. In the anguished silence between them, Sancha was almost undone. With a pained little gasp, she wrenched her fingers from his hand and ran toward the blurred haze of the lantern.

A servant was lighting the wall sconces when Hugh followed Sancha and the monk into a small solar laid deep with

Saracen carpets. In the hearth a fire had been rekindled, and sounds of activity came from the chamber beyond.

Arnaud de Severies came into the light, squint-eyed from sleep, his hair in disarray, and wrapped in a fur-lined robe. The sight of his niece struck him speechless. His gaze staggered from the disheveled girl to the young man whose open jacque revealed a blood-soaked shirt. "By the risen Christ," he stammered. "Dominique! How is it you have come to me? My God! But—but what of your affliction?"

"My affliction was born of poppy juice and deceit, and meant to silence me, to keep me from carrying the truth to Madame, to you my uncle, and to all the world." Sancha's impassioned narrative of the grisly events at Windsor held de Severies enthralled.

Hugh collapsed in a chair. Every fiber of his body ached. He sat there trying not to think, half-listening to Sancha's rapid words, and understanding none of it. After a time, he leaned his head back and closed his eyes.

A flurry of female voices and rustling silks preceded a gaggle of women who swept into the room. With cries of recognition the women embraced Sancha, and after a moment, escorted her toward the door.

Hugh, now alert, followed her with his eyes. All at once he leaned forward with an odd uncertain movement, as if he intended to rise from the chair. It occurred to him that he would never see her again, and he wondered what else he might have said to her, to keep her, to make her stay with him. Realizing the uselessness of his thoughts, he sank back in the chair.

She had not so much as sent him a backward glance. A sharp, searing pain stabbed through his chest. He would have believed it was his heart breaking, had he not felt a fresh trickle of blood ooze from the wound in his shoulder.

Twenty-three

"May God visit it on me if I speak untruthfully," de Severie said to Hugh, after the women had departed. "I was completel duped by Swynford. I had no notion of his treachery." He pace the room. As he spoke an astonishing range of expression crossed his dissipated features—sorrow, guilt, grief, and bitter ness. At times his eyes moistened with tears, and the tone c his voice altered as if it might crack with emotion. Despite hi passion, or perhaps because of it, Hugh thought him not alto gether sincere.

"Dominique will be safe, hidden among the women of m entourage." De Severies was adamant. He went on to say wha a comfort his niece would be for Madame Isabelle during thei return to France. "Madame has suffered much heartache fo one so young. At times she refuses to eat, to sleep. I fear fo her health, her mind, you understand?"

In the heat of the room, Hugh's shoulder began to throl De Severies, noticing his discomfort, asked if he might sen a servant in search of the bishop's physician. Hugh declined

The faint lilting sound of women's voices filtered into th chamber, and de Severies, taking a second wind, said, "I blam myself entirely for Dominique's misfortunes. The poor chil has been terribly wronged. I swear on our Saviour's blood tha once she is returned to court, I shall make amends. I owe great debt to you as well, monseigneur, and I am prepared t compensate you for your efforts."

"I did not come seeking payment. I want only your sworn word that no further harm will come to Dominique."

"That I freely give. I will defend her with my life." And pausing, he asked again, "Will you not allow me to have someone attend your wound?"

"No," Hugh replied, getting to his feet. The required effort sent the blood rushing to his head. "I have leagues to go. There is one favor I would ask of you. Have you paper and ink?"

"But of course." De Severies motioned to the small, bland-faced servant, who moved quiet as a ghost from where he had been sitting.

Hugh moved stiffly to the table, sat down, and asked, "Which Holy Father does your king address as pope?"

"His Holiness Benedict," de Severies replied. Thus informed, Hugh began to write with rapid strokes. Completing his thoughts, he glanced over his Latin words, uncertain at the last, then offered the letter to de Severies. "Will this satisfy your curia?"

De Severies eyes moved rapidly down the page, his mobile features betraying every word. He raised his head. "Yes, certainly, there will be no question. An annulment will be granted. It is a noble gesture, monseigneur. With this, Dominique will again be marriageable. Are you certain I may not offer you some payment?"

"No." Hugh was insistent. His manner was now brisk, his face swept clean of emotion. He wanted only to be on his way. There was the matter of Swynford. Hugh had said nothing of Northumberland's plot to seize the queen, nor the force of men who waited many leagues south. He could not bring himself to trust de Severies.

At the door, Hugh halted. "There is something else you might do for me," he mentioned, fumbling through his jacque, for a moment unable to find the ring. At last discovering it, he looked at the blood red gem as if he were debating with himself, then said, "In time Dominique will have many fine jewels, more than I could hope to offer her. But this ruby is unlike other stones, its color is deep and true. Will you give her this for me?"

In the courtyard, Martin was waiting with the horses. "Are we bound for Evistone?" he asked, passing the black's reins to Hugh.

"We've another call to make, at Chalford Priory."

"Chalford?" Martin wondered, leading the bay palfrey as he turned his horse toward the gates.

"Yes, I'll tell you as we ride."

The sky lightened by degrees. Martin listened. Finally, he shook his head. "What do you suppose will happen?"

"Who can say?" Hugh muttered, rummaging through his jacque once more for the keys his half brother had given him. The keys were large and easily found. "Here, you may as well have these."

Martin's quick hand snatched them from the air. "What's this, then?"

"The keys to Aubry's keep. You are its steward, at least for as long as I might walk a straight course between Northumberland and Swynford."

They rode at a leisurely pace; there was time enough to spare. Chalford Priory lay but four leagues east, and it was Hugh's intent to be there during de Severies's visit. For already, he was obsessed with the idea that he must glimpse Sancha one last time, even if only from a distance. It was a foolish notion. He did not know what he hoped to gain from it, beyond more pain.

The village of Fawley lay in their path. Even at that early hour the noise of trade was in the air, the shouts of merchants and the squeaking of cart wheels. It was the same in the village market where men and women moved about preparing for the day's business, and the heady aroma of food cooking over open fires drifted on the sun-dappled mist.

Martin set off on foot to purchase whatever was edible. Hugh remained with the horses, beneath the trees at the edge of the market grounds. He was asleep when Martin returned with bread, a slab of cheese, and a leather sack of wine. Hugh used a portion of the wine to wash his wound; the rest they drank.

Inside Chalford's walls there were more of Swynford's soldiers in evidence than nuns, and possibly more dogs and cats than either. A scarred, red-bearded yeoman standing guard at the doors to the prioress's residence gave Hugh an inquisitorial stare when he demanded to speak to Thomas Swynford.

Moments later, Swynford, having been advised that a young noble wished to speak to him, strode out onto the balcony of his suite. His jaw dropped with recognition, and, rushing back into the room, sent a servant to hustle Hugh into the residence.

"My God," Swynford declared, "you look like death!"

"I have ridden all night," Hugh told him, surveying the room and slumping down on an upholstered bench. As he did he noticed the squints on the opposite wall. Fashioned as an ornate latticework of fanciful vines and flowers, the stonework provided a sweeping view of the chapel below.

A servant brought Hugh wine. When asked by Swynford about his bloodied shirt, Hugh casually laid the cause on a lance blow suffered in a melee at Warkworth the day before. A nuisance, no more, a wound broken open from long hours in the saddle. "I had no means to contact you on such short notice, other than to come myself."

Hugh related briefly how he had ridden from Warkworth with only his steward. He had not been followed. Hopefully Northumberland believed him en route back to Evistone. He told Swynford then of Northumberland's plot to kidnap Richard's queen and to slaughter the French entourage. "You must delay handing the queen over to the French, at least delay their journey south."

Hugh and Swynford were still talking when a servant brought news of the French courtiers' arrival. By then Swyn-

ford had called in his captain and several of his sergeants, an
was in the midst of ordering them to gather troops at Pickerin
before attempting to rout the kidnappers. "I want prisoners,
Swynford told his commanders. "Those still able to give evi
dence against their masters."

Earlier in the courtyard, a servant had come up to Marti
where he stood with the horses, and directed him toward th
postern gate. "Wait for your master there," the servant said to
him.

Martin sighted past the chapel, beyond a low stone wall
There he saw a garden much like the one at Evistone, thoug
many times larger. He was gathering up the horses' reins whe
a chorus of barking dogs and the shouts of guardsmen heralde
the arrival of the French courtiers. Martin delayed, watching
wondering if his master's French wife would be among thei
number. Curious, he pressed his way into the crowd of on
lookers.

Dressed in silks and swathed in a velvet cloak, Sancha ar
rived amid a group of French noblewomen. Alighting from
charette with their pale faces deep in their tasseled hoods an
their arms laden with gifts for the little queen, they appeare
one no different from the other. They walked toward the chape
past the lines of gawking soldiers and servants.

When Sancha saw Martin's good and honest face in the fore
front of the crowd, it seemed an answer to her every praye
As she came even with him, she caught his eye, then contrive
to tip the basket of silver pomanders she carried on her arm
In the excitement she leaned close to Martin's face and aske
hopefully, "He is here?"

"Aye." Martin stooped to retrieve a pomander and placed i
in her hand. There was no mistaking the look of anguish i
her dark eyes.

"I must speak to him," she said in a hushed, breathless whis
per.

Martin had only time to say, "I've been told to wait by th
postern gate, yonder, through the garden," for a guardsma

came toward them, drawn by the commotion, and Martin melted once again into the crowd.

At the doors of the chapel, Sancha glanced quickly back over her shoulder, but Martin was lost to her line of vision.

The sight of Madame, small and frail, praying in the chapel, forced Sancha to put aside her own heartache for a time.

It had been arranged by her uncle that Sancha should be placed beside Madame Isabelle, Marie, and Alene. Their reunion was one of silent tears and guarded smiles. And there beneath the eyes of the English guards, Sancha, in whispered words, told her little queen of Richard's death. Not the gory sight that she had seen, for it would have been too much for her to bear. Instead, she told of the damning words she had overheard, and how Bolingbroke and his cronies had sought to silence her.

Throughout, Isabelle remained white-faced, without expression, a child who had suffered a woman's loss, a poor, sad child. Perhaps it was something in her eyes, a sereneness beyond the pain, for Sancha suspected she had always known that he was dead, that her beautiful, golden Richard was lost to her forever.

While the nuns sang the praises of the Virgin, Isabelle, with tears glistening in her eyes, pressed her cool hand to Sancha's, and murmured, "Dear, dear Sancha, I feared I would never see you again. You must not blame me. I was told you were grievously ill. The young man they brought before me swore to care for you with kindness. Did I do wrong to give you to him?"

"No, Madame. He has ever sought to protect me. It was he who gave me leave to come."

"Then he has risked much for love of you. Monseigneur de Severies has said you will return to France with me?"

"If it is your wish, Madame."

"My only wish is that you shall know happiness. Come with me, if it is your choice, but look first into your heart, for it must be without regret."

Above the chapel, Northumberland and his commanders were still locked in a discussion. Hugh wandered across the room, a goblet of wine in his hand, to gaze into the chapel where Richard's child queen and her father's courtiers knelt in prayer. Looking down upon the still figures Hugh could not determine which of the lavishly cloaked and hooded noblewomen was his wife—had been his wife.

The soldiers departed, and once more Swynford and Hugh were alone, save for the silent servant. Swynford inquired, "How did you come by this information?"

Hugh turned back. "That I dare not say. Though you may know it is from Northumberland's breast."

Swynford chuckled. "A woman, then?"

"Does it matter?"

"Fair enough," he said with a laugh, and then as an afterthought, he asked, "How fares your wife?"

"Poorly."

"That is unfortunate. Well, know that you have done a great service for your king. And now, it is best you ride north. I would not have you sacrifice the future for the present. I will have need of you in times to come. Northumberland, the old hellpuck, will not be dissuaded from lusting after Henry's crown, not until he's stone-cold dead."

Swynford walked Hugh to the door. "William did well to claim you; you are very like him. God keep you on your journey."

Swynford's parting words burned Hugh like a brand. It was true, he thought, bitterly. For at that moment all that he had disliked about his father, he saw in himself. He had claimed his legacy, he held both Evistone and Aubry, but it had cost him that which he loved most.

A servant directed Hugh toward the garden and a postern gate, where his steward awaited him. Stepping out into the cool sunlight, Hugh entered the garden. It reminded him of Sancha, and he felt again the emptiness and longing.

Near the gate he thought he saw something move at the

edge of his vision. He halted and turned his head in time to catch a glimpse of a cloaked figure hurrying past a row of black-barked trees and mass off golden foliage, a figure coming swiftly toward him down the path that curved away from the rear of the chapel.

In that instant it seemed his heart ceased to beat. He recognized the light smooth step, the set of the small shoulders, the smiling face beneath the hood, the tilt of her nose. It was Sancha!

She rushed toward him, stumbling a little as she reached him, but his arms were ready and he caught her, closed her inside. "I could not leave you," she gasped, breathless. "Who would there be to care for you? Poor fool, who does not know a daisy from a rose!"

Hugh could not speak, beyond a wordless sob of joy. He buried his face in the softness of the velvet, felt it snag against his stubbled jaw. He kissed her swiftly, and with a hand round her waist took her down the path. His only thought was to get her safe away, home again to Evistone.